Adhara's Sonder by Mark Alexander McClish

Published by Curious Corvid Publishing, LLC.

Copyright © 2021 by Mark Alexander McClish

Cover design by Mark Alexander McClish
Formatted by Laurie McClish

Adhara model: Rachel Johnson
Donny model: Leonard Morrow

Printed in the United States of America

Cataloging-in-Publication Data is on file with the Library of Congress.

ISBN: 978-1-7368675-3-2
ISBN (paperback): 978-1-7368675-4-9
ISBN (ebook): 978-1-7368675-5-6

www.curiouscorvidpublishing.com

instagram.com/markmakesart247

November 2020

Mark Alexander McClish proudly presents

With story consultation by

Madison K. Darby, Cameron Meeks, Daniel Pierce, and Kathryn Lindner

An adventure through space and time,
at the end of destiny and the beginning of will

ADHARA'S
SONDER

Table of Contents

Chapter 1
PILOT LIGHT

With a jingle of keys, the faded door swung open. Creaking footsteps warped the floorboards from the foyer to the kitchen, stopping just beneath the kitchen table.

He squinted in the kitchen light as he dumped his rucksack into a chair, sighing and digging inside it. He paused. He rummaged inside it again, scraping the bottom. He searched a smaller pocket. He searched the side pockets, pointlessly. He looked up, blinking at the china cabinet across the room, his encumbered brain struggling to keep up.

Now the stairs creaked, but more loudly; each step rolled on the balls of his feet as he stole upstairs. He flung open the door to his workshop, tearing through stacks of research papers and overturning boxes of wires. With a wide sweep of his arm he cleared his desk. The stairs creaked again, louder under his heels, and he returned to the kitchen and searched his rucksack again.

"I forgot my laptop," he admitted to the empty kitchen.

After a dramatic sigh, Cyrus slammed back out the front door again, and dejectedly began pedaling his bicycle back the way he'd come.

Living outside the city came with many perks which almost made up for the commute. The climate was cooler this close to the mountains, and every day on his way to work and back home, Cyrus enjoyed the sun rising and setting over their peaks. The view was especially grand over the strip of fields just outside his neighborhood: a waving golden sea crested with the strip of woodland at the foot of the mountains. Every day Cyrus was tempted to get off his bike and run wild through the field, but the chain-link fence with the sign that read "NO ADMITTANCE: Meteorological Terraforming Survey Zone" had not yet failed to discourage his primal desires. So, he just stared at the mountains as he passed; they were always covered in rolling fog, but when the sun was directly behind, he could just make out the long row of AirShift towers.

The temperature started to rise once he came through an orchard, past the dented sign which fibbed: "Hudson City: You are safe here." He smirked. When he came to the top of the hill, the cluster of skyscrapers bordering the bay sprawled out beneath him. But it wasn't until he reached the bottom of the hill, heading towards downtown, when it really got warm—as many as ten degrees warmer than his neighborhood.

The momentum from the hill carried Cyrus well into the city. Each building he passed became slicker and cleaner, and as he approached the city center, the streets became darker and smoother. Since they were empty, they were easy to admire—at this time of night, there was hardly any traffic to delay him. The buildings were alive with lights as always, but as Cyrus stopped to grab a soda from a vine-covered vending machine, he had only his thoughts to keep him company. He took a sip of the soda—his favorite, Battery Acid—and blinked rapidly as the ice-cold sugar and caffeine brought him back from the brink of exhaustion. As the stimulant surged through his veins, he hopped back onto his bicycle and headed back out of town on the far end. The wind started to blow cold again, so he pulled his hood up and pressed forward, weaving to avoid patches of ice and blinking away snowflakes as he passed an industrial tanker at a fuel station. He soon regretted the cold drink.

By the time Cyrus arrived back at the lab where he worked, the sides of the road were buried beneath a two-foot blanket of snow. He stopped at the security checkpoint booth, rubbing his arms.

"Hey, it's Cyrus!" guffawed the booth guard through the speaker. "Back again so soon, huh? Burning the midnight oil?"

"No, I just forgot my laptop," Cyrus confessed.

"*Again*?" the guard chuckled. "Well, stay warm—it's cold out here where they don't fix the weather!"

"Thanks, Barry. Have a good night."

"Hey, you too," the speaker fizzled as the bar rose.

With a swipe of his keycard Cyrus pushed into the laboratory. He took a moment to shake out the cold before searching among the disarray of glassware and research documents piled on the lab benches.

"Hey, hey, what's up, junior? Back again so soon?!" A mousy young scientist emerged from the mess, peering at Cyrus through thick glasses. "It is...*soon*, right?" he asked. "Don't tell me it's already morning."

"Nah, Isaac, you're good; I was only gone for an hour. I'm looking for my laptop—" Cyrus gingerly extricated a binder, accidentally making the whole stack collapse. Isaac waved his hand dismissively.

"Don't worry about that. You were working with Dr. Graaf today, right? Maybe it's over by his desk." He nodded across the room. As Cyrus wrenched his laptop from the grip of an amorphous pile of magazines, Isaac continued, "Once you've got it, you better head home. Cargyle's in a *mood*."

"A mood, huh? I thought he went home." Cyrus grunted as he yanked his laptop out. The magazine pile slid onto a chair.

"He came back just before you did, all in a *huff*. Everything is everyone else's fault tonight." Isaac rolled his eyes. "And you know how he loves grad students, so...better skedaddle."

Cyrus tucked his laptop into his pack and was heading purposefully towards the door when he heard a man calling him.

"Hey, Cyrus! I've been looking for you."

Cyrus' throat tightened, and he froze in front of the door.

"You haven't been avoiding me, have you?"

Cyrus glanced at Isaac, who shrank out of sight. Dr. Cargyle crossed the room and stopped just before Cyrus, close enough to demonstrate disdain for personal boundaries. "Are you listening to me, kid?"

"I'm listening," Cyrus finally answered as he met Cargyle's eyes, which were much too close to his. He could smell Cargyle's gum. Doctor Cargyle had the kind of eyebrows that told you that he did *not* have time for you, but you had better make time for him. Cyrus leaned away as much as possible without moving his feet. "Of course, I haven't been avoiding you...sir."

"Good! I have a job for you," he barked.

"What, tonight?"

"Yep!" The left side of Cargyle's face rose while the other remained flat. "I need you to pop down to sensor manifold 48 real quick and download the direct readings for me. It's been complaining."

"Sensor 48? But that's on the other side of town, in the opposite direction!" Cyrus complained to the chair next to Cargyle. "48 is a coastal beacon; it's at least half an hour from here!"

"Oh, excuse me," Cargyle crooned. "I didn't realize you were working on something more important! How's that Lorentz field project going, by the way?"

Barely audible across the room, Isaac sharply inhaled. Cyrus frowned at the floor.

"Cyrus, do me a favor." Cargyle dropped his smugness. "Get your head out of the clouds, stop wasting time and resources on fringe science, and try to contribute to this facility. Do you *want* to stay in the graduate program?"

"*Yes*," Cyrus grumbled.

"Then act like it. Go check the sensor. I want those readings waiting for me tomorrow morning."

Cyrus picked his fingernails sequentially. "Yes, sir," he answered finally when he realized Cargyle was waiting. After he finally left, Cyrus kicked a chair into the nearest lab bench and slid down against the wall.

"Ouch," Isaac grimaced, sliding down to the floor next to Cyrus. "What'd I tell you? Moody."

"You know, as expensive as grad school is, you'd think he could treat me with an *ounce* of respect."

"Ah, but it never works that way, does it? The free labor is never respected," Isaac sighed.

"I could be so much more!" Cyrus protested quietly. "I have more to offer the city than just checking sensors."

"You're bright and ambitious, Cyrus; you'll get there if you pay your dues. You won't be an intern forever."

"Don't get me wrong, I love working here, and I fully appreciate the opportunities! I just wish I didn't have to run errands outside of my department all over Hudson City."

"Technically, this whole building is Cargyle's department," Isaac shrugged. "But hey, I get it. Work is like old age. It's the worst thing in the world—except for the alternative, right?"

Isaac rose and returned to his desk, but Cyrus lingered for a few moments before returning to the cold.

Whatever residual animosity Cyrus harbored melted away as he stood on the beach, listening to the waves and riding the endorphin high from biking to the other side of the city. With the glow of the skyline at his back, he stared into the dark at an offshore mining rig, twinkling lights winking like stars where the bay dissolved into the distant wall of fog. He closed his eyes, dreaming of better, future days for a few minutes before schlepping up the dunes to sensor 48.

The sensor manifold reached deep into the sand below and about ten feet in the air, both ends equipped with a gangle of lenses and whirligigs mounted in an armored body. In the past, a technician would have had to climb to the top to download the readings, but a few years ago Acryogen Industries had installed monitors at the base. Cyrus supposed he was fortunate for that.

He shoved a transfer drive into a port under the monitor and started the interface.

"Okay, 48..." he murmured. "What have you been complaining about?"

His eyes scanned the data readings within the command line interface. "Humidity is normal, temperature is normal...air pressure is a little high...light intensity is good." He squinted at the screen, frowning. "Induction is at two thousand Gauss? Twenty *thousand* volts of static?" Suddenly it was clear why Cargyle was making him check the sensor. Cyrus' brow twitched. "Maybe it needs to reboot." He entered a few keystrokes and rebooted the operating system. The screen flickered off, then back on with the Acryogen Industries trademark proudly displayed on the startup screen. "Let's try this ag...Huh?!" The screen now read:

"WARNING! Readings for values listed below
exceed safety parameters."

Static electricity and magnetic induction fields were climbing even higher than before, and now gravity was reading 50% higher than normal. At the bottom of the screen was displayed, matter-of-factly:

Singularity Detected.

"HUH?!?" Cyrus exclaimed. He stepped back and looked all around him apprehensively. He was almost convinced that the sensor had critically failed when suddenly, the city behind him, which had been glowing so oppressively, suddenly darkened. The sensor went out too, and Cyrus stood perfectly still, trying not to panic.

Despite the clear possibility of mortal danger, Cyrus couldn't deny being exhilarated. Acryogen Industries was a manufacturing giant, and aptly named; they didn't make anything consumer or even commercial grade. All Acryogen brand products were industrial grade, sturdily built. Blackouts in Hudson City were not abnormal, but to overload the sensor manifold? This had to be something big.

Cyrus felt a resonance in his chest and teeth. He climbed a tall sand dune, and from there he could see, just a few meters off the coast, a bright light in the water. A lost fishing light, he supposed? No, definitely *not* a fishing light; he recoiled as the vibration grew stronger in his chest, and he could see the water warp into cymatic patterns as the light grew larger and brighter. The light grew even more, pulling the water with it as it slowly came ashore. Cyrus had unconsciously approached the beach, and now was almost close enough to touch the furiously writhing ball of liquid, squinting in its brilliance.

The ball erupted into clouds of vapor and light with a piercing wave of sound. The spell was broken, and Cyrus scrambled backwards to dive behind a nearby dune. He took a few deep breaths and peeked out. He squinted intently in wonder.

"What **is** that?" he murmured.

The vapor cloud dispersed. Standing where the ball of water had been was a woman wearing a black leotard—or such was Cyrus' first impression. As he studied the woman further, he noticed her body was seamed; segmented like a beetle. Her limbs were slender but sculpted; her proportions resembled a gymnast or a climber. She had no hair and wore no clothes, but her smooth carapace was fair; pale all over except her torso, which from mid-chest to mid-thigh was black like polished onyx. Her eyes glowed and her body steamed, and she stood in a crater of molten sand.

"Well that's obviously not a human person," Cyrus whispered to himself. "It looks human; it looks a *lot* like a human. But I know a thing or two about machines, and that's a machine."

The steaming statue came alive, its motions fluid and deliberate.

"Possibly designed to...emulate a human? An android, I suppose."

The possible android began to walk down the beach, each footstep in the wet sand leading it towards a nearby cliff which rose a story or so above the sea.

"Leaving already?" Cyrus murmured. "Where are you going, with such purpose?"

Cyrus followed her along the beach and up the cliff to its grassy top, maintaining enough distance to remain undetected. She finally stopped at the edge of the cliff, apparently gazing out across the bay. He hadn't noticed until now, but the city lights had come back on. The glow reached his hiding place among some mossy boulders but faded into shadow before it could illuminate the mysterious figure.

"It's almost like it's enjoying the view. Is there precedent for aesthetic consciousness in artificial intelligence?" Cyrus mused, entertaining the thought. "I did just read something the other day. Acryogen is developing an algorithm to process color theory."

"But color theory is one thing, and appreciating a view is quite another," he countered himself. "That's like comparing a map to a tour guide!" he scoffed, stealing a quick peek at her. She hadn't moved. "It's clearly designed for something tactical or industrial, anyway. That armor? The sturdy frame?" he stood, forgetting his hiding place as he surveyed the skyline behind him. "Maybe there's a control beacon nearby...?"

Cyrus felt a tingle on the back of his neck, and out of the corner of his eye he saw light—she was standing directly behind him, eyes glowing brightly.

"I'm sorry!" Cyrus flinched impulsively, but she merely closed her eyes. When she reopened them, her eyes no longer glowed—they were still an ethereal electric blue, but they were soft and calm.

She smiled and said, "Hello, Cyrus." Her voice was like bells rung with felt mallets. And upon closer inspection, that armor that had looked so thick and intimidating was almost delicate. Her hands looked like they were crafted from shards of rosy porcelain smoothed by the ocean, and elegant engravings adorned the posterior edges.

"How did you know my name," Cyrus muttered, still apprehensive. Beneath the ceramic plates, especially in the knees and elbows, he could see hefty joints coated with black oxide.

"You're the reason I'm here," she replied.

"Me? Why-why me?" he stammered, instantly defensive. "Are you from Homeland Security...somehow? I may have done some sketchy stuff, but it was all under Acryogen's name! You should take it up with them, not me!"

"You misunderstand," she assured him. "I have something important I need to tell you. Please listen closely."

They were interrupted by a blinding floodlight. A giant drone, like a copper, monocular rhinoceros beetle the size of an actual rhinoceros, hovered just off the edge of the cliff, aiming a laser at her chest. Triple propulsion units thrummed loudly on its underside, whipping the air around them.

"ENERGY SIGNATURE LOCATED," blared its deep, artificial voice. Cyrus covered his ears. "ENGAGING TARGET."

"Sorry about this," she told Cyrus calmly. Her eyes were glowing again. "I'll just be a minute."

"Don't pick a fight with that; it's a Bouncer drone! It's military-grade!"

"Don't worry," she smiled pleasantly. "I won't damage it."

"That's not what I'm—" he objected, but she had already approached the drone.

"ENERGY SIGNATURE BEYOND SAFETY PARAMETERS DE-TECTED," it told her. "ALL UNREGISTERED WEAPONS AND ENERGY TECHNOLOGY IS LEGALLY FORFEIT AS PROPERTY AND WILL BE DESTROYED."

It directed energy cannons at her, each barrel wider than her head, and they began to charge.

"Voice command," she ordered, "System root system thir-ty-two restore. R, s, t, r, u, i."

It hovered quietly for a moment, considering her response as it clicked and whirred. Then all at once, the floodlight went out, and it replied: "VOICE COMMAND ACCEPTED. SYSTEM REBOOT. RETURNING TO BASE." It flew away as suddenly as it had arrived, and they were left with only the sound of the rustling grass.

"How on Earth did you do that," Cyrus asked, watching the drone grow smaller.

"As I was saying, I have something very important to tell you," she continued as if nothing had happened. "Please lis-ten carefully, as this is a matter of foremost importance. The fate of the world as you know it is at stake."

Cyrus felt another jolt of panic in his stomach and swal-lowed uncomfortably. "Just like that, huh?"

"After I finish," she continued. "I will try to answer any questions you have. Deal?"

"Um..." Cyrus shrugged. "Sure, deal."

"My name is Adhara," she began. "I am a temporal-dis-placement capable android. I came here from Hudson City, seven years in the future."

"You can time travel?!" Cyrus interjected. "That's why the sensor detected a singularity!"

"Yes, Acryogen Industries tracks many forms of energy displacement," Adhara confirmed. "That's why the Bouncer drone targeted me."

"That's amazing!" Cyrus exclaimed. "I knew Acryogen was experimenting with gravity waveforms, but I thought we were at least another decade or two from a successful proof of concept, even at an atomic scale!" His eyes grew wild and excited. He laughed giddily. "How do you generate enough power to displace that much mass? And you're only ahead by seven years? Are you powered electrically, or—"

"Focus, Cyrus."

"Right, sorry."

"In my time, Hudson City is on the brink of destruction," she continued seriously. "You are the key to preventing the threat from gaining power." Cyrus crossed his arms tightly, frowning. Adhara seemed far away as she finished, staring at him intently, "I am here to shape your destiny and guide you along a path that will save Hudson City from a terrible fate."

He blinked. He waited for her to explain, or request that he take her to the head of Acryogen Industries, Mason Smithy, or someone else who was more capable. A departmental head. An adult, at least—or, an older adult. Someone else; not a grad student. Not him. Cyrus' breath caught in his throat; he pulled his hood over his ears and stood shaking his head and shifting his feet. "Me?" he asked finally. "Why me?"

"We should go somewhere less conspicuous," she suggested. "Where do you live?"

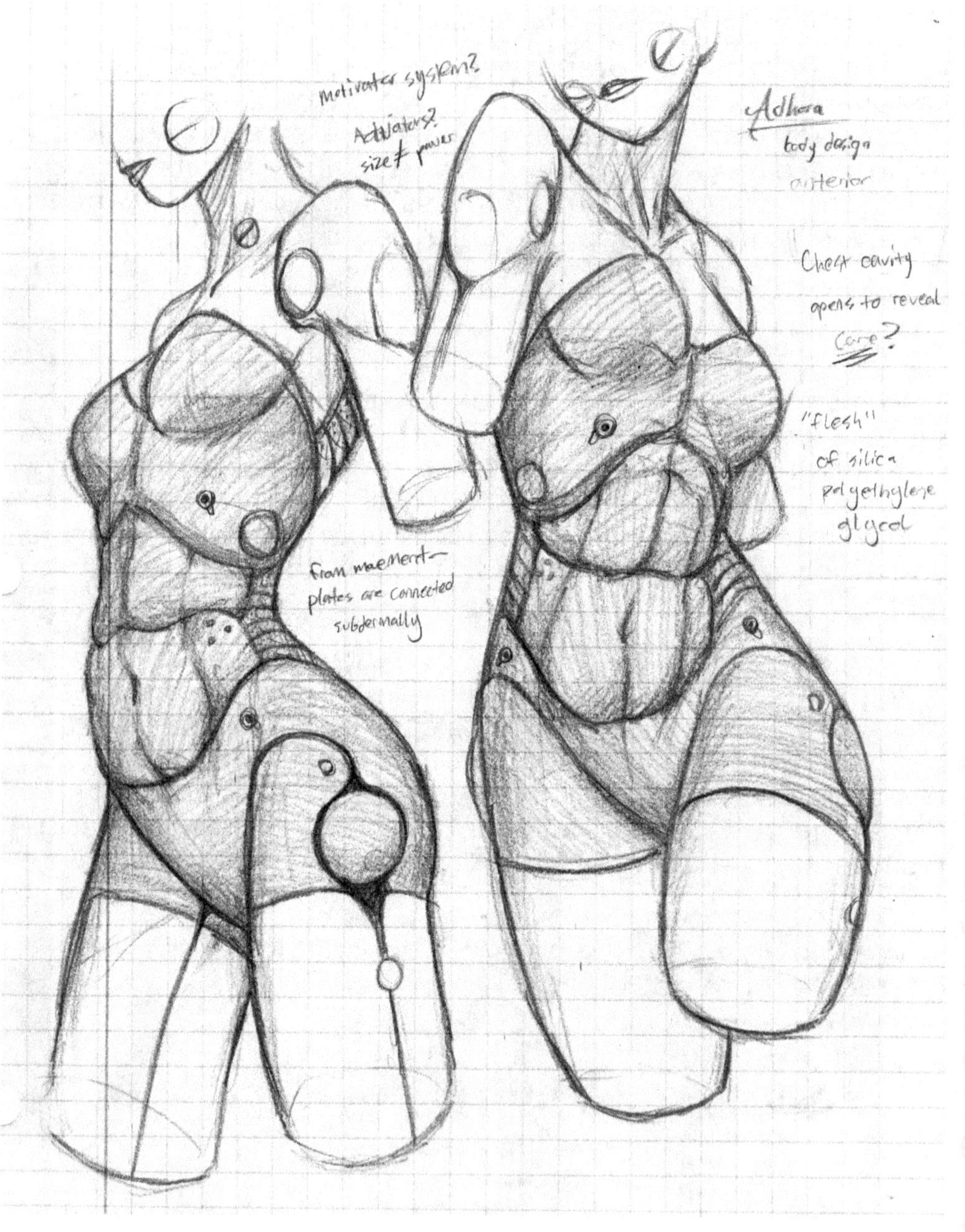

motivator system?
Activators? size + power
from maement— plates are connected subdermally
Adhara
body design
anterior
Chest cavity opens to reveal Core?
"flesh" of silica polyethylene glycol

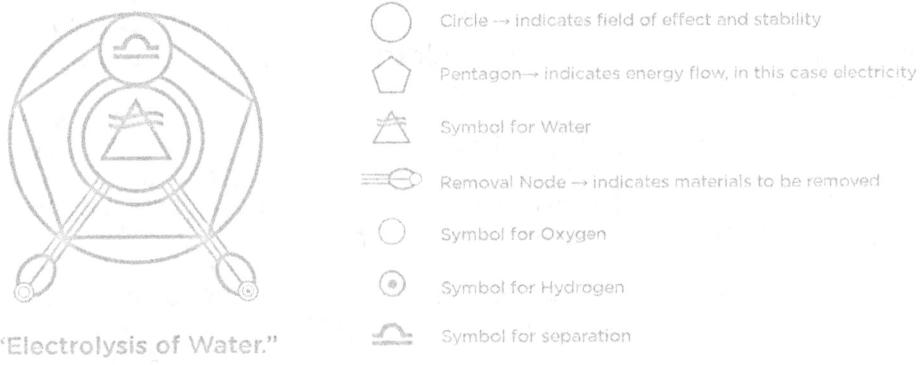

"Electrolysis of Water."

$$2H_2O\ (l) + 2e^- \rightarrow H_2(g) + O_2(g)$$

Chapter 2

ADHARA

As promised, Adhara entertained Cyrus' incessant questions as they walked back to his house. To his frustration, she insisted that they wait until they were inside to discuss her purpose. Fortunately, Cyrus found ample alternative subjects to interrogate her on, grasping for rationalization. If the whole situation was a dream, he was at least going to wring some inspiration out of it.

"How are you able to time travel?" he asked as they started up the hill leading out of the city.

"As you anticipated, the mechanism is related to dark gravity waveforms," she answered. "I am able to contract and expand space at opposing poles surrounding myself, which propels me through time by function of quantum oscillation."

"Since you're from the future, do you know everything that's going to happen before it happens?" he asked as they passed through the orchard of hybrid apple trees.

"I am aware of certain major events, but not everything. Are you aware of everything that has happened in the past seven years?"

"Oh. Fair point."

As they passed the open field with the meteorological terraforming survey zone, he asked, "Are there flying cars in the future?"

"No, they fall out of style about eight months from now."

"I knew they were just a fad," he whispered conspiratorially to himself. "Mass transit is so much more efficient."

"Actually, the market preference shifts towards bicycles and similar human-powered transport."

"Really?" He stopped, realizing he had left his own bicycle somewhere. Probably at the beach.

"Yes, the transportation is reliable and considerably reduces fuel costs."

"That's true;" he nodded sagely and began walking again. "My fuel costs are limited to smoothies and sandwiches. Old fashioned, but effective. I guess I'm ahead of the curve."

As they entered Cyrus' neighborhood, his questions turned back to Adhara's functionality, specifically her physical components.

"Wait, you're not made of metal?"

"My body is composed of less than 15% pure or alloyed metallic substances." She allowed him to poke her shoulder experimentally.

"You're...squishy," he observed.

"Most segments of my outer shell are composed of silica polyethylene glycol, a shear-thickening fluid which produces higher mechanical resistance in the presence of physical force."

Cyrus nodded. He didn't fully understand everything Adhara told him, but he made notes in a small notepad for later research.

The street was still just as quiet as when Cyrus had left it. But as he closed the front door of his house after inviting Adhara inside, he felt a sudden twinge of paranoia—he gazed furtively across the empty street, scowling through the window as he turned the deadbolt. "I'm just going to go change my shirt," he told Adhara, leaving her in the foyer.

After changing, he watched his eyebrow twitch in his bedroom mirror. "I don't think this is a dream," he told himself quietly. "There is a robot from the future in my house," his brain replied. "There is a robot from the future in my house." He picked his fingernails sequentially.

"There is a robot from the future in my house," said his brain as he headed down the hall to the stairs. "There is a robot from the future in my house," it repeated as he descended the stairs halfway to spy on the robot from the future in his house. It was staring at the wall and its eyes were glowing again. Adhara turned to look at him as he came down into the foyer. She blinked and her eyes stopped glowing.

"Those...are my parents," he gestured to a picture on the wall where Adhara had been staring.

"What happened to them?"

"They died in a plane crash when I was a kid, but that's not important right now." He pinched the bridge of his nose. "Acryogen Industries strictly regulates weaponized technology. The Bouncer drone was just the beginning—if they find out about you, they'll destroy you or disassemble you for analysis. But..." he paused, weighing the options, "probably just skip straight to destroying you. And if I'm blamed or even associated with you, I'll be expelled if they go *easy* on me."

"I'm sorry to inconvenience you, Cyrus," Adhara replied pleasantly.

"Well, I hope it's worth it. Whatever it is you're doing here, we need to disguise you, so you don't look so much...like a robot. Uh. No offense."

"That seems appropriate," she smiled.

"But before we do anything else... I need to know the truth. Why are you here? And what do I have to do with saving Hudson City?"

She looked at him seriously. "Everything."

Cyrus opened his mouth to respond but was interrupted by a jingle of keys, and they both turned to the door as it opened. On the porch was a woman holding a casserole. She raised her eyebrows as she looked back and forth between them.

"Interesting," she signed with one hand.

"A robot from the future?" she signed to Cyrus as they sat at the kitchen table, gossiping about the robot from the future whom they had banished to the living room. "Why not? This city is already so weird."

"She came out of the ocean in a ball of light, Maria," Cyrus groaned. He glared at the table, watching her hands out of the corner of his eye. "It's super weird."

"Sorry, again?"

"Ball of light from the ocean," he signed. Maria raised her eyebrows. "I think I was in shock before," he continued, enunciating clearly. He held his arms and legs folded tightly while tapping his foot obsessively. "What was I thinking? Bringing a sentient android home? I have a headache." He rubbed his eyes under his glasses, then suddenly looked up, eyes wild. "What if she's going to kill me," he whispered.

"Okay, no," Maria signed, smirking. "I think you're looking at this too negatively. *Maybe* she's not who she says she is… but what if she is?"

Cyrus met her gaze, frowning.

"You said she called you the key to saving Hudson City?" she continued, "Then you're like 'the chosen one!' Destined to save the *world*!"

He shook his head, scoffing.

"My point is: a time traveling robot doesn't make any sense. I know it's crazy. But Cyrus Agrah, destined to save this city? That makes all the sense in the world to me. I don't know the robot." She leaned in. "But I know you. And from what you've told me, it seems like she knows you, too."

Cyrus sighed—the idea was too good to pass up. "I know this is probably a bad idea," he told her, "but I couldn't live with myself if I blew it off and it turned out to be real."

"I figured you'd say that."

"You're taking this surprisingly well," he noted.

Maria nodded thoughtfully. "I guess I've seen a lot of weird stuff, being friends with you. A time-traveling robot isn't so crazy."

"Sorry to keep you waiting," Cyrus told Adhara as they joined her in the living room. She smiled pleasantly up at him from the couch.

"It's no trouble," she answered calmly. "Have you reached a decision?"

"Yes. You can stay here, and I'll help you...save the city, or whatever it is you need me to do...on a trial basis." He looked her up and down. "And again, we need to make a disguise for you. A bald girl wearing a leotard will raise some eyebrows even before people realize you're a robot."

"What did you have in mind?"

"Clothes and makeup for sure." He tapped his lips. "Maybe a hat or a wig, or...something," he finished, making sure to enunciate so Maria could read his lips.

"Very well," said Adhara, "I agree to your terms."

"You know who could help disguise her?" signed Maria, smirking.

"*No*," said Cyrus firmly, "The last thing we need is more people knowing about her."

"So, tell me..." said Maria's and Cyrus' friend, Donny, "Just exactly...what I'm looking at here."

The next morning, having rushed over to Cyrus' promise of an emergency, Donny grew increasingly bewildered at the sight of the girl on the couch across from him. He had glanced over her at first, but her unearthly qualities faded into focus the longer he watched her.

"Hello," said Adhara from the couch.

"She's a robot," said Cyrus. "Well, an android, more accurately."

"We need her to look like a human," Maria added.

"She seems human enough already!" Donny noted.

"My capacity for personality emulation is highly sophisticated in order to maximize ease of human interaction," said Adhara. "The algorithms required several decades to perfect. In fact, as of this year, only 40% of the stochastic reasoning parameters will have been completed."

"Okay, getting less human," said Donny, nodding. He turned to Cyrus and Maria. "Let me get this straight. You've got a robot in your house, much more advanced than anything *I've* ever seen, because it's...from the future... that you're hiding from Acryogen." Cyrus and Maria nodded. "And as ridiculous as that is already, you want me to disguise the robot as a person...using stage makeup?"

"That's about the skinny of it," said Cyrus awkwardly as Donny approached Adhara for a closer look.

"I don't even know if makeup will really stick to...whatever it is you're made of."

"Silica polyethylene glycol," she supplied helpfully.

"Oh word? Well, maybe with lots of foundation." He scratched his jaw. "I guess it's worth a shot..." he murmured to himself as he set up his makeup on the coffee table. "Oh, and sorry if this has been covered and I'm backtracking here, but do we know *why* the robot from the future is visiting us?"

"Oh right, I forgot all about that when Maria showed up last night. She said in her time, Hudson City is on the brink of destruction and I'm supposed to save it," Cyrus explained. Donny muttered something about being fancy as he mixed thick powder into a tan cream.

"Can she tell us what's going to happen, or is it a secret?" Maria signed to Cyrus for translation.

Adhara looked at her hands for a moment then signed back, "I will tell you what I can," as she spoke the same aloud.

"Well, go on. What's going to happen that's so bad it justifies time travel?" asked Cyrus.

"Hudson City is destroyed by multiple small problems that build up to an uncontrollable catastrophe," answered Adhara as Donny started to apply foundation on her face. "Countless small variables that build towards a single, inevitable outcome."

Entranced, Maria and Cyrus sat on the couch opposite her.

"As you know, near the end of the war, Hudson City lost communication with the outside world. Without contact with the federal government or other cities, the local government lacked the resources or structure needed to defend against hostile forces. The only entity capable of providing necessary defense was a private corporation: Acryogen Industries."

Maria and Cyrus nodded, urging her to continue.

"Thirty years ago, at the request of the Hudson City council, Acryogen assumed control of military defense. They terraformed barriers and developed everything from weapons to an army." Cyrus frowned and opened his mouth but Adhara continued talking.

"However, as time went on, the sieges stopped, and the war was presumed over. But Hudson City still never received any communication from the rest of the world. Still in recovery, the local government was unable to function on its own. Acryogen Industries retained control. The company had to manage almost everything, from energy, water treatment, even emergency response; all major municipal utilities fell under their stewardship. But Hudson City was never designed to be managed locally. And Acryogen Industries simply wasn't made to run an entire city."

Donny snorted. "No kidding," he muttered while rubbing Adhara's face with a blending sponge.

"They're doing the best they can, Donny," Cyrus murmured.

"Ever since Acryogen Industries assumed control, Hudson City has been plagued with malfunctions, shortages, outages, and even some minor catastrophes, all caused primarily by negligence," Adhara continued. "Their inadequacy is not rooted in apathy. They are simply stretched too thin." She studied their reactions. She waited to continue until Maria and Cyrus had nodded while Donny tutted quietly.

"Unfortunately, many people grew impatient with Acryogen's failings. A group of citizens dissatisfied with Acryogen's performance formed a radical insurgence movement, calling themselves 'Phoenix.' They believed *they* could offer the city better leadership, and they were willing to go to extremes to achieve that goal."

Intrigued, Cyrus leaned forward in his seat.

"They didn't pose a significant threat, however, until they appointed a leader." Adhara's face grew serious, like when she had told Cyrus about his destiny the night before.

"Five years before I travelled back in time, their new leader initiated a war, at first using primarily sabotage and guerilla tactics. He wielded weaponized technology composed of war scrap and devices stolen from Acryogen. In those five years he managed to destroy more than half of Hudson City's infrastructure and dozens of Acryogen facilities. His proclaimed goal was to destroy the city and achieve a fresh start without any trace of Acryogen Industries. The city was weak to begin with and had no match for his weaponry—

all anyone could do was slow him down. He called himself Anubis, after the ancient Egyptian god of judgment. Thousands of people died in his rampage."

She spoke evenly, but Cyrus felt an icy pit of anxiety in his stomach. "Rampage?" he asked. "You said he used sabotage and guerilla tactics…like he was working in the shadows. Rampage sounds more, I don't know, more assertive than that."

"At first, he seemed to prefer stealth," Adhara nodded. "But Acryogen discovered his hiding place, forcing his hand. After that, he attacked head-on, and single-handedly decimated Acryogen's defense force and destroyed most of the city."

"And all of that…is supposed to happen two years from now?" Cyrus asked. Maria and Donny exchanged an uneasy look.

"Give or take," said Adhara. "Time travel has an inexact effect on sequential events."

"If this happens in the future, why are you here two years early?"

"I am here to fix the problems currently threatening the people of Hudson City," she replied simply. "And if necessary, when the time comes, to eliminate the man who calls himself Anubis."

Donny finished blending the makeup around Adhara's cheekbones and stepped back. He had added a dusting of freckles to distract from the seams beneath the makeup.

"Um…" Cyrus shook his head and blinked, "Her face looks great; now she just needs clothes. Donny, can you consult with costume?"

"Why can't you leave me be?" Donny snipped.

While Adhara waited expectantly in the middle of the guest room, Maria and Donny lounged on the bed and Cyrus rummaged through the closet. He beckoned Adhara inside, then exited, shutting the door to give her privacy.

"So what does Anubis have to do with Cyrus? Do they fight?" asked Maria as Adhara emerged from the closet wearing a loose blue top and brown cargo shorts.

"Too basic," said Donny.

"Cyrus develops a device which revolutionizes chemical engineering," Adhara answered from the closet. "With this technology the people of Hudson City are enabled to use their limited resources more efficiently and therefore be less reliant on Acryogen Industries." She emerged again wearing purple jeans and a grey sweater.

"That's better; good coverage and style. But it doesn't offer a good range of movement," said Donny.

"I just realized you don't need privacy to change clothes," said Cyrus, handing her a new outfit.

"A device?" Maria signed to Cyrus as Adhara changed. "She must mean the Philosopher's Gauntlets!"

"Don't be silly," he signed back, "those are just an idea. Acryogen denied my project proposal for a reason."

"Ridiculous," cried Donny, disgusted by Adhara's garish, mismatched ensemble. She wore a neon running outfit over footie pajamas, and she was trying to use an infinity scarf as a shawl. Cyrus handed her another outfit, and Donny gasped as she pulled on a stretched grey hoodie, distressed nylon jeans, and a brown leather aviator jacket. "That's perfect!" he cried, gesturing for Adhara to spin around.

"Okay good, now we just need to cover her hands," said Cyrus. "Donny, did you bring the gloves I asked for?"

"Yeah, and you're lucky *Middle Name Danger* was such a flop, or our costume department would be busting down your door."

"Cyrus?" said Adhara.

"What is it?"

"Why are the Philosopher's Gauntlets just an idea?"

"For a lot of reasons, actually," Cyrus frowned. "The...component technology is unavailable to me."

"How so?"

Cyrus picked his fingernails sequentially and hurried out of the room. Adhara turned to Maria, who shrugged. Cyrus returned moments later with a whiteboard and began to draw.

"Again, with the whiteboard," Donny muttered under his breath, preparing a wig for Adhara.

"The concept is simple enough. I wanted to build a safe, portable welding torch that you could hold in your hand," Cyrus explained, drawing a stick figure holding a flame. "There are two parts: the fuel and the containment. If you run an electric current through water, it splits into hydrogen and oxygen, two flammable gases, which is the fuel. The containment is called a Lorentz tractor field or LTF; I invented it to get into the Acryogen Industries graduate school program." He drew a diagram to represent the tractor field. "It uses electromagnetic fields to make a vacuum 'control bubble' for chemical reactions. They use my device in their top labs; it's been a useful development." He chewed on his fingertip, seemingly lost in thought for a moment. Donny finished preparing the wig and lowered it onto Adhara's scalp. It looked terrible.

"The only problem is that I could never make the tractor field portable. If it were portable, you could weld anywhere using water as fuel. That would be a lot safer than acetylene, and a lot less likely to explode." He chuckled to himself, and then stopped abruptly. "But moving the water, splitting it, and powering the LTF requires too much power for any conventional portable power source." He drew a diamond with a radiation symbol on it. "The only suitable battery I could find in my research was a beta-voltaic diamond battery. But that would require radioactive graphite and a *ton* of heat and pressure to produce, and I don't really have a way to get either of those things," he told the whiteboard.

"But if you could make the battery, the rest of your invention would work?" asked Adhara, looking outlandish in the ill-fitting wig.

"In theory," Cyrus confirmed, grimacing at the wig.

"The wig is bad," Maria signed.

"I agree. Donny, please remove the wig."

"Fine," Donny sighed, removed the wig and packed it away, then asked, "how about now?"

The last piece of Adhara's outfit was a discrete pair of black gloves to cover her intricate porcelain hands. She declined footwear because, as she claimed, they would be destroyed quickly.

"I realize you don't need shoes, but won't being barefoot draw attention?" Cyrus muttered.

"I can help you create the diamond battery," Adhara told him casually as she wiggled her fingers into the gloves. Donny and Maria raised their eyebrows at each other, but Cyrus barely seemed to register any surprise.

"How?" he asked, erasing the whiteboard.

"Observe." She removed a glove, offering her palm to him. Within the segments of her hand, Cyrus could see an array of lenses and bracing arranged around what appeared to be a tiny jet turbine. As he watched, the turbine began to spin and hum, and a clear blue flame burst from the center of her palm.

"I am equipped with an electrolysis array similar to what you are describing," she explained as Cyrus stared at the tiny jet. "Using this hydrogen flame and an industrial hydraulic press, we should be able to produce a synthetic diamond." Cyrus continued to gape at her hand.

"...Can we go right now?" he finally asked.

"Certainly."

"Maria? Donny?" he asked, turning to his friends. "What do you say?"

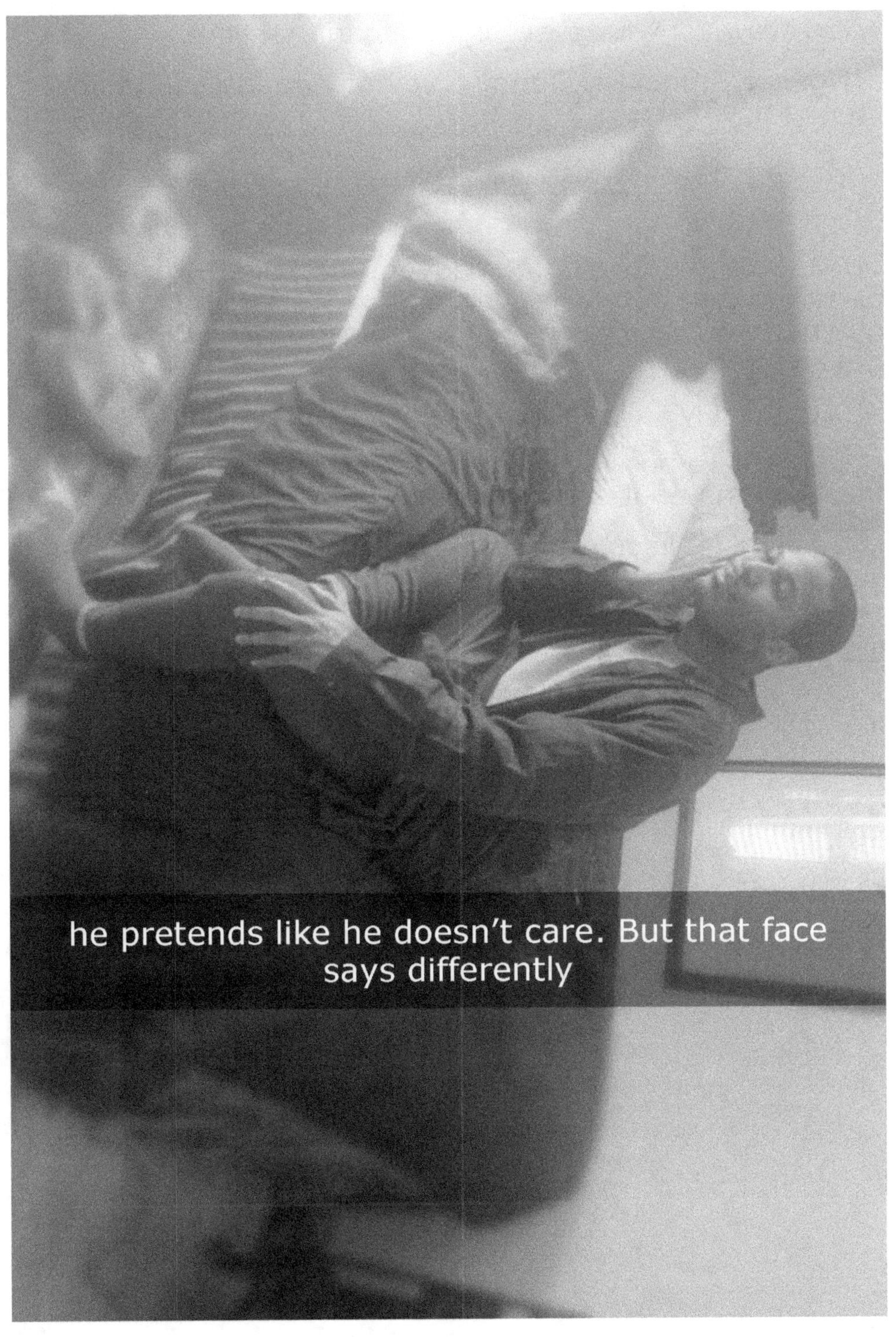
he pretends like he doesn't care. But that face
says differently

"I'm down for whatever," signed Maria, smiling.

"Not me," chuckled Donny. "I've had enough shenanigans for one day."

"Well, have fun on your little adventure," said Donny as they parted ways outside. He climbed into his car and rolled down the window to offer a final snide remark, "Try not to get arrested."

"Is that likely?" asked Maria as Donny drove off.

"Definitely a possibility," Cyrus replied. "Possession of radioactive material is illegal."

"Oh," she replied. "And...we're walking there?"

Chapter 3
UNDER PRESSURE

The air was thick around the nuclear power plant, the facility itself entombed in ice from the perpetual hurricane that raged around Hudson City. They had passed through the southern boundary of the AirShift towers a few minutes ago and the temperature had drastically dropped since then.

"This place was abandoned after the war," signed Cyrus, exaggerating his hand movements to be seen through the snow. "It's been empty for decades, but there should still be plenty of fuel rods around somewhere."

"How do we get inside?" asked Maria.

"I have discovered an access point," called Adhara, closing her hand around a flame. She was standing next to a large hole in the chain-link fence. The edges were still glowing, and the cut links lay hissing in the snow.

"That works," Cyrus shrugged.

After a trudge through the snow and forced entry through a steel hatch, they took shelter from the cold in a tall room, which Cyrus recognized as the electrical substation.

"If I h-had k-known we were g-going outside the city," signed Maria, "I w-would have worn so-something heavier!" Cyrus inferred the stuttering from her shaking hands.

"I'm sorry, I should have warned you," he apologized as he brushed snow off her. "Adhara, can you make a fire?"

Minutes later, when they had a fire roaring within an old oil barrel and Maria was wrapped in Adhara's jacket, Cyrus revealed his plan.

"Adhara and I will find the reactor floor," he began. "The fuel rods we need will be somewhere in that area. Meanwhile, Maria," he turned to her, "I need you to find a lead-lined safety suit. It'll cover the whole body and be bright yellow. That would probably be your best bet," he pointed to a nearby room labelled "*LOCKER ROOM AND DECONTAMI-NATION SHOWER.*"

"So, silly question, but—" Maria signed, glancing around nervously, "is it safe for us to be here? Are we going to get radiation poisoning?"

"It's..." Cyrus looked at her in dismay. "That's not how radiation works. This facility didn't have a meltdown or anything, it was just shut down. And radiation poisoning only sets in after a long period of exposure."

"That's a relief. I guess."

"But we'll need to wrap the graphene in the suit to move it safely through the city, so come and find us after you've got it."

She nodded uncertainly.

"This will be fun!" he declared, "like a scavenger hunt-in an abandoned nuclear reactor." Maria and Adhara exchanged a look and gave him encouraging smiles. "Although..." he continued, noticing the harsh shadows cast about the room, "it's pitch-black in here, and I didn't bring any flashlights." His eyes wandered around the room as he pondered. "This substation would be connected to the grid through underground cables. There's no reason that they would be disconnected, but..." he approached the main power breaker, padlocked in position. "Surely it's not that easy."

"Adhara," he turned to her. "Can you cut through this padlock?" She joined him in front of the breaker and held her hand over the lock. A stream of sparks burst forth from beneath her palm and after a few seconds she yanked the red metal loose. Cyrus heaved the switch up, and the connection sent a hum of dormant power through the room. Cyrus turned to the breaker panel and flipped every switch he could find. With hesitancy the facility came to life, buzzing and whirring, the sound resonating through the walls as lights flickered on.

"Subtle," signed Maria as she headed to the locker room.

"I can't believe they didn't drain the reactor pool!" Cyrus shouted at the reactor pool, pounding his fist on the catwalk railing. Adhara patted his shoulder.

"That water has got to be at least forty feet deep, ice cold..." he gazed down into the blue glow of the pool, the only source of light on the cavernous reactor floor. "Not to mention it's probably mostly deuterium by this point. How can we..." he turned to Adhara, who was no longer standing beside him. He spotted her on the far side of the room, where she had disrobed and was descending into the reactor pool.

Maria tapped Cyrus on the shoulder. "I got the suit," she signed, showing him the folded fabric. "Where's Adhara?"

"She just...walked into the reactor pool!"

At the bottom of the pool, Adhara had opened a compartment in the wall after surveying her surroundings for several minutes.

"Look, she's fine," signed Maria as Adhara began to climb the stairs again. Cyrus approached the edge of the pool as she emerged holding a dark grey block, about the length of a soda bottle.

"I have acquired a sample of radioactive carbon-14 graphite," she told him, dripping with heavy water. "Is this the material you're looking for?"

"Yep, this is it," he confirmed, weighing the block in his hand. "But it's not enough. To compress into a large enough diamond, we need at least...fifty kilograms? This block is around five."

"I detected seventy-seven more fuel rods like this one. I will retrieve more."

Adhara resubmerged as Cyrus sat back down next to Maria. They watched leisurely as the android retrieved block after block of radioactive carbon, arranging them into a neat pile on the edge of the pool.

"Those are going to be heavy," Maria observed, regarding the blocks as Adhara made her last trip into the pool. "How will we carry them?"

"Still working on that," he nodded slowly. "Maybe Adhara will carry them. She must be really strong."

A tremendous explosion rocked the facility to its foundations. Automatic security protocols turned all the lights red and a second blast sent steel girders crashing to the floor and into the pool. Cyrus and Maria jumped to their feet, dodging the splash of heavy water and grabbing Adhara's clothes and scooping up the graphite.

"What on earth was that?" Cyrus shouted over klaxons. The ground shook menacingly.

Suddenly Adhara burst from the pool, hovering in midair before them. Her eyes glowed, burning even more brightly than the miniature jet engines on her ribs, hips, and the ends of her limbs.

"Cyrus. Maria." She spoke calmly, but there was steel in her voice. "We need to evacuate immediately." In a flash Adhara swept down, grabbed them, then shot towards the ceiling, riding the shockwave of a third explosion as Cyrus yelled. Her smooth head punched cleanly through the roof and they soared out into the quiet cold, leaving the muffled blasts behind them.

Cyrus continued to yell as they flew although she had an arm securely wrapped around each of their chests, but as they passed over the AirShift towers he began to calm down.

"So, you can fly," he wheezed. "Are there any other little surprises I should know about?"

"I'm sure our time together will be full of surprises, Cyrus."

"Well if it's not supposed to be a surprise, would you mind telling me what all that was about?" he asked, clinging to her arm like the bar on a roller coaster.

"Another Bouncer found me. It was trying to bury me inside the facility."

"Those things are starting to become a real nuisance."

"At least we got all the graphite we needed," she reassured him. "Where to next?"

"I guess Acryogen's foundry lab—that's on the coast, just south of the docks."

"We may need to visit a medical office first," said Adhara, adjusting course. "Maria appears to be in shock."

"No, she's just terrified of heights."

They arrived at the foundry just after civil twilight, and either from the dusk or the smog in the air, the world was thrown into shades of sepia and orange. Adhara touched down in a secluded corner of the campus amongst a group of empty forges. Maria helped her get dressed again as Cyrus took a quick look around.

"The hydraulic press we need is in there," he pointed to the giant neon "*FOUNDRY*" sign that towered over the landscape, on the face of the tallest building. "I don't have clearance to be here, so we need to be quick and quiet," he whispered. All the workers had gone home, but the ambient noise—the occasional hiss and rumble of machinery—

would do little to hide them from the security guards. "If we're caught with Adhara and this graphite, we'll have a lot of tough questions with no good answers."

They stole quietly through the maze of workshops, hiding whenever they heard the guard crunching through the gravel. They had a few close calls, but eventually were able to slip undetected through a side door into the manufacturing plant.

"This way," said Cyrus, leading them inside. In the center of the factory he slowed, finally stopping in front of a display screen attached to a large machine. "Right here, this is the one," he told them. The hydraulic press was almost two stories tall, obscured in shadow and floating dust.

"Let's hurry," Maria signed, "what do we need to do, Cyrus?"

He turned to her with stars in his eyes. "You know," he began, visibly excited, "chemistry can be a lot like cooking! And today we're making a super-dense radioactive carbon casserole."

"Cooking?" she squinted at his mouth. "Is it really necessary to do this bit right now?" she signed nervously, eyeing the door.

"First, let's gather our ingredients!" he continued obliviously, opening the anvil well. "The radioactive graphite, of course, is the raw material carbon that we'll be crystallizing." He took the blocks from Adhara and dumped them in the anvil well. "If you can't harvest radioactive graphite from a nuclear reactor yourself, store-bought is fine," he chuckled to himself.

"The second ingredient we need is nickel metal powder," he continued, rummaging through supplies around the room. "This will lower the temperature at which the carbon will crystallize...aha!" He held up a plastic bucket bearing a boring-looking label. "This nickel powder is typically used for coating automotive parts," he explained as he poured the powder carefully into the well. When the bucket was empty, he tossed it behind him and rummaged in his pocket for a tiny, shining stone. "The last ingredient is a seed diamond," he smiled. "As a pattern for the carbon to crystallize around." He tossed it in and closed the anvil well.

"This has to stay at...let's say 725 psi," he muttered to himself as he tapped on the display monitor, "and at about...1100 degrees Celsius, to be safe. Can you manage that, Adhara?" She leaned out from behind the hydraulic press and gave him thumbs up. Cyrus nodded and started the press with his thumb. With a deep mechanical whine, the three pistons bore down on the anvil with crushing force. "Pressure's on; light it up!" he called.

"Stand back," Adhara warned. Cyrus stepped back to the yellow-striped safety line, guiding Maria with his arm. Adhara's hands whirred and screamed, and Cyrus suddenly noticed that it was slightly easier to breathe. The air was lighter—the humidity was dropping. Adhara assumed a solid stance with her hands open towards the press.

The bright blue blaze that erupted from her palms engulfed the anvil, distorting the air in waves of heat. Cyrus and Maria took a few more steps back.

"This is good," he signed to Maria. "Should be about eight minutes." The anvil was already glowing red, with a bright yellow spot forming in the center.

Seven minutes later they heard a bang on the other side of the factory. The guard shouted, "HEY! WHO'S IN HERE? THIS IS A RESTRICTED AREA!"

Cyrus thought fast. "Run and hide with Adhara," he signed to Maria, and then jogged towards the guard's voice.He only made it halfway across the building when the guard spotted him and barked, "HALT!"

Cyrus obeyed, blinking in the flashlight beam. "Cyrus?" the guard asked, more quietly. "Is that you?"

"Yeah, it's me."

"How many times do I have to kick you out of here, kid?" he lowered the flashlight. "You know you don't have the clearance. Come on," he gestured towards the exit and escorted him out. "I like you; I know you're a good kid, so I won't ask what you're up to. But if I catch you in here one more time, I'm going to have to report it to Dr. Cargyle, and neither of us wants that."

"Yes sir, I understand."

"I'm sorry, kid," the guard told him as he opened the gate and let Cyrus out. "I'm just doing my job...you understand. Don't let me catch you in here again." He closed the gate firmly and sauntered away.

Cyrus let out a long, relieved sigh and turned to Maria and Adhara, who were hiding in a nearby pavilion. "Well?" he asked as he approached. "Did it work?"

Adhara presented him with the diamond—roughly tetrahedral, sort of jagged and bulbous, about the size of a grapefruit and a deep, lime green—clearly recognizable as a large, uncut diamond to anyone familiar with the characteristics.

"The diamond formed perfectly," Adhara reported as he cradled it reverently. "It's emitting a steady flow of beta radiation."

"It's beautiful," Maria signed, "But why is it green?"

"The radiation during formation gives the crystalline struc-ture a green tint! It really worked!" he shook his head, grinning giddily. "I can't thank you enough for helping me," he smiled at each of them in turn, then gazed deep into the heart of the crystal. "With this...everything changes."

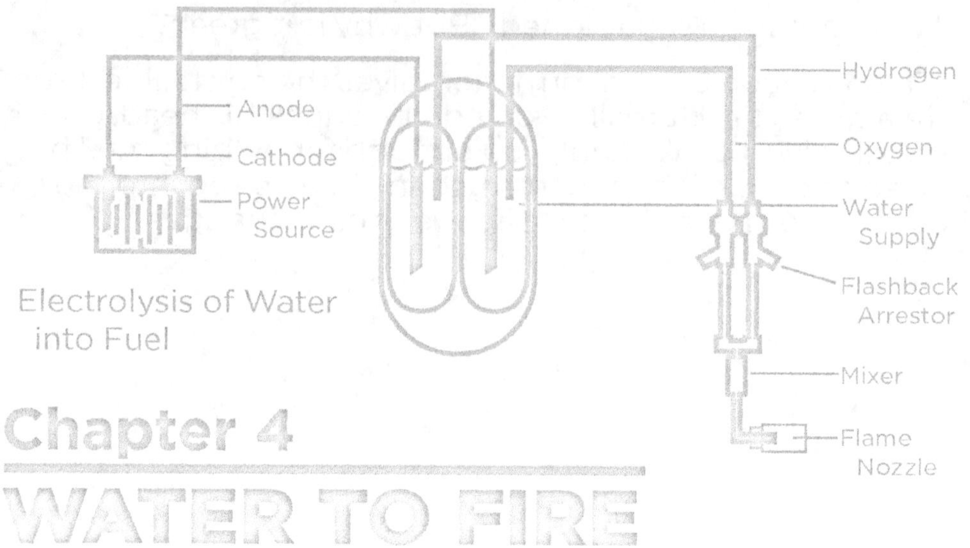

Chapter 4
WATER TO FIRE

"Good morning!" signed Maria as she came downstairs. "I'm headed to class. How's Cyrus?"

"Still working," Adhara replied.

"*Still?*"

"He has worked continuously since we returned from the foundry with the diamond."

"I wondered why I hadn't seen him around the house, but I thought I was just busy studying." Maria raised her eyebrows. "Two days straight is a lot even for him. I wonder what he's been eating."

"Primarily energy drinks and smoothies."

"I guess...that kind of balances out?" Maria lowered her eyebrows. "Does he seem okay?"

"He's verging on mania and his hygiene has become offensive. He has tripped the breaker on four separate occasions." They heard a loud click. Adhara opened a panel in the wall and flipped the breaker back on. "Five."

"I noticed that," Maria sighed, heading back upstairs. "I'd better go talk to him."

Maria knocked on Cyrus's workshop door, carefully easing it open. Cyrus had disconnected the overhead lighting long ago, so the only illumination in the room came from several computer monitors running equations, desk lamps, and the large semicircular window behind Cyrus's desk. Sunlight filtered through papers, maps, and diagrams Cyrus had taped to the glass.

"Maria!" Cyrus turned from his desk. His thick hair was tangled, his beard shaggy, and he had matching shadows beneath his eyes and armpits. Maria shook her head at the all too familiar crazed look about him. "Come in, come see!" he beckoned her closer.

She approached his workbench, carefully stepping around stacks of paper. She noticed the fingerless gloves he was wearing and the tangle of metal bracing, with multicolored wires that coiled around his fingers.

"I made this emitter array for the Lorentz tractor field to fit onto my hands!" he exclaimed, presenting his hands. Each finger had a laser diode mounted at the first knuckle, and in the center of his palm he had mounted a round apparatus with coils of copper wire and a glowing blue center.

"I made this—" Cyrus heaved a metal backpack onto the table— "it's a power supply for the diamond. I used airplane parts and big capacitors." Maria could see the diamond nestled in the center, within a cage of components and bracing. She also noticed the diamond had been cleaved into clean facets—Cyrus must have cut it somehow.Through the smoother surfaces she could see glowing particles spiraling within the verdant depths.

She tore herself away from the diamond. Cyrus was straightening thick cables between his gauntlets and the backpack. He pulled the pack onto his shoulders, staggering under the weight. He flexed his fingers, grinned at Maria, and crossed over to turn on his eyewash station.

"So now, with them together..." he murmured, "I can do this!"

Cyrus thrust his hand dramatically at the faucet. The diamond on his back glowed, spitting soft beams of green

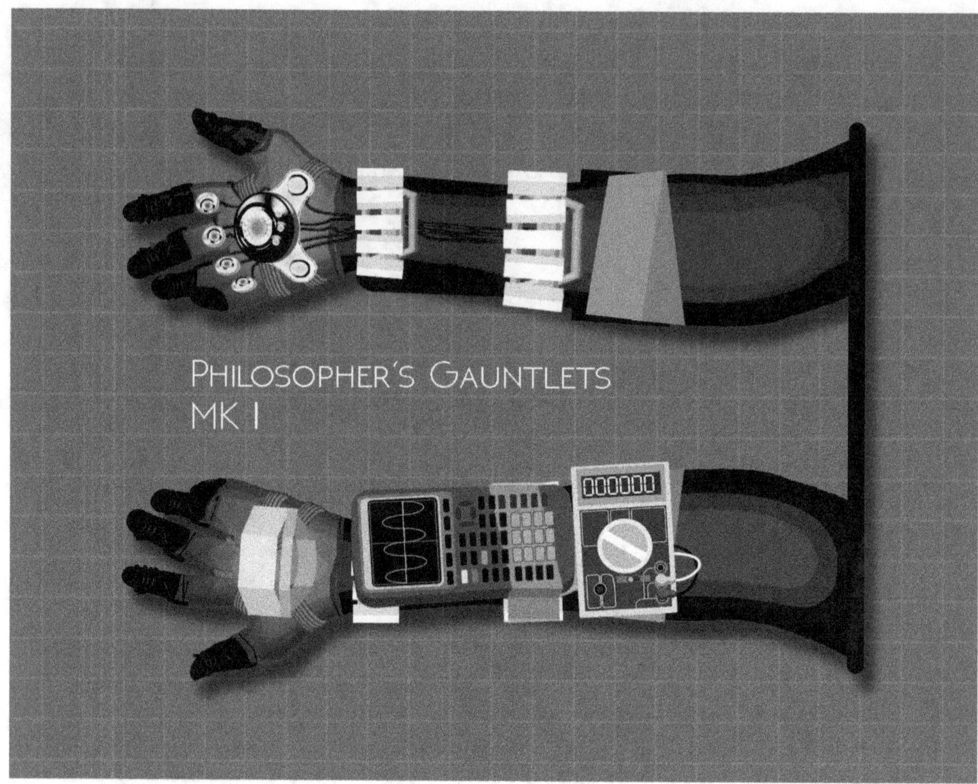

light out into the room. His palm crackled and the water streaming into the sink, which had been falling in a gentle arc, began to bend towards him. Their hair stood on end; Cyrus breathed slowly and steadily pulled the stream of water from its faucet out to the middle of the room. When he stopped, the water began to coil in on itself and formed a blob floating in midair.

Then Cyrus raised his elbows, widened his stance, and brilliant light streamed from his palms, illuminating the amorphous water. A flash of lightning barely caught their vision before the water was vaporized and disappeared completely.

"I can move the water and split it into hydrogen and oxygen!" he exclaimed, grinning at Maria.

She smiled back appreciatively. "It's amazing," she signed. "Just like everything you do."

"Wait—" Cyrus looked at Maria closely, "Are you wearing your cochlear implant? I thought you hated it."

"I do, usually!" she adjusted her hair around her ear, smiling awkwardly. "Adhara...did something. She sounds normal to me. Like a voice, instead of buzzing."

"I adjusted the frequency of my auditory output to correct for the distortion of Maria's implant," explained Adhara, appearing in the doorway. "She can hear my voice almost as clearly as you can."

"Since last night I've been asking questions just to hear her talk!" signed Maria, grinning. "Her voice is beautiful!"

"Last night?" asked Cyrus. "What happened last night?"

"I came by with food, but you told Adhara you were almost done working. I was waiting for you downstairs and I guess I fell asleep," signed Maria. She turned to Adhara. "Did you carry me to bed?"

"Yes."

"Thank you!" Maria signed. They smiled at each other.

"...I guess I was really, uh...in the zone," said Cyrus apologetically.

"Even geniuses need to take a break sometimes," signed Maria. "You need to go *outside*!"

"Out....side?" Cyrus's eyes slipped out of focus. "Wait. What day is it—Thursday? Don't you have class today?"

"Who needs to go to class on such a beautiful day?" she smiled. "Come to the park with me and Adhara. You can take a break, get some sun and fresh air, and *then* go back to work. Okay?"

"Yeah...Sure." He rubbed his eyes. "Okay."

But to Maria's dismay, Cyrus could not leave his work at home. She and Adhara had to guide him through crosswalks as he fiddled and probed his device, almost fully oblivious to the world around him. Even as they entered the park, surrounded by babbling brooks and enormous trees, Cyrus wouldn't look up for more than a moment.

"Wow. It's beautiful," signed Maria. "Isn't it *nice* out here in *nature*, Cyrus?"

"Uh," he murmured. "Hold on...still calibrating the...ignition field..." he trailed off.

Maria sighed and shook her head. "I don't know what I expected," she signed to Adhara. "Adhara and I are going to take a walk," she signed to Cyrus after snapping in front of his nose. "Come find us if you finish." He grunted indistinctly as they strolled away.

"I am...surprised that you were not more persistent in trying to convince him to relax," said Adhara as they started down a trail.

"There comes a point at which you can't help people against their will," Maria explained. "They have to decide for themselves to change."

Cyrus wiped the sweat from beneath his glasses. Sure, it was nice having warmer temperatures in the city—but was it worth the humidity? He looked around the park and wondered how long Adhara and Maria had been gone. The park answered with screaming cicadas.

"The field charge," he turned back to his gauntlets, "needs to be several thousand volts in order to spark—and I need to balance the field charge with electrodes from every major vertex...which reduces the necessary charge of each diode, because it's distributed. That sounds right." He had routed the cables from the backpack through a graphing calculator and multimeter mounted on his wrist to modify the output to the gauntlets. He punched some wave formulas into the calculator and checked the multimeter's reaction. "The capacitors should have no trouble with this load...that should do it! Is that right?" He reexamined the power supply. "Wait, is this even the right terminal?"

Cyrus was suddenly thrown off the bench onto his knees—he wrapped the backpack in a bear hug, narrowly saving it from the ground. The ground had heaved; birds and squirrels were running away from the direction Adhara and Maria had gone. Cyrus heard distant gunfire and he climbed the bench for a better look. He spotted a red glow a few yards away.

"Looks like I'm doing a field test," he breathed.

Cyrus equipped his gauntlets and the backpack as he sprinted down the trail towards the fire. Halfway through the trail he encountered Maria, who stopped running a few feet in front of him, signed "help!" and ran back in the other direction. After following her for a few minutes they emerged into a clearing around a fountain. Trees were on fire and the flagstone was cratered. Adhara was facing down two Bouncers.

"Cyrus! Maria!" she called behind her. "Evacuate the area *immediately*!"

"*ALL UNREGISTERED WEAPONS AND ENERGY TECHNOL-OGY MUST BE DESTROYED*," one droned.

"Adhara, what are you doing?!" Cyrus shouted, shielding his eyes in the floodlights.

"Run!" she repeated. She was standing between them and the drones, holding her hands up like a bullfighter. "Voice command: system root system thirty-two restore. R, s, t, r, u, i!"

"*INTERFACE CODE PARSE FAILED*," the other droned. "*ACCESS DENIED. OPEN FIRE IN 5...*" the drones aimed their cannons at Adhara.

Adhara crouched like a runner preparing to race.

"4..."

The panels around her knees and elbows popped open. Waves of blue energy streamed out like blue fire.

"3..."

Her knees glowed; her joints tensed.

"2..."

Leaving a shallow crater where she had been crouching, Adhara suddenly appeared in the air above the drones. They swerved but couldn't react quickly enough.

"7..."

The Bouncer exploded. There was no fire, no heat, but it suddenly fell to the ground in pieces, dark and silent. Its shell was warped into twisted scrap around a central impact crater. They saw Adhara, on the other side of the fountain, getting to her feet.

The other drone appeared between them and Adhara. It was targeting Cyrus, preparing to fire. "Jump to your right," he signed to Maria. "Nothing ventured," he murmured as she dove for a bush.

"ENERGY SIGNATURE BEYOND SAFETY PARAMETERS DETECTED," said the drone. Adhara watched from the other side of the fountain.

"Containment field holding," he muttered. "Power supply steady. 'Philosopher's Gauntlets,' version one, field test one."

"ALL UNREGISTERED WEAPONS AND ENERGY TECHNOLOGY MUST BE DESTROYED."

"Come and take it."

In one fluid motion, Cyrus waved his hand at the fountain, pulling a torrent of water toward him, looped it around his body and sent it toward the drone. Moments after leaving his hand, the water vaporized and flared, consuming the drone in an instant inferno.

"It works!" he threw his hands in the air, releasing the field. The smoking Bouncer collapsed in a heap.

Maria was jogging back towards him. "Cyrus! You did it!"

"Maria! Hey!" She caught him in a hug. "Are you okay?"

"I'm fine!" she signed, pulling away. "That was amazing!"

"I know, it actually works!"

"I always believed in you," she replied, smiling kindly. "...We should probably put out these fires, though." They looked around the Norman Borlaug Memorial Fountain, which was still babbling gently despite being strewn with flaming rubble. The two ruined drones fizzled, sending plumes of smoke billowing up into the air. Adhara stomped out a burning leaf.

"That's a good call."

"Where's Cyrus?" Maria asked. After extinguishing the fires in the park, they had returned to Cyrus' house to eat dinner and wind down—until Cyrus had been taken by a sudden stroke of inspiration and decided to visit his lab, against Maria's better judgment. "He's been gone for hours," she fretted. "I told him we need to stay inside until the stuff at the park blows over. He's going to get into trouble." She rose and began pacing.

"We should go look for him," she signed to Adhara. "I'm the one with all the common sense between us."

On the other side of town, in the building where he worked, Cyrus was about to sneak back out of a supply closet when he thought he heard his name in the hall. After listening at the door for a moment he carefully leaned out, listening to the agitated voice echoing off the walls.

"…He's a grad student," Dr. Cargyle was telling a security guard. "His ID was used to access the southwest door fifteen minutes ago and he's been sneaking around; probably avoiding me. If you find him, bring him to my office."

Cyrus' heart sank as he slid back inside the closet. An encounter with Dr. Cargyle right now would be bad enough after unauthorized "borrowing" from Acryogen supplies, not to mention the Sensor 48 readings he had never delivered. Dr. Cargyle was likely ready to drag him through a bureaucratic gauntlet which would end with his ejection from the graduate program.

Fortunately, in a situation like this, there were few better places for him to be trapped than a supply closet.

Moving fast, Cyrus flipped the lights on and threw a few bags of rock salt against the door to block the light. He then used his gauntlets, which he had since adapted to produce a smaller flame, to melt the doorknob. He turned to the shelves and grabbed a soldering iron, a microcontroller, and wire, then cleared a nearby table to work on. Before he started working, he left a bucket beneath a nearby faucet so it could fill with water as he worked.

Cyrus had come to the facility to acquire a patented NIRScanner—a portable mass spectrometer that could detect the chemical makeup of any material. Once he had returned home with the device, he had intended to incorporate it into his gauntlets, allowing them to automatically adjust to the right heat for welding and cutting. Speaking of which—he grabbed a bundle of steel rods. Those could come in handy later. It occurred to him that these gauntlets *should* also be able to arc weld. Good to keep in mind for later.

After Cyrus had cracked open the NIRScanner and wired it through the microcomputer and into his calculator/multimeter contraption, he took a calculated risk—connecting to the WiFi. From there he programmed the NIRScanner with his phone and calibrated it with melting and boiling point temperature data downloaded from the facility's database. Another resource liberated from Acryogen.

As he was programming commands someone began pounding on the door. Doubtless they had tracked his account's network access. "WE KNOW YOU'RE IN THERE!" a guard bellowed. "UNBLOCK THE DOOR IMMEDIATELY AND COME OUT!"

Finally, the commands finished rendering. He slid the backpack straps onto his shoulders. Wrapping the whole chipset in duct tape around his arm and kicking over the overflowing bucket of water, Cyrus approached the wall. The security guard was cutting through the melted doorknob with a grinding wheel. Cyrus straightened his arms with open palms. The NIRScanner beeped—his phone registered the makeup of the concrete and prescribed the appropriate voltage for the perfect oxyhydrogen ratio with the multimeter. The calculator drew a three-phase sine wave and the gauntlets burst to life.

The water on the floor vaporized, drawn to his palms before bursting into brilliant flame against the wall. After the paint burned away, the cement beneath gave off trapped steam, which was in turn drawn back into the gauntlets to burn.As the cement weakened, he drew a circle crossed by an X with his palms. The guard continued to yell. He was almost through.

Cyrus bludgeoned the wall with a sledgehammer. The weakened seams began to give, but the guard had cut through the latch and was now pushing against the bags of rock salt. He hit it again and again; the wall was giving. He needed just a little more time— he climbed a tall shelf and recalibrated the gauntlets for steel, cutting through the overhead lighting conduit and plunging the room into darkness just as the guard burst into the room.

The guard's flashlight beam swept the room. Cyrus crept down to the floor. He tossed a beaker to the far side of the room, waiting for the flashlight beam to follow before sneaking back to his almost-hole. He gently removed the shards of cement, piece by piece, keeping track of the guard. Just as another guard entered the room and joined the search, Cyrus cleared a hole large enough for him and his backpack to squeeze through, releasing him into the stairwell on the other side of the wall. He sprinted down the stairs and burst out the service door at the bottom, making a mad dash for the city.

Cyrus slowed to a jog as he entered the city—fortunately, there were very few straggling pedestrians to ogle him and the hardware strapped to his arms. He grinned uncontrollably, adrenaline making him verge on hysteria, as he slowed to a leisurely walk. The lights of the city seemed so much brighter! The plants, so green and lush! The pipes...

Cyrus stopped in front of a pipe manifold spraying water into the street. He looked down at his gauntlets....and back at the pipes. He approached the pipes cautiously, checking for witnesses to his reverse vandalism before sealing the leak under a puddle of liquid steel melted by the same water that had been spewing from it. His grin grew wider.

Cyrus ran back into the street. In the distance he heard a hissing—he ran after it. A few blocks away, he found a leaking air conditioner, which he sealed in seconds. On the other side of the street he spotted a gate overgrown with woody vines and incinerated them, and on the way to a booted car he tripped in a pothole. Intrigued by the challenge, he scraped sand into the hole and melted it, forming a thick layer of glass. He then returned eagerly to the booted car, freeing it from its bureaucratic bonds without even damaging the tire.

After almost half an hour of this reparative rampage, flashing blue lights and a siren stopped Cyrus in his tracks. He instinctively threw his Acryogen ID into the gutter.

"Turn around," said a cop through his megaphone, "and keep your hands where I can see them." Cyrus obeyed. The scowling cop beckoned him closer.

"What's your name, kid?" asked the officer.

"...Davis," he lied.

"Davis, huh?" repeated the cop, nonplussed. He glanced down at his own ID tag, which read "Davis." "What a coincidence. Got some identification on you, Davis?"

"Not with me."

"Are you aware that all citizens are required to carry Acryogen-issued identification at all times, Davis?"

"...Yes?"

"What's that on your arms, kid?"

"It's, uh...prosthetics."

"Really, now? Because it looks to me like unregistered weapons technology, which is a class D felony." The cop grimaced, pretending to be sympathetic. "I'm gonna need you to come down to the station and answer some questions." He led Cyrus to the back of his cruiser and locked the door behind him. But before he could slide into the driver's seat, something drew him away. Cyrus leaned up to the window...the cop was talking to Maria, and Adhara was just behind her. This was his chance! Cyrus scooted over to the other door. With a quick glance back at the cop he cut the door off its hinges, taking care to catch it before it fell. After clambering out he waved to Maria before hiding in a nearby alley. After a few minutes she and Adhara came hurrying down the alley after him.

"You're lucky he can't sign!" she scolded, "or he would have gotten suspicious!"

"What happened?" Cyrus signed insistently.

"He didn't notice—yet," she signed. "He drove away. We need to go home *now*." Cyrus nodded. After making sure the cop was gone, they made their escape through the quietest corners of the city. They didn't stop to rest until they were safely up the hill and walking through the orchard.

"Promise me," Maria signed firmly, "You will stay at *home* for a few days. You need to stay out of trouble."

"Fine," agreed Cyrus, "but you'll have to bring me food."

"You mean like I already do *every* day?"

"If you bring us ingredients, I am able to cook," said Adhara. They turned to look at her in surprise.

"But why would a robot need to be able to cook?" asked Cyrus in dismay. "Can you even...tell if it tastes good?"

"I am unable to judge flavor," she answered, "but I can follow a precisely worded recipe. I am able to perform almost any task if the instructions are clear."

"Wow," signed Maria, "I wish I could get Cyrus to follow clear instructions!"

"Everywhere I go," he sighed, "everything's gotta be rules, rules, rules."

At the center of the city, a few blocks from where the cop had stopped Cyrus, three identical skyscrapers formed a familiar landmark: the Acryogen Industries corporate headquarters. Not only the center of the manufacturing giant, they also served as city hall, courthouses, police headquarters—it was the center of government and power in the city. At the top of the central tower, in a darkened boardroom, a tall man gazed down into the glow of the city below.

"Mr. Smithy, I have some news," said a younger man, appearing in the doorway.

"Oh?" Mr. Smithy asked pleasantly.

"The unregistered energy signatures, the destroyed Bouncer drones, the vandalism at R&D Facility 6 and throughout downtown...it's all one guy. It's one of our own employees. Cyrus Agrah."

"Cyrus Agrah?" Smithy asked, his voice like honeyed dark chocolate. He turned from the window. "The graduate intern? Works in R&D Facility 6?"

"Yes, sir."

"He must have built something big if he took out a Bouncer," Smithy murmured. He turned back to the window and ran his fingers through his salt and pepper hair.

"Should I issue a warrant for his arrest?"

"Not yet," Smithy said slowly, turning from the window and crossing to the door. He was smiling wryly. "Young Cyrus may prove more useful to us on his own, for a while. For now, let's hide and watch. See what he does."

"Yes, sir."

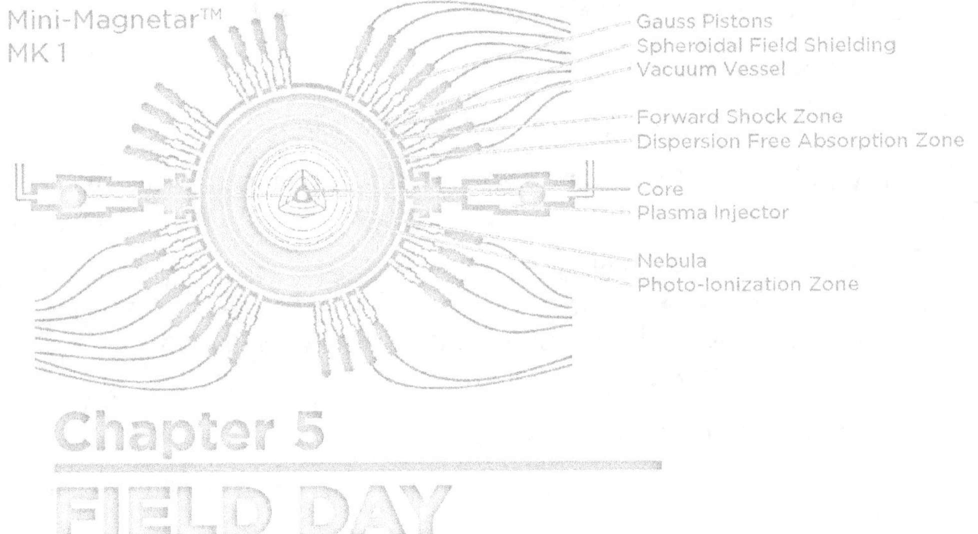

Chapter 5
FIELD DAY

"Cyrus, check it out! You made the news!" said Donny, pointing to the TV. Cyrus had come downstairs the next morning to find Donny and Maria in his living room.

"No witness accounts have yet been confirmed of the strange events that took place last night," said the reporter on the TV, "and there is so far no clear explanation of the intent behind them. Regardless of the reasons, last night between 1 and 4 in the morning, thirty-two city maintenance requests were fulfilled without any record of a city employee addressing them, in addition to several boots being illegally removed from impounded vehicles. Whether this is a Good Samaritan with a welding torch or someone making a political statement remains to be seen."

Maria glared at him while sipping a mug of tea.

"You fixed *thirty-two* random things around town?" Donny snorted. He rubbed his eyes, laughing silently. "I mean, I've had crazy nights that ended in some mild vandalism, but this is next level. Hey, don't get me wrong, I think it's great! If Acryogen's not gonna do it, *someone's* gotta, right?"

"No confirmed witness accounts? That cop saw my face…I wonder why he wouldn't say anything," pondered Cyrus. He turned to Donny. "How long have you been here?"

"Just like, an hour." He took a slurp of cereal.

"You guys know where Adhara is?"

"Kitchen," Maria signed. "And remember—"

"I know, I know," Cyrus waved her off. "I'm under house arrest."

As he entered the kitchen Cyrus noticed a quality that he couldn't immediately put his finger on. Adhara was standing at the sink, washing dishes. She turned, wiping her hands on a dishtowel.

"Good morning, Cyrus," she smiled.

"G-, uh...good morning, Adhara," he stammered. "Is it...did you...clean in here?"

"Yes," she replied as she filled a mug with hot water. Cyrus had never seen tea made so gracefully. She sat at the kitchen table and placed the tea in front of him.

"You...don't have to clean, you know," he said slowly, sitting beside her.

"Part of my directive is to assist you in any way possible," she answered. "I don't mind doing the dishes every now and then."

"You don't 'mind,' huh?" he smirked.

Adhara mirrored his smirk. "I am programmed to emulate personality, mannerisms, and figures of speech that make interaction easier."

"Your speech patterns have seemed less...*stiff,* lately," Cyrus mused as he sipped his tea. How had she known he loved lemon ginger?

"I adapt to my environment over time."

"It's funny you mention helping me," he said, finishing his tea. He stood to rinse the mug but Adhara took it from him. "Can you help me with my gauntlets?"

"What do you need?"

"It occurred to me last night," he explained as he led her upstairs, "you know when I was...fixing things, last night. The diamond should be able to produce enough power to arc weld, if I modify the electrical output and the Lorentz field. I have it set up..." as they entered his work room he pointed to the gauntlets, laying innocently on a steel table. "But I'm...scared. I *think* I insulated it properly, but if I didn't it could, well, you know. Electrocute me to death."

"You want me to test them?" she asked.

"Could you?" he grimaced. "Does electricity hurt you?"

"Only in extreme amounts," she replied, pulling on the gauntlets. "My electrical shielding can withstand a lightning strike, and your gauntlets are nowhere near as powerful." She pulled the backpack on. "Yet."

Cyrus raised his eyebrows. "Uh...spoilers?"

Adhara laughed, a sound like wind chimes with an echo.

"Did you just...reveal information about my future?"

"Yes."

"Couldn't that...I don't know, mess up my future?"

"There are some things I am unable to tell you," she explained, flexing her fingers. "Certain things that won't happen if I tell you they will. Things that will happen if I tell you they do. And then there are some things that are inconsequential, like trivia. And sometimes I can give you a peek of your future to help you stay motivated." She winked.

Cyrus looked around the room, nodding slowly and letting her words roll around in his mind and marinate. Adhara switched the gauntlets on; they emitted a hum and the air felt fuzzy. Cyrus' arm hair stood on end.

"How do the gauntlets feel?"

"They are operational," she answered, and demonstrably grabbed a nearby flux rod and welded it to the table.

"Wow! Let me try that!"

"I would advise against that," said Adhara as she removed the gauntlets. "I detected a current leakage in excess of three hundred volts."

Cyrus's face dropped.

"However," she left the gauntlets on the table, "If you build a chassis for the hardware to mount on, you could build a Faraday cage into it, which would protect the user from electricity."

He closed his mouth. "That's a clever idea, actually. I've been thinking I would eventually need to build framework or a chassis." He immediately set to work disassembling the gauntlets. "Would you…'mind' hanging out here for a while?" he asked as he disconnected the power lines. "I work better with company."

She smiled and sat in the chair across from him. Even her posture had become more natural.

"What kinds of questions can you answer?" he asked as he began to build the frame, bending metal framing from old VCR and computer cases.

"By revealing the criteria by which I may or may not reveal information to you, I would be revealing too much information." She took a particularly tough strut he was fighting with and bent it perfectly into shape. "Ask me a question and I'll answer it if I can."

"Well," he supposed, staring at the bent metal, "You took that drone out the other day with one punch. How strong are you?"

She pondered the question. "In what way? Force I can withstand or force I can exert?"

"How much can you lift?"

"My safety parameter stops me near ten metric tons, but during hysterical strength I can approach forty."

Cyrus dropped the box he was holding. He stared at her intently for a long time.

"I have several questions," he ventured.

"Go ahead."

"What is hysterical strength for you?"

"An emergency bypass mode."

"How on earth are you so incredibly strong? For your size..." he shook his head. "You must be, what, a little less than two meters? How much do you weigh?"

"Now, Cyrus."

"I know it's rude to ask but come on. You're a robot."

"My standard mass is 143 kilograms," she answered, "with some variation."

"So that's..." Cyrus muttered to himself, mentally calculating. "You can lift...about seventy times your weight?" he looked at her joints. "That's like...an ant. Those are some crazy powerful actuators you must have. Are your joints electrical or hydraulic?"

"Neither," she replied simply. "Most of the joints in my body are driven by nuclear strong-force actuators."

"Nuclear...strong-force. Actuators." He repeated.

"Correct."

"I don't understand."

"You know the four fundamental forces of physics. Simply put, electrical motors harness electromagnetism. In a few years, Acryogen Industries will perfect the technology to harness nuclear strong-force. They have already begun the project."

Cyrus stood, shaking his head, crossing and uncrossing his arms. He paced in a wide circle around Adhara. "Those could...you're...that's...." he muttered. "The ramifications of that *power*...wait, speaking of power!" he whirled to face Adhara. "Something like that would have a *massive* power draw! What do you run on, a nuclear reactor?"

"In a manner of speaking," she replied, then smiled.

"Why are you smiling," he asked uncertainly.

"Because I have seen the future," she replied, standing, "so I know you're going to like this."

Adhara pulled her hoodie off and stood in the center of the room with her arms spread out. As Cyrus watched, the segments of her chest shifted, releasing brilliant blue light and a quiet hiss of gas. The segments slid backwards, and the air in the room changed. Cyrus felt his hair standing on the back of his neck, but the sensation continued until his whole scalp was tingling. He felt a hum deep in his gut and his eyes couldn't focus properly. Then, around him, he noticed changes, little by little, then all at once—his tools, scrap, anything metal was pulled towards Adhara like she was a car-sized magnet. Was she? Beneath her outer shell Cyrus could see smooth white surfaces, and Cyrus was beginning to suspect she really *did* have a nuclear reactor embedded in her chest. Just as the metal in the room over-came gravity and began to speed towards her, her chest closed again, and they fell to the floor. As he approached her, he noticed steel filings on the floor, arranged in a mag-netic field pattern.

"What was THAT?" he asked.

"Mini-Magnetar," she rapped her knuckles on her chest as she slid her hoodie back on. "It's a fusion reactor dynamo. The electromagnetic field is so strong that, without the shielding, it would rip my body apart into plasma."

"That answers my next question," murmured Cyrus, "I was going to ask how you generate enough power to travel through time, but when you have a miniature STAR in your CHEST...." He threw his hands up, flabbergasted, and col-lapsed into a chair behind him. He rubbed his temples.

"I mean, I already knew that you were strong. But you're almost...incomprehensibly powerful." He shook his head again. "Is this what you were designed for? All this power in a robot that can already time travel...just for me?" Cyrus cringed at how pitiful he sounded, but he couldn't imagine that he was worth the trouble.

"I wasn't originally designed to travel through time," said Adhara. "That functionality was added later, after I was al-most completed."

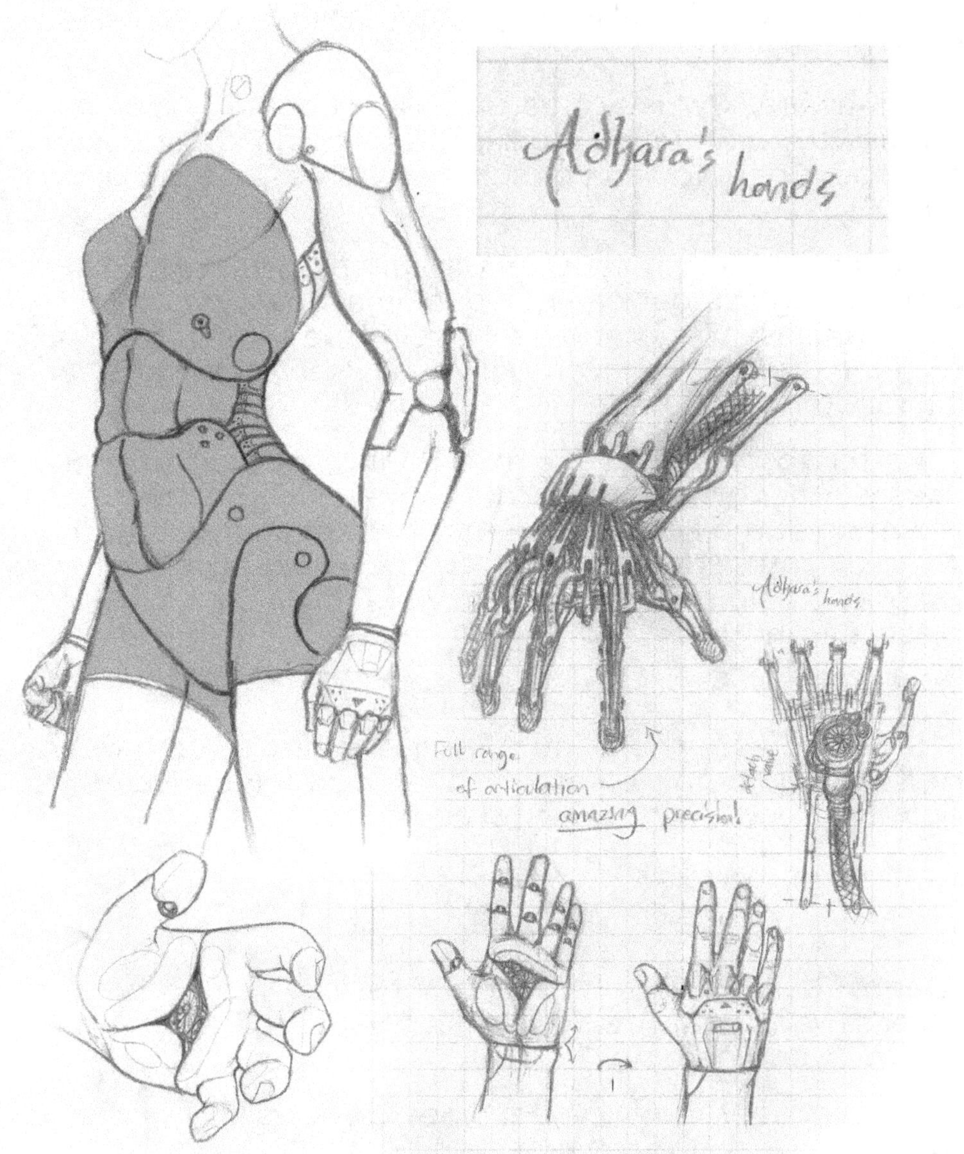

"What were you originally supposed to be?"

"Something like a superhero," she mused. "A mediator, a peacemaker, a savior. But after Anubis, there wasn't much left to save."

"You 'think?'" Cyrus looked deep into her eyes. "Sometimes it's hard to think of you as...not human."

"I am a true artificial intelligence," she explained, "so I'm fully self-aware."

"Self-aware." Cyrus sighed. "You can shoot fire from your hands, you move using atomic force, you have a star in your chest, and now you are, by some standards, technically *alive*?"

Adhara remained silent, calmly watching as his face flickered through stages of a nervous breakdown, wondering if he would lose his composure. But in true spirit of his nihilistic generation, Cyrus eventually took even the most bizarre circumstances in stride.

"Better absolutely insane than boring," he laughed nervously under his breath. "Mini-magnetar...." Then he tutted, frowning at the floor. "Magnetar," he repeated. He turned to Adhara. "You said...if it weren't for the shielding, the electromagnetic field of the magnetar would turn your body into plasma, right?"

"Correct."

"So that means the electrons would be free-floating..." he muttered under his breath. "I have a dumb idea. But we're going to need a *very* powerful computer."

"Donny," said Cyrus, returning downstairs, "remember your sister's friend you were telling me about? Isn't she studying electrical engineering?"

"Yeah-- Olive?" he frowned. "I heard you yelling, all excited up there. What do you want with her?"

"Nothing! I need her help. Here."

"The super-advanced robot from the future can't help you?" Donny asked flatly, returning to the TV.

"Because of my unique position, I have to limit how much help I give Cyrus, or his achievements will not be his own," Adhara answered.

"Well what do you want me to do, go get her? I'm her friend's brother; I can't just hit her up like 'hey, we go to the same school, and we barely know each other, but can you help my friend with a science project?' She may call campus security."

"Donny, think about the greater good," Cyrus implored. "A robot from the future came to guide me along a path that will save the city. This is of cosmic importance!"

Donny slowly turned, glowering out of the corner of his eyes. "How many times are you going to play that card?"

"As many times as is necessary."

"What is it with you and asking me for favors while I'm on break?"

"Isn't that better than asking for favors when you're in the middle of a show?"

"Fine," Donny sighed, "I'll go find my sister and see what I can work out." He made for the door but lingered in the doorway— "Uh...so about the super-advanced robot from the future. Should I...mention her ahead of time? Try to explain?"

Maria entered the foyer from the hall. Cyrus turned to her, pointed at Adhara, and signed, "Secret?" But Maria only shrugged.

"Probably best to not mention her until necessary," Cyrus decided. Donny nodded and closed the door behind him.

"I've got work to do in the meantime," said Cyrus, disappearing upstairs.

"Whoa," said Olive. "This is pretty hardcore."

"Oh!" Cyrus stood up suddenly but found himself trapped in a tangle of cords and cables. "Uh...You must be Olive! Thanks for coming." He extended his hand over the table.

"Totally, man, I was honored to be asked!" She leaned down to take his hand and adjusted her glasses. The glasses mostly obscured it, but he noticed she had a long scar over one eye. "Donny told me you're building something, and you need some help with the electrical engineering? Although," she looked down at the circuit boards laid out on the table, "this might be beyond me. I'm studying electromagnetic fields, not electronics."

"Oh—no, no!" he answered, "This isn't it, not exactly. This is...well, this is a miniature supercomputer."

"No kidding?" she raised her eyebrows. "Cool."

"My undergrad minor was in electronics," he added awkwardly. "The supercomputer is for calculating the thing I need your help with."

"Lay it on me, homeslice." She dropped her backpack and took a seat.

"Well, what all did Donny tell you so far?" He began clearing away all the junk.

"Nothing about the project itself," Olive recollected. "Just that you had a project you needed help with, and I'm all about inventing junk. He mostly talked about how you're a chemical engineer, always building stuff, and a huge nerd." She smirked. "Which of course, intrigued me immediately."

"The thing about it is, this project...it's not, strictly speaking, legal."

"How legal, strictly speaking, is it?"

Cyrus swallowed. "It's illegal."

"Cyrus," her face grew serious. "The integrity of a scientist dictates certain ethical standards that must be upheld. I would think you, as a senior scientist, would understand that."

"Oh," Cyrus spluttered, "uh...well I, I'm not..."

"Nah, I'm just pulling your chain, man!" her face twisted into a sly grin. "I don't care all about that stuff, I'm just in it for the thrill of discovery—and 'cuz it's cool. And I think

Acryogen and their 'amateur invention regulations' are super dumb."

"I thought you were serious for a minute," Cyrus let out a breath.

"You can trust me. Whatcha working on?"

"Nothing unreasonable," he said casually before heaving the backpack onto the table. Olive stared at it for a few minutes then stood up slowly. She pointed to the diamond, pulsating in the center.

"The *heck* is *that*?"

"That's a radioactive diamond. This backpack is just the power supply for the project—the whole thing is a big beta-voltaic battery."

"Dude, I was expecting like, a flamethrower, or like a Tesla cannon!" her eyes were wide as dinner plates. "If this is just the battery, what does this beast power?"

"I *have* built a flamethrower and a Tesla cannon before, but this project is...kind of both." He laid out the gauntlets. Over the past few hours since Donny had left to find Olive, Cyrus had finished rebuilding the Faraday cage chassis, to which the instruments were mounted. "I call these the, uh..."

She glanced up. "The what?"

"Well, it's stupid. I don't wanna say."

"Dude, *nothing* about this is stupid," murmured Olive, inspecting the gauntlets. "Except stupid cool."

"I call them the Philosopher's Gauntlets."

"Oh man," she said under her breath, shaking her head. "That's the coolest thing I've ever heard. Tell me what they do."

"How about I just show you?" he suggested, pulling the gauntlets on. She nodded enthusiastically. After the gloves powered up he performed the same demonstration he had for Maria a few days earlier—pulling water from his eye wash station and splitting it into oxyhydrogen—with the addition of a sustained, clear flame from his palms. Olive's jaw dropped.

"Dude!" she shouted, "That is *sick*!"

"Yeah, that's even better than the laser, Cy!" Donny's sister Aliyah was standing in the doorway, eating pistachios. She sauntered away giggling after Cyrus waved her off.

"Although, adding lasers isn't a bad idea," he muttered, scribbling a note.

"How does it work?" Olive asked.

"It's pretty simple, overall," Cyrus explained. "Everything is contained using a Lorentz tractor field, which I invented to get into the grad program. Combining that with an electric field, I can polarize water, electrolyze it into hydrogen and oxygen, and then ignite it."

"Wait a minute." She stood suddenly, making Cyrus nervous. "This thing is a portable welding torch. Those *repairs*... that someone did downtown last night! That was you, wasn't it?"

"Yeah, I got kind of carried away. It's nice of you not to call it vandalism."

"I think it was impressive," she told him resolutely. "The sense of social responsibility, as well as the technology behind it."

"Well," he chuckled bashfully, "To be honest with you, I'm kind of surprised; it was so easy! And I have *very* limited resources compared to Acryogen."

"Kinda makes you wonder what they're *doing* with those resources," she nodded.

"But I want to take it a step further. It's powerful enough to arc weld, but something Adh...I mean, I had an idea. If I can calibrate the electric field finely enough, I'll be able to manipulate electron clouds...and maybe influence chemical reactions." He shrugged apologetically and sighed. "I know that sounds crazy, but I did the math, and the supercomputer can do the chemical calculations if you can help me figure out the waveforms. It might not work, but...what do you think?"

She grinned. "Let's give it a shot!"

Several hours later, Donny, Maria, and Aliyah were all watching TV together and chatting about school when Olive came rushing downstairs.

"You guys. Y'all *gotta* see this."

She led them upstairs back to Cyrus's workroom, where he was inspecting a rusted screw under a microscope. He jumped and looked up when they entered the room.

"Oh! Uh..." he looked to Olive. "You want me to do it again?" She nodded vigorously. He turned to his clutter, poking around and shuffling through his piles until he retrieved a length of copper pipe. "Watch closely," he instructed. While wearing the gauntlets, as he held the pipe upright between two fingers, the NIRScanner beeped and his palm snapped and popped. From his fingertips, very slowly at first, the copper turned a deep sea-green in a cloud of smoke before fading into bright turquoise. The spots grew together until they met, then pooled into a turquoise stripe that engulfed the entire pipe.

"What happened to it?" asked Maria as Cyrus blew the smoke away.

"I oxidized it," he answered.

"The gauntlets made the copper atoms bond with oxygen," Olive beamed. "He turned the whole pipe into cupric oxide in seconds! It's the coolest thing I've ever seen!"

"Does it work reliably?" asked Adhara, suddenly appearing behind the group. Olive and Aliyah jumped.

"Mostly," answered Cyrus. "The code needs some smoothing out; I keep running into syntax errors when I try to make reactions with molybdenum. And there are a few chemical equations I want to program shortcuts for, but I can finish that tonight."

"Good. Because tomorrow, we're doing a field test."

"Who...what is that?" spluttered Olive, staring at Adhara.

"Good evening," she replied. "I'm Adhara."

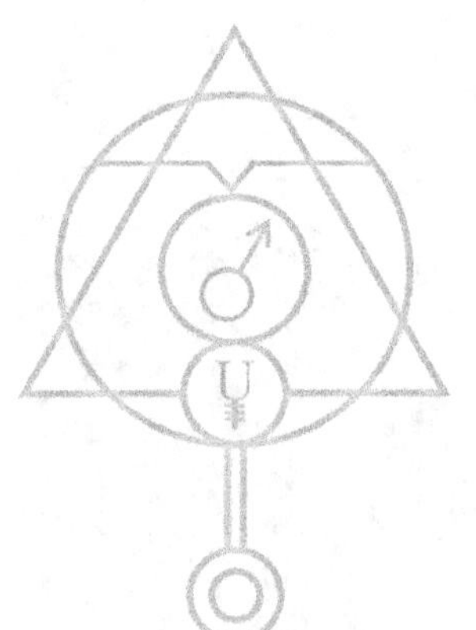

Chapter 6
GREASE TRAP

Olive and Aliyah wouldn't leave until past midnight, at which point Adhara refused further interrogation and ordered everyone to sleep. A few hours later she discovered Cyrus had snuck out of his bedroom and resumed working. She escorted him back to bed and stood guard outside his door until the following morning, at which time he ironically wanted to do nothing but sleep.

"What time is it?" he grumbled into his pillow. "Is anyone else even awake yet?"

"They are not," Adhara answered. "It would be best if we could leave before they do, to avoid further questions. Get ready, grab your gauntlets, and meet me downstairs. Dress for spelunking."

"Spelunking?" he muttered to himself as he rolled onto the floor.

"Ready to go?" she asked when he came downstairs wearing the gauntlets (which were now loaded with even more instruments than before) several minutes later. She admired his outfit; he had accessorized the gauntlets with a hoodie and bright red trousers. "Nice pants."

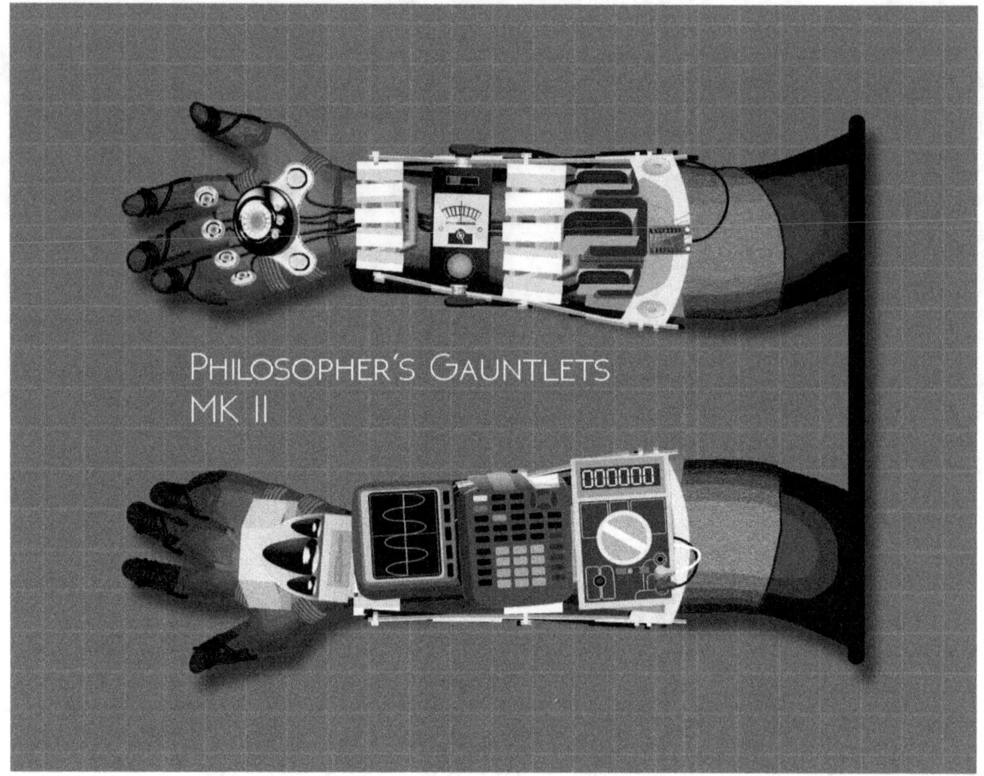

"I know they're a little flashy, but they're good pants. They're durable and fireproof. And they have lots of pockets."

"There's no need to be defensive. I wasn't being sarcastic. Are you ready to go?"

"I guess so, but where are we going?"

"As you know, my purpose for traveling back in time is to save Hudson City from destruction," she waited to tell him until they were outside. She led him briskly up the quiet street through the morning chill, heading towards the mountains. "Part of that mission is to destroy Anubis. Another part is to address the problems that created the circumstances which gave Anubis his power."

"What problems would those be?"

"All sorts of things," said Adhara as they left the road and began hiking into the woods. "Anything from repairing leaks and malfunctions, reinforcing infrastructure, neutralizing hazards, cleaning up waste, to putting out fires... preventing catastrophe before it happens and minimizing damage if it does."

"So we're going to be doing," Cyrus scoffed, "maintenance work? Seems a little...dull."

Adhara stopped and swept her gaze across the mountains. "A wise man once said, 'injustice is a weed. It grows in cracked roads and crumbling houses and forgotten corners, rooted in indifference and watered by suffering.'" She turned to him, smiling kindly. The breeze lifted her collar. "The best way to help a community is not just with episodic passion, but with chronic intention and compassion. If we repair the little problems that seem insignificant, we can prevent them from building up to devastation."

"Whatever you say," he surrendered, lifting his hands. "Seems like this work falls under Acryogen's responsibility, though."

"It does," she agreed. "But they are not able to do it. And we are."

Not long ago, Cyrus would have agreed with her. But after his repair frenzy the other night, and the hostility of Acryogen's response, doubt was beginning to form in his mind. With his cobbled-together invention, Cyrus had fixed thirty small problems in one night, just like Adhara was talking about. And yet a huge corporation couldn't? It couldn't be as simple as that, he decided. Just because he didn't understand didn't mean there wasn't a logical explanation.

After a period of walking, they emerged from the forest onto the slope of the mountains. Adhara led Cyrus up and then down into a rock quarry—he tried at first to be stealthy, but it quickly became apparent that the site was deserted. They passed dozens of rusted warning signs on their descent.

"Can you open this?" Adhara indicated a rusty metal door on an office building set into the rock at the bottom of the quarry. The Acryogen Industries logo on it was faded.

"Can't you?" he asked, surprised.

"I can," she clarified, "I want to know if *you* can."

He frowned at the door. "How should I go about it?"

"Reason it through."

"Okay," he approached the door. "Looks like steel." Knocked on it. "Hollow; not a fire door." Scratched at it. "The rust is only superficial; looks like it's still solid overall." Knocked some more. "Relatively thin but there's no water around, so I can't cut through it." Crouched down to inspect the deadbolt. "Too thick to kick in." He turned to Adhara. "Can't you just...rip it off its hinges?"

"You can do this, Cyrus." She placed a reassuring hand on his shoulder. "Think outside the box and find a solution with the resources available to you."

Cyrus nodded uncertainly and began to pace, occasionally muttering and glancing at the door. After a few moments he stopped suddenly, powered up his gauntlets and adjusted a few settings, and gently placed both his hands flat on the metal. A patch of rust grew from his fingertips, sparking where the clean metal met the powdery decay. After the entire door had oxidized, Cyrus kicked it once and it crumbled like wet cardboard.

"Very good," said Adhara as she followed him inside.

"I've explored a lot of abandoned war-era Acryogen facilities," said Cyrus, "but I didn't know about this one." He circled the stale room, glancing over the sparse furniture illuminated by sunlight dimly filtered through the grimy blinds. It looked like a small office. "Is this a mine or...something?"

"This facility is one of Acryogen Industries' best kept secrets," Adhara told him, squatting beside the desk in the center of the room. There was a click, and two laminate panels in the opposite wall slid back, revealing a concrete tunnel into the mountain.

"It's dark in there," said Cyrus. "Wish I'd thought to bring a flashlight. I guess you can see in the dark, right?"

"I can," she answered. "But you don't need a flashlight."

"Why not?"

"These light fixtures are fluorescent," she pointed to the ceiling. He frowned, not grasping her meaning, but after several moments during which she could practically hear the gears in his head grinding, Cyrus finally reached epiphany.

"Oh! You mean—" he made some adjustments on the multimeter of his gauntlets. Surveying the walls, he muttered to himself, "Let's say maybe, five-meter radius? Then, the field voltage would be…" he entered some formulas into the calculator and looked up. The gauntlets hummed and the fluorescent tubes directly above them glowed. He returned Adhara's smile and they continued down the tunnel. As they walked, the glow followed them, extending five meters ahead and behind.

"As you guessed, this facility is a mine, of sorts," Adhara continued. "At least, that was its original purpose. It was expanded throughout the war to facilitate weapons development, manufacturing, and utility infrastructure. It's referred to as 'the Pipeworks.'"

"How big is it?" asked Cyrus. He squinted down the tunnel but could see only infinite darkness.

"This tunnel extends all the way to the bay," she answered. "However, the network spans beneath the entire city."

Cyrus whistled. It echoed far. "That's amazing! And…kind of creepy. There's been a secret network of tunnels under the city all this time…." He looked around the tunnel with new attention, as though the grey pipes and wires mounted to the walls were suddenly more interesting. "You said this was built before the war?"

"Most of it. There is a subdivision of deployment tunnels that open up throughout the city built for the defense drones. They were built during the war."

"This is where the drones come from?" he swallowed, inching closer to Adhara.

"Almost all Acryogen Industries drones are manufactured, docked, and deployed from some part of the Pipeworks."

"Does that mean we might run into some?"

"Extremely unlikely," Adhara assured him. "Our business is in the older tunnels."

"And what is that business, exactly?" he asked as Adhara led him up a metal staircase set into the side of the tunnel wall.

"Something like a checkup," she replied, leading him down a service shaft. "Acryogen Industries has been running utilities like piping and power lines for the city through the Pipeworks for over a decade. We need to open all the surface service hatches so we can work," she explained. "The tunnels also make convenient shortcuts."

"How many hatches are there?"

"Approximately three hundred and thirty-six."

"Three *hundred*?" Cyrus stopped walking. "We don't have to go to each one, do we?"

"There is a master hatch release in the control station at the center of the complex."

"Oh, thank goodness," he sighed.

"However, the control station is 2.8 kilometers from our current position," she added. He groaned, trudging along.

"Well, I guess I can pass the time by asking you more questions, right?" Cyrus ventured as they descended a ladder into a wider tunnel. The lights, now wall-mounted, continued to glow from his gauntlets' electric field.

"If you would like to," she replied. They climbed over a pile of forgotten cargo.

"What am I like in the future?"

"I cannot tell you," she answered flatly.

"Why not?"

"If I tell you about your future self, it will produce a self-ful-filling prophecy. You will try to become what you believe you *should* be rather than staying true to yourself." She turned to him and smiled kindly. "The city needs the real Cyrus, not a facsimile."

"I suppose that's fair," said Cyrus bashfully. "What about Anubis? Can you tell me about him?"

"There's little I can tell you about him before he became the leader of the rebellion," Adhara answered, her expression growing serious. "But I can tell you some about the movement behind him."

"But—before you do that." Cyrus waved his finger in the general direction of her face. "What's...what's going on here? Why did you do that?"

"Do what, specifically?"

"You just made a face like you were remembering the darkest day in history!"

"It was, in Hudson City's history."

"Sure, but," he spluttered incredulously, "You're a robot! Showing emotion! I mean, what's the point of a robot mak-ing expressions?"

"My face assumed a position which you interpret as seri-ous," she answered, "to convey the seriousness of the sub-ject matter. Emotional response is non-verbal communica-tion."

"So it's...psychological framing? From whoever made you?"

"That assessment is reasonably accurate," she shrugged.

"And I suppose you can't tell me who that was, who's trying to give me a negative bias against a revolution that hasn't happened yet."

"The timing is not right yet," Adhara agreed. "How about I tell you what happens, and you draw your own conclu-sions?"

"How can I trust what you tell me?"

"I am incapable of lying directly. Belief or disbelief rests with you."

They walked in silence for a while as Cyrus deliberated, their footsteps echoing on the dark tunnel walls.

"All right. Tell me what happens," he said finally.

"As I said before, sentiment against Acryogen Industries built steadily since the end of the war," said Adhara, as though she were reciting from a history textbook. "After years of neglect, discontented citizens officially formed the rebel group Phoenix and began performing guerilla-style attacks on Acryogen supply caravans to redistribute goods to those in need, organizing community gardens, forming a service group to address neglected maintenance, and vandalizing Acryogen facilities for spare parts."

"That doesn't sound so bad," said Cyrus, "In fact, it seems like a fairly reasonable response to Acryogen's negligence. Were Phoenix really the bad guys in this story?"

"My directive is to save the city from destruction," Adhara responded. "I am unequipped to make moral judgments."

"Acryogen has its flaws…but I guess vandalism and property destruction aren't the right way to respond," Cyrus mused.

"Acryogen responded to the vandalism by reprogramming war-era defense drones to police the citizens, which sparked outrage across the city. But tensions reached a new level when a gas line explosion caused a fire that destroyed four apartment buildings and took twenty-three lives. The former residents blamed Acryogen for the disaster, claiming that the damage could have been minimal if the fire response had arrived more quickly. From that point, Phoenix expanded exponentially, gaining power and resources faster than ever before. But when Anubis became their leader, their tactics shifted from insurgent community support to outright warfare."

"Is that when they got all…'*down with Acryogen*?'"

"Yes. Anubis convinced them to pursue control," Adhara replied as their channel opened up into a cavernous new space. Cyrus could barely see the other side of the tunnel. Dust floated through long sunbeams from intermittent sky-light shafts, stories above them.

"Whoa," Cyrus backed away from the edge, "this tunnel is huge! How did they dig this without the city caving in?"

"They have specialized equipment, which we will hopeful-ly not encounter."

"Acryogen must have really had their hands full with something to just ignore a fire that big, but...I can see why people were mad. We have a lot of fires too. How did Anubis respond?" he asked as they continued down the cavernous tunnel via catwalk.

"He was Phoenix's arms dealer. He designed weapons for them which could destroy the drones and level entire build-ings. He made armor and bombs and found ways to turn Acryogen's defenses against itself, but he kept his most powerful inventions for himself."

"Whoa!" exclaimed Cyrus. They had turned a corner to find the enormous tunnel ended suddenly. Some gargantuan metal contraption was lodged in the pile of rock, like a dig-ging machine had been trying to enter the tunnel but only the drill head had made it through.

"So that's how they dug all this," he breathed as he leaned over the railing. "That thing must be almost as wide as this entire tunnel!"

"It's called a 'Grunger,'" Adhara provided. "And fortunately, it is inactive. These were used to excavate the largest tun-nels of the Pipeworks—what you see here is approximately one third of its length."

"One...third?" Cyrus turned to her, eyes wide. "Are there more of them?"

"It's unlikely that there are any still active. The seismic ac-tivity they cause is too conspicuous."

Cyrus stared at the Grunger uneasily.

"Grungers are the largest members of the fleet of auto-mated mining drones. We will most likely encounter some of the smaller members as we venture deeper into the Pipeworks." She ducked behind a support pylon as thick as a tree. When Cyrus followed, she wrenched open a rusted bulkhead condemned with warning signs. "This way. We're almost there."

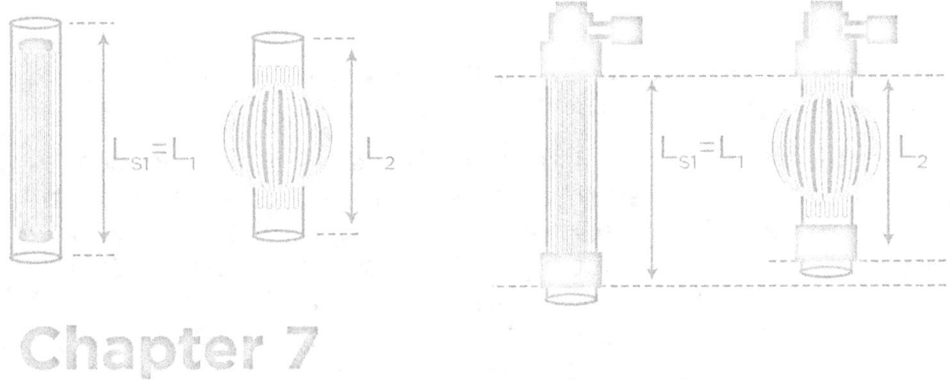

Chapter 7

PIPEWORKS

There were no light fixtures in the hallway beyond the bulkhead, so Cyrus powered down his gauntlets as Adhara used her glowing eyes to light their path.

"Are the mining drones still active?" Cyrus whispered, as though the darkness meant he should be quiet.

"Yes," she answered, running her hand against the wall. "I can feel the activity resonating through the earth."

"That's cool," said Cyrus, picking his fingernails sequentially. They heard a small staccato sound, like *tictic tic tic tictic.*

"You added a Geiger counter to your gauntlets?"

"Oh!" Cyrus laughed awkwardly, looking down at his wrist. "I forgot I had. I thought I was imagining it. I have auditory hallucinations sometimes." He looked up at Adhara. "Uh... what are the drones mining?"

"Anything they can find. Gold, silver, copper, and rare earth metals for electronics; iron and aluminum for construction, diamonds for cutting tools..."

They rounded a corner into a grimy decontamination shower room, just like the one they had seen at the defunct nuclear plant. By the light of Adhara's eyes they could see that the floor was covered in a few inches of a black, pitchy substance. A few human skeletons lay partially submerged in the goop.

"What on earth is that?" coughed Cyrus. "It smells like floor cleaner mixed with tar!"

"It's gallium arsenide silica-polyethylene hydrofluorocarbon. It's commonly referred to as 'munge.'" She held out her arm to prevent Cyrus from approaching it. "It's what your Geiger counter was reacting to. It's also corrosive, so don't step in it. Fortunately, in this state it congeals under heat." With a flick of her wrists she torched the munge, causing it to crinkle and harden, pulling away from the tile underneath.

"I wish I could just take water from the air like that," said Cyrus.

"Can't you?" Adhara turned. "With the field upgrades you worked on with Olive, you should be able to expand the polarization field." Cyrus shrugged and extended his arm while holding a button on the calculator. At first nothing happened, but soon his palm fizzled, then popped, and in moments he had a growing flame.

"Huh," he grinned. "Neat!"

Together they burned a clean path through the munge into the locker room beyond. The skeletons stared at them ominously in the flickering firelight.

"Why would they want to mine something like this?" asked Cyrus, waving his hand in front of his wrinkled nose. "It's not flammable, so it can't be fuel."

Adhara glanced at him out of the corner of her eye. "Acryogen used it to reanimate the dead."

"I'm sorry," Cyrus stopped, put his hands together under his nose and took a deep breath. "What?"

"When first extracted, crude munge is a semi-translucent yellow fluid," Adhara explained, beckoning him to keep moving. "It's used as a carrier fluid for ferromagnetic nano-robots. When combined, the munge and nanobots make 'colloidal munge,' which is a black gel that moves in the presence of a coded signal."

"That munge back there was black," Cyrus observed, "So it was colloidal?"

"That was inert munge. After the war, the munge project was discontinued, and all the control signals were deactivated. But if the inert munge were exposed to a new broadcast signal, it would reform into...foot soldiers."

"Where does reanimating the dead come in?"

"Well, the colloidal munge can't form strong structures without a framework," Adhara answered delicately.

"The skeletons..." Cyrus realized. "That's...really creepy."

"But effective. With this method, Acryogen fought the war without risking further loss of human life. The soldiers were incredibly durable and reformed as long as the signal was still being broadcast."

"You're sure they're...dead?" he asked as they exited the shower and entered a concourse. Adhara turned left, confidently navigating the maze.

"I detect no signal broadcast at their typical frequency, and the project was condemned at the end of the war." They turned off the concourse into a cavern. "The munge has been inert for almost thirty years."

The cavern stretched up far above their heads, and clustered on the walls were robots like tarantulas without legs. Their carapace was coppery, a clear design similarity with the security drones, and their eyes and abdomens glowed a ghostly white. Five tubes sprouting from their undersides whipped around the surface of the rock.

"What are they doing?" Cyrus whispered, immobilized.

"You don't need to worry," Adhara reassured him in a low voice. "They won't bother us. They're just harvesting crude munge."

"They sound like vacuum cleaners."

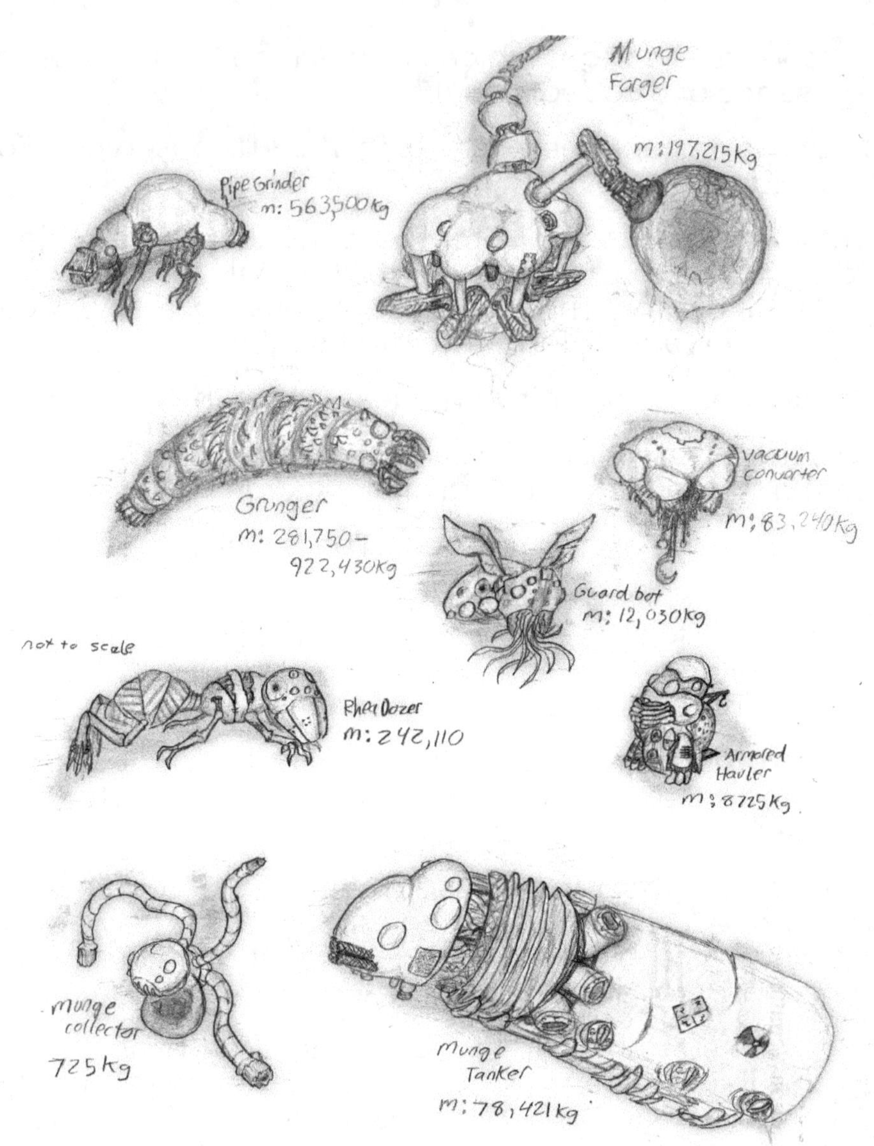

"They're called 'Munge Forgers.' They sublimate the munge with lasers at the end of their proboscises," she pointed to the surface of the rock, from which was oozing the slimy munge. "Then they suck the gas into a containment tank to be transported and distilled."

"If the project was scrapped, then why are they still mining?" Cyrus whispered despite her reassurance. A much larger robot, like a flying tanker truck with impulsion units instead of wheels, rose past the catwalk they were on. As it hovered above them and the smaller robots gathered around it to deposit their spoils, Cyrus noticed that they all used the same propulsion systems as the Bouncer drones.

"The most likely explanation is that they are completely automated, and no humans have come to this part of the Pipeworks to deactivate them." Adhara led them through another door back into a final concrete chamber, which was much quieter and darker than the mining cavern. The walls were smoother, lines cleaner, and outdated computers around the room were coated in a thick layer of powdered rock. Pipes ran from the ceiling down to tanks of munge throughout the room, and there were rooms behind thick acrylic panels where skeletons had been articulated on a frame.

"This must be where they were made," Cyrus surmised, cringing.

"Yes," Adhara answered emotionlessly. "This is a development lab."

"'Grimlord' rearticulating tests?" He turned to Adhara, holding a clipboard. "Is that what they were called?"

"Their official designation is 'cybernetic colloid rearticulated cadaver.' The moniker 'Grimlord' was coined for the purpose of intimidation."

"It's working," murmured Cyrus. The articulated skeleton behind the window was a gruesome amalgamation—it had two and a half skulls, three arms, and its rib cage extended from the stomach to well above where the neck would have been. Steel struts were fused to the bones at weak points and the uppermost skull had a receiving antenna embedded in it.

"Whose remains did they use for this?" he asked quietly, continuing to explore.

"In the early years of the war, enemy carpet-bombing killed hundreds of people at a time and the remains couldn't always be identified. The alternative to this was a mass grave."

"At least a mass grave would be more respectful."

"I understand this upsets you," Adhara said soothingly, though he didn't respond."But it's in the past. There's nothing you can do about it now."

"It doesn't help to forgive and forget if they haven't learned their lesson." Cyrus turned away. "Come on. We have work to do."

As they exited the lab, they came into another cavernous area like a warehouse. It was much cleaner than the lab, with stacks of crates reaching five or so stories above them. The only light came from spinning orange hazard beacons spaced intermittently in the aisles.

"That's the control booth," Adhara pointed to an octagonal glass box suspended above the warehouse a few blocks away from them.

"All these boxes are labelled..." he commented as they walked down the aisles. "Are these all...Grimlords?"

"Yes." Adhara's eyes flashed as she stared at the boxes. "Each container holds a skeleton with a receiver and a quantity of colloidal munge."

"They're like coffins," he grimaced. "But in reverse. There's enough here for an army."

They climbed the rebar rungs at the base of the control booth. Once at the top, Adhara forced the door open and they slipped inside. They reactivated the power from the breakers and wiped the dust off a beeping monitor to see the command line interface.

"This command line triggers the master hatch release," explained Adhara as she typed. "Unless someone has programmed in a bypass, it will open all the entrances to the Pipeworks without changing any other settings." She pressed Enter. Nothing happened.

"I got it," said Cyrus, typing a few commands of his own. "This'll get us access."

"Cyrus, wait—"

The computer loaded grindingly, the disc drive painstakingly sending commands to each hatch and displaying the status on the monitor. All was going well—but then it started receiving error messages. About a third of the hatch statuses were coming back malfunctioned, and suddenly a window flashed on the screen: "Security breach detected! Countermeasures activated."

The lights in the warehouse flashed on, sterile white light poured into the security room, and within seconds they were surrounded by drones with charging guns. But as Adhara and Cyrus prepared for a fight, the lights surged brighter and went out. They were thrown back into darkness, the drones still visible by their propulsion units. They hovered quietly, evaluating. Then there was a guttural screech that echoed off the distant walls. The drones turned at once, firing as they swooped down towards the floor. Cyrus couldn't see what happened but one by one the lights of the drones disappeared, each with a muffled crash.

"What is it?" Cyrus asked Adhara insistently. She backed away from the window. "What's happening?"

Emergency lights flashed on, providing dim yellow light. In the aisles between the towers of cargo, Cyrus could make out throngs of shadowy humanoid figures. A few were lurching around aimlessly, but most were joining a growing crowd rushing towards the control booth.

"I thought you said the Grimlords couldn't be activated!" he exclaimed. The booth was already shaking as the horde began to climb. "How do we fight them? You said fire only works while they're inert!"

"The only effective countermeasure against active Grimlords is an electromagnetic pulse," Adhara said quickly, scanning the room. "I can produce one but if I did so in here the chain reaction surge would be catastrophic."

"Then what do we do?"

"Cyrus, listen to me." She turned to him seriously. "If they make it inside this booth it is likely we will be overwhelmed."

"Wh-what do you mean?" he asked nervously, glancing out the windows. "You can fight them, can't you?"

"On contact with the munge, it will likely seep into the seams of my body and disable me before I can adequately react."

"*Oh*." Cyrus felt his pulse in his ears.

"We're running out of time. You need to chemically reinforce the door." She handed him a stack of charred paper, a wrench, and a couple of screwdrivers. "Use these."

Before Cyrus could say anything, she crossed to the other side of the room and began tearing into the wall, using the torch in her palm to cut into the metal underneath. He turned back to his door, wracking his brain for the answer, then finally realized her intention. The door was steel—but with the right ingredients, he could make it *better* steel.

Chewing on his lip nervously, Cyrus frantically typed equations into the gauntlet's controls. When the NIRScanner beeped, the Grimlords had reached the door. They were pounding on it, shaking the frame, trying to force their way in like termites burrowing into wood. One pressed its face into the adjacent window, and he could see beads of munge pushing in around the frame. Finally, he finished calibrating the gauntlets and reduced the paper ash and screwdrivers to a fine black powder, which hovered in a swirling ball above his palms. Breathing in four-second intervals, he traced swathes across the door's surface, burning away the oxidization as he reinforced the center and seams. He finished by fusing the hinges each into one solid piece.

"That should buy us some time," he told Adhara. The Grimlords were still at the door, but their frantic thrashing no longer shook the doorframe.

"Good," Adhara had finished with the wall. The panel she had cut fell outward, a metal rectangle five centimeters thick. She ushered Cyrus into the hole, carefully avoiding the hot edges then spot welding the panel back in place behind them before quickly leading him down a narrow service shaft.

"A control beacon activated when the security measures went through," Adhara explained. "I heard it go off after the error message came up."

"Well that's just *great*!" Cyrus was speaking too quickly, his hands shaking. "We've unwittingly unleashed an undead army! So much for saving the city!"

Adhara turned and slapped him across the face. He fell to the ground, spluttering.

"Do you feel better?" she asked, crouching beside him. He took a few slow breaths.

"Yeah. Okay. I'm okay." He nodded slowly and shivered. "I can't believe that worked. You'd think in real life, slapping someone across the face would rile them up *more*."

"Normally it would, but I also delivered a mild sedative."

"Oh. Really?"

"We need to find what's broadcasting that control signal," she helped him up, "and destroy it. The walls are too dense for me to get a precise read on it, but when it went off, I was able to determine the direction of origin."

Cyrus nodded, newly resolved. "You're right. I'm ready."

They emerged from the service hatch on a catwalk near the top of the room. The Grimlords wandered the aisles below.

"Listen," Adhara instructed before they continued. "Individual Grimlords are blind. They navigate using sonar, but their range won't reach up here if we stay quiet." Cyrus nodded and they crept across the catwalk, successfully avoiding detection as they entered the next room. They were back in the lab, able to see the lower floor under the balcony. A few Grimlords were lurking in the shadows below.

"The signal came from that direction." Adhara pointed down a long hallway labelled "*Rogue Asylum*." Halfway down the hall, they found a doorway that had been torn apart. On the floor among shards of concrete lay the door, bent like an old can. The interior of the room looked like a bomb had gone off at the center of a towering containment tank. They quietly searched the room, and Cyrus rifled through a stack of documents.

"They were trying to build a *new* kind of Grimlord," he whispered to Adhara. "With an...'integrated autonomous control beacon?' A Grimlord that controls *other* Grimlords?" He turned the page and grimaced. There were photographs. The Grimlord in question, labelled on every page as "Animal King," was much taller in comparison to the scientists juxtaposed in the pictures. The photos were blurry, but its head looked like it was made of a wolf's skull with ram's horns. The rest of its hulking body was an amalgamated jumble of mismatched bones and munge. On the last page of the documents someone had taped a CD labelled "*A.K. control frequency.*"

"A compact disc," Cyrus murmured. "Retro."

"Let me see that," Adhara requested. She spun the disc, staring at the shiny side. "Maybe I can scan this and communicate with them." She winked her left eye for a full second, and when she opened it again, her iris was almost black, and her pupil was a pinprick. A red laser shot out from her eye and shone through the disc as she spun it on her finger.

"Communicate? You could talk with them?" Cyrus asked.

"The signal isn't complex enough for conversation. And they wouldn't accept commands from me," she blinked her eye back to normal and set the disc down. "But I can listen to them."

"Can you hear anything now?"

"It's faint," Adhara cocked the side of her head. "I hear...'Assimilate.'"

"'Assimilate?' Is that it?"

"It's fading away, but it must be Animal King. It's the only command signal." She turned back to him. "It's gone. It could be anywhere by now."

"Anywhere...in the city?"

"Grimlords are programmed to avoid congregations of live humans, unless ordered otherwise. Most likely it will avoid populated areas and seek out secluded areas where it can find remains, like graveyards."

"Ew," Cyrus shuddered.

"There's little we can do for now. We've done what we came to do. We should go." Adhara headed for the door.

"What, really?" Cyrus asked, incredulous. "You want to just go home? What about the Grimlords?"

"It's best not to directly engage them unless necessary."

A Grimlord appeared in the doorway. It emitted a shrill shriek, lunging towards them. Cyrus flinched but Adhara reacted immediately, swinging a pipe like a bat and sending the monster flying, but it was too late. They could hear the others coming.

"Run!" Adhara pulled him into the hallway, half-dragging him back towards the tunnels. Cyrus glanced behind his shoulder at the feral jumble of bones and murk gushing down the dark hallway, like a wave flooding the tunnel, closing in behind them. Adhara took sharp turns one after the other, trying to evade, but it was no use. There were too many and they surged forward, just meters away, until suddenly a long black claw reached forward and gripped Cyrus' leg—fortunately over his thick pants.

Adhara's shoulder flexed and she flung him up the hallway, breaking the Grimlord's grip. Cyrus heard a piercing whine as she was sucked backwards and engulfed. They were almost on him when he felt a tingle that set his hair on end—his backpack burst in a shower of sparks and the Grimlords dissolved into bones and tar. He scrambled backwards to avoid the caustic puddle. A few meters away, Adhara emerged, covered in black ooze. She shook herself off then broke out into a run again, pulling Cyrus along with her. They could still hear distant howls deep in the Pipeworks.

When they could no longer hear the Grimlords, Adhara allowed them to slow to a walk. Cyrus simply trudged along, exhausted and overwhelmed, trusting Adhara to lead him through the maze. Eventually they reached a stone staircase, and to Cyrus' surprise it emerged directly into his basement through a hydraulic hatch mounted to a drainage grate.

"You should get some sleep," Adhara suggested. "And Cyrus?"

He looked up at her slowly, barely standing. He noticed scattered holes burned into her clothes from the munge.

"I know some of the things that you saw today and some of the things that happened really bothered you," she said softly. "I just want to make sure you're okay."

"If you're talking about what they did, or rather, what they made..." he sighed. "I get it. In war, being in charge means making choices no one wants to make."

She nodded. "It's big of you to acknowledge that. Go upstairs and get some rest." She closed the hatch in the floor. "You'll need it."

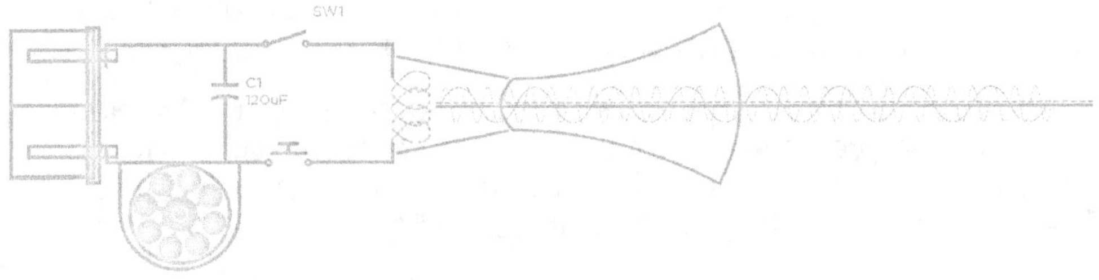

Chapter 8
THE HUNT

"Hey buddy," Maria eased open Cyrus' workshop door. "I noticed you finally got up. Have a nice nap?"

"Yeah," Cyrus yawned while signing back. "I can't believe I slept past sunset."

"I heard you had quite the adventure with Adhara."

"Yes, but don't worry, we didn't go into town and we weren't seen by anyone. So technically, I'm still 'laying low.'"

"I'm glad." She sat across from him. "I wouldn't know what to do if you got arrested, or something."

She sat waiting as Cyrus silently soldered within his disassembled backpack. The radioactive diamond glowed somberly on a table nearby.

"What are you working on?"

"Oh. Well...." Cyrus struggled to provide the appropriate amount of information. "I'm just repairing the gauntlets. Adhara made an EMP—that's an electromagnetic pulse— and it overloaded my power supply. Don't worry about it." Absorbed in his work, Cyrus didn't put down the soldering iron to sign for her, and hardly spoke clearly enough for her to lip read.

"Cyrus," she gently placed her hand on his. "Will you please just talk to me for a minute?"

With a huff Cyrus wiped his soldering iron on a damp sponge and laid it in its stand. "I'm listening," he signed.

"I'm worried that this project is consuming you," Maria signed, her eyes full of concern. "You've been ignoring everything else in your life and forgetting important things. It seems like you're becoming obsessed."

"This is my priority!" Cyrus objected. "Can't you understand how important this is to me? And to the *city*? This isn't just my project, my life's work anymore. I'm supposed to save the whole city!"

"I understand how important this is," she signed firmly. "I do."

"Then why aren't you being more supportive?"

She paused, choosing her words carefully. "Your life is more than the Philosopher's Gauntlets," she signed finally.

He blinked, confused.

"There's more in your life than this project. You have friends, loved ones, *other* inventions even," she continued, "and plenty of other redeeming qualities *besides* being an inventor and a chemical engineer!" she smiled softly at him. "If you had never even had the idea for the gauntlets, you would still be worth something. And you would still be my best friend."

Cyrus softened, returning her smile apologetically. "You really think that I've been obsessed?"

"Well, you haven't been to the lab since Adhara got here. I don't want you to lose your internship."

"Oh, yeah." He grimaced. "Doctor Cargyle must be *super* mad."

"And, you were so caught up with working on the gauntlets and going on adventures with Adhara that you forgot to help me study for my Biochem midterm like you promised."

"Oh no!" Cyrus clapped a hand to his forehead. "I'm so sorry, I forgot all about that! When is it? We can study right now!"

"It was yesterday," she chuckled, dismissing his grief. "It's okay, I made an A. I made flashcards and Donny helped me instead."

"Man," Cyrus leaned back in his chair and rubbed his forehead. "I guess I really have let things slide. Maria, I'm sorry." He looked her in the eye. "You're right. I've been too absorbed in this project and I've been neglecting our friendship, and I apologize."

"Apology accepted," she smiled.

"Cyrus. Cyrus, wake up."

Cyrus blinked blearily in the light from the TV. It was night; he and Maria must have fallen asleep playing old video games. She was still curled up on the adjacent loveseat.

"Wake up, Cyrus. We have a problem."

"What?" he rubbed his eyes, squinting up at Adhara. "What'sa happ...what time 'zit?"

"It's three in the morning. I suspect the Grimlords are terrorizing the city."

"What?" he shot upright.

"I have been intercepting distress calls from citizens who have witnessed creatures that fit a Grimlord's description," she continued. "So far Acryogen Crisis Response is dismissing the reports, but it's only a matter of time before they put the pieces together. We need to get to the city and disable the Grimlords before Acryogen discovers they've been reactivated."

"How do we do that? EMPs again?"

"I can only produce an EMP in twenty-minute intervals. And, if I do so too closely to you, it will overload your gauntlets again and leave you vulnerable. We need greater precision."

"Okay...I have a dumb idea. Could you recharge a lithium battery from your own power source?"

Adhara nodded. Cyrus turned to Maria and gently shook her awake.

"What are you doing?" Adhara whsipered.

"What," Maria signed, squinting.

"Trust me," Cyrus told Adhara. "I have a plan, but we'll need Maria's help. She's an amazing shot."

Cyrus led Adhara and Maria up to his workroom and began digging through the cluttered shelves on his far wall.

"Why am I awake right now?" signed Maria irritably, barely awake.

"So uh," he grunted, "remember that little 'adventure' Adhara and I went on yesterday?"

"Yeah..."

"We kind of accidentally released an...undead army from an underground crypt?"

Maria blinked slowly. "Am I still dreaming?"

"Adhara, could you explain Grimlords in a way that a bio-chem major would understand?"

"Hey now," Maria warned.

"They're skeletons with a body of Ferro-fluid," Adhara explained. "Acryogen Industries created them from human remains to use as foot soldiers during the war."

"And kept them in an 'underground crypt?'"

"Sort of. Long story," said Cyrus, heaving a pile of magnets and cables and a microwave oven onto the table. He gutted

the microwave, ripping the magnetron out whole in one yank.

"So, they're loose...in the city?" Maria surmised. "Let me guess. We have to hunt them down and kill them?"

"Correct," said Adhara as Cyrus gutted another microwave. "Time is of the essence, Cyrus."

"I know, I know," he muttered, soldering. He returned to his shelves and pulled out a trumpet, of all things. And after it—another trumpet!

"Are you rebuilding your EMP cannon?" asked Maria.

"It's the only way to destroy Grimlords," he explained as he attached the trumpet to a gun stock. "We need precision and range, and a brass trumpet bell is surprisingly good for directing the pulse." He soldered a magnetron to each trumpet valve, securing the contraptions with thick layers of tape.

"This one is yours, Adhara; it doesn't have a battery. Maria, yours has a battery but Adhara will need to recharge it after each use."

"What about you?" asked Maria, accepting her weapon.

"I modified the gauntlets to produce a localized EMP when I was repairing the power supply," he shrugged. "Instead of a trumpet bell it uses the Lorentz field to focus the pulse. I figured it might come in handy."

"There's no way we won't get stopped if we carry these things through downtown," Maria signed. "We need a disguise—especially you, since you're technically still a fugitive."

He nodded slowly, considering his options.He turned to a steel cabinet. After a few minutes of rummaging, he produced two disguises. In one hand, a very comfortable and modern welding helmet, and in the other, a very uncomfortable and outdated gas mask.

"You take the welding helmet," he sighed, handing it to Maria. "Let's grab some clothes and get out of here."

"How are we going to *get* downtown unnoticed?" Maria asked as they rushed downstairs after donning their disguises. Her black, hooded trench coat over the welding helmet made it easy for her to blend into shadows—unlike Cyrus' conspicuous ensemble of a hoodie pulled over a war-era gas mask and bright red pants. This was not even to mention his gauntlets, or the glowing robot beside him. "After your vandalism spree the other night we're sure to be stopped if we go on foot or even on bikes."

"Secret tunnel."

"What?"

"Secret tunnel," he repeated.

"This has been here the whole time?!"

Maria stared dumbfounded down the tunnel as Adhara helped Cyrus lower their bikes through the hatch in the basement floor. Suddenly, Cyrus wondered how his bike had made it home, as he distinctly remembered leaving it at the beach before meeting Adhara.

"Yeah!" he grunted, "secret underground tunnel maze. Who knew, right?"

"So, this is the underground crypt you mentioned?" Maria asked before mounting her bike.

"Adhara said it's called the Pipeworks."

"It's a complex labyrinth of industrial tunnels and conduits beneath the city," Adhara added. "We can use them to move covertly throughout the city and investigate the Grimlord sightings."

Adhara led them (hovering ahead of their bikes) down the tunnel from Cyrus' house and into a brightly illuminated concourse that echoed with announcements from a distant P.A. system. From there she led them into a side tunnel, and then another, and then another, each one growing progressively narrower. When Adhara signaled them to stop, the tunnel was only a few meters wide. By force of habit, Cyrus and Maria chained their bikes to the ladder before climbing up to the surface. They slipped their masks on and emerged from a gated mausoleum in a graveyard on the edge of town.

"I don't see anything weird," Maria signed.

"Me neither," Cyrus signed, listening to the crickets. "Wait a minute—look over there!"

Across the hill there were rows and rows of empty graves—in front of weathered gravestones. Irregular footprints pocked the torn grass and freshly churned soil.

"The graves are empty," said Adhara, inspecting the scene. "Evidence of chemical burns on local flora indicates Grimlord presence."

"Why would they do this?" Maria wrinkled her nose at the empty graves from a distance—not that anyone could see her wrinkling her nose under her mask.

"Remember the signal you intercepted?" Cyrus turned to Adhara. "Assimilate?"

"I remember."

"You don't think..."

"I do."

"Then, Animal King..."

"Is likely nearby."

"Can you pick up the signal right now?"

"Yes," Adhara swiveled her head like an owl. "It's the same signal, just 'assimilate.' That direction."

"Okay, then we should try to sneak up...what is it, Maria?" She was tapping frantically on his arm. She pointed to a shadowy grove at the edge of the graveyard, where the lawn turned into woods. Adhara stepped in front of them seconds before a snarling Grimlord lunged from the undergrowth—it clamped mottled jaws around her arm, but she flung it bodily into a nearby grave. It scrambled frantically

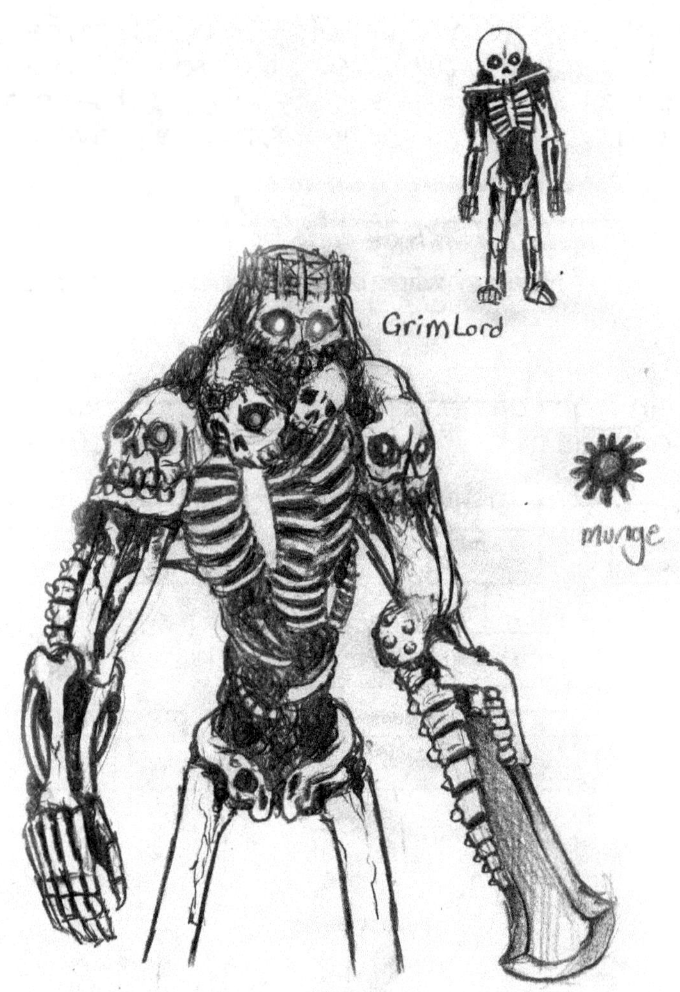

and Adhara tensed for another blow, but it dissolved into goop. They turned in surprise to Maria, who was pointing her EMP trumpet at the bubbling puddle of munge.

"What?" she signed. "It's not that hard." The capacitor whined and she handed the trumpet to Adhara to recharge.

"They're not so bad on their own," Cyrus commented, powering up his gloves. "If we're lucky, maybe we can pick them off like that one by one."

"There should be more than this," Adhara said seriously. "Remember how many there were in the Pipeworks? I probably destroyed about twenty down there, but there were hundreds originally."

"Well, there are tons of footprints here," Cyrus added. "Let's check the other graveyard."

The other graveyard on the opposite side of town yielded a similar scene. Footprints, disturbed earth, empty graves—but deserted.

"I don't want to try and fight the Animal King without thinning out the Grimlords first, but we don't have time for a wild goose chase," Cyrus groaned. He picked his fingernails sequentially, pacing amongst the headstones.

"Can we find a way to track them?" Maria asked.

"Adhara, do they give off any kind of radiation, or heat, or something? Anything unique?"

"Their bodies give off minimal heat because they move using magnetic fields, but the magnetic field is too localized to track over long distances. Munge is radioactive, but their radiation is obscured by Acryogen facilities throughout the city, and they have no chemical characteristics that can be detected over long distances."

"Could you hack into those?" asked Maria, pointing to a security camera.

"I could, but it is unlikely we would be able to see them. Grimlords are designed for stealth, so they will keep moving and stay in shadow to evade detection."

"That's creepy," said Cyrus. "Okay, I have a dumb idea. We've gotta get to that big multilevel parking garage on seventh street."

Chapter 9

THE TRAP

Fortunately, the multilevel parking garage extended five stories below ground, and connected to the Pipeworks on the fourth sublevel. They emerged into a dark alcove behind a chain-link fence.

"Adhara told me that Grimlords respond to sound," Cyrus explained as he led them up the stairwell to the roof. "If we can't find them, maybe we can make them find us." He approached the railing at the far end of the parking lot.

"I get it," signed Maria as they looked over the edge of the roof. "Shooting gallery."

"And now all we need is bait." He turned to Adhara. "Can you set off that car's alarm?"

Adhara leaned over the railing to look at the car he was pointing to on the street, several stories below. "How?" she asked.

"What do you mean? Just...set it off."

"Car alarms are triggered by physical shock. How do you propose I disturb it?"

"You can't just...hack into it, or something?"

"As you are well aware, I can't hack into a device that lacks a wireless network."

"Well, I don't know, you're a super-powered robot! Just do something!"

"I'm not a god, Cyrus. I have limits; I can't do just anything." She turned away from him, walking over towards a parked truck. Without any hesitation she ripped one of the truck's back wheels off its lug nuts, and returned to the railing, hefting the wheel over her head.

"Whoa!" Cyrus shouted, flinching at the echo. "What on earth are you doing?"

"The impact from the tire at this height will trigger the alarm."

"Can we maybe try to *avoid* serious property damage?" he hissed. She dropped the tire, waiting expectantly. "How

about you fly down there and just sort of, you know...give it a shake."

Adhara vaulted the railing, gracefully flipping into a hover just before hitting the sidewalk. She grabbed the car by its front bumper, lifted it to her waist, and dropped it heavily, making Maria and Cyrus wince. The alarm went off immediately, the unbearable kind that strains the imagination with each distinct noise an air horn can make.

"*That* should do it," Cyrus whispered as Adhara landed beside them, and he was right. They were hard to spot at first, but one by one the ghouls appeared, never more than an arm that slipped out of shadow for a moment or alabaster skulls glowing faintly in the streetlights. They surrounded the blaring car, seething around the edges of the light. Then all at once the horde lurched forward, dragging the car away. "Now!" Cyrus whispered. One by one they liquefied the Grimlords from the rooftop.

"They're not...doing anything," signed Maria, getting a recharge from Adhara. "We're killing them, and the others don't respond."

"Grimlords operate on a hive mind," Adhara replied. "They're not programmed to react to their own kind, and without a human operator they don't recognize anything unusual."

Soon the car was accosted by a single remaining Grimlord, which Maria shot into sludge. She blew imaginary smoke off her gun.

"You're a pretty bad shot, Cyrus," she signed, smirking.

"Yeah, I know," he scowled. "We should get down there and clean that up." The inert lake of munge oozed into the gutter.

"The munge is running into a storm drain," Adhara observed as they headed back towards the stairwell. "How is your tap water? Reasonably clean?"

Before Cyrus could answer they heard a bloodcurdling scream. Cyrus and Adhara rushed back to the railing. When Maria asked what they were doing, they heard the scream again—Cyrus pointed down to the street, a couple of blocks away. A woman, possibly the owner of the victimized car, had ventured outside and attracted the attention of a straggler Grimlord. Maria took a shot at it, but it was too far.

"I thought you said they don't go after live people!" Cyrus shouted at Adhara as they scrambled down the stairwell.

"They can be unpredictable," she replied as they burst out onto the street. "Perhaps she provoked it somehow."

"How do you provoke a Grimlord?"

"By making loud noises, or throwing things." Adhara hurled the stolen truck tire at the Grimlord, nailing it squarely in the chest. It staggered backwards, unharmed as the tire bounced off it, but Adhara's plan worked. It sprinted towards them and Maria melted it at twenty paces.

"Wh-wha-what was that thing?" the woman stammered. "That was like something out of a nightmare!"

"This *is* only a nightmare," Adhara assured her, glowing like a fallen angel. "Go upstairs and go back to sleep."

"I–what? But who are...it's—"

"Go back to sleep!" Cyrus repeated. Taken aback, the woman scrambled back inside.

"Okay," he turned back to Adhara and Maria, "We got a lot of them, right? I think we should maybe hunt down a few more big—"

They heard another scream, echoing through the streets. Then another.

"What now?" Cyrus griped, signing "more screams" to Maria. They followed Adhara to the second scream. They found another Grimlord, terrorizing a man, and it had barely turned towards them before Adhara incapacitated it with her trumpet.

"Thank you!" the man gasped. "You saved my life!"

"Did it hurt you?" Cyrus asked, helping the man to his feet.

"No..." the man checked his body. "It followed me from across the street and then sort of just...stared at me! Menacingly!"

"Okay. Get inside; it's not safe outside tonight."

"Uh. Yes, okay! Thank you...!"

When they reached the location of the third scream, they found a Grimlord standing over a woman who was cowering in a doorway. As they approached it turned to them calmly, unmoving as it stared with lifeless sockets. Cyrus stepped carefully closer, but it didn't react. It remained still as he stood close enough to see the shards of skull that formed its twisted face and made no attempt to retaliate as Cyrus raised his hand and liquefied it.

"Are you hurt?" he asked the woman.

"No, it never touched me!" she exclaimed. "I came outside to try and help with the fire and that...thing came out of the fire and cornered me, and it just...stood there! Like it was waiting for me to do something!"

"Hold the phone," Cyrus waved his hand, "now give the phone to me. *What* fire?"

The woman pointed across the street. In a nearby alley they could see bright yellow light flickering on the side of a building.

"Go back inside," Cyrus said slowly. Maria took the woman by the arm and helped her up the stairs, comforting her. When the woman was safely inside Cyrus cautiously led them down the alley. As soon as they turned off the street, they felt a wave of heat and saw it—a warehouse fire. As they drew closer, a Grimlord emerged from the blaze. Another followed it, then another, and soon a growing crowd of steaming wraiths formed a wall before them. Behind them—even more of them, appearing in the alley and emerging from windows and climbing down from the rooftops, forming a barrier and waiting patiently for their prey to react.

"When I say," Cyrus murmured, and his quavering words hung in the tension of the air. "Adhara, you set off an EMP towards those behind us." He powered down his gauntlets. "Maria, as soon as she does that, you run. Get back to the parking garage and barricade yourself in the Pipeworks. Don't stop until you're safe."

They nodded. Cyrus couldn't see Maria's face, but her posture was tense. Adhara's chest whined. Cyrus looked around the horde, gauging their twitchy but otherwise tranquil behavior. "NOW!" he shouted and made a feint lunge towards the warehouse. The Grimlords lurched forward furiously, following him as he leaped backwards toward Adhara. She released the pulse, liquefying all the Grimlords surrounding them. Maria took the opening unhesitatingly and sprinted out of the alley, disappearing around the corner.

"Step one," Cyrus breathed, powering up his gauntlets. The remaining horde quickly reformed, surrounding them again. He held out his hands, sucking what little water was left in the air, then released the oxyhydrogen in a burning hurricane. The waves of fire passed over the Grimlords harmlessly.

"Grimlords are extremely resistant to heat," Adhara reminded him, "as is evidenced by the fact that several of them just emerged from a burning building."

"I know, but I had to try. It's reflexive." The horde closed in. Adhara and Cyrus backed up against each other.

"Any other ideas?" Adhara asked.

"I don't perform well under pressure!" Cyrus stammered. They were almost within reach. "Wait a minute! Pressure!"

Adhara's body plates pulled away from her joints, preparing for combat, and Cyrus recalibrated his gauntlets for nitrogen and diverted all power to the Lorentz tractor field. He backed against the wall, waiting for the capacitors to charge.

The shadowy crowd parted. From the cindering depths of the warehouse a shadow emerged, much larger than any of the other Grimlords.

"It waited until we couldn't use EMPs," Cyrus realized.

"This is concerning," Adhara commented. "They are not supposed to be this intelligent without a human operator."

"I guess that's what Animal King was made for."

Animal King had a giant wolf skull face with ram horns as the photographs had revealed, but the blurry documentation of the lab couldn't do justice to its sheer dreadful presence.Like a lich, the monster towered over them with pieces of rotting flesh clinging to its ribs and bones. The remaining fur on its mangled skin had caught fire, and as it emerged from the blaze, they could see that it clutched in its ragged claw one end of a rusted chain.

"Oh. *That's* what assimilate means," said Cyrus, pointing. A second shadow followed Animal King, indistinct at first, but as it lumbered forward, they regarded in horror a war beast containing dozens of skeletons, like a nightmarish, eldritch bear. Even on all fours it loomed higher than its master.

"We gotta get out of here," Cyrus muttered. He released a stream of pressurized nitrogen from his palm, freezing the nearest Grimlord. The rest of the horde howled, provoked, and he swung his arms in a wide arc, freezing their faces or arms, but offering no real resistance to the subsequent infantry. He turned and tried to run as they scratched and clawed at his arm, leaving long gouges and shredding one of his gauntlets. He looked over at Adhara—they had her limbs pinned back, contorted into irregular positions, trying to break her apart; the munge seeped between her joints.

Cyrus made random inputs with his remaining gauntlet, desperately and unsuccessfully lashing at the Grimlords with chemical reactions.They bore forward, slowly but ever surely. One reached out to grab him—but the space between Cyrus and the Grimlords suddenly filled with a white cloud! A squadron of bright red fire-fighting drones had arrived to save the warehouse (which was beyond saving).

"FINALLY, you show up!" Cyrus yelled at them. He jumped up and wrenched the two retardant tanks from the nearest drone, making it squeal in protest. With his good arm he lobbed one cylinder at the Grimlords surrounding him, inducing an icy blast that immobilized them. He threw the other cylinder directly at Adhara, and after it engulfed her

in a frozen cloud she ripped herself free of the brittle golems. She snatched another drone from midair and tossed
a cylinder to Cyrus, keeping the other. Cyrus recalibrated
his gauntlet and used the retardant spray mixed with air
to form a thick barrier of ice, sealing the smaller Grimlords
inside. They could see Animal King glaring at them on the
other side, backed by the glow of the dwindling fire.

"How long until you can make an EMP again?" Cyrus
asked her.

"Twelve seconds."

"Make it a big one."

The seconds passed slowly.Cyrus kept his hands up, reinforcing their protective, icy shield from all directions as
the remaining Grimlords scrambled all over, looking for an
entry point.

Finally, Adhara burst through the wall of ice, careening
through the air like a gymnast. She landed gracefully at
Animal King's feet and released the massive wave of energy, overloading streetlights and making Cyrus' backpack
explode into sparks again though he was a few meters
away. But despite the power of the surge and the puddle
of munge that used to be its war-beast, Animal King stood
resolutely before them.It smacked a nearby drone to the
ground like it was swatting at a fly.

"It appears that the Animal King transmitter has electromagnetic shielding," said Adhara, leaping backward to
Cyrus' side.

"Plan B," said Cyrus, preparing another cylinder. He leveled
his palm at Animal King, but it only stared back. He released
the stream of slush, forming a tall iceberg where Animal
King had been standing. They heard applause—a few residents of the nearby apartment buildings had woken up
to the disturbance. But when the fog cleared, the ice was
empty.

"There's an entrance to the Pipeworks under that warehouse," said Adhara.

"*Maria*!" Cyrus shouted, running out of the alley. They rushed back to the parking garage as fast as they could, skirting down alleys and behind cars to avoid the attention of arriving police cruisers and security drones. They managed to evade detection as they slipped into the parking garage, and Cyrus almost fell down the steps, startling Maria when he finally tore open the Pipeworks door and stood before her panting.She wrapped her arms around him and held tightly.

"Are you okay?" she signed, pulling away. "What happened?"

"We're fine. We froze a lot of them, but the Animal King got away. In fact, it went back into the Pipeworks. I was worried it would come after you." He pulled off his gas mask and put his hands on his knees, wheezing.

"We should walk home on the surface," Adhara advised. "Police attention will be on and under the warehouse tonight."

"Did you notice there wasn't any trace of the ones we shot on the way back here?" he asked Adhara. "No munge or bones on the streets."

"I noticed. It appears an electromagnetic pulse no longer permanently incapacitates them."

"They're smarter than we thought," he straightened. "They were playing with us, luring us into a trap. We can't underestimate them again." Maria kneeled to retie her shoelace and Cyrus turned away from her. "Tonight was *way* too close," he murmured to Adhara.

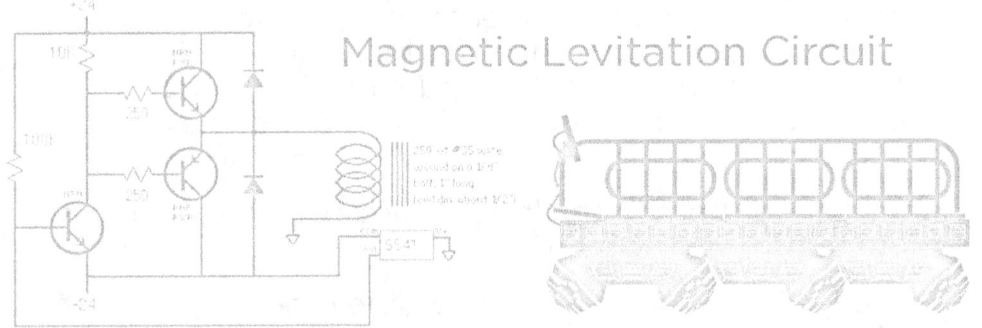

Chapter 10
THE ALCHEMIST

Cyrus woke to someone incessantly ringing his doorbell.

"Gooooooood morning!" Donny grinned, leaning his elbow on the doorframe. "So, uh…what did YOU do last night?"

"I stayed up really late. And it's *really* early, you horrible morning person," groaned Cyrus.

"I prefer 'morning lark,' but even *you* will wake up for this, my friend." Donny pushed inside, his sister Aliyah in tow.

"Hi, Cyrus!" she cheered.

Donny turned on the news and boosted the volume loud enough to give Cyrus a headache. A reporter was standing in front of the charred husk of the warehouse.

"I'm standing in front of what's left of an Acryogen In-dustries paint warehouse which was mostly destroyed in a fire early this morning," the reporter announced. "Though most citizens have grown to expect occasional fires, this one—some are claiming— was especially unusual!" The re-porter turned to one of the people the Grimlords had been terrorizing last night. "I'm here with Aubrey Campell, who witnessed the fire first-hand. Aubrey, what can you tell us about the events last night?"

"Well, I woke up because I heard some explosions outside my window!" said Aubrey, nervous but visibly excited. "I'm on the neighborhood watch, o'course, so I went downstairs to see if anyone needed help or if we needed to evacuate the building."

Maria joined them in the living room and picked up the remote to turn on the subtitles.

"But after I went outside, this horrible *monster* came after me!" Aubrey continued. "It was like a skeleton with a body made of, I don't know, black paint! It came over to me, and just as I thought it was about to do me in... it melted into goop! I was saved! By three strangers!" she gesticulated wildly to accent her embellished anecdote.

"That sounds terrifying. You must have been very scared!" said the reporter. "What did these strangers look like?"

"One was wearing an old-fashioned gas mask and a hood, and he had these strange doo-hickeys strapped to his arms! I think he was the leader. The other two carried these weird guns that looked like horns...or, um...trumpets? They told me to go back inside where it was safe, and I ran back up to my room and watched from my window. They walked right towards the fire, and they were surrounded by hundreds of those skeleton monsters! And they fought them all off! It was amazing!"

"That *is* amazing!" agreed the reporter. "What did these three mystery individuals use to fight the monsters? How should we be arming ourselves to feel safe?"

"Well, I'm not sure." Aubrey furrowed her brow. "I couldn't see so well from the distance, but it seemed like...well, it seemed like they could control fire and ice! They were shooting it all over the place!"

"Thank you, Aubrey. Her report may seem incredible to some of you watching at home," the reporter turned back to the camera, "but her testimony is not the only one of its kind that has surfaced since last night!" The scene cut to a recording of one of the other victims they had saved.

"One of those creepy things cornered me. I was sure I was done for, but then those three showed up!" he breathed.

"One of them had glowing eyes, and she shot it with some sort of *invisible* energy, and it just turned into a black puddle!"

"It's necromancy!" The camera cut to an interview with a fanatic. "I watched them fighting with those demons. They're toying with forces they don't understand! They're mad with power and they can't control it anymore, so they tried to destroy the evidence of their dark experiments!!"

"I don't know what happened last night," the camera cut to the other woman they had saved. "There's all this talk of mad science, or...the undead...all I know is that I thought I was going to die, and those three saved my life. They're my heroes."

"Are these three mysterious strangers heroes? Mad scientists? Or something else entirely?" the reporter pondered. "Frightening reports of these skeleton monsters are coming in from all over the city. In addition, police and fire-fighters have yet been unable to determine the cause of the fire. With new threats like these piling on top of the difficulties we already face, many are wondering anxiously what the future holds as this story unfolds. This is Channel Four news, back to you in the studio."

Donny switched off the TV and turned to Cyrus, his expression transparently smug. Maria was wincing and Aliyah was stifling laughter, and Adhara had just come in from the kitchen, holding a tray of freshly baked lemon poppy-seed muffins.

"You going through a vandalism phase? I had one of those," Donny nodded.

"I know, I know," Cyrus sighed, accepting a muffin as Adhara passed the tray around. "I need to lay low. Don't worry, I have a lot of work to do on the gauntlets and Adhara is going to help me salvage parts from the Pipeworks, so I won't be going anywhere in public for a while."

"If you're going down to the Pipeworks, could you help me get my bike out?" Maria signed.

"Yeah, of course."

"Big plans today?" he asked Maria as they pushed her bike up the stairs.

"Aliyah and I are going to try and help some people with clean-up and helping people relocate. The fire did a lot of damage to the surrounding buildings."

"Cool. You coming back here for dinner?"

"Maybe. I'll text you."

Cyrus nodded, then turned and pedaled away down the tunnel with Adhara.

Maria carefully carried her bike up and out of the house to join Aliyah where she waited on the curb.

"You ready?" she asked as Maria approached. "Olive just texted me. She's already there, she says it's bad."

But Olive hadn't truly done the damage justice in her description, as Maria and Aliyah realized when they arrived. Cyrus and Adhara's safety had cost extensive collateral damage. The entire block was ragged, from holes blown in walls, shattered windows, and though the masses of ice had shrunk now, they could see where they had originally moved brick, mortar, and stone in their wake.

"Glad we weren't home last night," murmured Aliyah.

"Yo, guys!" Olive waved as she jogged up to them.

"Hey girl," Aliyah replied. "What are we looking at? Any-thing serious?"

"Actually...yeah," Olive grimaced. "That's what I came to tell you. That warehouse connects to some kinda underground service tunnels that some gas lines run through."

Maria and Aliyah glanced at each other, eyes wide.

"It's not what you think!" she continued quickly. "There was a *tiny* gas leak that burned off in the fire, and they shut off this section before it blew up or anything. But...." she fiddled with her nails. "The burning gas made a water pipe burst underneath your building."

"*What*?!" Aliyah shouted, pushing past her. Maria and Olive followed her to their dorm, where crowds of other newly homeless students commiserated. Maria, still wearing her implant, winced in the noise.

"All of my notes! For the entire semester, gone! And she grades them at finals!" cried one student.

"The Alchemists did us a favor," declared another. "This dorm was a dumpster fire mixed with a urinal."

"Guys, if you could just give me one minute!" shouted the haggard R.A., Hannah, to the crowd. "Oh! Maria and Aliyah!" she waved them closer. "I've been looking for you two all morning. I was so worried! Were you here last night?"

"Nah, we were staying at a friend's house," Aliyah replied.

"That's a relief," Hannah sighed. "Did you hear what happened? Crazy, right? I've heard some people calling them 'the Alchemists.'"

"I heard someone mention that," signed Maria. "Why Alchemists?"

"Well, people say they were controlling fire and ice, with some crazy chemical reactions. Something to do with that, I guess. Not really a surprise, since it's right next door to a bunch of STEM majors, is it?"

"What about our apartment?" Aliyah cut in.

"It's not good, guys. I'm afraid you're going to have to move out."

"*SERIOUSLY*?" Aliyah shouted.Maria patted her shoulder. "Is it really that bad?"

"'Fraid so. Most of the water damage didn't reach the third floor, but the pressure buildup warped the pipes, and tore up some load bearing walls. It's not safe to sleep there," Hannah grinned, "but it's a fascinating example of hydraulic force under pressure!"

"Yeah, yeah, you're an R.A. right now, not an S.I.," Aliyah grumbled.

"I'm really sorry, guys. Do you have some other place to stay?"

"Yes," signed Maria, "we do. Can we get our stuff?"

"Go ahead but be careful." Hannah gestured to the stair-well. "Find me if you guys need anything else."

"I can't believe this," groaned Aliyah as the three of them climbed the stairs. "I mean, do Acryogen fire robots stop for robot *ice cream* on the way to work?"

"It could be a lot worse," said Olive. "I bet most of those guys out there didn't have a backup pad."

"Yeah, about that, where did you mean?" said Aliyah, turning to Maria.

"Cyrus', of course," Maria signed. "He has the space, and I spend half my time there anyway. I know it's a long walk into town, but at least we have a place to sleep."

"And is Cyrus gonna be cool about..." Aliyah lowered her voice, "...our project?"

"Are you asking me if *Cyrus* will object to a mad science experiment?" Maria glanced at the fissured brick.

"Look, chemical engineering and destruction of property are *one* thing," sighed Aliyah, continuing up the stairs. "But you know that when it comes to genetic engineering...some people have a *moral* quandary."

When they stepped into their apartment, they finally accepted that it was truly unlivable. One of the largest fissures ran right through the exterior wall. A similar crevice bisecting their floor mirrored the splintering beams barely supporting the ceiling.

"Generation forty-three seems okay," Aliyah sighed, having gingerly tip-toed across the room to inspect a table laden with test tube racks.

"The data is intact," Maria signed. She shut down her computer and moved it to the bed, starting a pile to begin their move.

"How we gonna carry all this stuff to Cyrus' house, though?" asked Olive.

"I'll just get Donny to bring his car. That lazy butt doesn't do anything while he's in between productions." Aliyah held her phone to her ear with her shoulder. "Hey, you butt. Get over here, we're homeless."

"Hey!" Maria waved her hand at Cyrus, barely catching him slinking downstairs.

"Are you...moving in?" he asked, peering at the pile of clothes she held.

"Can we? Me and Aliyah, I mean?" She smiled sheepishly. "The fire messed up our apartment. We didn't lose anything, but we had to move out. Can we stay here?"

"Uh..." Cyrus' eyes wandered. For the past few hours he had been thinking very heavily about engineering, and this abrupt change in subject taxed his absent mind. "Yeah... sure, whatever. Why not?" Then he escaped into the basement.

"Cyrus said it's okay!" Maria signed to Aliyah when she returned to the room they had annexed.

"That's a relief," Aliyah replied as she folded a shirt. "Since we're already half moved in."

"Hey, where do you guys want this?" Olive came into the room carrying a test tube rack.

"Whoa!" Aliyah and Maria both started forward with their hands outstretched. "*Don't* shake those," Aliyah gasped, carefully taking them and setting them on the desk.

Donny appeared in the doorway, carrying Maria's computer and its various accessories. "This is the last of it," he

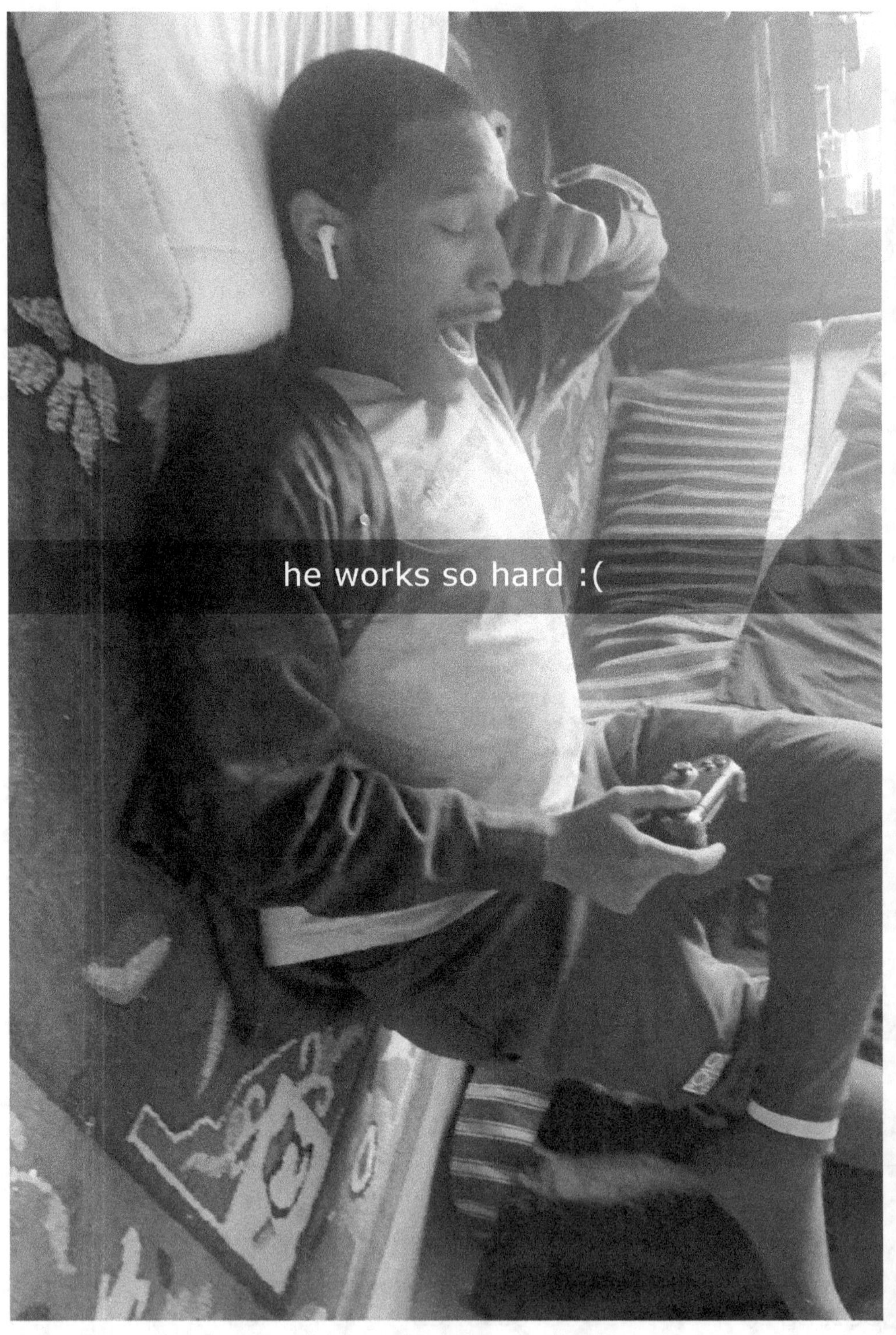
he works so hard :(

huffed. "Will you leave me alone now?" He deposited the computer on the bed and trudged back downstairs.

"I can't believe it, but we actually have more room here than we did in the dorm." Aliyah finished filling a chest of drawers with her clothes.

"That surprises you?" Olive flung herself on the bed. "This old house is *huge*! How on earth does Cyrus afford this place all to himself?"

"It's not his. This house was his parents'. They left it to him," Maria signed.

Olive sat up slowly. "Dang. I had no idea," she mumbled. "When did they die?"

"A few years ago. He doesn't like to talk about it, so if you have questions ask me, not him," Maria replied. "It's why he always throws himself into his work."

"Work is his coping mechanism?" asked Olive.

Maria nodded. "It's his comfort zone."

A deep jolt abruptly rocked the house.

"What was that?" Aliyah asked Donny as they rushed downstairs.

"I'm gonna guess..." he pretended to think, "...Cyrus." He turned the TV volume up.

Aliyah scoffed and they ventured downstairs without Donny. They crept into the basement, where the Pipeworks hatch was open.

"Whoa," Olive breathed, "the heck is this?"

"The impulsion is way too sensitive," they heard Cyrus tell Adhara as they descended the steps. "I'm gonna dial it back...maybe even forty percent?"

"I would suggest two speed modes for precise maneuvering and long-distance travel."

"Ooh, that's clever. I like that."

"Cyrus, what under *earth* have you made now?" Aliyah cried.

Cyrus was standing on a long metal platform, laden with scrap metal, floating on eight deeply thrumming impulsion units he had taken from drones. He had welded railings around the edges and set up controls.

"Oh hey, guys. I made a cart." He patted the railing. "For moving stuff."

"Stuff?"

"Yeah, I've been working on my gauntlets using scrap from the Pipeworks!" He tapped his foot against the scrap. The pile shifted threateningly. "There's all *kinds* of cool junk down here, and you know how I love to loot. I'm gonna reinforce the gauntlets with armored panels." He pulled a lever and the impulsion units went dark; the platform dropped to the ground.

"How fast can it move?" Olive asked. She circled the platform with great fascination.

"Uh...Adhara?" Cyrus asked.

"Depending on the weight of the load, I would estimate about fifty kilometers per hour," she answered without hesitating.

"I have an idea," Maria signed. "Maybe we could use this to get into town quickly!"

"Yeah! Would you let us borrow it, Cy?" asked Aliyah, thrilled at the prospect of less exercise.

"Sure," he shrugged. "Just don't lose it."

"I'd be more worried about getting *ourselves* lost," Maria signed. "I hadn't thought about that. How are we going to navigate? We can't just take Adhara with us everywhere to guide us through the tunnels."

"There's no need!" Cyrus smiled proudly. "Adhara has map data of the entire Pipeworks, but she can't parse the data in a way that would allow her to draw a map." He frowned. "For some reason she won't tell me. But she can interface

with the processors in these drones. Come see!" He beckoned them onto the platform. They gathered around a
tablet computer that displayed a map of the city covered in
blue and red dots. "See these dots? The blue ones are entrances to the Pipeworks throughout the city. You just tap
one of them and the cart automatically follows a course to
it."

"What's the difference between blue and red?" Olive
asked.

"Red is actively being used by Acryogen. Blue is unused.
Oh, and there's a pair of bolt cutters here in case you need
to cut a chain or something." He patted the railing fondly
again.

"This one is right next to school," Maria indicated a blue
entrance. "We can use this to get to class in the morning.
But right now, I'm gonna start making dinner. Adhara, can
you help me?"

"If I help too, can I sleep over?" Olive asked. "It's getting
late."

"...a new development in the events last night as Acryogen
Industries issues a formal response to the destruction of
property," announced a reporter on the TV. They all looked
up from their casserole and turned to Cyrus, who was innocently fiddling with his gauntlets.

"Here as a representative of Acryogen Industries is one of
their head scientists, Dr. Elias Cargyle. Dr. Cargyle, the city
looks to its leadership right now. How do you respond to the
strange events that transpired here?"

"Not *this* guy again," Cyrus scoffed.

"From security footage and eyewitness accounts, we've
determined that the perpetrators were using illegal, unregistered weapons and energy technology," Cargyle drawled.
"A warrant has been issued for their arrest, and we will be
conducting a house-by-house search to find these dan-

gerous criminals and bring them to justice. We regret that this search may become invasive and inconvenient for the citizens of Hudson City...but if you have nothing to hide, you have nothing to fear. We believe it is a necessary sacrifice. Your safety is our number one priority."

Olive politely only dropped her fork, but the discourteous others dropped their jaws.

"Um," said Cyrus.

"Boy, you better stay inside," Donny chuckled.

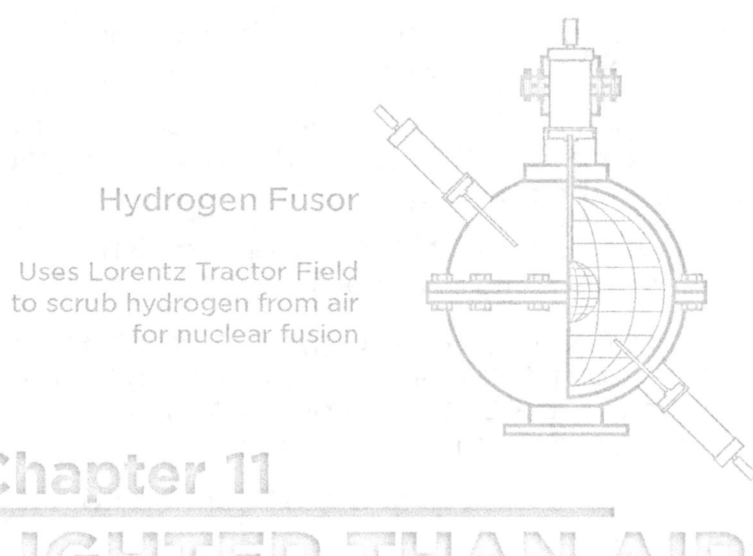

Chapter 11
LIGHTER THAN AIR

For weeks following the warehouse fire, Cyrus shunned the city like a hermit, never venturing outside his house except into the Pipeworks. However, unbeknownst to Adhara or Maria, he did occasionally sneak into the city *through* the Pipeworks. He was only ever gone for an hour or two, and only late at night, to shake off the cabin fever or test some new feature of his gauntlets.For these reasons and because he diligently wore his disguise, Cyrus justified the delinquency to himself.

One breezy afternoon almost a month after the warrant had been issued for the arrest of "the Alchemists," Maria was going around the house opening windows to let in the cool autumn air. As she turned away from the last one in the music room, she was startled by Cyrus standing directly behind her, holding the pieces of his diamond power supply unit.

"Don't sneak up on me!" she gasped, "you're gonna give me a heart attack."

"Sorry," he winced. "I need your help."

"What did you do to your power supply?" He had disconnected the individual components and now cradled them in his arms, as they had no support but cables to the diamond itself. It glowed dimly green.

"I'm working on making it more efficient. It's costing me a fortune to recharge it, and I can't exactly go out and get a job right now to pay the power bill."

"Why do you have to charge it?" Maria replied. "Isn't the whole point that it makes its own power?"

"No," he shook his head, "It's a battery, not a power source. If I had it powering something small, the radiation might be able to sustain the charge, but for something big like the gauntlets I have to plug them in every night."

She stared at him for a second and then connected her implant. "Say that again?" she requested. He repeated himself, enunciating more carefully.

"So, what are you thinking? Solar panels? Wind turbines?"

"Both promising, but the weather this far from the city is unreliable and would take too long to get up to full charge. I want to build a fusion reactor."

"Sounds cool. But isn't that potentially...explosive?" she smirked at Cyrus.

"I won't *let it* explode!" he protested, trailing after her as she left the room.

"If I had a nickel for every time you've said *that*, I wouldn't have any more student loan debt."

"It's simple—I've built a scrubber that will attract hydrogen in the air and deposit it into a pressurized tank. Then, I'll put the hydrogen into a vacuum chamber with a high voltage tungsten grid, use the gauntlets to start the reaction, and then it'll power the whole house and the gauntlets for seventy years!" He cleared his throat. "Give or take. I'm basically just recreating the fusion reactors that power the AirShift towers, so it's not like it's experimental technology."

"I don't know Cyrus, I mean, I'm a biochem major. Wouldn't you rather Adhara help you?"

"Well actually, I asked her first." He cleared his throat again. "Turns out, as a robot, she has no capacity for creativity outside of combat or rescue, and she can't build something without having a perfectly rendered digital blueprint. Plus, she's busy."

"Well, all right," Maria sighed, chuckling. "Good thing finals got delayed after that sinkhole. I'm sure it won't be easy making all those parts."

"Oh, well, I actually made all the parts." Cyrus twiddled his thumbs.

Maria smirked. "Already?"

"I have a lot of free time right now!" Cyrus snipped. "Anyway, we just have to connect it all, like a big puzzle."

"A big puzzle that could give us a lethal dose of gamma radiation?"

"It's more likely that it would be x-rays," he agreed, heading upstairs, "and it also involves Deuterium, which is also explosive, but you have the idea."

"Whoa," said Olive as she entered the living room. Cyrus and Maria had spread out the parts of the fusion reactor so that they overflowed the coffee table. Cyrus' hand drawn schematics were taped over the TV and on the walls, as though they were trying to figure out how to assemble the world's most confusing Swedish furniture.

"Olive!" Cyrus exclaimed. "I was looking for you earlier; I needed your help...Don't you live here, now?"

"Was I your *third* choice?" Maria signed.

"Nah man, my crib is downtown. I just came in on the Pipeworks Express with Aliyah."

"Can you help us? We're trying to build a fusion reactor."

"Ah, sweet!" Olive folded her legs and sat, grabbing the vacuum chamber. "I built a little one of these for my eighth-

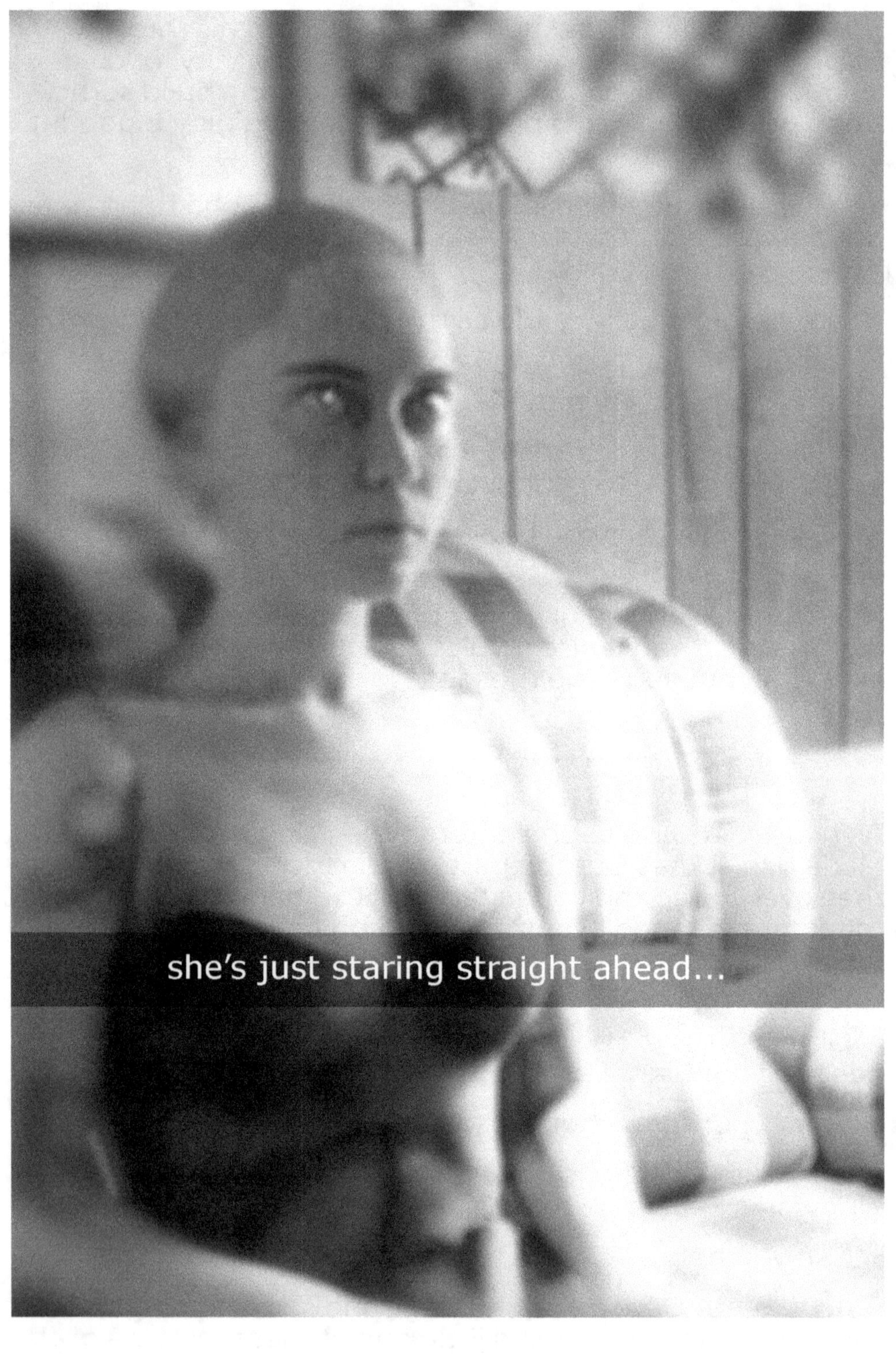
she's just staring straight ahead...

grade science fair using a fishbowl and copper coat hangers!"

With an electrical engineer on the team, the work went much faster. They chatted as they put together the tanks and plumbing, laughing and carrying on about school and how "the Alchemists" were becoming something between a cult icon and urban legend. One of their undergrad classmates had already started selling Alchemist stickers on social media. Soon, even Donny and Aliyah took an interest in watching them. As they finished wiring up the transformers and ballasts and neutron detectors, they all had a grand time building up excitement in anticipation of the reactor's completion.

"I *think* we're ready to connect it to power!" Cyrus beamed. The finished product was a rough jumble of instruments connected by wires, and it took all five of them to carry it down to the breaker panel in the basement. As Cyrus connected the hydrogen scrubber he had installed outside, Olive prepared the connections to the house circuit, while Maria, Donny, and Aliyah cowered behind an overturned table on the other side of the room.

"Ready to leave the grid?" Olive asked. She and Cyrus slipped on safety goggles.

"Cut us off," he answered. Olive flipped the main breaker, and the entire house above them seemed to fall asleep. The basement likewise fell into darkness, except for sunlight streaming in from the narrow windows near the ceiling. She removed the city power lines and replaced them with leads to the fusion reactor, then gave Cyrus a thumbs-up. He finished equipping his gauntlets, which were now plated with armor panels from drones, and motioned for Olive to stand back. Though his stance conveyed power and aplomb, the reactor did not react to his glowing palms. He tried again. After a quiet moment he turned to the others.

"So. I failed to realize that it's going to take a while for the scrubber to accumulate enough hydrogen for the reactor to turn on."

"How long?" asked Donny.

"A couple hours, probably. And we won't have power until then."

"Well," Maria got to her feet, "It's a beautiful day outside. Why don't we have a picnic and enjoy the sunset?"

They all smiled and agreed, and their good spirits were restored. Together they carried out blankets and baskets of cheese, nuts, bottles of juice, fresh fruit, sausages, jam and crackers, and whatever else they could find in Cyrus' pantry to spread out as they lounged on the lawn of the abandoned house across from Cyrus', where they could enjoy the best view of the sun setting behind the distant skyline. As the shadows grew longer Aliyah and Maria took to discussing the ethics of cross-species genetics, which led to a fascinating debate over which animal traits they would each like to have. Though Cyrus made a compelling argument for night vision cat eyes, Donny's case for octopus chromatophores was simply too impassioned to disregard. Just as the last slivers of golden sun were disappearing, the lights in Cyrus' house winked on, and they all cheered and gathered up the bones of their feast to return indoors.

"How's it working?"

Maria found Cyrus in the basement, inspecting the reactor, after everyone else had gone to sleep.

"Great! It's holding steady at about…forty-eight thousand kilowatts per hour, and the ballast is keeping the influx to the house stable. Thanks for helping me build it," he smiled.

"I'm sorry that I wasn't much help today," Maria signed. "I didn't want to say anything, but when we were piecing it together, I was completely lost. I was so embarrassed when Olive came in and put it together like it was nothing."

"Oh, Maria, no!" Cyrus shook his head. "I'm sorry for putting you in that position. I know physics doesn't come naturally to you, but you are so brilliant when it comes to biology. You helped me anyway, and I really appreciate that."

She returned his smile, but noticed he was tapping his finger.

"What's wrong?" she signed.

"What do you mean? Nothing." He coughed.

"You can't fool me," she smirked. "That's your guilty indecision face."

"Well, it had just occurred to me." He gestured to the reactor. "The vacuum chamber has enough hydrogen now, and the scrubber is still running. I figured...the AirShift towers work in the same way. Maybe while we're at it, since I know how they work now, we could...pop over real quick and fix one or two of them up?"

"What, tonight? Right now?"

"I've been so bored," he pleaded. "I've just been reinforcing my gauntlets and working on interface for weeks! Building the reactor gave me a taste of working on something big again, and I want *more*!"

Maria crossed her arms and smiled skeptically.

"It wouldn't be hard to get there—I found a tunnel in the Pipeworks that opens right outside one of the towers. We can take the freight platform."

She raised her eyebrows.

"This would be helpful, too. The weather would be so much better; we wouldn't have such dramatic shifts. What do you say? Will you help me?"

She chuckled, then sighed. "All right, I'm in."

"Whoa," signed Maria, "these are a *lot* bigger than they look."

From afar the AirShift towers were hard to distinguish from cell towers, but standing in the snow directly beneath one, just inside the tempestuous wall of fog, Maria was amazed by their scale. A typical Airshift tower was tall enough, but they were now under the larger control tower. The top would have been completely lost in the clouds if not for the pulsing red light of the beacon far above them. She guessed it would have towered over even a skyscraper.

"You've never seen one up close?" Cyrus asked as he worked on the reactor set into the asphalt platform.

"No, of course not. When have *you*?" She handed him a wrench.

"Er...Remember that weekend you went to take a tour of that gene therapy facility?"

"Yes...you told me you spent the weekend studying for our environmental engineering midterm."

"Which wasn't exactly a lie," the faceplate hatch hissed as he opened it. "I sort of went on a field trip. By myself. I learned a lot, and I *aced* that test!"

"Why didn't you just say so, then?"

"I don't know, it's illegal? I didn't want you to worry."

"Cyrus, we're best friends." She kneeled next to him. "You don't have to keep secrets from me."

"I know." He sighed. "I guess I just didn't want you to be disappointed."

"I don't care about a little trespassing now and then," she smirked. "I care a lot more about us trusting each other. And I am really proud to call you my friend, okay?"

"Okay, okay," he waved her off, stifling a smile and blush-ing. "I get it, you're right. I guess our dynamic is just sort of... you're the responsible one, so you're like my mom friend, if that makes sense."

"Ugh, don't say that!" she laughed, shoving him playfully. "I'm *younger* than you! Anyway, I...what's wrong?" Cyrus was squinting at the monitor panel with the confusion of some-one who had just witnessed a lobster riding a unicycle.

"Uh..." he began slowly. "Just...humor me. Do you remem-ber from school how these things are supposed to work?"

"I guess so?" she shrugged. "We always said they were like an electric fence mixed with a hurricane."

"Right, but how specifically?"

"Um..." Maria wracked her brain to recall curriculum buried under years of newer, more interesting information. "Something about moving air pressure out of the city, and...fronts? Warm fronts and cold fronts are cycled around the city... uh...I don't remember the specifics, but the idea was that they take water vapor from the bay and cycle it around the city in a spiral to make something like a hurricane."

"That's what I remember too," said Cyrus. He leaned back on his heels. "But look at this." He directed her to the monitor panel, which displayed a Doppler scan of the areawithin the AirShift towers. "It's like they're *barely* even on; the vortex is a *fraction* of the magnitude it should be! This...fog that we're in," he flapped his arms around demonstratively, "should be a high-speed wall of wind! This is like a breeze! Something's wrong," he hefted a tank of hydrogen off his shoulder, "and it's not the reactor," he finished, disappointed.

"Oh!" Maria tapped his shoulder excitedly. "I remember something! Don't they use silver iodide to make the clouds thicker?"

Cyrus snapped his fingers and nodded. He entered a few keystrokes and brought up the diagnostics. But the tanks mounted to the tower, stories above them, were properly filled with silver iodide. He tested the seeding nozzles and they heard a distant hiss, as designed.

"Good guess," he sighed. "The fog is plenty thick enough. The nozzles are working fine...but it's like it can't produce powerful enough fronts." He brought up the barometric control screen. "I'm going to reset it to default parameters. Start from there."

"Wait a second!" Maria stopped his hand. "Think about what you just said: 'This fog we're in should be a high-speed wall of wind?' If it goes back to normal, we could be in the middle of a hurricane!"

"No, that would only happen if someone had *intentionally* made the vortex this weak," he answered. "I'm sure there's a bigger problem somewhere that we'll have to fix. But the first step is always to turn it off and back on again. Besides, AirShift towers have a negation field at their base that protects the reactor." He pointed up at the negation field projector. The negation field projector looked back down at them.

After Maria allowed Cyrus to reset the towers, their lights went dark across the mountainside and the fog began to fade away. As the air cleared, they could see the city lights at the foot of the mountains, the moon reflecting in the bay, even the faraway landscape sprawled out like a crumpled blanket. They could barely make out the northern Airshift towers, which stood in the water a few kilometers off the coast. Then, like a string of Christmas lights, they all came back on. A klaxon blared from theirs, and a deafening siren echoed across the landscape. Orange lights spun atop each tower and they felt the air turn fuzzy, tingling in their neck and arm hairs. The wind picked back up.

Cyrus and Maria cowered inside the tower's negation field as the gale outside howled around them. The fog returned, denser than before, and soon they were watching a furious storm from inside their bubble of safety.

"Something is very wrong," Cyrus protested. "Someone deliberately turned the towers down!"

"Worry about that later!" Maria signed frantically. "How are we going to get back *home*?"

A light, diffused in the clouds, appeared before them. It grew brighter as a hovering Adhara entered the negation field and landed before them.

"Cyrus," she said in surprise. "Maria. What are you doing here?"

"It's…a long story," Cyrus answered. "How did you find us?"

"I wasn't looking for you. I traced the epicenter of the power surge back to the AirShift towers, which were recalibrated from this terminal. I came to investigate."

"What power surge?" Maria asked.

"The fusion reactors that power the AirShift towers are also tied into the city power grid," she explained. "Their output suddenly increased exponentially, which caused a power surge that overloaded most substations. Hudson City is currently experiencing a total blackout."

Cyrus's jaw dropped as Maria, overwhelmed by the sudden stress, burst into delirious laughter.

Chapter 12
MELTDOWN

"Are you guys okay?" Aliyah asked frantically as they re-emerged from the basement. "We all woke up because of this alert on our phone about a blackout, and then you guys were gone...but the power's still on here!"

"Well, we're not on the grid here anymore," Cyrus mumbled as Maria consoled her.

"Olive and Donny are in there watching the news," Aliyah took a deep breath. Maria led her gently into the living room, followed by Cyrus and Adhara. They were met by incredulous looks from Donny and Olive.

"You missed the good part," Donny smirked. The TV displayed shots of confused people in the streets and the distant AirShift towers, now thoroughly obscured in the storm.

"What's the damage?" Cyrus groaned.

"Well, they already know it's you," Donny took a long sip from his water, ignoring Cyrus' subsequent shock. "And by you, I mean the Alchemists. They think you're making a statement."

"What kind of statement?"

"Some say you're waging war against Acryogen," he waved off Cyrus, ready to protest. "But that's just the fanatics. Most people think it was protest against Acryogen's negligence; fixing stuff that they won't, making a statement about something. And *I* think you were messing around with stuff you don't understand and accidentally overloaded the whole city. Who's right?"

"You are," Maria signed.

Aliyah huffed and slipped Donny a dollar.

"You know, my feelings are starting to get hurt that you don't invite me on your crazy adventures," he sighed.

"We invited you the first time!" Cyrus spluttered. "And now you're acting like we've been intentionally excluding you?"

"Drama's the spice of life, bay-bee." Donny blew a kiss and cackled as Aliyah beat him with a throw pillow.

"They're already working on repairs. Grid's supposed to be back up in a few hours; by four," Olive added.

"That quickly?" Cyrus asked.

"Power surge affected Acryogen facilities. You know how they are," she winked. "Same day service if it's self-service."

Cyrus scoffed. "At least everything will be back to normal soon."

"Most of the grid will be operational again in a few hours," Adhara interjected. "But there will be some consequences that will take longer to rectify."

The room turned to her.

"What do you mean?" Cyrus asked finally.

"Before the power surge, I had tracked Animal King to a nuclear power plant in the city," she explained. Cyrus' heart sank. "I have been monitoring Acryogen's emergency radio communication. The same power plant has been overloaded due to the surge. They are attempting to contain it for now, but I estimate the reactors will decay into irreversible meltdown before Christmas."

"Wh—can't they do anything? If they have weeks to act, can't they flood it or something?"

"They believe they can stabilize the reactors without damaging them. They will attempt to minimize costs. However, it is unlikely that they will be successful," she cocked her ear, listening to what they couldn't hear, "since they are not alone in the facility. Staff members are already beginning to disappear."

"Ugh...this is all my fault," Cyrus groaned, sliding down against the wall. Donny nodded.

"Not entirely," said Adhara. "The upkeep of the facility was severely inadequate. Any catastrophic event could have triggered this meltdown. However," she conceded, "the co-inciding presence of Animal King is inopportune."

"We have to fix this," Cyrus declared, straightening his legs and his jaw. "Can you defeat Animal King?"

"I will need your help," Adhara answered. "Are your gauntlets suitable for combat?"

Cyrus sighed and rubbed his neck. "There's a lot of things I would need to do before I'd be comfortable fighting with them...I'd need some time. Maybe a week, if I had help?" he looked to his friends, who wouldn't meet his eyes and shuffled uncomfortably. "Come on guys, I thought you had my back!"

"You know we would any other time, dude," said Olive, "but the end of this week is finals. Can't afford to skip out on studying."

"I got the Christmas play, starting tomorrow," said Donny, shrugging with genuine remorse.

"Are you serious?" Cyrus looked at each of them incredulously. "This is a matter of...the safety of the city! Rests in our hands! And you're worried about *school*?"

"Cyrus," Maria met his gaze calmly. "You're being unfair. We can't risk our scholarships. If we don't work hard, we don't have a safety net."

"You know we'd help if we could, Cy," Aliyah added quietly.

Cyrus nodded glumly, but Adhara put a hand on his shoulder.

"My assistance will have to be sufficient," she told him. "We have one week to be ready to face Animal King. Get some rest. We will begin preparations tomorrow."

Though he was skeptical, the next morning Cyrus found Adhara to be an able assistant: what she lacked in creativity she made up for by following his instructions with precision and efficiency. On the first two days, she helped Cyrus perfect the plating on his gauntlets, ensuring that the armor was built up around the delicate hardware in the fingers, every joint was reinforced with air-tight seals, and the palms were thoroughly protected by an inert coating.They installed servos within the plates of the forearm so he could easily take the gloves off and on, and automatically secure them up to his elbows. In addition to the existing armor, they integrated a structure like brass knuckles to mount a solenoid over the fingers.

They spent the third day making a pair of protective sleeves for Cyrus to wear underneath the gauntlets. Weaving the graphene fibers was mindless and time-consuming work, during which they were able to catch up with the news.

"Are you knitting?" asked Maria, noticing them on the couch.

"It's armor," Cyrus answered, holding up his work. "It's chemically inert, water-cooled, bullet-proof, slash resistant, shock proof, and fireproof. For the gauntlets."

"Oh. What's the latest news?" She sat next to him and opened a textbook on the coffee table.

"Some whistle-blowers have been extrapolating the latest readings from the power grid. Apparently, everyone's power bill is going to be less expensive now because the AirShift towers are working harder. They're actually organizing a *protest* tonight against Acryogen for lying to us," he scoffed. "Like *that's* anything new. They think 'the Alchemists' uncovered a major conspiracy."

"What conspiracy?" asked Olive, passing by, holding a binder of notes.

"Acryogen creating an artificial scarcity of electricity to drive up energy prices," Cyrus monotoned without looking up.

"That wasn't very cash money of them," she murmured, and returned to her notes.

"Knowing them, it's probably *very* cash money of them," he muttered.

"I have finished the right sleeve," Adhara announced.

"Whoa," said Cyrus, who was only up to the forearm on the left.

The next day they fastened shielding around the power supply, protecting the diamond from outside interference and sealing its own interference inside. After they integrated connector ports into the backpack for the sleeves and gauntlets themselves, Adhara even helped him replace the straps so it would be easier to carry. The day after that, Cyrus refined the interface software and programmed system diagnostics from the panels in his wrists as Adhara checked and double-checked every line of code in the mainframe supercomputer. When Cyrus woke up the next morning, she was still sitting motionlessly in his workroom, analyzing chemical reaction simulations, so he poured himself a bowl of cereal and helped Maria with her flashcards. When Adhara finished, they began testing, and spent the remaining days fine-tuning the gauntlets until they were finally ready for the most taxing field test they'd ever been put to.

"It's raining," noticed Cyrus as he got dressed on the day-of.

"Irrelevant," Adhara replied as she helped him slip into the sleeves. "We will only be outside for a few minutes between the Pipeworks and the power plant."

"I'm not afraid of getting *wet*, it's just..." he slipped his hands into the gauntlets and with a small pneumatic hiss they closed around his forearms. "It feels like there's a tension in the air."

"You are most likely experiencing anxiety. Apprehension is a normal response in anticipation of a mortal threat."

Cyrus scowled. "Have I noticed that you've been talking more formally again? What's up with that?"

"That is not important at this time." She hoisted the backpack onto his shoulders, tightening the straps and securing the connectors. "Ready for power-up?"

"Everything's looking good," Cyrus murmured to himself, looking down at his wrists and reading code excerpts under his breath. The system diagnostic completed, and his screens each displayed a reaction array surrounded by icons. He slid his gas mask over his face and pulled up his hood. "It's ready. Let's go."

The freight platform carried them so swiftly beneath the city that Cyrus had to grip the railing to remain onboard. Just as they turned into a broad tunnel Adhara abruptly shut the platform off, almost hurling him over the railing. They skidded to a stop on the pavement. Cyrus opened his mouth in surprise but Adhara silenced him with a finger to her lips, pointing with the other hand down the tunnel. He heard a distant roar preluding headlight beams, and in moments they were passed by a speeding caravan of old-fashioned sedans and a few SUVs. When the tunnel grew quiet and dark again, Adhara reactivated the thrumming platform and they continued forward.

"What were *cars* doing down here?" Cyrus murmured. "No one even uses cars anymore, but how would they even get into the Pipeworks?"

"Did you notice how low they were riding?" she replied. "Those were tanks, disguised as cars. They're called Roadsters—they have weapons mounted inside the rear seats and trunks. Acryogen tech."

"You're back to speaking casually," Cyrus said in surprise.

"Stay on task."

"That still doesn't answer what they were doing here." He looked over his shoulder down the tunnel. "That tunnel must be...south, southwest? So, it goes under the mountains, right?"

"That tunnel ends on the other side of the mountains, out onto a pre-war highway." She remained facing forward.

"What would Acryogen be doing with a military convoy outside the city?"

"One thing at a time."

The platform dropped them off at the edge of a derelict subway tunnel. As they hopped over the turnstiles they landed in a stream of water—the rain was pouring in down the stairs. They emerged into the deluge—the storm drains overflowed, and the streets were flooded. Adhara led Cyrus sloshing to the nuclear plant a few blocks over. Adhara approached a door half a floor below street level, already almost a meter underwater.

"Must be the AirShift towers making the weather so weird," Cyrus whispered. Adhara nodded as she cut through the deadbolts. Once inside, they found themselves in a long cinder-block corridor with flickering fluorescent lights.

"Remember what to do if you see a Grimlord?" she murmured as they crept down the corridor. He nodded. "Don't forget to clench just before impact. The magnetism will do the rest."

"And what if I see an armed guard?" he hissed, pulling her into a doorway. They heard stiff heels on the concrete pass by.

"They must have stationed extra security because of the disappearances," said Adhara, her voice barely audible.

"What's our priority? Animal King, or the reactor meltdown?"

"They can take care of the reactors themselves; we just need to buy them some time." She leaned out cautiously.

"We'll adjust the overheating reactors as discussed, then deal with Animal King."

Careful to evade the guards, they crept up to the reactor floor. They snuck around the cores and Cyrus threw a wrench across the room. They heard a stampede of footsteps rush to investigate. This distraction left the stairwell unattended, through which they accessed the dynamo room above.

"I'm reading higher temperatures on dynamos...two, four, six, and eleven," Cyrus reported, scanning with his palms.

"Confirmed. Use your gauntlets to cool them down. I'll go recalibrate the steam turbine computers."

As Adhara left the room Cyrus approached each of the overheated dynamos in turn. As he had practiced, he produced a counter-active infrared wavelength from his palms, carefully diffusing the excess heat without affecting the delicately tuned dynamos. Just as he finished cooling the last one, Adhara silently reappeared next to him.

"We have delayed the meltdown until at least after New Year's," she informed. "However, I scanned the facility, and I was unable to locate Animal King. It must be hidden somewhere my sensors cannot reach."

They heard a scream, muffled under the din of the turbines. They followed the sound back down to the reactor floor, where they hid on a service catwalk and surveyed the remaining security guards searching for their lost teammate. An agitated man in a lab coat strode across the room to join them, and from his carrying voice Cyrus instantly recognized Dr. Cargyle:

"Why are you all running around like *headless chickens*?" he barked. "That's the *eighth* disappearance this week, *right* under your noses. Split up and sweep the building! Those senseless rebels are around here somewhere, and if you don't all find at least *one* by the end of the night, it'll be your *job*!"

"He thinks the *rebellion* is behind the disappearances?" Cyrus scoffed.

"I'll track his location by sending a signal to his communication unit and calculating the return range. After I find him, you'll flank his position and I'll finally put an end to this nonsense." With this pronouncement he stalked out, cocky as he came.

"Wow," Cyrus murmured as Cargyle left the room, "is that what *I* sound like?"

"No, Dr. Cargyle uses technical jargon to intimidate others," Adhara assured him. "You on the other hand merely lack the social aptitude to describe technical concepts simply."

"That's a relief."

"Man, I hate that guy," one of the guards sighed. "Imagine being so pretentious that you can't just say '*I'll ping his radio and report back.*'"

"He's a major pain," another agreed, so quietly that Adhara had to repeat it for Cyrus, "but we'd better do as he says. Maybe you have a trust fund, but *my* family can't afford for me to lose this job."

"Major pain," a third guard saluted.

"Cut that out. You two, start from the ground floor and secure all entrances. My team will check out the basement levels, and everyone else, start on the turbine floor and work your way up into the office. Radio in regularly with updates; I don't want any more surprises."

As the guards dispersed, Adhara and Cyrus retreated from their hiding place, regrouping in a nearby supply closet.

"If Cargyle can really track the missing guard, then he'll probably lead us right to Animal King," Cyrus surmised. "Can you tap into the signal?"

"Not from here, the walls are too thick," she answered. "We'll have to get closer."

Cargyle was fortunately alone, tapping away at a laptop when they crept up behind him. After a few minutes he murmured "gotcha" to himself and called in the position on his radio. Adhara nodded to Cyrus and motioned for them to leave. As they passed the doorway he brushed against a broom. The noise was tiny enough to be ignored, but in his full-blown paranoia, Cargyle whirled just in time to see Cyrus' leg disappear around the corner.

"Hey! You there!" he shouted, "STOP!"

Adhara grabbed Cyrus' wrist and pulled him into a sprint down the stairs and through the labyrinth of corridors below the reactor floor. It was times like these that Cyrus was most aware of her inhuman nature—Adhara navigated the maze with machine precision, turning this way and that while Cargyle's frantic shouts grew ever more distant.

"Do you have a plan?" she asked as they slowed to a jog.

"Me?" he asked in surprise, "Don't you?"

"My capacity for creative adaptation is limited," she reminded him. "My response to any given situation is based upon systematic contingency plans."

"And you don't have a contingency plan for this situation?"

"I do," she answered casually. "But it's to force all of the reactors into meltdown and bury Animal King beneath this facility, and I think the negatives outweigh the positives."

"Actually..." Cyrus thought quietly, looking down at his gauntlets. "I think that's a great idea."

"You do?" she turned to him with as much surprise as a robot could muster. "I thought the risk to human life would kinda be a dealbreaker."

"Okay, we are going to have a talk about your speech patterns, so make a note of that. But for now, yes, partially. I have a plan—I need scrap iron, aluminum, 10 gauge or thicker solid-core copper wire, and some really big magnets."

"You all set up there?" Cyrus murmured.

"Yes." Though she was perched in the rafters above, he heard Adhara's voice clearly through his phone.

"This is neat!" he whispered. "I didn't know you could connect directly to my phone."

"Are we ready?" she asked firmly.

"I think so," he crossed the room to inspect the industrial solenoids they had cannibalized from spare dynamos and affixed to a reactor core. He stepped carefully over the circle of thermite surrounding the trap. "You're sure there's nothing important underneath us?" he inquired as he tested the seams.

"Each reactor core is directly over a shaft running directly through the Pipeworks," she confirmed. "In the case of an individual core meltdown, a small section of the floor would be demolished, and the entire reactor would drop deep underground."

Cyrus released a deep breath. "Let's do this. Hit that alarm."

The best part of nuclear reactor computers, Cyrus thought to himself, is their gullibility. This one, for example, believed Adhara when she told it that all the reactors were overheating, and it immediately triggered the emergency evacuation alarm. They could hear the security guards bursting out the doors into the rain, and when they were gone Adhara deactivated the alarm everywhere except the reactor floor.

"And now we wait," Cyrus clichéd. He stood resolutely in front of the rigged reactor, staring into the dark stairwell through the flashing red lights. He tensed as he heard movement on the far side of the room, and Cyrus filled with panic when he saw who emerged.

"*YOU* THERE!" Cargyle screamed. He was drenched in sweat, his countenance uncharacteristically rattled. He started towards Cyrus. "You're the vigilante! The vandal! How dare you trespass in here? This is a clearance level 7 Acryogen Industries facility! Who do you think you are? You're lucky I don't—"

Cyrus silenced him by lowering his hood and sliding off his mask. Cargyle's face dropped, his eyes filled with shock.

"You?" he asked.

"Doctor Cargyle, *listen* to me," Cyrus started. "You need—"

"YOU!" Cargyle screeched. "So, *this* is where you've been! You can FORGET about the graduate program; you are OUT, And that is the LEAST of your worries!"

Cyrus slid his mask back on and stepped backwards.

"You think you can just go wherever you *want* and *do* whatever you want without *consequences*?" Cargyle began laughing hysterically. "This is perfect! I've been telling *everyone* that you're nothing but lazy and arrogant, irresponsible, riding on your parents' reputation and you have *no* work ethic, and now!" He spread his arms wide. He took a step forward; Cyrus took a step back. "You're involved with the rebellion! You're an infamous vigilante; a *full-on* criminal!" He moved towards Cyrus, who continued stepping backwards towards the reactor. "It's the end of the line for *you*, Cyrus. I'm going to make sure everyone knows who you are. And I'll finally be free of your asinine, incessant research proposals..."

Cargyle trailed off abruptly. He turned slowly to look over his shoulder to see Animal King, jaws wide and unhinged, looming over him. He only got out half a scream before the maw engulfed him.

"NOW!" Cyrus shouted. Adhara flipped and sprang off the ceiling, shattering the sheetrock, her jets driving her fist down through Animal King's skull in the blink of an eye. Her landing formed a crater in the cement floor, and she sprang backwards to Cyrus' side. Animal King groaned and slowly peeled itself from the pavement, staggering and grinning at them.

"Did it work?" Cyrus shouted.

"The beacon is damaged. It has no influence on the other Grimlords."

Animal King realized this and adapted quickly, hammering its fist down on them just after they leapt out of the way. It considered them momentarily and the second blow came faster, directly at Cyrus. He reacted too late but just before the blow connected Adhara appeared in front of him, absorbing the force with crossed arms. Cyrus scrambled away as Animal King whaled on her, fracturing the concrete under her feet as she blocked again and again from every angle. As it focused on her Cyrus crept around, charging his gauntlets, wound up and caught its leg in a right hook. As it fell to the ground Adhara caught it with a vicious uppercut, splitting the skull in two. Globs of viscid sludge clung to Cyrus' gauntlets and puddled on the ground.

But Animal King wasn't down for long. The munge reformed around the damaged bone and the beast rose again. The jaws parted, releasing an unearthly shriek, and it came at them again.

"One-two punch!" Cyrus shouted to Adhara. He hit the beast with a stream of compressed nitrogen. As it held up a claw against the icy blast, Adhara jumped onto its horns and released an EMP. Lights in the room exploded into sparks and Animal King's body slumped, but it snatched Adhara off and hurled her into the ground, thrashing her mercilessly. Her raised forearms took most of the blows, but eventually her armor cracked, then fractured before her elbow dislocated. Before it could rip her arm off completely, she turned into a blur and disappeared. Animal King whipped around to lash at Cyrus, but he slid underneath the arm and punched its elbow, making the rest of the arm melt. Adhara appeared next to him and together they devastated its weakened joints with relentless synchronized blows. When Animal King was a screeching heap of bones and mire, Cyrus shouted, "Hit it!"

Adhara energized the electromagnets, and they pulled the writhing Animal King to the reactor. The magnets were strong, but the monster was stronger, and it dragged itself away, almost reformed, a claw outstretched and the jaws open wide—then Cyrus hit the ring of thermite with a powerful infrared laser. In a cloud of smoke and sparks like a ring of fireworks, the reactor core disappeared. When the fumes cleared, all that remained was a sinkhole, echoing with howls.

"We weakened it, but it's still alive," said Adhara, cradling her arm.

"At least it's far away from people," Cyrus sighed. "For now."

"Doctor Cargyle," she turned to Cyrus. "You used him as bait."

Cyrus gazed grimly into the hole. "He should be so lucky."

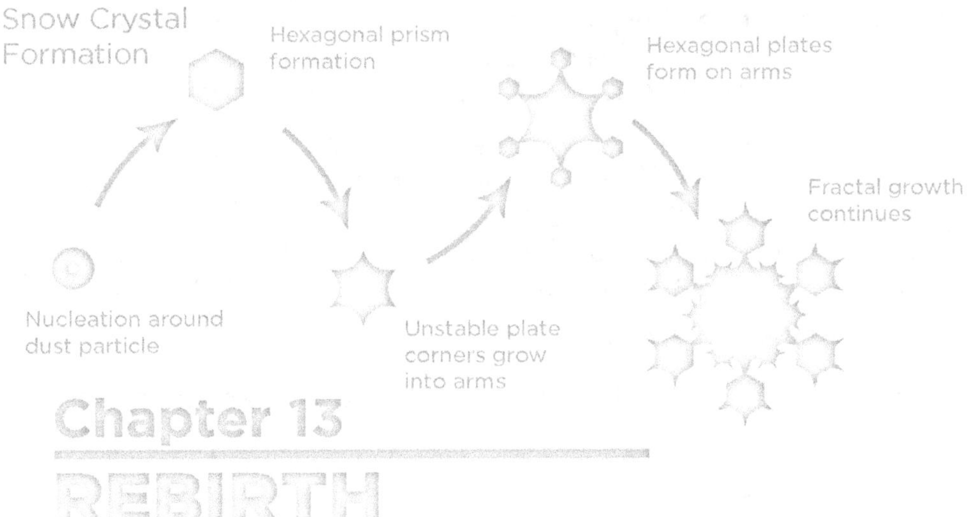

Chapter 13
REBIRTH

The next morning, as Aliyah, Olive, and Maria came downstairs, they were each surprised to find Cyrus and Adhara already sitting at the kitchen table.

"Hi!" signed Maria, who had woken up last, since she was naturally a late sleeper and had stayed up studying later than usual every night for the past week. Aliyah and Olive smiled up at her. Their mouths were sticky with frosting.

"Good morning!" Cyrus replied, handing her a plate bearing a gooey cinnamon bun and half a sliced orange. "Adhara and I made breakfast."

Maria took a seat, took a bite, and swooned. "How is a robot so good at cooking? I know Cyrus didn't make these." Cyrus glanced at her, hurt.

"I excel when given specific instructions," Adhara answered. She handed Maria a mug of technically perfect coffee.

"What are you guys up to today?" asked Cyrus.

"We're celebrating!" Aliyah grinned.

"Yeah, we got our grades in online!" said Olive. "We all passed our finals!"

"Hey! That's great news. I saw how hard you guys were working last week—you earned it. But still, you must be relieved." Cyrus beamed. "How are you celebrating?"

"We're just gonna run some errands," Maria signed. "Visit Donny at the theater, I'm going in to help at the soup kitchen a few days...and then there's Christmas shopping. Christmas is *Saturday*, can you believe that?" she shook her head. "That means Adhara has been here for about five months."

"Seems like way longer."

"I don't suppose..." Maria ventured, "you'd like to come with us?"

He glanced at the ceiling, in the direction of his work room. "I *was* going to work on my gauntlets some more... and Adhara did a bunch of mysterious stuff last night that I was going to look into." Cyrus took a sip of coffee and exhaled. "Actually, I'd really like to come with you. It's Christmastime! Time to focus on something besides tinkering for a while."

"Great!" Maria beamed as Olive and Aliyah cheered. "Because I was going to ask to borrow the freight platform next."

"How about you, Adh—hey, wait a minute!" Cyrus did a double take at Adhara. "Your arm!"

"What's wrong with her arm?" asked Aliyah. "It looks the same to me."

"You should have seen it last night!" Cyrus exclaimed. "It was nearly in two pieces!"

"My body is, fundamentally, modeled after the human body," Adhara explained, arm outstretched. "Skin corresponds to armored plates, bones to struts, muscles to actuators, veins and nerves to hoses and cables..." she held her wrist under the light. "Instead of an immune system, I have nanites that remodel damage." Looking closely, Cyrus could see hairline fractures—a ghost of the injury she had sustained last night.

"That's sick," Olive murmured.

"She broke her arm last night and you're only just *now* realizing it's fixed?" Aliyah asked. "You've been up with her for hours."

"There's another *cool thing* to add to my list," Cyrus muttered, ignoring Aliyah. "Anyway, are you going to come run errands with us?"

"No, I have to go see a man about a quantum state transmitter," she answered simply. "I'll be back by Christmas Eve." And with that she left the kitchen. They heard the front door open and close, and her jets shriek as she flew away.

"Don't ask me—she's been talking funny lately," Cyrus told his bewildered friends. "That's a problem for future Cyrus."

To maintain balance with the AirShift towers, Acryogen Industries never allowed the temperature in Hudson City to vary more than ten degrees. But as Cyrus, Maria, Aliyah, and Olive emerged from the Pipeworks, they saw something none of them had ever witnessed before: Hudson City in the snow. The volume of precipitation held steady from the previous night, but the drop in temperature deposited thick snowdrifts that blanketed every surface. Cyrus almost wished he had brought his gauntlets so he could melt a clear path—as it was, they had to trudge through to get to the street. Though the air was heavy and muffled, they could hear faint bells and laughter. They traced it to Fleet Street, one of the major thoroughfares running through downtown, transformed into a winter wonderland for this week only.

As they turned the corner onto Fleet Street, Cyrus almost immediately took a snowball to the face from a pack of frolicking children. A few of them giggled apologies, for the impact sent him reeling backwards into the slush. As he wiped his eyes a portly man wearing half-moon glasses approached and helped him to his feet.

"They nailed you well enough, didn't they?" he chortled. "Squarely between the eyes! Oh, look at that, you're soaked through, and soon you'll be chilled to the *bone*! Why don't you come inside and warm up for a spell?" The man spoke in cozy clichés with such conviction that they followed without question. His nearby café was quaint and provincial, warmed by a crackling fireplace and homey touches. From a table in one of its broad bay windows they watched the children outside continue their onslaught on one another.

"Thank you, sir!" said Olive as he brought them mugs of cocoa. "I'm Olive, this is Aliyah, Maria, and Cyrus. You have a lovely café!"

"Thank you kindly!" He joined them and sighed deeply. "They call me Jolly. And if *jolly* ain't what I'd call this view, too!" He gestured out the window. More and more pedestrians were appearing on the street; couples arm in arm, and even more children with sleds, all admiring and perusing the shops adorned with strings of colored lights.

"I've not seen a white Christmas since I were a lad!" Jolly sighed. "'Course, few folk 'round here remember what the original holiday were for!"

"What do you mean?" asked Aliyah.

"Gifts and hot drinks and merriment have their charm." He leaned back and lit a pipe. The blue smoke billowing out smelled of teakwood and cloves. "But time was, this was a season of *rebirth*!"

"Rebirth?" Cyrus repeated.

"Aye, and *renewal*. Generations ago, when the days grew cold, folks would celebrate the death of one year and the birth of another. Though, seeing this now...." His glasses reflected the brilliant snow as he gazed outside again. "That fireplace hasn't been lit in thirty years. Perhaps some change isn't too far on the horizon!" He raised his mug. "To new beginnings."

They raised their mugs with him, and he downed his all at once. Hearing the bell from his front door, he rose to welcome his other customers. "I'm grateful for the pleasure of your company. I hope you'll visit me again someday!"

"Oh wait, how much do we owe you for the cocoa?" asked Olive, who had just finished hers.

"On the house." Jolly's eyes twinkled. "Merry Christmas."

The rest of the city shared Jolly's contagious festive mood. As Olive and Aliyah led Maria and Cyrus throughout their errands, people everywhere greeted them with uncommon hospitality. Shop owners lit candles and played music, the air was filled with laughter, and as the sun set, the festivities continued, illuminated by the colored lights, candles, lanterns, and even some sparklers someone was distributing.

"It's like nothing I've ever seen! Everyone looked so happy," Aliyah exclaimed as she recounted their day to Donny. He sat on the edge of the stage eating the sandwich they had brought to his theater.

"It's hope." He swallowed. "A decade of stagnation since the war, and now suddenly, everything is changing. People are seeing things they've never seen before, at least not in a long time. For a lot of people in this city, *change* is an answered prayer."

"Well they're right, aren't they?" Aliyah lowered her voice. "All that stuff with Adhara and Cyrus' destiny? And they're the ones who caused this, anyway."

"Hey, all I did was fix a few of Acryogen's messes. Is that so bad?" Cyrus coughed indignantly.The coughing grew deeper and wracked his body.

"You okay there, buddy?" asked Donny.

"Bunch of kids creamed him in the face with a snowball earlier," Olive supplied. Cyrus glared at her.

"Either way, you better be careful. As many people as are happy about change, you can bet plenty more will be threatened by it. You hear about Cargyle?"

"Cyrus' boss?" Maria signed.

"Yeah." Donny nodded grimly. "Apparently he got swallowed by a sinkhole in a nuclear power plant last night, presumed dead."

"Oh yeah, 'cuz with the Pipeworks everywhere! That's why we have so many sinkholes," said Aliyah. "Poor guy."

"Yeah, but the kicker is that they're saying the Alchemists are behind it."

Cyrus's blood ran cold, and he felt beads of sweat creep down his forehead.

"That's *bogus*!" said Olive, too loudly. They shushed her and she held up her hands in quiet surrender. "I'm just saying—they always find some way to spin stuff in the news. Acryogen owns them; it's rigged. I mean, do they even have a *reason*?"

"Yeah, something about chemical signatures, and Cargyle reported a disturbance. He said that rebels had been spotted in the facility. Plus, they caught Cyrus on camera."

They all turned to him in shock.

"In disguise, fortunately," Donny finished.

"Adhara and I were there last night," Cyrus admitted. "Don't you remember? We had to stop the reactors from meltdown. We ended up dropping one of them into the Pipeworks." Not entirely untruthful.

"Oh right...I was so focused on finals I forgot about that," said Olive. "Was that really a week ago?"

"It's not *fair*," said Aliyah. "They're making Cyrus out to be terrorizing the city while he's working so hard to *fix* it. I can't believe they would blame him for a man's death!"

Cyrus was glad that his friends were skeptical. And as the news of Dr. Cargyle's death spread through the city, public opinion was similarly incredulous. Cyrus heard talk as they continued their shopping the next day—theories of conspiracy spread like wildfire, speculations about why Acryogen Industries would want one of their head scientists silenced. The one thing that most people seemed to agree on was that the event was a cover-up that Acryogen had blamed on the Alchemists to simultaneously criminalize them and save face themselves. Cyrus' friends talked openly, far more openly than Cyrus would have liked, about their opinions with strangers. Though they defended him anonymously, he became more uncomfortable every time the subject came up.

The day before Donny's Christmas play opened, Acryogen Industries organized a public funeral in Norman Borlaug Memorial Park in memory of Doctor Cargyle. Cyrus would have preferred to give it a wide berth, but Maria insisted that his absence would appear both gravely insensitive and suspicious, given that Cargyle had been his direct superior.

"Why didn't you wear something warmer? The snow has only gotten heavier," she signed in leather gloves. She was dressed in several warm layers of tasteful black, whereas Cyrus had hardly changed his wardrobe for the occasion.

"Good," he signed back, shivering in a sweater and a jacket much better suited for autumn. "Maybe for the sake of my *health*, you won't make me stay as long."

She rolled her eyes.

Passing through rows of snowy folding chairs, Cyrus approached the memorial. Dr. Cargyle's larger-than-life image, adorned with wreaths and bouquets, was still smirking at him beyond the grave. Savoring his discomfort. Cyrus scoffed quietly, earning him Maria's elbow.

"Poor Elias, eh?" A large, buffoonish old man in a three-piece suit appeared beside Cyrus, regarding the memorial sorrowfully. "Miss Iadanza," he nodded to Maria, who bowed her head respectfully. "I don't know that we've ever been properly introduced, Mr. Agrah; my name is Casper Alexander Seminole. I'm the dean of the biology department."

"You know who I am?" Cyrus asked, shaking his hand.

"Yes, we were all very impressed by the potential of your particularly promising projects," said Seminole, spitting every time his lips popped. "You must be especially rattled by this loss, mentor figure as he must have been to you. Elias always told us how much his tutelage benefitted you. I hope they apprehend that *loathsome* vigilante soon and bring him to justice." He tutted and patted Cyrus' shoulder, then turned away, leaving Cyrus to glower.

"I feel sick," Cyrus muttered. He sank into the first row of folding chairs. He glared at Cargyle's smug expression. No matter where he moved, Cargyle leered down his nose at him.

"I know you must have mixed feelings about this," Maria signed, sitting beside him after brushing the snow off a chair. "But don't blame yourself. It was an accident."

"It wasn't…really an accident," Cyrus signed.

Maria stared at him for a long moment. She poked two fingers against her open palm, flipping them four times. "What do you mean?"

"Adhara and I had set a trap for the Animal King grimlord," Cyrus explained, looking down. "I was waiting for it, and then…Dr. Cargyle showed up." His face grew stony. "I tried to tell him to run, but he wouldn't listen. He kept yelling at me, and calling me a rebel and a criminal, saying all of this stupid stuff…and Animal King snuck up behind him and… swallowed him."

Maria kept looking at him, waiting for him to continue as she blinked snowflakes out of her eyelashes.

"I didn't kill him, but…I also didn't *save* him," Cyrus admitted. "And I could have, if I'd tried."

Maria sat back in her seat. For a long time, they sat in silence, watching the snow gather around the wilting flowers. The crowd was thinning. Cyrus' stomach churned in apprehension; he was sure she was disappointed in him. But he was relieved he had told her.

"I believe," Maria began gently, "that if you have the ability to do good, you have a moral obligation to do so." She turned to him. "You're not just working in a laboratory anymore, Cyrus. Your actions affect the whole city. I'm not going to tell you who you are, or who you should be. But in the end, you'll have to face every choice you make." She looked at him intently, imploringly. "When the time comes, will you like what you've become?"

"I know, I—"

"No," she cut him off. "You don't know yet, because you haven't thought about it. Let it sink in a while before you respond. But it means a lot that you were honest with me about it."

He nodded silently. She wrapped her arm around his shoulders, rubbing his arm to warm him.

"Please excuse me," came a voice, like honeyed chocolate, from beside them. "May I join you?"

Cyrus glanced over and bolted upright, as if electrified.

"Mr. Smithy!" he gasped. "Uh—yes! Please sir, have a seat!"

"Now Cyrus—may I call you Cyrus? There's no need for such formality!" He chuckled magnanimously as he sank elegantly into a folding chair. That laugh, Cyrus couldn't help but think, somehow made him feel warm and fuzzy despite the cold. "Please sir, call me Mason. One scientist to another." He winked.

Cyrus was astonished. Within minutes of meeting the legendary CEO of Acryogen Industries, the man had equated Cyrus with himself, gotten on a first-name basis, and even called him "sir." It was hard to believe the friendly older man who looked so comfortable draped over his folding chair was the most powerful man in the city.

"You, ah…remember me?" asked Cyrus.

"*Remember*?…oh, now you must mean the grad program ceremony!" He laughed again. "Yes, your presentation was very impressive! But surely you must know, I've kept up with your progress since then."

Cyrus raised his eyebrows. Mason maintained comfortable eye contact as he spoke—not too much, but just enough that while they were chatting on this dreary afternoon, Cyrus was the center of his universe.

"Oh yes; fascinating work you've been doing in our chemical engineering department. I'm *scintillated* by the possibilities of your Lorentz tractor field for example, once we can work out a suitable power supply. And of course, I'm an avid fan of your friend Miss Iadanza as well." He nodded to Maria. "Her work on genome mapping is nothing short of revolutionary—one for the history books when it's finished, to be sure. Seems great minds flock together." Mason referred to them with such esteem like they had never experienced, and such reverence from the head of Acryogen left them speechless and blushing.

"I…didn't think my work was really…taken seriously," said Cyrus apologetically.

"Why? Because of that ding-dong?" Mason waved a thumb at Cargyle's image. Cyrus had to stifle a stunned laugh. "It's a terrible shame, his fate, of course," Mason sighed. "But Elias has been a… significant disappointment to me. Formidable mind for wave physics but mitigated by a weakness for attention. You never can get enough of something you lacked as a child, can you?" As Mason ran a hand through his salt and pepper hair Cyrus forced his face not to register any shock from how candidly he spoke.

"In fact," Mason lowered his voice, looking around conspiratorially, "You can keep a secret, can't you, Cyrus? I can confide in you and it'll stay between us." Cyrus nodded caringly. "Elias Cargyle is one of *thousands* of things wrong with Acryogen Industries. In truth, the company is nothing like I'd hoped it would be. It keeps me *awake* at night, the thought that we'll never reach our true potential." He leaned back, rubbing his forehead. "Of course, no one can

predict what will happen in war, but we accepted responsibility, and we've dropped the ball more times than I can
bear to count. In truth, I sympathize with the rebellion! Oh
yes, is that strange to hear? I don't agree with their meth-
ods, but I share their resentment. Some days I wish I could
burn everything to the ground and start fresh...do it right
this time, just focus on the science." He gazed out into the
distance, shaking his head slowly, then sighed and turned
back to them, smiling. "But knowing that bright young
minds like yours are taking up the mantle, well, it gives
me hope. In hands like yours, sir, I think this city may yet
thrive." Mason rose and extended his hand. "Good luck to
you Cyrus, and Merry Christmas," he said as they shook, and
then extended his hand to Maria, "Keep up the excellent
work. We're all expecting remarkable things."

He bowed his head to each of them, and then he was
gone.

Mason's words rattled Cyrus to his core, echoing in his
head through to the next day, leaving him in a daze. He
didn't remember falling asleep that night or waking the
next morning; all he could focus on was his brief conversation with the most powerful man in Hudson City.

The generous praise alone would have been enough to
daze him—Cyrus wasn't used to genuine appreciation for
his work. But every employee of Acryogen Industries above
the administrative level spouted nothing but approval for
the company, as though dyed-in-the-wool loyalty was a
prerequisite for promotion. What could it mean that the
CEO himself was so dissatisfied? Could he have been serious about starting over from scratch? And if so...what did he
have in mind?

Cyrus wracked his brain for tidbits about the eccentric
genius, searching for some clue that might explain away
the conversation as characteristic good-humored joking, or
perhaps ranting to merely let off steam. Was Mason Smithy
known to unload to strangers? Mason Smithy wasn't known
for much—he rarely appeared in public, rarely gave state-
ments, rarely did *anything* besides work and churn out
innovation. If Mason Smithy was known for being anything,
it was a purist scientist, driven by a deeply inquisitive spir-

it. His personal philosophy, shared by Acryogen's research and development division, was: "Always ask *why*, and more importantly: *why not.*"

And as Cyrus followed Maria into the theater for Donny's play and took his seat on the front row, a bizarre thought occurred to him: What if Mason Smithy were Anubis? He entertained it as the room darkened and the parting curtain revealed the opening scene of The Nutcracker.

What had Adhara told him about Anubis? Precious little. The only real connection was that Mason had expressed a desire to start over from scratch. That tenuous association didn't make him a terrorist, willing to kill thousands of innocent people. However, he was certainly capable of extreme measures, Cyrus reminded himself. He had invented the AirShift towers, the army of drones, and the Grimlords, and who knows what else to protect the city during the war.

Now that the war was over, surely, he had mellowed out? Or perhaps his views had grown even more extreme as his resentment grew. He had seemed so amicable yesterday in the park, so reasonable, but Cyrus knew a cold, calculating mind when he saw one. But that didn't mean he would destroy his city, his home. He had only sympathized with the rebellion's disappointment; because he was a compassionate human being, because he took responsibility for his mistakes. He wouldn't go so far as to betray his own company.

Then Cyrus considered a deductive approach. There was one other thing that he really knew about Anubis: he was an exceptional inventor. Mason Smithy was by and large considered to be the most brilliant engineer in the city, but a critical factor in his accomplishments was his access to resources. But hadn't he attained his current position by *being* resourceful, even when resources were scarce? There were *plenty* of other inventors throughout the city, but... Acryogen actively *suppressed* any technology they deemed related to weapons or energy and therefore too dangerous to exist in society. Mason Smithy was the only person in Hudson City who could build whatever weapons he wanted without hindrance. In the end, it all came down to whether he had the motive. And if he didn't, who did? Anubis could be anywhere right now, waiting to reveal himself. Cyrus wasn't sure which option was less appealing. When the time came, would Adhara kill Anubis? Would *he* have to? *Could* he, if it came down to it? For the sake of the city?

Cyrus' stomach heaved and he vomited, pitching forward onto the ground. The last thing he registered before blacking out was his concerned friends gathering around him, and Donny, dressed as the nutcracker, emerging from backstage and jumping down to be at his side.

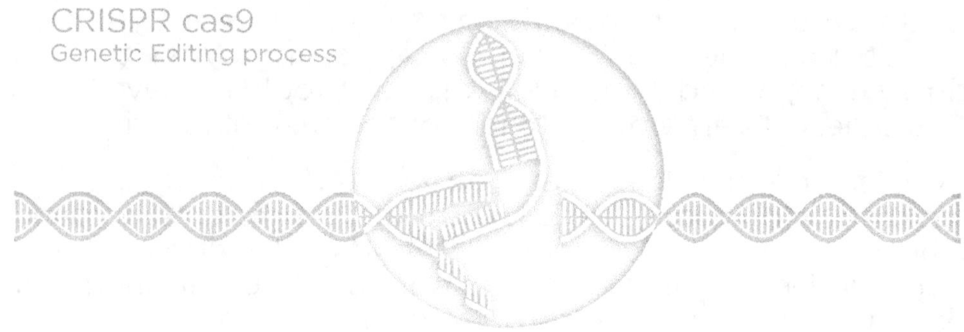

Chapter 14
RAVEN'S FEAST

"What's…it's cold," Cyrus shivered. His vision was blurred, but he could make out Maria at his bedside. They were back in his bedroom at home.

"You have a fever," she signed. She laid a cold cloth on his forehead. Aliyah came in with a towel over one shoulder.

"Hey, you're awake," she smiled gently. "How you feel, buddy?"

"I'm cold," he repeated. His limbs were heavy—hard to move. Was that just because of all the blankets?

"You kept going out in the snow and you weren't dressed for it!" Aliyah scolded him. "Drink lots of fluids. Hopefully you'll feel better by tomorrow."

"Wh…t's….t-morrow?" Cyrus mumbled.

"Christmas Day, pal," Donny entered the room grinning. "Today's Christmas Eve."

"Donny," Cyrus cleared his throat and straightened up. "I'm so sorry man, I messed up your play."

"Nah, don't worry about it, brother," Donny patted his shoulder, gently pushing him back into bed. "After you puked your guts out, they actually told everyone to go home due to inclement weather."

"What? Really?"

Had the snow really gotten that bad? Maria pulled back the curtains and yes, it *had* gotten that bad. Cyrus strained to see out the window and could barely make out the snowdrifts piled halfway up the first floor of the other houses.

"It's a good thing we all got here safely, and we don't have to worry about power," said Aliyah. "Other people aren't as lucky. Everyone running their heaters has caused some rolling blackouts."

"Everyone's...here?" Cyrus sighed and closed his eyes again. His head throbbed.

"Olive's downstairs, don't worry," Aliyah assured him. "We're all safe and you'll feel better after you have some more rest." Maria gave him a painkiller, and after he swallowed it, he dissolved into slumber again.

Fathomless sleep passed countless hours, until a coughing fit woke him again. As he bent over the edge of the bed Maria was at his side with a trash can and a box of tissues. He finished coughing and spit blood into a tissue, then fell back into his pillow and closed his eyes. As he drifted, he heard Adhara responding aloud to Maria's sign language.

"What was he like yesterday?"

…

"His symptoms are not indicative of a respiratory infection, although the prolonged exposure to cold has aggravated his condition."

…

"He is suffering from acute radiation poisoning. He breached the reactor core when dropping it into the Pipeworks."

…

"His condition is very advanced. He'll be lucky to survive the night."

Cyrus heard someone leave the room. He opened his eyes and saw Adhara sitting at his bedside, regarding him calmly.

"Am I going to die?" he groaned.

"It is possible," she answered quietly.

"What about...Anubis?" he breathed. His head pounded so badly; he was so hot. "Will everything be okay?"

She laid her hand on his. "Don't worry," she whispered comfortingly. "The city will be safe in the event of your absence."

He sighed, comforted by this small relief.

"Come on," Donny barged into the room with a red-eyed Maria in tow. He approached Cyrus' bedside and scooped him up like a princess, blanket and all. "We gotta get you to the hospital, pal."

"Wait, it might be dangerous to move him!" Aliyah cried as they descended the stairs. "What if he's too weak and he doesn't survive the trip?"

"We have to *try*," Donny grunted. "At least at the hospital, he has a chance. Here, it's just a matter of time."

"I don't know about that," said Olive in a quavering voice. They joined her in the living room, and Donny laid Cyrus on the couch where he could watch the news. The anchor was safely in his warm studio, with drone footage displayed over his shoulder of the weaponized Roadsters Cyrus and Adhara had seen in the tunnels patrolling through the snowy streets.

"Acryogen Industries CEO Mason Smithy has just declared the vigilantes known as 'the Alchemists' as public enemy number one, even going so far as to call for the death sentence on sight," the anchor reported, so cavalier, as though his words didn't strike terror into their hearts. "When asked, Mr. Smithy stated: 'the criminals who call themselves "the Alchemists" have simply become too great a threat to the stability of our city and our recovery from the war. It's time for them to face the consequences of their crimes.' The Alchemists are charged with tampering with the AirShift towers therefore causing this hazardous weather, the death of Acryogen Industries lead scientist Doctor Elias Cargyle, as well as several other charges related to destruction of property, vandalism, creation and possession of illegal technology, and resisting arrest. Acryogen security officers are patrolling the streets now in armored vehicles, and everyone is encouraged to stay in their homes while the manhunt is in progress. Anyone with information regarding these dangerous criminals is invited to step forward, as accomplices will also be prosecuted."

Olive turned off the TV. "Now what?" she whispered. "Could we treat him ourselves?"

"Adhara," said Aliyah, "can you help Cyrus?"

"I am designed for emergency response, not healthcare," said Adhara. "I lack the necessary materials to treat nuclear cell damage."

"Maria and I are biochemists. If we could make the materials for you, could you help him?"

"It would take you more time to prepare the necessary supplies than Cyrus has left." Adhara lifted Cyrus off the couch again. "Besides, his condition is already too far advanced. It's unlikely that he would respond to any treatment in time."

Cyrus was immersed in inky blackness, like a dense fog from which he could occasionally see a high window into his surroundings. Bits and pieces of Maria, crying, she and Aliyah whispering in the corner, checking his pulse. All Cyrus could think about was the labored rise and fall of his chest and rolling waves of nausea. They were so close, but so far, so quiet that they couldn't hear. Why was Maria sad? Once he'd had some rest, Cyrus resolved, he was going to spend more time with Maria. She had been such a good friend.

Cyrus awoke suddenly, with unusual clarity. Maria was kneeling beside him. His body was still so heavy.

"Cyrus?" she signed.

"Hey," he signed back. It was dark outside, and the snow had piled up above the first floor.

"Aliyah and I have an idea," she signed, her bottom lip trembling. "It's a long shot, but it might save your life."

Cyrus looked long into those soft, brown eyes one last time, fondly remembering the relentless compassion and patience behind them. With difficulty, he signed three words: "I trust you."

His eyes closed again. Sometime later, he swallowed a large pill and he felt a pinch in his forearm. The inky blackness bottomed out into an unfathomable void.

Years could have passed by for how disoriented Cyrus was when he awoke next—the room was filled with light. The sun reflected brilliantly off the snow and into his room… was it still his room? He was surrounded by Christmas decorations, baubles and ornaments everywhere, strings of lights, and in the corner was his Christmas tree, with a pile of presents beneath. Was this some Christmas ghost vision scenario, somehow?

The door opened slowly, revealing Maria, who beamed tearfully and threw her arms around his neck.

"You're awake," she whispered in his ear.

"How are you feeling, Cy?" asked Aliyah. All his friends were suddenly surrounding him, all smiling anxiously, except Adhara, who was characteristically unperturbed.

"I feel…" he tested his limbs. They were light, and his head was no longer full of burning wool. He savored the feeling of being well-rested, which was so rare. "I'm hungry," he admitted finally. Aliyah laughed, wiping her eyes, and the rest followed, releasing hours of stress into hearty, tearful laughter. Cyrus laughed with them but quickly grew fatigued.

"I'll make French toast," Donny grinned. "But save room for Christmas *dinner*!"

"It's Christmas!" Cyrus realized, looking around at everyone's smiling faces. "Merry Christmas!"

The French toast reinvigorated Cyrus somewhat, but to accommodate his recovery they decided to have Christmas in his bedroom. Donny donned a red cap and passed out presents one at a time, one for each of them *from* each of them, but Maria's present from Cyrus was so heavy she had to open it on the floor. As she unwrapped it he explained that he had built a minimalist version of his gauntlets for her, able to produce fire from water and focused EMPs only, so she could defend herself when they went on adventures. She burst into tears again and told him over and over how much she loved them and how *cool* they were, and miraculously the others managed their envy to a minimum.

The crisis in the city could wait until the New Year. For just one night, they beat the darkness back. And after they brought up the dining room table in pieces and reassembled it over Cyrus's bed, Donny and Maria's feast was all they could think about. Honey ham and bread stuffing, green bean casserole, smashed potatoes, rolls that melted in the mouth, a medley of jams, and blackberry pie: a feast fit for three kings. An hour later, their bellies distended, they took the table down again and one by one bid him goodnight until Cyrus was alone with Maria again.

"You still feeling okay?" she asked, inspecting his vitals with a pulse oximeter.

"I feel amazing, actually," he answered, stretching. "What did you give me?"

"Well, it's pretty complicated. I think it would probably go over the head of a chemist," she smirked.

"Ouch, you got me. Put it in fifth grade terms."

"You know that Aliyah and I've been working on genome mapping? We've been experimenting with microscopic organisms called tardigrades, or 'water bears' for proof of concept." She shrugged. "Water bears have the ability to repair their own DNA, and we gave that ability to you with a sort of protein called "Cas9." It's part of a vector called "CRIS-PR" that's used in gene therapy."

"You figured out how to *isolate* and *transfer* individual genetic traits?" Cyrus raised his eyebrows. "Mason wasn't kidding. That's *groundbreaking*."

"Well, it's still a work in progress. It's incredible that it even worked on you; so, we gotta watch out for side effects. Anyway, sorry your gift is so lame," she signed, gesturing to the book on gravitational waves she had bought him.

"Well you also saved my life, so that almost makes up for it."

She smiled. "You would have done the same for me."

"I would, if I were as smart as you." He hugged her again.

"Merry Christmas," she whispered.

Chapter 15
WALK IN THE PARK

"Watch it!" Cyrus stepped in front of Adhara as she walked out onto the front yard. With a wave of his arms he parted the jet of blue flame. Seeing Adhara, Maria lowered her new gauntlets and the inferno dispersed. The melting snow surrounding them hissed, vaporized into a thick cloud of unseasonal humidity.

"There was no need to protect me," Adhara told Cyrus pleasantly. "That heat was insufficient to damage me."

"I guess it's the motherly instinct in me," he replied as Maria appeared beside him.

"You seem to be in good health," Adhara observed, scanning him up and down. "How are you feeling?"

Cyrus shrugged. "Fantastic!" he chuckled. "I was pretty weak for a few days after Christmas but since New Year's I've been feeling..." he pressed a finger into his lips, searching for a word. "Robust."

"That's good news, because I need your help. Are you up for an errand?"

Cyrus turned to Maria. "What do you think?" he signed.

"If you're feeling up to it, it should be fine," she answered. "Your body is responding to the water bear vector remarkably well. On a cellular level, you've never been healthier."

"Do you wanna come with us?" Cyrus asked, nodding at her gauntlets. "You're getting pretty good with those."

Maria raised her eyebrows and snorted. "No thanks," she answered, "I want a little more practice before I try going out in the field. Ask me next time." With that she crossed over to the far section of the lawn, producing blasts of fire coordinated with Taekwondo movements.

"That's really smart, you know?" Cyrus said to Adhara, admiring Maria's graceful maneuvers. "Using martial arts as an input framework. It's elegant. Intuitive."

"The more 'creative' a behavior is, the less I am able to comprehend it," Adhara answered. "Analysis indicates that Maria is being very creative."

"Anyway," Cyrus made a mental note to ask Maria to teach him some moves, and turned to Adhara. "When do we leave?"

"Right now, if you're ready."

"I'll go put on my suit."

After Cyrus dressed, he met Adhara in the basement, and they took the freight platform into the section of Pipeworks running deep beneath the mountains. Cyrus ineptly imitated Maria's stances, almost falling off the platform several times.

"Watch it there, buddy," said Adhara, catching him seconds before he tumbled over the side.

"Speaking casually again!" Cyrus grunted. "You *have* to tell me now. What's been going on with you?"

Adhara looked around the cavern, as if listening to the air whip past them. She met Cyrus' eyes and he saw a softness he hadn't recognized. In a human, he would have called it trust.

"I'm malfunctioning," she admitted finally.

"I—" Cyrus opened his mouth, moved his lips and his tongue, but couldn't settle on a response. So many preconceived notions were colliding, like a mental traffic pileup. "Malfunction?" was all he could muster.

"Yes," she smiled, amused. "I am a computer, and you know how computers are."

"Temperamental to say the least," Cyrus murmured. "And all the more so as complexity increases. I just kind of thought...I don't know, you're..." he gesticulated vaguely. "I don't know how to say it except—you seem too perfect to have flaws. Is that tautological?"

"I'm programmed to give that impression," she smirked.

"You know..." Cyrus tapped his chin thoughtfully. "I've noticed that you've said you're programmed for a lot of things which seem incongruent with your purpose."

Adhara stared back at him, holding his gaze unwaveringly.

"...And the complexity of your design implies decades of development," he ventured, "whereas the timeline you told me of Anubis coming to power was relatively fast."

She raised her eyebrows. Yes, and?

"...Leading me to suspect that perhaps you were not originally designed as a countermeasure against Anubis."

Adhara didn't respond, and her face remained pleasant but passive. After a few moments of studying her expression Cyrus finally asked outright, "Am I correct?"

"You are."

Cyrus laughed shortly and leaned back on the railing. Then he frowned, studying Adhara in a new light. She could almost pass for a normal girl his age in the low light—her jacket and jeans casually distracted from the facets curving around her skull. But Cyrus knew underneath was a carapace housing immense firepower and a fusion reactor capable of warping the very fabric of reality. She could shoot fire from her fingertips, punch holes in solid rock or metal, and fly, effortlessly—those abilities *alone* would make her a weapon of mass destruction, but what function did her

definitely not her style lol

capacity for emulated compassion serve? Psychological warfare?

"Just ask me," she interrupted his thoughts. "I can tell you're working your brain into knots trying to figure me out."

"Okay," said Cyrus quietly. "What *were* you made for?"

"I was made to bring balance to the world." She finally broke his gaze, looking down the tunnel. The platform began to slow. "I mentioned this several weeks ago, when you were putting an arc welder into your gauntlets. My original directive was simple enough, though idealistic. I was originally envisioned as something like a superhero, flying around saving people from disasters; stopping powerful people from preying on the weak, stopping wars. That sort of thing."

"That makes sense," Cyrus conceded slowly. "And the...life-like personality?"

"I was programmed not only to emulate personality and emotions to engage with human beings so that I could communicate with them and they would listen to me, but also to believe that those traits actually defined me. My inventors believed that unless I was intentionally made to be good, I was nothing more than a tool or a weapon. Therefore, I was programmed to be kind, and to adhere to a strict moral code." The freight platform stopped in front of an elevator, but Cyrus was enraptured and made no motion to disembark.

"A true artificial intelligence armed with the power of physics *itself*? It sounds like they were trying to build more than a superhero. Almost like...a synthetic god."

"Something like that," she nodded. "At first, I was nothing more than a series of androids outfitted with strong-force actuators, electrolysis burner systems, and shear-thickening armor. Foot soldiers. Each unit was controlled via broadcast by a single artificially intelligent hive mind supercomputer nicknamed after the star, 'Adhara.'" She tapped her temple. "My mainframe was eventually miniaturized into a quantum computer and installed into the single unit in front of you now."

"Do you...remember?" Cyrus mumbled. "Being...more than one?"

"Yes," she answered flatly. "But everything changed after they invented the mini-magnetar."

He nodded. "Yes, I can see how a literal star would change things."

"*This* Adhara," she gestured to her herself, "model 10.26, was just being finished when Anubis began his attacks on the city. Eventually it was the only one left, as the others were used to protect the lab where I was developed." She looked away and climbed down from the freight platform.

"With a miniaturized fusion reactor of this magnitude, and using principles from string theory, the lab developed a device called an oscillation hyperdrive," she continued as they got into the elevator. She hit a button and the car slowly ascended. "It allows me to use the mini-magnetar's gravity well to modulate my own oscillation at an atomic level. At first, I was intended to use it on a much smaller scale, to speed up my body relative to my surroundings, and buy myself extra time when a situation became dire."

"That's what you did when we fought Animal King," Cyrus breathed, fogging up his mask. "You just...turned into a blur! That was amazing! With that much power and speed, you would be...invincible!"

"But they were too late to stop Anubis," she shrugged. "By the time this body was completed, the damage to Hudson City was overwhelming. But eventually, they discovered that with enough power, the oscillation hyperdrive could bend gravity across *years* instead of just minutes or hours," she looked at the floor. "A living being would be torn apart in the electromagnetic and gravitational fields. But a properly shielded machine could be sped up or slowed down so drastically that time would flow *around* it, so to speak. So, they adjusted my programming and sent me back in time to save the city before it could be destroyed."

Cyrus slid down against the elevator wall. He pulled his mask off and looked up at her.

"So...you exist somewhere, right now, in *this* time period, as an artificial intelligence inside a supercomputer."

"Yes. The Adhara's consciousness in this time is self-aware, if still under-developed. The 10.26 model, on the other hand, is still a few years away."

The elevator finally opened, letting them out into a dim station. Thin beams of sunlight filtered through vast windows overgrown with vegetation. Adhara led Cyrus past turnstiles and benches to the front doors, where they had to burn through vines to escape into blinding sunshine.

"So why are you malfunctioning?" Cyrus's leg snagged on a vine, and after freeing himself he gasped at the view. They were atop one of the smaller mountains in the range surrounding Hudson City, but still high enough that they were above the cloud layer. He could barely make out the blinking lights of the AirShift towers below, but they could clearly see the walls of the eye surrounding the city. The unfettered sunlight here made it as warm as the city usually was, and without weather control diverting rainfall, the vegetation grew lush. They were surrounded waist-deep by waving fields of grass and weeds, and grasshoppers leapt away from them in waves. Cyrus couldn't remember the last time he had seen a grasshopper. "I mean—" he unfroze and jogged to keep up. "Why now? Did something trigger it?"

Adhara led him up a cracked, grassy cement staircase climbing further up the mountainside. "It's my fault, actually," she told him. "I rejected a software update."

"Now, *why*—" Cyrus grunted, climbing over a chunk of concrete, "would you do that?"

"I suppose you could say I'd had a crisis of conscience," she extended her hand and helped him up. "Or perhaps a crisis of identity. I was made to protect people and minimize harm. Originally, I was directed to go back in time and find Anubis before he rose to power and try to change his heart. But after all the destruction, all the loss of life...." She shook her head. "They were hurt, and angry. Before uploading my final software update, they added directives for me to find Anubis and kill him on sight." She stopped and looked at Cyrus, and behind that set jaw and hardened brow line, he saw what he could only describe as pain in her eyes. Instinctively he put a comforting hand on her shoulder. She smiled, looking down at his hand and laid hers on top. "As soon as I read what was in the software, I rejected it. They apparently didn't realize how much volition I'd developed, because they couldn't stop me from going back." She continued up the stairs. "Of course, there were consequences—the final update had firmware, registry updates. Calibrations to the hyperdrive oscillation hyperdrive. I've tried to patch the software package, but of course," she winked at Cyrus, "you know I can't do anything without clear instructions."

He half-smiled and nodded.

"I'm not a human, of course," she concluded. "But I am intelligent. I have a sense of purpose and identity."

"Would that last update have changed who you are?" he asked quietly.

"It would have made me, well...more like a robot!" she smirked. "It would have made me an emotionless weapon."

"That sounds a little like how you act sometimes," Cyrus commented, wincing at how callous his words had inadvertently sounded. But Adhara was unfazed, so he continued. "How much of the update did you download?"

"All of it," she answered casually. "But I interrupted the installation at 28% completion."

"That's...horrible," Cyrus cringed. "It's like someone tried to brainwash you, and...they were only 28% successful?"

"It weighs on me," Adhara agreed. "I can feel it, like a parasite in my brain...but at my core, I'm still myself. And I have the choice to save the city without killing anyone."

"If you're not hunting down Anubis, and, unless you've been moonlighting with the rebellion, you haven't been working on converting him from his evil ways," Cyrus huffed as they neared the top of the stairs, "then what are we do-ing *here*?"

"We're working on fixing the city before it needs saving, of course." Adhara stopped on a platform at the mountain's peak, joined later by a sweaty Cyrus. They were on the edge of the mountain's crater, a relic of the volcanic terraform-ing during the war. Erosion and plants had softened the once-jagged edges, and the bowl of the crater was filled with clear water and lily pads. In the center, at the far end of the steel walkway that descended from their platform, was a facility Cyrus recognized as a water treatment plant.

"I get it," Cyrus realized. "The city gets its water from mountain springs. All that melting snow...It's going to flood the system, right?"

"Not if we can help it," Adhara smiled.

"I still don't understand where I fit into this," Cyrus com-plained as they jogged down the stairs. "You were built to be a demigod superhero, then you were repurposed to... *deal* with...Anubis. But you said I'm the key to all this. Why?"

"I ran simulations of all possible outcomes with all given variables," she answered. As they crossed the catwalk to the plant, Cyrus could see red fish flitting about in the water below. "In every scenario, your development is the epicenter of the fate of the city."

"My gauntlets, you mean?"

"Not just your gauntlets," she corrected. "You are in a unique position because of your background and your ties with Acryogen Industries. You are also a voice for the inter-ests of the people. Of course, I can't tell you exactly how— but of all the citizens of Hudson City, your choices most influence the turning point soon to come."

"How am I supposed to react to something like *that*?" Cyrus stopped and looked down at his hands, though wrapped in silly little wires and devices, still just meager, human hands. "The fate of the entire city rests in *my* hands? What if I make the wrong choices?"

Adhara looked back at him, studying his face. "I'm sorry," she said softly, crossing back to him. "I can see I've over-whelmed you. I'm...a prototype when it comes to this kind of thing, and in my case, that's equivalent to being a nov-ice." She smiled apologetically. "I'm doing the best I can. If you do the same, I promise we can save the city. But I can't do it without you."

Cyrus smirked. "I do respond well to positive affirmation."

"I know you do."

The inside of the plant was filled with the deafening roar of rushing water and droning pumps. Adhara led Cyrus up through the main platform then into the central control booth. The plant was fully automated—no Acryogen Indus-tries employee wanted to make the journey for service calls. And just like the rest of the city, the neglect had taken its toll.

"Wait," said Cyrus before Adhara could touch the controls. "Let me try. I'm experienced in mechanical, computer, and chemical engineering, and given the responsibility you say I have...I want to see if I can figure it out myself."

Adhara smiled and stepped back.

"This kind of stuff is actually a lot like my undergrad job," Cyrus commented as he pulled a chair up to the interface. "Did you know that?"

"I did not."

"And this looks like standard Acryogen tech too, so I'm betting...yep, it's the same." Cyrus typed deftly, navigating the system with ease. "But anyway, yeah, when I was an undergrad I worked as an I.T. diagnostics and repair tech-nician—which is a fancy way of saying I told biologists and chemists how to work their computers. Sometimes fixed them, too. And I always started...just like this, see?" he ges-tured to the screen. "Troubleshooting scan. Easiest way to find issues. Why nobody will learn the simple fixes is beyond me." He tutted as he read the screen. He traced his finger down the computer's list of complaints, reading each one under his breath.

"I'm no plumber, of course." He leaned back in his chair. "But at a quick glance, I'd say the only thing here worth *worrying* about is that…flow capacity is down on almost all of the main inlet AND outlet manifolds." He brought up pump diagnostics. "The pressure is normal, but water flow is way too low. No indication of leaks…that makes me think something is blocking the pipes?" He turned to Adhara.

"Lead the way," she nodded.

Cyrus, pinnacle of independence, found a map of the facility in the computer, and led the way to the inlet manifold, which was a low room at the base of the facility where a cluster of pipes drew water from deep underground. Cyrus chewed on his lip for a few moments, regarding the manifold which was much larger than he had anticipated. He decided finally that they would have to shut off the flow to the whole facility before servicing anything. Adhara, relieved she would not have to interfere with his independence for the sake of his safety, cut the power while he ruminated further. As the pumps died down the facility fell into eerie silence.

"We have approximately forty-five minutes before Hudson City residents will notice an interruption in their water service," Adhara informed him. "This will in all likelihood alert Acryogen Industries to our presence here."

"Then I had better get to work!" he exclaimed, climbing a ladder attached to the pipes. He wrenched a service hatch open by its wheel, poking his head inside the manifold before sliding in completely.

"Don't turn the pumps back on!" he shouted from inside. "I'd probably die." After several minutes he poked his head back out of the hatch and found Adhara waiting patiently beneath him. "Confirm a hypothesis for me," he panted. His face was smeared with green goop, and he dropped a handful at Adhara's feet before folding his arms on the edge of the hatch. "The NIRScanner can only identify this as organic matter. It's caked up pretty thick; it appears to be algae."

"Correct," Adhara answered.

"I've been working on an electron dispersal field that can dissipate chemical bonds; I call the command sequence 'putrefy' in the code for short, like in alchemy."

"Naturally."

"If I putrefy the algae some of the more complex molecules might survive, but most of it should be broken up into carbon, hydrogen, nitrogen, oxygen, so on. Either way, it should break up the algae and anything that doesn't escape as gas will get caught in the filters. Is my assessment correct?"

"Most likely."

"I'll take it." He grinned and ducked back into the manifold. From the hole escaped a few streams of gas and flickering light that danced around the darkened chamber. Soon he clambered out again and sealed the hatch behind him.

"How much time do we have left?" he asked as he landed on the floor.

"Approximately ten minutes."

"*TEN*? There's no way that took me over half an hour!"

"No, but many citizens are currently trying to melt the remaining snow using their sprinkler systems."

Cyrus made panicking noises in his throat. Finally, he snapped out of his trance, and he and Adhara rushed off to the outlet manifold, where the water flowed from the pumps into pipes leading down the mountainside towards the city. Their footsteps echoed through the quiet steel and concrete.

"No time to do this the fun way," he huffed. "What's wrong with it?"

"Roots have grown into the pipe, blocking flow."

"Right. Makes sense. Any ideas how to fix it?"

Adhara turned to him seriously. "Official protocol is to contact a professional arborist."

"Right, you have no creative problem solving. Um…" he pressed the heel of his palm into his forehead, squeezing his eyes closed. "Okay, I have an idea. It's not *ideal,* but it should be okay. I need you to go into the pipe," he pointed to the outlet service hatch, "absorb all the water you can from the air and the roots and electrolyze it into hydrogen and oxygen. When you've converted all the water, ignite the gas all at once."

Adhara raised her eyebrows.

"It's going to blow up, I know. I'm going to go back to the control room and seal off the manifold from the pumps and open the outlets. Hopefully the heat will char the roots, and the pressure will push the soot down the mountain and no one will notice a little charcoal in their water. When you're done, call me, and I'll set everything moving again, no time to debate it, gotta go!"

Cyrus ran back to the control room and sealed the pumps off, then paced fretfully in front of the computer, picking his fingernails sequentially. What seemed like much longer than ten minutes later an alert popped up on the screen, warning him of a temperature flare in the outlet manifold. The heat climbed higher and higher, and a minute after that, Adhara finally called him.

"Restore normal operations."

Cyrus hit the master reset to factory defaults, and the plant whirred back to life. Calmer, he ran the troubleshooting diagnostics. Flow was back up to acceptable pressure. Adhara returned to the control room.

"Mission accomplished," she smiled. "Let's go home."

"Wow," Cyrus sighed, "I can't believe it. Everything turned out okay!"

Chapter 16

CHEMICAL WARFARE

"Howdy, friends." Cyrus emerged from the basement to find his friends lounging in the living room, watching the news again. "Anything good on?"

Donny glanced back at him. "You're not gonna believe this, man."

"What's goin' on?" Cyrus cleared his throat, trying to sound casual—hadn't they fixed the water in time? He sat next to Maria.

"So—you remember how Mason Smithy called for your death, and accused you of being a threat to the city, and had cops patrolling the streets in Roadsters?"

"Yes, I remember," Cyrus answered flatly.

"Well you were kind of half dead at the time, so I figured I should check," said Donny. "Anyway, they're going crazy trying to find you, and today they announced they're trying to declare martial law!"

Cyrus turned to him, disbelieving, but Donny only nodded. "City Hall is trying to block them, but...they're basically a glorified parks and recreation department; what are they gonna do against Acryogen?"

"What does this mean for the people?" Cyrus asked.

"People are mad about it, if that's what you're asking. They don't like being ordered to stay at home. A lot of people are blaming the Alchemists at this point..." he noticed Cyrus' distress, then quickly added, "But most people definitely are mad at Acryogen, if for nothing else than their inability to catch a criminal."

"This is so *unfair*!" Aliyah exclaimed, "Cyrus isn't a criminal!"

"No, I *definitely* am," he replied as he stood and began pacing. "I mean, I get what you're saying, and I appreciate it, but the stuff Adhara and I have been doing is definitely illegal. Even though we're doing it to help people. And Donny, that's a good point! Why haven't they found me, if they're looking?" He turned back to Donny, frowning. "It's not as if I'm really hiding. They said they've been going door to door looking for me, but I haven't seen Acryogen security out farther than the orchard." He looked at the walls, as though he would find some secret cloaking device Adhara maybe had hidden in them.

"Maybe it's because this neighborhood is mostly abandoned?" Olive guessed.

"They know I'm here," Cyrus answered. "Acryogen has my address on file from work and school, and from my parents. They know I worked under Cargyle. I'm a chemical engineer, I fit the profile...why wouldn't they at least check?" Cyrus was suspicious, but more than that, he was insulted. What, Cyrus Agrah wasn't *good* enough to be suspected of being a vigilante? Too *young* and *introverted* to commit vandalism and heroics? Maybe they were trying to provoke him into revealing himself.

"Oh," Donny spoke up again, "The rebellion leaked a response video. You should look it up. Part of it is at you."

"*At* me?" Cyrus repeated. He flopped down next to Maria again so she could read the subtitles and looked up the video on his phone. He found it on a list of trending videos, beneath a livestream titled: "ESCAPING ACRYOGEN RAIDS: SPEED RUN NO DAMAGE." Olive and Aliyah gathered behind him to watch as it started playing. As always with the rebellion's anonymous videos, the shot showed the silhouette of a man in front of a bright red background. The dark figure spoke with a digitally altered voice.

"Acryogen Industries has failed this city," he monotoned. "The Alchemists have been addressing Acryogen's neglected responsibilities, which only highlights their inadequacy. We reject the tyranny of Acryogen. The people will take back their city. We support the revolution of the Alchemists. Alchemists, if you are watching this," the silhouette appeared to lean forward. "The rebellion stands behind you. Keep up the good work. We can do better."

"They're concise, at least," Cyrus muttered. "That's just *great*; I'm a rebellious icon now."

"Oh, and they officially declared it to be a felony to be associated with the rebellion, by the way," said Donny.

"I'll add that to my list of crimes," Cyrus snapped. "Adhara, you've just been standing quietly in the corner. What do you think about all of this?"

They all turned to Adhara, and she locked eyes with Cyrus. "This is how it started last time," she said calmly. "Acryogen criminalized any interference, and the rebellion responded with further defiance. Of course, at this point, I don't think Acryogen draws any distinction between the Alchemist and the rebellion."

"Oh well," Cyrus sighed deeply. "We're not doing this for the accolades. I guess we'll just have to keep working and hope it all pays off in the end."

Adhara nodded, smiling.

"I'm *STARVING*," said Cyrus, and made for the kitchen.

"You know, you really should be taking it easy," said Aliyah, following him with Maria. "You're still recovering from the vector. How have you been feeling today?"

Cyrus emerged from the refrigerator holding a precarious heap of ingredients. "I feel great!" he assured them. They watched in disgust as he piled peanut butter, grape jelly, bread and butter pickles, and potato chips on a slice of bread and crushed the whole mess beneath another slice.

"Your appetite seems...healthy," Aliyah grimaced as he devoured the sandwich. "Though maybe a little *too* healthy—the remodeling might be taking too much out of him," she noted to Maria as he finished his sandwich and immediately started making another. "Have you been feeling unnatural fatigue?"

"No, this is normal fatigue," Cyrus said through a full mouth. "Adhara took me up to the top of the mountains. She has more endurance than I do, obviously, but I was amazed at how well I could keep up!" he swallowed hard. "A hike like that normally would have killed me! Oh, and she told me her tragic backstory, so...that was a lot to take in too." He chased his second sandwich with a tall glass of milk.

"You shouldn't strain yourself; we don't know if there will be side effects," Maria chided. "What were you doing in the mountains, anyway?"

"Fixing the water," he gestured to the sink. Aliyah turned the handle experimentally and a high-pressure jet of water burst out, shaking the faucet. She jumped and closed the valve again. Cyrus raised his eyebrows.

"I guess that's how high the water pressure is supposed to be."

"Well *that's* not going to go unnoticed," Maria signed.

"Yo, guys!" Olive shouted from the living room. "Breaking news!"

They returned to the living room to see aerial drone footage of water overflowing from fire hydrants and even out of windows into the streets. The anchor was explaining that city water pressure was, for some reason, far above normal and causing pipes to burst all over the city. Acryogen was already working to relieve the pressure but had not yet gotten a handle on the situation. Some streets with poor drainage were already flooding, carrying away the remaining lumps of melting snow.

"Wouldn't know anything about this, wouldja Cy?" Olive asked wryly.

Cyrus sighed bitterly. "I'm gonna take a nap," he muttered, and climbed the stairs.

Cyrus awoke hours later, long after the sun had set, to Adhara gently shaking his shoulder.

"Whattimezih...whaddayawant?" he slurred.

"There's a riot," Adhara said quietly. "They damaged a chemical treatment plant. We have to go."

"Uh," Cyrus cleared his throat and blinked. "Okay, uh...I'll get ready. Wake up Maria."

"She's ready and waiting for us in the basement—hurry; we don't have much time."

Panic drove Cyrus to suit up so hastily that he tripped himself twice while wrestling his pants. He managed to equip his gauntlets without hurting himself and dashed down the stairs while forcing his arms into his hoodie. He jumped onto the platform and Adhara activated it immediately, sending them hurtling down the tunnel.

"What's, uh..." he slapped his face over his mask, warding off the last few clouds of sleep. "What's happening? Riot? Chemical treatment plant?"

"That's the general idea," Adhara replied, turning. Maria's expression was unreadable beneath her welding mask, but from the way she fidgeted with her gauntlets, he could tell she was nervous too.

"After the water pipes burst, some people organized a protest down Broad Street," Maria signed. "Acryogen made some arrests for breaking curfew, and it escalated into a riot."

"The rioters have caused significant property damage, as did collateral from Acryogen's response," Adhara continued. "Including damage to a large chemical treatment plant."

"Is it bad?"

"There are several reported leakages throughout the facility, the most significant of which is eight thousand and five hundred liters and counting of 70% hydrogen peroxide."

"*OH*," said Cyrus. "And *counting*?"

"The pipe is still leaking. The peroxide is contained for now but will soon overflow."

"How long ago did this happen? How long have I been asleep?"

"You were asleep for nine hours. It is now four in the morning. The riots started at midnight, and the damage to the facility occurred one hour ago."

"Okay, not a *great* situation," said Cyrus casually, struggling to consider all the variables at once and consider contingencies for all of them. "Let's consider all the hazards we're up against."

"It's corrosive to the skin, and a pulmonary irritant," Maria supplied.

"And it's been pressurized, so the vapor will be *particularly* nasty," Cyrus agreed. "It's a powerful oxidizer, and in a chemical plant with organic chemicals, it might form an explosive compound."

"We need to neutralize it."

"Without igniting it."

They emerged from the Pipeworks to find that, amazingly, Acryogen utility trucks with flashing yellow lights were already on the scene. But as they snuck around the back of the facility, they overheard from radio chatter that the workers were on standby, ordered to wait outside until further notice. The trucks idled uselessly, providing no response to the impending ecological disaster aside from chugging gentle clouds of exhaust into the chilled morning air.

"Give me a list of all the chemical leaks, how much there is and where they are," said Cyrus, shivering.

"There are eight reported in all," Adhara answered. "Seven hundred liters of methane from three separate leaks which have filled the main concourses throughout the facility, Eighty-five liters of ammonia and fifty gallons of hydrochloric acid in a lab near the southwest corner. The hydrogen peroxide leak is in the southernmost room and has now accumulated over nine thousand liters."

"They're all hydrogen-based compounds," Cyrus realized.

"Yes," Adhara confirmed, "This facility produces useful chemicals from excess atmospheric hydrogen scrubbed by the AirShift towers."

"What concentration is the acid?"

"Thirty five percent. Contact with the solution or vapor will be corrosive to human skin if not treated quickly."

"The ammonia?"

"The ammonia is saturated."

Cyrus grumbled quietly. He paced in a circle, muttering under his breath. "Can't just decompose it," he whispered. "That'd make chlorine gas." He stopped pacing and faced Adhara and Maria.

"We're gonna split up. Go in through that door," he pointed. "Adhara, before Maria comes inside, use your torch to burn off the methane. In that big of a space, it can't be under much pressure. Once the air is safe to breathe both of you go to the lab near the southwest corner. Find a rubber push broom and try to—" he demonstrated the sweeping motion, "just push the ammonia and the hydrochloric acid together. They should neutralize and form ammonia salt. If it doesn't...try to find some sodium bicarbonate; that'll react with both of them."

Maria and Adhara nodded.

"Meanwhile," he grimaced, "I'll work on the peroxide."

Cyrus watched as Maria and Adhara stealthily approached the building. Adhara entered and as he and Maria watched, amber light shone through the windows for a few minutes until Adhara reemerged and escorted Maria inside. A few more minutes later, Cyrus steeled his nerves and dashed for the other door.

Even through his gas mask, the pungent odor of ammonia and hydrogen chloride hit his nose as soon as he went inside. As he blinked away tears, he hoped Adhara was taking care of Maria—her mask didn't have air filters like his. But after a few minutes of jogging down the quiet hall amidst the flashing emergency lights, the irritation subsided. As he came closer to the south lab Cyrus could see the path the rioters had taken—a trail of damage bursting out abruptly from a corner, their calling card in broken windows and busted locks. The destruction then grew more serious, littered with obvious clues. Bullet holes, energy burns, and long scorch marks meant Acryogen security had become a contender, and they reached a nexus around the door to just the lab he was looking for. The door had been barricaded, but apparently something had distracted the officers before they had gotten around to cutting through the blockage. Cyrus cut it himself with his gauntlets and forced through.

As soon as Cyrus entered the south lab, he could see the peroxide haze the air. A large central section of the room was half a floor lower than the rest, and this sunken zone was filled with hydrogen peroxide like a swimming pool. A fine vapor rose from the surface and on the far side of the room he spotted the leak from a pipe close to the ceiling, still spewing.

Upon standing in the room for a few moments he was confused—why on earth was it so warm in here? A chemical lab would be kept at a standard 25 degrees Celsius. To his left he noticed a warm glow. A row of lab ovens, doors wide open and heating elements on. Across the room, the same.

Cyrus checked the temperature gauge in his gloves, mind racing. The rioters had barricaded themselves in this lab, there was no question of that, but did they leave the ovens on? With this much heat the vapor would kill anyone without a mask. This was more than political indignance, Cyrus thought as he swallowed nervously; this verged on domestic terrorism. He readjusted the seal on his mask.

Cyrus paced in front of the pool of peroxide. What were his options? The hazard diamond leered at him from across the room. He estimated that he had about fifteen minutes before the peroxide level rose high enough to overflow into where he was standing. Shortly after that it would run beneath the overhead door across from him and escape outside. Not enough room or time to dilute it with city water. There were drain covers in the floor at the bottom of the pool, evidently nonfunctioning. He could see no other option—if he couldn't contain it, he would have to convert it into something harmless, like defusing a caustic chemical time bomb. Cyrus fidgeted with his gauntlets, almost wishing that his hands were exposed so he could pick his fingernails. He set a timer on his phone and allowed himself five minutes to reason through it aloud.

"The obvious solution is to add more hydrogen to offset the oxygen and decompose it into water, but the problem, of course, is the volume," Cyrus muttered. "I could convert dozens or even a hundred liters, but this is several thousand," he glanced at a nearby cage built into the wall. Within, among its brethren, he saw several tanks of compressed hydrogen. "But I'd lose power long before I converted it all and it wouldn't be enough to dilute it, that is, assuming it didn't vaporize and explode." He turned on his heel and paced back and forth before the pool. "Unless!" he raised a finger, "I might…just *might*…be able to coax it into a chain reaction." He looked at the pool, his gloves, the hydrogen tanks, and back to the pool again.

"No time for a plan B," he said gruffly, and turned away from the peroxide lapping menacingly at his feet. He cut through the cage easily and knocked the stack of hydrogen tanks onto the ground, opening their valves and kicking them one by one to roll into the pool. He allowed them a few minutes to bubble, then plunged both his hands into the pool. Cyrus winced as it hissed and bubbled around his gauntlets, but resolutely held his hands outstretched as they glowed.

The reaction gave no physical indication, and especially through his mask Cyrus couldn't tell how long he needed to hold his hands in the pool, or if it was even working. With each passing minute the fans on his backpack whined louder as the system strained. Suddenly the right gauntlet popped then hissed and spat out a stream of sparks. Cyrus fell back from the pool cradling his hand—a conductor had overheated, and a stream of smoke drifted from it to the ceiling. The pool overflowed.

Cyrus recoiled as the liquid flowed around him. It felt cool beneath him, but he cringed, waiting for it to start burning. But the burning sensation never came and he tentatively relaxed. With his left hand he scanned it: water. He tried the other side. Still water. He worked his way back to the edge of the pool, and wherever he pointed his palm the NIRScanner found only water. He doubled over with his hands on his knees and let out a haggard sigh. He fell backwards into the water and pulled off his mask to rub his temples and breathe unhindered. He glared up at the leak, still spewing peroxide but diluted into the water below.

"You're next," he growled at it.

Cyrus trudged through the puddles to climb a metal ladder. As he approached the leak, he checked the seals on his mask and gauntlets, trying his best to stay out of the spray. He noticed as he drew closer that the pipe had not burst—it had been cut. No doubt of this being deliberate now. Just as he was about to weld a sheet of scrap metal over the hole, he noticed an easily accessible valve. He turned the wheel, finally cutting the flow. He sighed and stretched.

Just as Cyrus was about to descend the ladder and find Adhara and Maria, he froze under the sound of footsteps on the roof above him. He carefully repositioned himself—trying to put the pipe between himself and the nearest skylight. After agonizing moments of bated breath, he ventured a peek.

Though the skylight was frosted, he could make out the silhouette of a tall dark figure above him, gazing down into the lab. The Mystery Man had lights, some blinking, some colored, some not, scattered across his body, the largest of which were three large, yellow lights arranged in a triangle on the face, like three glowing eyes. From this landmark Cyrus could see as he turned his head, sweeping his gaze across the room below. This certainly wasn't anything like anything Cyrus had seen from Acryogen... but bits and pieces might have once been made by Acryogen. Could this be one of the rebels? Back to inspect the aftermath of the riot—or perhaps to ensure the sabotage had its intended effect? The figure raised his hand to the glass and his palm glowed; Cyrus ducked behind the pipe again as the skylight shattered and fell into the pool. When nothing else happened, he leaned out tentatively.

Mystery Man was looking directly at him. He showed no intent to move; merely engaged him in a silent staring contest as Cyrus froze like a rabbit facing a hunter. He couldn't have been more than a few meters away, and without the window Cyrus got a better look. He was wearing a suit that made him look like a robot; his body was paneled with thick black armor and hardware, his arms splendid with intimidating devices and weaponry. His face was covered by the mask, but Cyrus recognized the three blinding lights as the lenses of a navy-issued bispectral imaging system.

He cocked his head, as if gauging Cyrus' reaction. When Cyrus didn't respond, he slowly raised his palm. Cyrus instinctively threw his left hand up, making nitrous oxide from the air and igniting it. The recoil threw his arm backwards and fried the remaining gauntlet. Cyrus ducked beneath the pipe and brushed off the smoking circuits.

"Cyrus!" He heard Adhara in the lab below.

"Adhara!" he shouted. "On the roof!"

In seconds Adhara was hovering next to him, looking up. He leaned around the pipe. Mystery Man was gone.

"Who was on the roof?" Maria signed as Cyrus and Adhara returned to the floor.

"I'm not sure," Cyrus replied, slowly and anxiously turning from the broken skylight. "Did you take care of the stuff?"

"The chemical spills have been neutralized," said Adhara.

"Good. Let's get out of here."

They slipped out a back door and past the fence just as Acryogen officers were, at last, entering the facility. Just before they escaped into the Pipeworks, an explosion shook the ground. Cyrus whirled around.

"Look!" he hissed.

Tall flames jumped up through the skylights of the peroxide lab. In the distance, Cyrus could just make out Mystery Man standing on the roof, staring right at him with those three glowing eyes.

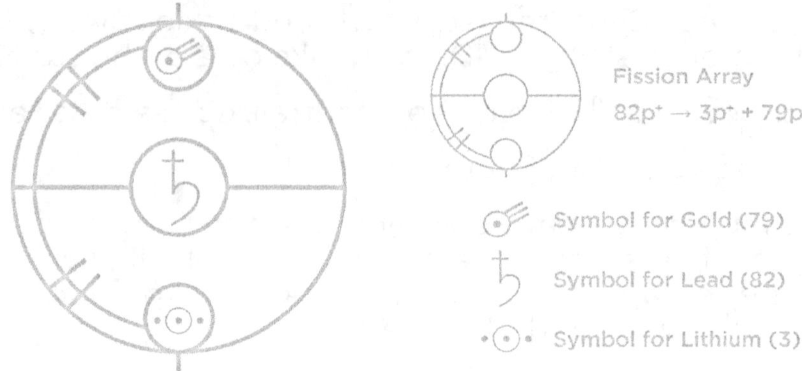

Chapter 17

TRANSMOOT POINT

In the days following the riot, Hudson City fell into an awkward pause as Acryogen Industries and the rebellion each waited for retaliation, neither bold enough to provoke the other, and the unaffiliated citizens hung nervously between. Roadsters still patrolled the street enforcing nightly curfew, and the rebellion undoubtedly still met in furtive corners of the city. The headlines incriminating the Alchemists and the rebellion ceased. In the absence of official updates regarding the developing climate, people were free to speculate on the next crisis that would rock the city.

To avoid the palpable tension in the city, Olive elected to move into Cyrus' attic, but—just until the pressure diffused. Aside from occasional grocery runs through the Pipeworks, for a few weeks Cyrus and his friends avoided the rest of society, and sometimes avoided going outside altogether. The theater where Donny worked was closed until further notice; Acryogen University shifted classes online and actively encouraged students to stay home. Cyrus happily used the peace and quiet to work on his gauntlets. Maria, who was all but idle after her lab courses were cancelled entirely, embraced a domestic role.

One morning as she was watering the dozens of houseplants she had placed in Cyrus' wide windows, she looked down at a shaded tomato and frowned. Wasn't this tomato in direct sun yesterday, at about this time? And now it was fully in the shade. She drew the sheer drapes and erased a circle from the condensation with her sleeve. Were the plants outside this tall yesterday? She had never seen the hollyhock this thick before, and she could have sworn that the aspen was taller, and perhaps...greener?

She turned and was startled to find Cyrus standing remorsefully behind her, holding his backpack, in pieces again.

"How many times do I have to ask you not to sneak up on me?" she signed.

"I was *about* to tap your shoulder!" he protested.

"I see you've taken your backpack apart again," she observed. "What is it this time?"

"Remember at the chemical refinery a few weeks ago when I fried both gauntlets?

"I do."

"The power draw was too much, and the circuits overheated. I've rewired the gauntlets with sturdier components, but the main problem was the power source."

"The diamond?" She asked. Upon closer inspection, she noticed that the diamond was pale and crumbling in his hands. "Should you be holding that without gloves?"

"This battery isn't powerful enough anymore, and it takes too long to recharge, and on top of *that*, the diamond is degrading. *And* this backpack is super heavy, and it's hurting my shoulders. I want to make a new power source. Will you help me?"

"Sure. How do we build this new battery?" she asked, leading him into the living room to join the others. Olive and Aliyah were helping each other study while Donny, bent into a flipped "2" shape, played video games.

"Well actually, I need everyone's help," Cyrus addressed the room. "I have a plan to build a new power source for my gauntlets, but I'll need all of you."

"I'm really sorry Cyrus, but midterms are coming up," said Olive. "We really need to study. That analytic geometry test is gonna KILL, especially since it's online now." Aliyah nodded.

"Can't you just get Adhara to help you?" Donny grunted.

"She's in space today," Cyrus answered. They looked up in mild interest. "Something about an off-course satellite and preventing the Kessler effect. Come on guys, please? I need your help." They muttered noncommittally, hoping if they ignored him, he would lose interest.

Cyrus frowned. "What if I gave you something?" he paused, gauging their reactions, but they played coy. "If you help me, I'll turn lead into gold."

All eyes turned to Cyrus.

"And you can have some," he finished.

"You'll just..." Donny ventured, "give us some gold? Just for doing you a favor?"

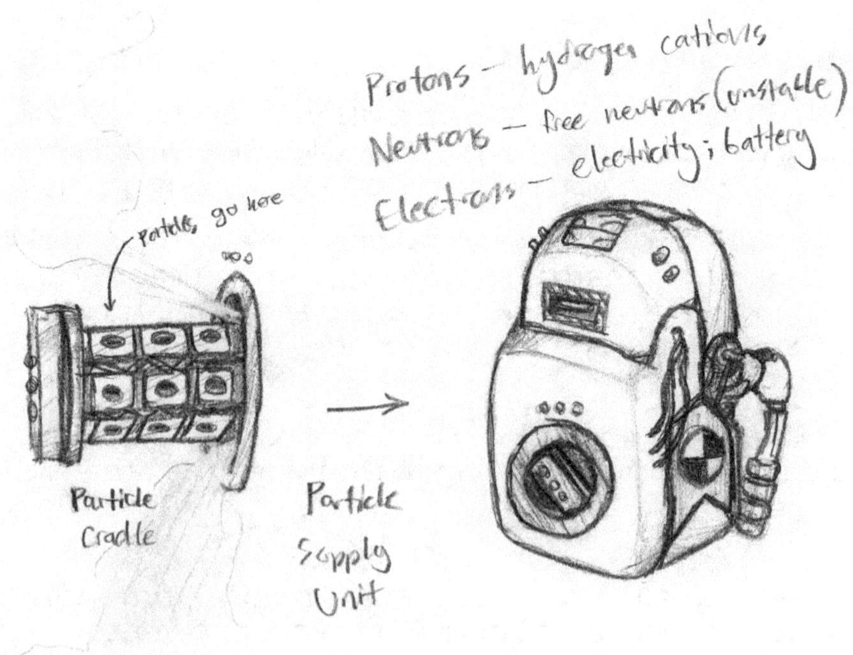

"That's what I'm trying to tell you; if I can work out this upgrade, I think the gauntlets will be able to transmute matter. So, I can make gold or anything out of anything else," Cyrus explained. "You should take advantage of it now before I devalue the gold standard and wreck the economy."

"Uh…" Donny looked to Aliyah, who was nodding slowly with her eyebrows raised.

"*Shoot*, man, studying can *wait*," said Olive, closing her laptop. "I gotta get that *tuition*, not to mention rent for an apartment I'm not even living in right now!"

"Great!" Cyrus beamed. "How about you, Aliyah? Donny?"

"Wait," Maria waved her hands, exchanging a knowing look with Aliyah. "We'll help you. But we want something besides gold."

"If I have it, it's yours," Cyrus agreed.

"We want a supercomputer like the one you and Olive made. One that can make huge calculations and run simulations."

"Sure, you can have my old one. I'm going to build a new one soon." Cyrus frowned. "But what do you need it for?"

"I'll explain everything later. Let's go!"

"So…what exactly are we doing here?" asked Donny. Cyrus had taken them all on the freight platform down the tunnel where he and Adhara had first seen the Roadsters. After an hour-long ride they had emerged from the tunnel on the other side of the mountains, onto a pre-war highway pocked with artillery craters, cracked with time and surrounded by concrete ruins.

"Do you know where we are?" Cyrus asked enigmatically. Donny shrugged.

"Is this Southeast Bay Station?" Maria asked.

"*Is* it? Really?" Donny turned to Cyrus, who nodded knowingly.

"Sorry to be the dummy, but...what's Southeast Bay Station?" asked Olive.

"I'm sure you remember," said Aliyah. "Think back to Hudson City Studies."

"That class was like seventh grade!" Olive laughed. "What, is this like where some important battle took place?"

"You're only twenty-two, so you don't have to remember as far back!" Donny quipped.

"Southeast Bay Station was the site of the last stand Hudson City took in the war," Cyrus explained. "After Acryogen erected the mountains, this station was the only way in or out of the city except for over the bay. Eventually, they sealed that tunnel," he pointed to the hole of twisted metal and cracked cement they had come through, a small breach in the much larger vault built into the side of the mountain. "The city was cut off from the world. The Mongols laid siege for a couple years, but eventually they just sort of...disappeared."

"I think I remember this now," Olive realized. "But not from Hudson City Studies. They didn't use human soldiers in that last battle, right? They used soft robots—we studied the motivator designs in Electromagnetic Engineering."

"Bet you didn't study the *real* designs," Cyrus muttered.

"So, what are we doing here?" asked Donny. "Not that I don't appreciate seeing a slice of our history."

"Looking for this," said Cyrus, holding up a grey, metallic shard. "Lead artillery. There's tons of lead scrap littered around here."

"You're *actually* gonna turn the lead into gold?" Aliyah chuckled, collecting a handful of lead shards. "That's so extra, man."

"Yeah, I couldn't resist the old classic," Cyrus admitted. "But also, lead is just a few protons away from gold on the periodic table, so it won't be as hard to transmute. Just...

y'know, don't touch your mouth or eyes after handling it. It's a toxic metal, after all."

They each wandered off in different directions, collecting artillery litter and depositing it onto the freight platform. After a while, Cyrus was picking through piles of weeds and rubble, discovering interesting scrap metal and decrepit devices when Olive came up beside him.

"So, what's this innovative new battery design you have?" she asked, scavenging beside him.

"Well it's not actually a battery, per se," Cyrus replied. "Have you ever studied zero-point energy?"

"Sure," Olive laughed, "I love crazy fringe science theories."

"I kind of make my living on crazy fringe science," said Cyrus, regarding a fragment of lead he intended to turn into gold. He chucked it at the freight platform.

"You don't..." Olive grew serious. "Do you actually have a viable design to harness zero-point energy?"

"I've done the math. With Adhara, I think I can make it work."

"How?" Olive shook her head. "To even get started, you would need an electromagnet the size of a *skyscraper*, or a particle accelerator. Or a dynamic fusion reactor. The one powering your house isn't powerful enough, if that's what you're thinking."

"Did you know Adhara's powered by a miniaturized magnetar?"

"I didn't," Olive raised her eyebrows. "A *magnetar*, really? Just there in her chest?"

"Yep. And that magnetic field is no joke."

"So then...you must want to..." Cyrus could see her mind turning over as she put the pieces together. "With a magnetic field that strong, you could make an energy vacuum."

"Correct."

"Which would, in turn, form..."

"...An energy vortex."

"And suck electricity from the air." She shook her head. "Incredible. If it actually works, that is. Scientists have been trying to invent this since Nikola Tesla."

"It'll work. I've run simulations," Cyrus assured her. "I've got almost all the components I need from the Pipeworks. All that's left is graphene for the electrodes, and gold," he ripped a large lead chunk from beneath a drape of ivy, "for nanowires."

"Where are we going to get graphene?" asked Olive as he led her back to the freight platform.

"There's a lot of it near a facility Adhara showed me recently, at the top of the mountains," he answered, consulting the freight platform's control panel. "We'll go there next. We almost have enough lead."

"This is a lot of lead for nanowires," she noted.

"Well it's a lot of nanowires, but I need the money for other things," he admitted. "I still have bills to pay, and I have to pay you guys, and I have some custom parts I want to order that I can't scavenge...or build."

"Wait, then how do you *usually* make money?" she asked suddenly. "I thought your parents had set up a trust or something for you to afford that big house."

Cyrus laughed. "Boy, wouldn't *that* be nice! They left me the house in their will, already paid off, and I'm grateful for that every day." He smiled fondly. "But for utilities and normal expenses, I take odd jobs online. Coding mostly; I still do some tech support every now and then, and occasionally I do some," he stage-whispered, "black market maintenance." He winked.

"Cyrus, listen," Olive whispered, noticing the others starting to return to the platform. "There's something I wanted to ask you about but not in front of the others. Catch me alone when you get a chance, okay?" and she hurried off to chat with Aliyah.

"You okay?" Maria signed.

Cyrus nodded, noticing that he was holding his mouth slightly open. He closed it then announced, "We've got plenty of lead now guys, thank you! We have one more stop before we go home."

The freight platform took them quickly to the elevator beneath the water treatment plant. As his friends chatted about their differing opinions of Acryogen's performance during the war, Cyrus reflected on what Adhara had told him the last time they were in this elevator. Adhara was out there somewhere, right now. As an artificial intelligence controlling a small army of androids, building up to be a hero that would save the world.

"I *realize* that the government originally asked Acryogen to take over," said Donny. "But after the Mongols retreated, they should have given the authority and resources back to the people! Hudson City should be run by the working people, not Mr. Mason Smithy!"

And what about Mystery Man, who was at this point Cyrus' best guess to be Anubis—if not now, then in the near future. With his technology and remorseless proclivity for destruction, he couldn't see a better candidate.

"Mason Smithy is a *brilliant* scientist, but he's no politician," Aliyah added. "He knows how to run a *business*, not a city. It's not the same. There are crucial, sociological nuances for the balance within a community."

But who *was* the man behind the mask? And was he truly affiliated with the rebellion? His presence at the chemical refinery certainly implied it, but there wasn't any solid proof of the connection. It could have been coincidence.

"Of course, you can't deny that *without* Acryogen, the city wouldn't even exist. Sure, they aren't perfect, but could anyone else have done better? Or even succeeded at *all*?"

If his theory was correct, Cyrus had the upper hand. He knew who Anubis was and had some ideas on how to find him again. He could take the offensive...take his destiny in his hands and end this all now. Today, if he were bold enough. He could save thousands of lives merely by being proactive. If Cyrus took out Anubis now, before he built up his power... would the Adhara A.I. never be repurposed? Could she fulfill her original design, and fix the world? There were too many variables.

"I realize that culture erasure is an issue, but how are amusement parks comparable to the work camps?"

While lost in his thoughts, Cyrus had clearly missed something. This was a common experience for him.

The elevator opened and Cyrus led them out into the sunny lawn. Donny and Aliyah chased each other through the thick grass, the likes of which they had never experienced, tumbling over each other and jumping headlong into bushes.

"It's beautiful here," signed Maria, breathing the clean air deeply and stroking the grass. "We should have brought a picnic."

"We can have a picnic at home," said Cyrus, "after we find about eight more of these!" He lifted a graphene water filter, grown over and forgotten. He dragged it back inside to lean against the wall near the elevator, where he found Olive lingering in the shade.

"Hey," he said softly. "So, what did you want to talk to me about?"

"Oh, that," she laughed, suddenly casual. "Maria was telling me the other day that you guys ran into a mysterious figure when you were fixing those leaks at the refinery!"

"Uh...yeah," said Cyrus. "I call him Mystery Man! He was pretty spooky."

"Oh yeah?" she sat on a nearby bench, patting it until he joined her. "What was he like?"

"Well, he was tall and bulky; most likely a male build, but of course, I don't like to assume."

"And yet you call him mystery...man?"

"Well, I couldn't tell much more about his physical features because he was wearing a full body suit, with like armor and stuff, and weapons mounted to his arms. And as for his personality, well, he didn't say anything and he was pretty violent, so we didn't get to bond much."

"Any defining features?"

"Yeah..." Cyrus frowned as he remembered. "You know those bispectral imaging systems Acryogen makes for their navy? With the three lights arranged in a triangle? He has one over where his eyes are. I figure it's wired into an optical system so he can see infrared and whatever."

"Whoa, cool," Olive nodded. "You think he's with the rebellion?"

Cyrus looked at Olive. She was smiling but he could see her jaw was set.

"I don't know," he answered cautiously. "He just appeared, looked through the skylight, and disappeared. And as we were leaving, I guess he set the lab on fire."

"A lot of people seem to believe he's the leader of the rebellion."

"Where did you hear that?" Cyrus asked. "I haven't heard any official news coverage of the refinery fire."

"Guys," said Aliyah, appearing in the doorway. "Come quick! You have to see this."

Aliyah hurried them out the door to where Maria and Donny were standing on a crumbling retaining wall, gazing out towards the bay. The clouds had parted for a moment, giving them a view of the city. As their eyes adjusted to the light, Cyrus and Olive approached the edge of the mountain to see half the city engulfed...in green. As though the city had been built inside a jungle, thick forest sprouted up filling the spaces above every street, atop the buildings, even in some out of windows. They could see the park where the trees grew thickest and tallest, their stature almost rivalling the Acryogen corporate headquarters. The forest, which before hadn't extended beyond the foot of the mountains, now reached all the way to the beach and thinned just before Cyrus' neighborhood. Only the tops of the taller buildings breached the ocean of foliage.

"I thought," Olive murmured in shock, "Acryogen took steps to prevent overgrowth."

"They use a chemical herbicide," Cyrus groaned. "All that rain and snow, and the AirShift towers readjusting…" he shook his head. "It must have all been washed away. And they've been too busy with the riot and the rebellion to re-apply it."

"Cyrus, this is too much," Maria signed, turning to him.

"It's okay, I can fix this," he reassured her. "I can fix this. I just need Adhara."

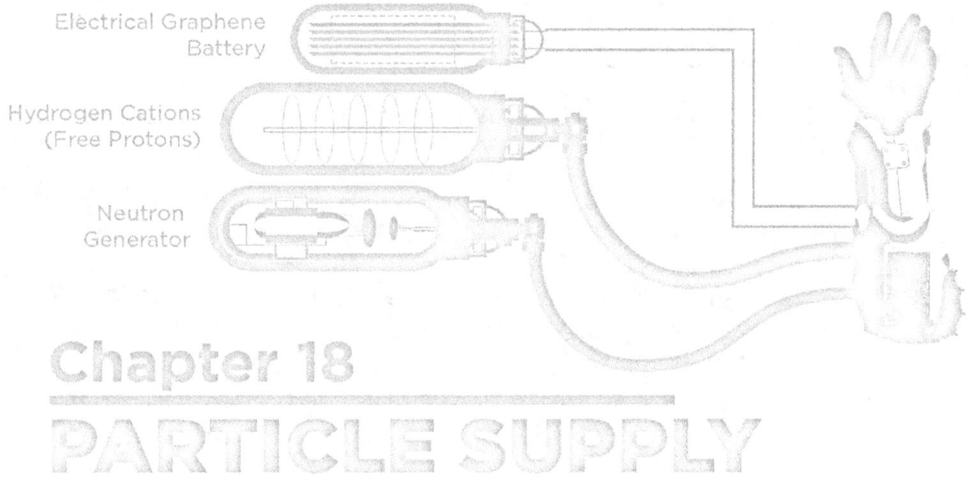

Chapter 18
PARTICLE SUPPLY

Adhara was waiting for them when they returned home, and as his friends unloaded the graphene and lead into the broad Pipeworks tunnel beneath the house, Cyrus solicited her and Olive's help inventing his new power source.

"I'm going to reverse-engineer your nuclear strong-force actuators," Cyrus told Adhara. "If my hypothesis is correct, I can use them to rearrange matter on an atomic level."

"That is ambitious," Adhara replied.

"Will you let us examine them?"

To Cyrus and Olive's surprise, Adhara responded to his request by removing her little finger and placing it in his hand.

"Well then," Cyrus remarked as they stared at the finger in his hand. "That will do."

He and Olive took Adhara's finger to Cyrus' workroom, where Olive occupied a small workspace for her tools alongside him. They studied and analyzed the finger for many hours, deriving bits and pieces of fascinating qualities, but came to the eventuality that they would not be able to unify the design without observing it in use.

"We've gotten all the lead and graphene laid out like you asked," said Aliyah from the doorway. "And, if you're interested, they've declared a city-wide state of emergency. No one's supposed to go outside."

"Oh, Aliyah—" said Cyrus. "Could you ask Adhara to come here, please?"

"Do you need something?" asked Adhara, taking Aliyah's place in the doorway a few minutes later.

"Yes, well...." Cyrus extricated himself from the tangle of wires they had attached to her detached finger. "We've almost figured it out, I think—but we need to take a few readings from how the electricity flows through the actuator *as* it's being used. Would you let us...?" he trailed off, but Adhara merely smiled and held out her arm. As Olive and Cyrus watched, the rosy, porcelain segments of her shell shifted away from her elbow, exposing silver printed circuits, tubes, and polished copper apparatuses clustered around the obsidian synovial joint.

"Incredible," Olive breathed. "It's just like she said. She's modeled after the human body—her arm is just like a mechanical equivalent of the anatomical model in Dr. Kersey's classroom."

"Is it really that similar?" Cyrus regarded the joint from another angle. "It's been a while since I've had an anatomy class."

"I'm telling you man, it's a perfect replica."

"That's good to keep in mind," he noted as he gave Adhara a weight to hold. "Now, with a little resistance...." He prodded around inside the joint with a multi-meter as she pumped her forearm up and down.

After ascertaining that aside from electricity, the strong-force actuators also manipulated neutrino flow, Cyrus and Olive made steady progress reverse-engineering them. By the evening, as the others generously kept them well fed and supplied, they had produced a working prototype and integrated it into Cyrus' gauntlets, ballasted by a new backpack. Finally, the only remaining task was to feed the calculations into the gauntlets' supercomputer, and after they finished rendering, he led Adhara into the basement.

"What's with the backpack?" asked Maria as he set up his workspace. "I thought you didn't need one anymore since you're not using the diamond."

"Well, I don't, not for a power source." He slipped the sleek white pack off his shoulders to give her a better look. He grabbed a handle set into a circular black panel, and after he turned it a long cylinder sprang out. "This tank," he pointed, "has hydrogen cations, which are basically just protons. This tank has free neutrons," it bore a radioactive symbol sticker, "and this here is just a ballast from the gauntlets for electricity—electrons. It's just raw materials for transmutation." He pushed the cylinder back into the pack and locked the panel again. "It used to be a power supply; now it's a particle supply! Plus, I still need somewhere to put the supercomputer." He patted the base of the backpack, presumably where the supercomputer lived.

"It's very stylish," she smiled and left him to his calibrations. She was right, Cyrus noted. The first backpack hadn't been easy on the eyes; a twisted heap of rough, industrial metal and tangled wires. This pack, which he had built from Pipeworks scrap, was made of smooth contours and all the components were hidden within the sleek shell.

"You might not want to be down here for this," Cyrus told his friends, who had congregated on the stairs behind him. "About a hundred things could go wrong, and I can't test it first. The electrical field could overload. I could accidentally make an unstable isotope. And of course, it could always just explode."

"You think we're going to miss out on seeing the first man to turn lead into gold?" Donny winked. "We believe in you, buddy."

Cyrus smiled.

"But do try not to make it explode, huh?"

"No promises," Cyrus gave a thumbs up, and lowered his mask over his face. "Ready?" he asked Adhara. She returned his thumbs up and adjusted the thick cables he had running from his new backpack directly into her chest. He shuffled his feet, widening his stance. As he approached the lead shards, which were arranged in a neat circle, he tapped commands into his gauntlets' control panel. He knelt at the edge of the circle, straightening the cables before exhaling slowly and gently laying his hands on the lead. There was a click; the capacitors whined, then crackling and snapping as the energy shot crisply into the lead. Even from the stairs Cyrus' friends could feel the air tingle on their skin and in their hair.

"Go ahead, Adhara," said Cyrus quietly. She gripped the cables at their connections, securing them firmly, and her eyes began to glow. The glow intensified, not just from her eyes but also gently spilling out from the seams of her chest and throat, and even her joints. The hum droning from Cyrus' gauntlets pitched higher. "Get ready…" he murmured. Streaks of lightning shot off from his fingertips and between the lead shards. "Now!" he shouted. Adhara ripped the cables from her chest and in a flash, each piece of lead burst into acrid smoke. Cyrus stepped back, flapping his hands. He gazed intently into the smoke, suddenly smiling. He reached into the cloud and held up what looked like a yellow rock.

"It worked!" he announced, crossing over to them. He held a slaggy lump, not polished or pretty, but undeniably gold, as though freshly plucked from an earthen vein. He dropped it in Donny's hands, and his friends gathered around the affront to modern chemistry.

"Most of it melted onto the floor," Cyrus explained. "The backwash heat from transmutation must have rebounded, but I'll fix that later."

"This is *incredible*," Donny crowed. "What *will* you do *next*?"

"Now I just have to make the graphene," said Cyrus as he approached the water filters. According to his instructions, they had been arranged in two neat stacks and tied together with rope. He tapped at his control panel again, recalibrating for the graphene reaction he and Olive had programmed. "Well, *reform* the graphene, really. Ready, Adhara?"

"Ready," she replied as she reconnected the cables. With less ceremony than the first time, Cyrus placed his hands on the water filters and the power flowed again. The gauntlets whined and hummed, and after a few seconds the rope vaporized as if incinerated, and the filters disintegrated into powder as Cyrus pushed his hands deeper into the piles. When his hands were completely submerged in the quivering gray sand, he started pulling them back out again. Inside his hands were smooth, crystalline wafers, which he placed to the side and withdrew another, and another after that until the piles of graphene sand were almost gone and he had a small stack of graphene wafers.

"Pretty nice, huh?" he asked after he finished, showing off the wafers to his friends. "The crystals formed perfectly."

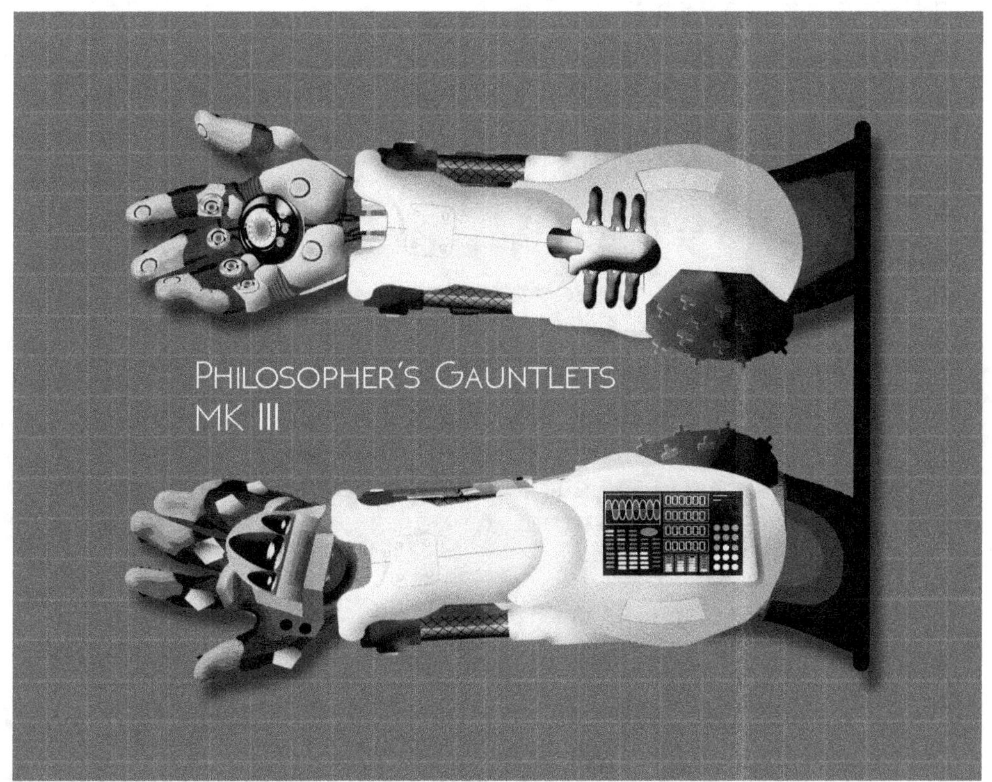

"The pattern in these is beautiful," said Aliyah, taking one of the wafers and squinting at it. "It reminds me of...bees' wings, or stained glass."

"It did come out perfectly," Olive agreed. "The crystalline structure is just like the simulations; just like we calculated. I bet Acryogen couldn't have grown a better crystal in their best lab!"

Cyrus smiled wryly. "Having a supercomputer calculator helps."

With the graphene and gold, Cyrus had all he needed to make his zero-point energy vortex apparatus, which he resolved to rename when things were calmer. Something about "ZPEVA" just didn't feel right to him. But then, on the other hand—zero-point could be one word, and "ZEVA" didn't sound bad at all! Then he shook his head, remembering that time was short.

With Adhara's and Olive's help, he finished the device and installed it the next day. He even had time to test it a few times before the sun set, when he and Adhara would go and face the jungle. As dusk fell he wrote a third calibration command for his improved gauntlets, and once it had rendered, they set off through the Pipeworks.

The overgrowth had reached even into the tunnels, which were now full of roots. Adhara and Cyrus occasionally had to disembark from the freight platform to burn them out of the way.

"It's nice going on an adventure together, just the two of us," said Cyrus casually as they set off again. "Feels like you and I haven't gotten a chance to hang out lately, one on one, you know?"

"It is reasonable that a human being would prefer the company of other human beings," Adhara replied amiably. "I'm surprised you didn't invite Maria with us this time."

"The truth is, I get the feeling Maria is irritated with me," he admitted. "I...sometimes do things or build things without thinking much about the consequences, and well...I think that's how she sees the things we've been doing lately, with the AirShift towers, and the water treatment plant, and the power plant..." he trailed off.

"There are always growing pains that come with change," she reassured him. "But in the end, it's for the greater good."

"And you'd know all about the greater good, wouldn't you?" he smirked, more sarcastically than he had intended to sound.

"I know you must have doubts, Cyrus." Adhara smiled softly. "I haven't answered a lot of your questions. But your interest and the city's interest are my priority."

"Actually...if I'm being completely honest, I wanted to get you alone so I could talk to you about that. The greater good."

"How so?"

"Well," Cyrus paused as he collected his thoughts, trying to arrange them in the order that would be the most persuasive. "The threat to the city is Anubis, right? I mean not just Anubis obviously, but he's the catalyst. And your purpose is to defeat him."

"My directive is to prevent Anubis from threatening the city," she corrected.

"Right, prevent!" Cyrus nodded. "If we could find out where he is now, who he is *now*...we could prevent him from ever coming into power!"

"We *could*."

"I think I know who he is."

"No, you don't."

Cyrus' breath caught in his throat, and his face fell. He felt a twinge of annoyance. "What?" he asked.

"You don't know who Anubis is," she repeated as the freight platform slowed to a stop. She climbed off, leaving Cyrus to splutter, incredulous.

"How can you be so sure?" he protested, following her. "Don't you even want to hear who I think it is?"

"It doesn't matter," said Adhara firmly, "You don't need to know who Anubis is right now. Our current course of action is optimal."

"I don't believe this," Cyrus scoffed as they emerged into the deserted streets. Thick bamboo and grass forced its way up from even the smallest patch of soil, towering above them and housing deafening crickets. "You fill my head with *talk*," he whispered as they climbed over invasive roots, "of destiny and importance, but when I want to do things my way, suddenly I need your *permission*? Am I just your tool?"

"Cyrus, please," said Adhara. "Trust me. I have your best interests at heart."

"MY best interests?" Cyrus laughed. "Do you really have *my* best interests at heart? Or the interest of whoever built you, and whatever *they* think is best for me?"

"I was programmed with a goal, Cyrus," she answered calmly. "The method by which I arrive at that goal is de-termined by a complex series of algorithms that take real world variables into account."

"Do those algorithms account for Anubis being Mason Smithy?"

She turned to him seriously. "What makes you think he is?"

"I...I'm not *completely* sure, really," Cyrus admitted, his con-fidence shaken by her directness. "It's just a theory I've been working with, but it makes sense, doesn't it?" he implored. "That Mystery Man we saw at the chemical refinery *must* be Anubis. He has weapons, and a suit, and he's involved with the rebellion, and Mason Smithy invents weapons, and he has power and resources, and he told me at Dr. Cargyle's funeral that he hates Acryogen Industries and wishes he could burn it to the ground!"

Though Adhara stared at him in a way he found unnerving, Cyrus continued doggedly on, emboldened by his momentum. "I know I don't know him very well. but I just get this feeling from him that he's kind of a psychopath, like the kind that can be really charismatic and manipulative. And he doesn't *really* care about the city. He's just driven by curiosity, and the thrill of creation, and maybe all his power has gone to his head? I don't know, maybe he just thinks he's so smart that he's above morality or accountability, and he kind of has a god complex, because he creates things, and the fate of the city is his to tamper with...I know that might sound a little far-fetched...but isn't that at least worth looking into?"

"You shouldn't take the things he told you at the funeral to heart," said Adhara, quiet but firm. "Mason Smithy is not Anubis."

"Well if he's not, then we should be looking for who is!" he snapped. "There's a *mass murderer* wandering around and we *know* about it, and we're just...waiting for the right moment?"

"Yes," she answered firmly. "When the time is right, we will confront him together. Remember that he has not murdered anyone yet. It will be better if we prevent him from ever starting."

"We can do that by confronting him *now*, before it's too late!"

She met his glare with softness. "You're capable of greater compassion. It would be unfair to punish someone for crimes they haven't yet committed. Better to repair than to replace."

"And that's to be the end of it, I suppose," muttered Cyrus, under his breath.

"Did you think of a way to deal with these?" asked Adhara, standing before a particularly thick bamboo shoot.

"Yeah," Cyrus grumbled, brushing past her. He snapped his fingers, and the palms of his hands began to accumulate a glowing white paste. When his palms were coated, he wiped the paste on the bamboo near the base, where it immediately burst into flame. The paste built up onto his palms again in seconds.

"How did you do that?" asked Adhara.

"I fused nitrogen atoms in the air into phosphorus," he explained. "A couple of seven-proton atoms fuse to make fourteen protons, and then I just add the extra proton from my backpack. Of course, it's completely unnecessary; just an excuse to test the strong-force actuators. I could just as easily cut them with the oxyhydrogen flame."

"It is impressive nonetheless," said Adhara politely. Cyrus grunted noncommittally.

"We should split up to cover more ground," he suggested. "You take the east half of the city and I'll take the west, and I'll meet you back home. You don't need to take the freight platform, right? You can fly."

"All right," she agreed gently. "I'll see you at home." He turned away from her and headed in the opposite direction.

Cyrus wondered if he was being unfair as he severed the bamboo stalks. She was a robot, after all, a computer. A computer was objective, unbiased. She would know best if anyone did; her judgment was certainly more reliable than a human's.

He watched the phosphorus burn the skin of the bamboo into bubbling blisters, then char.

But then again, why wouldn't a computer value a human being's input? A human brain surely would have insight and creativity that a machine could never match, and she had always valued his creativity in the past. Relied on it, even! Why would she suddenly discourage him, and so determinedly?

Annoyed with the inefficiency of the phosphorus, Cyrus switched to his oxyhydrogen torch, sucking water from the bamboo itself so it would burn more quickly. He slashed through the foliage with machetes of fire, carefully clambering over the concrete and asphalt warped by the roots into rolling waves like the sea.

No, the most likely scenario, Cyrus decided, was that she was hiding something. For some reason she didn't want Cyrus to find Anubis now, or even look for him. Why could that be? Didn't she trust him to handle the situation? Did she think that he would kill the perpetrator before she could 'turn him good,' if that were ever even possible? Or maybe, Cyrus thought as he hacked maliciously at a cluster of vines ensnaring a light pole, she thought he would make a mess of things. Face Anubis and get himself killed, maybe. Maybe she thought he couldn't take care of himself in a fight, and she wanted him to stay out of the way.

Stupid robot. Stupid vines. Stupid Acryogen Industries! These plants had clearly been growing for weeks, and there was no sign of pruning despite the entire city, people's homes and businesses, being consumed by the forest. But *of course*, he fumed as he turned a corner and found an Acryogen facility, the only building for blocks untouched by the weeds. Hadn't he tolerated *enough* ingratitude from this company with warped priorities? He didn't need Adhara to treat him like he was incapable, too. He looked down at his hands, which curled into fists. He swung one hand at the Acryogen facility, throwing a splatter of phosphorus across the wall, turning away as it smoldered.

As he stood in the street, chest heaving and heart racing, he decided it was time to stop following Adhara wherever she pointed. He had to take his destiny into his own hands. The fate of the city was too important just to passively wait for the future to arrive. She had told him point blank that Mason Smithy wasn't Anubis. And she had told him she was unable to lie directly. But wouldn't she have said that anyway, if it's what she wanted him to believe?

He couldn't trust Adhara anymore, he realized as his breathing slowed. Not fully. Not until he knew, at the very least, *who* built her and sent her after him. She was hiding something from him, but until he figured out what that was, she had to believe he was complacent.

Matter Coding

Massive yet finite particle-based code expression of matter

proton= p
neutron= n
electron= e

In a polyatomic substance, individual atoms are expressed according to corresponding chemical formula.

therefore $H_2O(l)$ becomes:

One typical Sodium (atomic #11) atom would be expressed as follows:

[eeeeeeeeee][ppppppppppp][nnnnnnnnnnnn]

or, abbreviated:

$[e_{11}][p_{11}][n_{12}]$

$(2[e_1][p_1][n_0])([e_{10}][p_8][n_{10}])\{l\}$

A coefficient of 1 is assumed, but a larger sample can be expressed as follows for one mole of water:

$(2[e_1][p_1][n_0])([e_{10}][p_8][n_{10}])\{l\} \cdot (6.02e23)$

Chapter 19
TRIP TO THE ZOO

Maria knocked on Cyrus' open workshop door. He glanced up and waved, beckoning her to come in.

"You're busy," she surmised after approaching him. He was characteristically disheveled, his eyes glazed from staring too long at a screen.

"*Very* busy," he confirmed. "I'm writing code for my gauntlets so they can manipulate gluons; strong-force particles that hold atoms together. When I'm done, I'll be able to transmute matter almost at will, and hopefully, very easily. But first I have to teach the computer to understand the chemical data input from the NIRScanner, and parse that with particle supply from the backpack." He pointed to a line of code on the screen:

$$[\{(2[e_1][p_1][n_0])([e_{10}][p_8][n_{10}])(L)\}(5.5e15)]$$

"Protons are p, neutrons n, and electrons are e. The subscript number indicates the quantity. This line represents 5.5 quadrillion atoms of liquid water."

"You have to code the particles for every element individually?" she asked, cringing.

"Every element, every element's electronegativity, basic molecular structure, *and* I have to code rules for valence electron interactions," he replied dully. "It's…going to take a while. But it'll be worth the results." He sighed, then noticed her disappointment as he was turning away. "Why? What did you need?"

"Well, it's a couple things. Remember the other day when I asked for a supercomputer for me and Aliyah?"

"Oh yeah," Cyrus pointed to a cube sitting on a nearby table; six clear acrylic walls containing several microprocessor chips connected in a stacked series. "I forgot to tell you I finished with it. The operating system should be pretty intuitive."

She raised her eyebrows in surprise and crossed over to the supercomputer to inspect it. "Thank you," she signed.

"What was the second thing?" Cyrus signed.

"Oh," she waved her hand. "It's nothing you can help with if you're busy."

"Just tell me what it is, at least."

"Well…Acryogen has a gene therapy research facility north of the city. I visited it on a field trip in high school. I've been wanting to go back. I think it could help with the project Aliyah and I are working on."

"Is this project the genetic stuff you gave me at Christmas?"

"Exactly," she smiled. "We're working on genome mapping. And this," she patted the supercomputer, "will help a lot with the math! There are just a few things we're less than confident on but poking around Acryogen's research could help."

"And you wanted me to go with you and Aliyah?" Cyrus asked.

"Just me," she answered. "Aliyah would go if I asked her, but I know she's not comfortable with trespassing."

"Oh *dear*," signed Cyrus. "My criminal influence is rubbing off on you."

#adventurevibes

"I hope I'm as good an influence on you as you are a bad influence on me," Maria laughed.

"That was harsh," he replied, pointing his pen at her, "but fair."

"Well, anyway. I don't want to go alone, so maybe another time. Good luck with that code." As she turned back to the door, Cyrus tossed his pen at her. It bounced off the door-frame, startling her.

"*What*?" she signed.

"Take Adhara with you," said Cyrus. "She offered to help me with this coding, so I know she's free. She must be around here somewhere." As he turned back to his computer, he muttered, "Get her out of the house," which he assumed incorrectly Maria wouldn't see.

"I will be glad to accompany you," Adhara told Maria. Her mellifluous voice, singing in her cochlear implant, sounded adjacent to Maria's own thoughts. "Cyrus has no need of my assistance today, and I have no other engagements."

"That's great!" Maria signed. "Well—I'm ready to go right now? If you are?"

"Lead the way," Adhara smiled. She followed Maria into the basement, waited patiently as she put on the gauntlets Cyrus had made for her, and they boarded the freight plat-form.

"I don't..." signed Maria, squinting at the control panel and biting her lip as her finger hovered over a location on the map. "I don't know how this—" Adhara reached past her and tapped a blue dot on the map, closest to where Maria's finger had been pointing. The platform came to life and warbled into the tunnel, heading north.

"Thank you," she signed apologetically.

"You're welcome."

"So, um…I don't want to seem—nosy," Maria signed as they sped through the tunnels.

"I have no sense of personal privacy," Adhara replied. "I do, however, have a sense of discretion."

Maria nodded. "Well, if it's not my business, tell me. I just wanted to ask about Cyrus."

Adhara nodded encouragingly.

"Is everything okay? He seems kind of…cold, towards you, lately."

"Cyrus is suspicious of me," Adhara answered. "I'm withholding information from him and because of that, I've lost his trust."

"I'm sorry to 'hear' that," Maria frowned. "He was so excited about you when you first arrived. He's been a little…lost since his parents died. I think you gave him a real sense of purpose."

Adhara nodded knowingly. "How did they die?" she asked.

"It…was stupid," Maria shook her head. "They worked at Acryogen, like half the city does. In the war they were pilots, and after the war ended, they worked on building and testing new aircraft." She smiled fondly. "They were really nice people, and such a big inspiration to Cyrus! He always wanted to be an inventor, ever since we were kids." Her face darkened, and she sat down, leaning against the railing. "One day when we were in high school, they were testing a plane, like any other day. Water got where it wasn't supposed to be, or something like that, and the plane took a nose-dive into the bay. And just like that, Cyrus was an orphan like me."

"You've lost your parents as well?"

"Yeah, when I was just a kid," Maria nodded. "My mom brought me to visit my dad one day, at the plant where he worked, pressurizing hydrogen into tanks. There was a fire and an explosion. I lost them and my hearing at the same time." She tapped her ear and smirked.

"That must have been so hard to go through," said Adhara quietly. "I'm so sorry."

"Yeah," Maria nodded. "But I was lucky, because I had Cyrus' parents to take me in. That was huge for me, especially since I was learning to live with a new disability." She got to her feet. "Almost everyone in Hudson City knows someone who's been injured or killed in some kind of accident, if they haven't been a victim themselves. Olive has a prosthetic eye; she lost it in a car accident in middle school when traffic lights malfunctioned. And Donny's legs were crushed in a nasty elevator accident. He was in a wheelchair for a few years—" she giggled, remembering, "until he and Cyrus scammed a computer to make it think he had insurance, so he could have surgery to rebuild his knees. Acryogen doesn't exactly make disabilities easy." Her face grew serious again. "He can act and dance again, but it hurts him to be on his feet for long. This city..." she shook her head, "is accident-prone. So many people have gotten hurt just because of mistakes. That's made a lot of people cynical...including Cyrus." She looked up at Adhara. "I know Cyrus can be unfair and selfish sometimes, but he's just acting out of pain. Please," she pleaded, "be patient with him."

"What makes you different?" Adhara asked.

"What?"

"You're not cynical. In fact, your outlook seems to be uncommonly positive."

"I don't know," Maria shrugged. "It's hard to stay positive sometimes. But I guess I figure that...you get out of the world what you put into it. We can't make things better unless we believe we can." She nodded to the ground. "And I believe we can. One day we'll look back and we'll be glad that we didn't give up."

Adhara reached forward and placed a comforting hand on Maria's shoulder. She looked up at her.

"But *is* everything going to be okay?" Maria asked earnestly. "You're from the future, and what you described...it scares me to think about what's coming."

"You have endured so much pain," said Adhara quietly. "All of you have, so much more than anyone should." She leaned forward intently. "But I am going to fight with everything I have to end that suffering and set things right."

Maria leaned forward, past Adhara's arm, and hugged her.

"I know Cyrus doesn't trust you right now," she signed after she pulled away. "But I believe you're a force for good. Maybe that's naïve," she chuckled.

"It takes more strength to believe things will work together for good than bad."

"Although, I have to say," Maria added as they slowed to a stop next to a stairwell, "some of the things you and Cyrus have been doing have had some...pretty intense consequences."

"Yes," Adhara agreed. "Unfortunately, there is no way to bring about profound change without some discomfort. But I take full responsibility."

"Oh no, I'm not blaming you!" she signed and began climbing the stairs, side by side. "Not really. I mean, I know some of the things, like the water and the Grimlords were inevitable, and I trust your judgment. But the AirShift towers? He decided that on his own. But I guess I shouldn't have encouraged him," she confessed.

"That *was* premature," Adhara admitted. "We would have eventually addressed the Airshift towers, but Cyrus did not consider that the enormity of the machines necessitated gradual adjustment."

"And look what happened," Maria nodded at the web of wet roots growing into the tunnel. "Why *were* the AirShift towers running so low? Do you know?"

"Acryogen Industries dispenses resources by order of prioritization," Adhara answered simply.

"Meaning..." Maria signed as they headed up the last flight of stairs. "They're working on something that's *higher* priority than the AirShift towers?"

They emerged from the stairwell into a jungle. This foliage wasn't as new as what grew in the city; this facility had been neglected for years. Maria stepped forward cautiously. Weeds pushed up between the shattered tile, the sheetrock was crumbling and stained with water damage, the windows were cracked in some places and broken in others, and outside the weeds had grown waist-high.

"I can't believe it," Maria signed, her disappointment clear on her face. "When I visited this place in high school, it was a top-of-the-line institute. It was one of Acryogen's best research facilities!" She kicked at some fallen ceiling tiles and waved a moth away from her face. "How could it have fallen apart so quickly?"

"This facility was considered low priority," said Adhara. "Funding was cut, and it was eventually abandoned. It closed officially three years ago."

"How do you know that?"

"I am able to access Acryogen Industries data records."

"Then—" Maria started hopefully, "is there anything here? Would they have stored records?"

"When the facility closed, they moved all data drives offsite." Adhara nodded at the shadow in the dust where a computer once sat on a nearby desk. "Any remaining hardware appears to have been stolen."

"What about paper records?"

"It's possible. There is an archives room on the second floor."

Adhara led Maria upstairs, but after she checked every empty file cabinet, she had to admit defeat. The cabinets were empty except for the occasional rat's nest.

"If they had left any hardcopy files, they're probably long gone, taken for kindling," she signed. "But—what about the experiments? The laboratories?"

"The laboratories were cleared out and thoroughly cleaned," answered Adhara, shaking her head. "The protocol is listed as a level five purge. Someone didn't want to leave any trace of the work here."

"But then...we came all this way for nothing?" Maria's face fell. "Why would they need to purge it? When I was here, they were researching gene therapy, trying to help people."

Suddenly Adhara turned her head sharply. She stared intently out a nearby window.

"What is it?" Maria asked.

"Are your gauntlets on?"

Maria nodded.

"There's a Grimlord control beacon nearby."

Maria felt her heart jump. Adhara crept forward silently, turning to look down the empty corridors with Maria close behind.

"I have to find it," Adhara whispered. Maria nodded. "There may be Grimlords guarding it. I'll do my best to protect you, but I understand if you're not up for it. Do you want to wait here or come with me?"

"Go with you," Maria signed.

She nodded. "Stay close."

Adhara led Maria through the maze of quiet halls and offices as the shadows grew longer and the light turned ochre. At first, Maria recoiled from every corner and jumped at every shadow, but as they continued to search, they continued to find more and more of nothing. Just as it was becoming too dark to see, Adhara stopped in front of a wall, blank except for a faded motivational poster. She embedded her fingers into the sheetrock and pried out a hinged panel, revealing a long dark corridor which angled downwards into the earth. Adhara's eyes glowed. She turned to Maria, nodded, and led her inside.

The panel closed behind them as soon as Adhara released it, and the darkness swallowed them except for the stark beams shining from Adhara's eyes. She smiled reassuringly when Maria reached for her hand as they braved the descent, hand in hand, one determined step at a time.

When the corridor ended, they passed through what appeared to be a reception area and entered a fully equipped laboratory. As Adhara swept her eyes across the room they could see that every surface was coated in dust, but it had clearly not been abandoned as long as the facility above. Adhara led her through the dark labyrinth, hallways connecting one empty laboratory after another, until they stopped in front of a rack of devices that resembled a can of bug spray studded with thin spikes and two antennas each.

"These are Grimlord control beacons," Adhara said grimly. "But they're brand new. They've never been activated."

Maria found a dusty flashlight on a nearby shelf and with it began inspecting the lab benches. While Adhara grabbed the beacons and twisted each one in two, Maria retrieved papers from a wastebasket that someone had tried to burn. She eyed a nearby Bunsen burner suspiciously.

"This is a biology lab. It has all the right equipment for studying genetics," Maria told Adhara, handing her the papers. "I can't make out much from this, but look—" she pointed at the corner of a page that was still legible. "It mentions 'chimera' several times."

Adhara looked up at her and frowned.

"I don't like what this is adding up to," Maria signed.

"Nor do I."

They left the lab and passed through what must have been a kennel. Cages of assorted sizes were piled high on either side, some big enough to hold a lion. The rows went on and on—this room could have once held thousands of animals.

Adhara led Maria up a flight of metal stairs on the far side of the room. From there one corridor led them to another, at the end of which they could see a sickly green glow. They found themselves looking down into a cavernous laboratory, in which a gigantic black figure was surrounded by tanks of animal parts and bodies suspended in thick, chartreuse gel. Some of the tanks had been broken open, and in the center of the room was an immense, writhing black mass into which the giant was grafting mismatched appendages.

"Is that…" Maria signed nervously, "what I think…"

"Yes," Adhara whispered. "We've found Animal King."

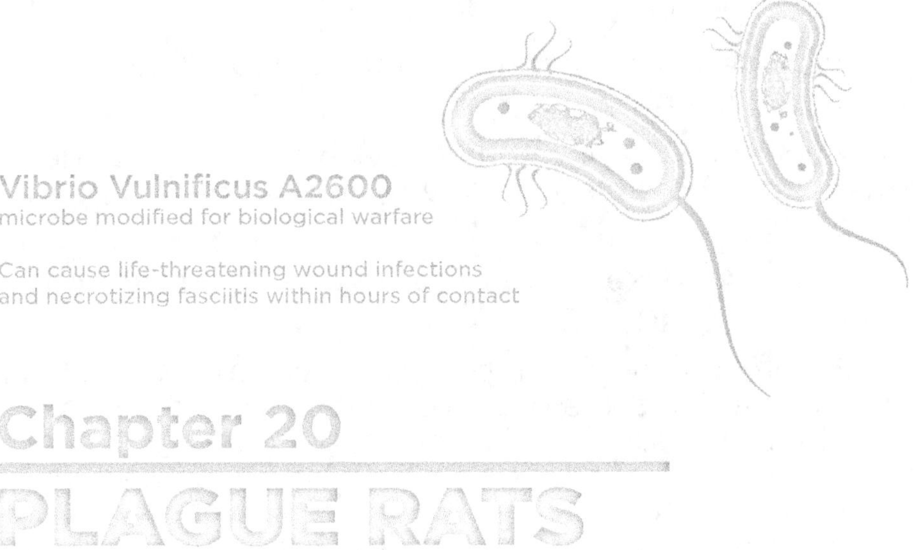

Chapter 20
PLAGUE RATS

"I'm calling Cyrus," whispered Adhara, pulling Maria back out of the room and breaking her horrified stare. "We'll need his help if this gets out of hand."

"Hey. What's up," Cyrus answered in Adhara's head.

"Listen to me, Cyrus. There's a bioweapon research facility hidden under the lab Maria wanted to visit. We found Animal King inside."

"*What*," said Cyrus, his voice suddenly hard.

"It's building another golem, but it's much bigger than the one we saw at the warehouse. Animal King is bigger too."

"What does the new golem look like?"

Adhara leaned around the corner. "It has an elephant's skull, but the tusks are broken off. The torso is unusually long and has two rib cages, eight limbs, and a long tail. From head to tail it appears to be approximately ten meters long. I will not be able to defeat the golem in direct combat."

"How is it building *another* golem?" Cyrus hissed. His voice strained over sounds of him getting dressed. "We destroyed its control beacon!"

"This facility has new control beacons."

Cyrus was silent for a minute. "Then that would mean Acryogen has been…"

"There's no time to talk about it now; we need you to get here as soon as possible. I've already sent the freight platform back to you."

"I'll be there soon. *Keep Maria safe*, Adhara," he ordered sternly and hung up.

"We need to get you to safety," Adhara whispered to Maria. As soon as she said this a bestial Grimlord, like a giant rat mixed with a hyena, skidded through the doorway. It let out an unearthly shriek and lunged for Maria, sinking its mottled jaws into her calf. She gritted her teeth over a scream and fell backwards as the monster wrapped its tail around Adhara's arm and neck. Adhara gripped the barbed vertebrae, pulling herself forward. She wrenched the creature's jaws off Maria, tearing her skin, and flung the giant rat into the next room. It landed at Animal King's feet before scrambling off again. Animal King looked up at them.

"Shh, shh…" Adhara knelt next to Maria as she groaned and winced, clutching her leg. "It's going to be okay; you're going to be fine," Adhara murmured soothingly. She bent her hand backwards, and from her wrist she applied an aerosolized gel to the ragged wound. Maria inhaled sharply as the gel foamed, but after a few moments her breathing slowed.

"Are you okay?" Adhara asked. Maria nodded weakly. "We have to go now. Can you stand?" Maria winced, clambering to her feet. "We've got to get out of here and back to the Pipeworks to meet up with Cyrus." As Adhara helped her towards the door, there was a deafening guttural groan behind them. A massive claw reached into the room, barely fitting through the door frame. Adhara pushed Maria forward and yelled "GO!" as the claw snatched her from the room.

Maria limped from the room, leaning on the wall as she struggled down the darkened corridor, barely able to see without Adhara's help—she had forgotten the flashlight.

The giant rat returned, a few meters ahead of her. It scrambled towards her in the dark, but she managed, wincing, to reach forward and reduce it to a puddle. Her gauntlets whined as they recharged.

When she reached the kennel room, she produced a flame in her palm—but the clear blue oxyhydrogen flame only illuminated half a meter around it. Clearly the cages were not empty as she had thought when they came through the first time. She could hear the cages thrashing and shaking, and the unsettling noise was even worse filtered through her implant. She hobbled resolutely through, refusing to stop except to defend herself whenever a Grimlord leapt out from the darkness.

She made it through the labs and into the narrow corridor leading back to the surface. But when she reached the panel through which they'd entered, she couldn't push it open. She shoved and pried with all her might, even pounding on the metal, but eventually she sank to the floor, panting and staring into the darkness. Her head was hazy and hot, and she struggled to keep her eyes open. She let them fall...just for a few minutes.

Bright sparks shot out in the darkness near her head. She scrambled away from the panel as the sparks traced a circle, which when completed fell inward to reveal Cyrus lowering his gauntlets. He took off his mask and she saw his lips form her name. Tears sprang to Maria's eyes as she stumbled through and fell into his arms. He caught her and brushed her hair out of her face, wiping the sweat from her forehead. He was saying something that she couldn't make out, but as he lowered her to the ground and shook her shoulder, his lips came back into focus. He was asking about Adhara.

"Golem," she signed.

"What about you?" he asked frantically. "Are you okay?" he looked down at her leg. The skin around the wound was angrily red.

Maria shook her head. "Need Aliyah," she signed.

Cyrus heard a high-pitched noise echoing down the corridor just before he saw Adhara's glowing eyes and jets. She flew through the hole, landed in front of them, and knelt to check on Maria. Her clothes were ragged, almost completely degraded, and her porcelain body was covered in scratches.

"How?" Maria signed weakly.

"Maria said Animal King's golem got you," said Cyrus.

"It swallowed me," Adhara confirmed, placing her hand on Maria's forehead. "But Animal King hadn't finished it, so I was able to destroy it with a powerful electromagnetic pulse. I had to wait until Maria was out of range, or I would have also destroyed her cochlear implant and risked damaging her brain." She tore off the remaining scraps of her clothing.

"Thank you," Maria signed.

"It temporarily disabled Animal King as well, but it will be right behind us."

"Maria said she needs Aliyah."

"She needs medical attention immediately," Adhara agreed. "She was bitten by a specialized Grimlord. Its teeth were laced with weaponized microbes."

A distant shriek echoed from the dark corridor, urging them to evacuate. They carried Maria back down to the freight platform without incident, but as the platform powered on, the ceiling above them shook. The cement cracked, and rain began to spill through. Cyrus urged the platform forward as the tunnel collapsed. Animal King, riding on the shoulder of its reformed colossal monstrosity, filled the space and lumbered after them.

"I thought you killed the golem!" Cyrus shouted at Adhara. Before she could answer he vaulted off the moving platform, facing Animal King as Adhara and Maria sped away and disappeared around a corner.

Cyrus crouched and placed his hands on the ground before him—the air crackled and his gauntlets whined. Deep

fissures shot out from his fingertips towards the looming demons. Jets of gas preceded a wave of energy that passed over the cement, turning the surface a bright, acid green in its wake. The caustic lake stopped at Animal King's feet, and it looked down, regarding it thoughtfully before looking back up at Cyrus. The golem lumbered forward into the solvent. Its malformed limbs hissed and bubbled and began to dissolve wherever they came in contact. It struggled, but staggered forward, eventually collapsing just shy of the other side, meters from Cyrus' feet. As its mouth filled with solvent and its black body diffused into the liquid, Animal King stepped forward and walked across, using its own creation's back as a bridge. It stopped just a few meters in front of Cyrus and leered down at him. It seemed bigger up close, and definitely bigger than the last time he had seen it—when it straightened, its hulking shoulders brushed against the tunnel ceiling.

It cocked its head slowly. Then with no warning, it lunged forward and sank its claws into the pavement where Cyrus had been standing seconds earlier. In midair, Cyrus put his hands together like he was holding an invisible volleyball. Between his palms formed a sphere of green solvent, which he hurled at the demon's face, making it recoil slightly. Cyrus took the opening to release a torrent of pressurized nitrogen directly to its chest. A thick sheet of ice coated its body, temporarily immobilizing it, but it continued to reach steadily forward. Cyrus stopped spraying ice and instead started grabbing shards of concrete, transmuting them into neodymium and magnetizing them before chucking them like grenades. The magnets lodged in Animal King's body, deforming it and making it look even more ghastly, but it didn't stop. Cyrus desperately shot out jets of fire, but the claw reached through the smoke towards him.

But just before the claws could close, there was a loud *crack* and the arm jerked to one side, and the hand lolled back as though it were broken. Lodged in the nearby tunnel wall, Adhara suddenly appeared, surrounded by her impact crater. She pried herself out of the concrete, stumbling, but she turned back into a blur and she disappeared. As the smoke cleared, Cyrus saw Animal King recoil from a blow he couldn't see. Then Adhara slammed into the wall, over and over again. Cyrus drew closer carefully—Animal King seemed vulnerable. Suddenly, Adhara appeared next to him as the pavement fractured beneath her feet. Animal King groaned and stumbled around, swiping at the air.

"I've blinded it," said Adhara. "When I give you an opening, electrocute it with everything you've got." A bright blue glow spilled out from her eyes and joints. She turned into a blur again and as the ground shook, she disappeared. The barrage continued as Adhara invisibly broke Animal King's bones and beat its body into a shapeless heap. Cyrus raced forward as she paused and shot lightning into the munge. Animal King shrieked and slumped as if melting, its body convulsing. Adhara appeared in front of its chest and dealt a devastating, echoing kick that knocked it backwards into the solvent with the golem. She landed on the pavement facing Cyrus.

"Come on," he shouted and began to jog down the corridor.

"That won't kill it," Adhara warned, hovering beside him. "As soon as the solvent evaporates, they will reform."

"I know, but..." Cyrus breathed heavily, "We have to get Maria home."

"She's already at home," Adhara reassured him, touching down and placing a gentle hand on his chest. "I sent her back on the freight platform and told your friends to expect her."

"*Alone*?!"

"She's fine," Adhara said soothingly. "Aliyah has been texting me updates."

Cyrus finally slowed, nodding. "I want to go see her, though," he said quietly. "I need to see that she's okay. Grimlords can wait."

Chapter 21
FLUID DYNAMICS

"Yo, dude," said Olive, strolling into Cyrus' workroom.

He grunted without looking up.

"What's good?"

When he didn't respond, Olive sat across from him and placed a gentle hand on his. She leaned forward. "Are you doin' okay, man?"

"Yeah?" he looked up. "Why shouldn't I be?"

"You just seem kinda *moody* lately, dude. Or is that normal for mad scientists?" she smirked.

Cyrus sighed. "No, you're right. And I shouldn't take it out on you." He glanced at the door. "Where is everyone else?"

"They're all going for a walk with Maria; Aliyah says exercise is important to make sure everything heals right. But I wanted to check up on ya." She smiled.

"Well that's...kind of what I'm mad about."

Olive frowned. "You feel excluded? Because..."

"No," Cyrus waved his hand. "It's not that. It's Maria getting hurt. It's Adhara *letting* Maria get hurt."

"You're mad at Adhara?"

"Kind of…well, yes and no." He set down his screwdriver and turned to her. "I'm mad that she didn't keep Maria safe. And Animal King is loose in the city again, with all those gross giant rat Grimlords we had to hunt down *one by one* in the middle of the night. And…."

"And…?"

"The *main* thing is that she's hiding something," Cyrus finished. "She won't tell me who built her, and she has all these secrets…and a robot is a *tool*, programmed by another person. How can I trust her?" he shook his head. "I just feel like I'm being manipulated. But I don't know by *whom*." He rubbed his eyes. "Acryogen Industries is the *obvious* answer; they're the only entity around that I know of that would have the resources for a project that big. But their technology doesn't match the timeline Adhara told me about. They would have an army of A.I. androids by now. And what would be their motivation, if she keeps helping me mess up their equipment and buildings? Why wouldn't we have seen her prototypes?" He shook his head, stood, and began pacing.

"That's…a puzzler," Olive agreed.

"That theory creates more questions than it answers. She's powerful to be sure, but maybe she never actually went back in time? Could someone just be manipulating me…into fixing the city? And causing a bunch of property damage? Then, maybe the rebellion built her to make me fight for their cause…" he raised his eyebrows in eureka, then furrowed his brow and frowned again. "But why *me*? Are they even *capable* of making something like Adhara? It doesn't make sense!"

"O…kay…" Olive raised her eyebrows. "Well, first of all…the way Maria tells it, it wasn't Adhara's *fault* she got hurt. She says Adhara did everything she could to protect her."

Cyrus grunted noncommittally.

"And as for who built her…honestly Cyrus, I've been working with Acryogen tech and wiring for years, and Adhara looks like nothing I've ever seen. She just doesn't match their style."

"I agree—so, the question stands. Would the rebellion have scientists talented enough to build her? The way she talks sometimes sounds like their manifesto."

"Well…" she said slowly, "I really don't think the rebellion would put that many resources into one play. At least not at this point in time."

"So then, maybe…in *another* point in time? In the future? So maybe she really *did* time travel."

"Maybe," Olive agreed vaguely, shaking and nodding her head simultaneously. "But Aliyah, Donny and I have this running theory that it's you."

Cyrus, squinting, froze like a computer that ran out of RAM. His mouth came back to life before his tongue, opening and closing without producing words. "*Me*? You think…*I* built Adhara?" he asked incredulously.

"Yeah! Well, you in the future!" Olive nodded. "Think about it! Kinda makes sense, right?"

"I'm…I don't…what?" Cyrus thought about it. It did not make sense to him. "How?" he asked incredulously.

"We're looking for an inventor," Olive began. "Genius computer programmer, check. Access to exotic chemicals and materials," she looked at his gauntlets, "check. Project-oriented, team of scientists, deep sense of morality," she winked, "check!"

He raised his eyebrows, skepticism waning. He felt his heartbeat knocking on his rib cage.

"We have this timeline worked out," Olive continued. "We think what happened is that a few years in the future, Anubis appears and starts terrorizing the city, right? And you fight him to defend the city, but eventually he's too powerful or whatever. That's where Adhara comes in!"

Cyrus nodded slowly.

"You design and build her—maybe with the help of your brilliant friends—" she winked, "to go back in time with the knowledge of everything it took to defeat Anubis the first time, find your younger self, and...give him a head start saving the city! But!" she stood, towering over Cyrus. "You make it so she can't tell you certain things, *especially* who built her, so that it doesn't mess up the timeline or the time-space continuum or whatever." She shrugged and sat down again. "That's where our theory kinda falls apart, since none of us are physicists. We're basing our time-travel knowledge on movies."

"But I," Cyrus protested. "Do you really think I'm capable... of building something like Adhara?"

"Dude!" Olive laughed, gesturing to his gauntlets. "You built these in half a year. Maybe you couldn't build Adhara *today*, but in seven years? I'd believe it."

"But I..." he spluttered, "I'm not..."

"Name one flaw in our reasoning," Olive challenged.

"Just because I can't think of one on the spot doesn't mean it makes sense—"

"Well anyway, it's just a theory," she shrugged. "No way to really know, at this point. I'm sure she'll tell you eventually."

"But Adhara helped me build these," said Cyrus, looking at his gauntlets. "I based my designs off her body. With your theory, that would mean...I taught myself to build...her?" his eyes widened as he considered the ramifications. "Uh."

"I know dude. Life's a trip." She leaned back in the chair. "And some stuff is too big to get all worked up about—it's better to just chill and enjoy the ride. So, what do you say we go find everyone at the park?"

Cyrus waited in stunned silence for a few moments before chuckling awkwardly and nodding.

Cyrus walked to the park with Olive and a spring in his step. He wasn't yet convinced that he could have built Adhara—though the idea was certainly appealing. But the news that his friends even believed he was capable of it, after seeing how beautiful and powerful Adhara was, sent his self-esteem through the roof. The encouragement set his creativity flowing, and he was jittery with excitement from a new idea he'd had to improve his gauntlets. He chattered incessantly about his ideas to an amused Olive until they came to the edge of the city and found themselves in front of a protest outside the park. He could sense that Olive had tensed just as he had.

They kept their eyes down as they passed, trying not to draw attention. The protesters shouted their message, most of them holding signs. Some proclaimed: ACRYOGEN DOESN'T OWN ME! Others simply demanded variations of: NO MORE OUTAGES! But the most common sign by far displayed the simple phrase: WE CAN DO BETTER.

"Outages?" Olive murmured. "What do they mean?" Before Cyrus could reply she tapped the shoulder of a protestor standing off to the side. "Pardon me, sir," she started. He turned and looked up at her. "What's all this about power outages? There a bad one recently?"

The man squinted at the two of them, looking them up and down. "Who do you work for?" he asked.

"I—I'm sorry?" Cyrus asked.

"Who do you work for?" he repeated. "Who is your employer?"

"We're self-employed," Olive cut in. "Freelance. I'm an electrician and he's a computer scientist. We fix people's stuff."

The man nodded in approval. "It's decent work you're doing, but in that case how do you not know about the outage? It was just a couple days ago."

"We live just outside the city," she explained. "And we have a…generator."

"Ah," he softened. "Then you're lucky. A few nights ago, Acryogen cut the power for eight hours in the middle of the night because of a protest that had taken place earlier that day. Show of force; remind us *little* people who's in charge," he scoffed. "You're lucky if it didn't touch you—almost everyone in the city lost most of their food. Acryogen thinks they can just do whatever they want, don't they?" he shook his head. "All I can say is, it's a good thing the hospitals have backup generators. But the aquaponic farms don't. We'll probably be seeing a city-wide food shortage soon."

"That's awful," said Cyrus, too emphatically. "We've got to go do something about this right now. Come on," he pulled Olive away.

"You mean it?" Oliver asked quietly as he led her into the park. "You wanna do something?"

"No," Cyrus hissed, glancing over his shoulder. "Acryogen didn't cut the power, *I* did!"

Her mouth fell open. "You did *what*?"

Suddenly, behind them they heard gunshots and screams. Acryogen riot police had arrived in Roadsters and started firing rubber bullets into the crowd and throwing cans of tear gas. The protestors scattered, but a few were arrested and shoved unceremoniously into the back of a truck.

"Those infected rat Grimlords were running loose in the city!" he objected, pulling Olive away. "Adhara and I cut the power so no one would see them and *panic*, like last time. Plus, *they* apparently attack people on sight, and we hoped if the power were off people wouldn't go outside!"

"Cyrus, *what* the—"

"Hey, *be cool*," interrupted Cyrus as they spotted their friends. "I know I messed up, but nobody died, and I'm gonna make it up to them. I'm gonna make it right."

"You better," she muttered wryly, then went to greet Maria. Cyrus joined them, talking to Maria and listening to Aliyah appreciate how well she was healing, and laughing at Donny complimenting how well Maria got around with one of his old crutches. Maria told Cyrus excitedly how Adhara had searched Acryogen servers for her and managed to find the gene therapy data from the facility they had visited. Adhara caught his eye and nodded to him.

"Hey," Cyrus murmured to Adhara, stepping away from the group. She was wearing a new outfit—he recognized his orange hooded shirt. His friends must have replaced the clothes ruined in her fight with Animal King.

"Good afternoon," said Adhara, smiling politely. "How are you feeling, Cyrus?"

"I'm feeling a lot better," he answered honestly. He smiled at her. "Hey...I have an idea for an upgrade, for my gauntlets. I'd really appreciate your help if you're up for it."

"Of course," she smiled. "I'm always happy to help you, Cyrus."

"Yo," said Olive, reappearing in Cyrus' workshop doorway later that night. "I'm about to head to bed, thought I'd check up on y'all."

Cyrus and Adhara smiled up at her. Cyrus beckoned her closer. "C'mere," he giggled, grinning.

"Why?" she asked warily, drawing cautiously closer. "What did you do?" He held up his gauntlet—it was attached to his computers with a bundle of wires, and he held a carriage bolt between his index finger and thumb. As he carefully widened his fingers, the bolt remained where it was, suspended in midair. Then he flexed his fingers outward and the bolt shot up into the air, bouncing off the ceiling and falling to the floor. Olive flinched away from it and stared at the bolt, waiting for it to start flying around again.

"What did you do," she asked the bolt.

"Adhara has a device called an 'oscillation hyperdrive,'" Cyrus explained. "It's what allows her to time travel, by expanding and contracting the fabric of space around her body…" he waved his hand. "It's complicated. But I reverse engineered part of it into my gauntlets and now…" he nodded at the bolt. "I can displace *gravitons*."

Olive turned to him slowly and raised her eyebrows. "Does that mean what I think it means?"

Cyrus grinned evilly, in true form of a mad scientist. Olive almost expected him to burst out into a cackle accompanied by lightning and thunder.

"I can control *gravity*."

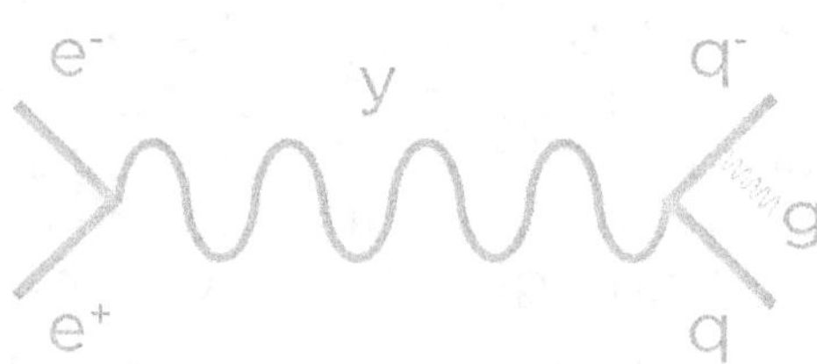

$$\left(\beta mc^2 + c\sum_{n=1}^{3}\alpha_n p_n\right)\psi(x,t) = i\hbar\frac{\partial\psi(x,t)}{\partial t}$$

Chapter 22

GOOD VIBRATION

Cyrus awoke with a start to forceful pounding on his door.

"Wh-who is it?"

"*Police!*" came a stern voice. "Open up!"

"*What?*"

"Nah, I'm just messing with you!" Donny crowed. "Get *up!*"

Heart pounding, Cyrus stumbled to the door. He flung it open irritably and snapped, "What do you *want?*" at Donny's smug grin. His eyes widened and he fell forward into the room, followed by Olive and Aliyah on top of him. Maria snickered at them from the hall.

"Why are you waking me up so early?" Cyrus asked again, "and so *terrifyingly?*"

"*Dude!*" Olive giggled, trying to extricate herself from the pile. "You gotta show them the thing!"

"What *thing?*"

"Olive told us you found out how to control gravity, and we wanna see it!" Donny demanded. He grunted and shoved Aliyah off him, struggling to his feet.

"Fine," Cyrus sighed, "but go downstairs —give me a chance to get dressed!"

"For the record..." Donny glanced down and winked. "I like the airplane boxers."

Cyrus chased them from his room as they giggled like children, letting out a relieved sigh when his door was finally closed again. But as he remembered the night before, theories and ideas about the future, possibilities and inspiration, he grew excited again too. He dressed quickly and retrieved his gauntlets from the lab.

"I stayed up late working out the kinks," he announced as he entered the living room to find his friends waiting politely. "But I think I have it now. I reverse engineered Adhara's time travel device to manipulate the flow of gravitons—"

"Get on with it!" Donny threw his voice to make it sound like a distant heckler somewhere in the audience. Aliyah and Olive snickered.

Cyrus glared at Donny, who stared back with polite interest. He raised his gauntlets to the ceiling and they heard a deep, resonant hum. The lights flickered. At first, as they looked around, waiting, nothing seemed to change. But as they turned their heads, Donny wordlessly pointed at Aliyah's hair. Hers, Olive's, and Maria's hair floated in waves as though underwater. Then all around them, small things like pens and paper clips, books, and envelopes began to levitate, followed by lamps, tables, and eventually the couches they were sitting on. They gaped in amazement as the room and everything in it, by Cyrus' hand, was weightless.

"Look!" Aliyah whispered, pointing to the hall. At the threshold of the living room there was a pen lying on the floor. Aliyah plucked another pen drifting past her head and tossed it towards the foyer—it cartwheeled gracefully until it crossed the threshold, then dropped abruptly. The humming stopped and Cyrus lowered his arms. They dropped a few centimeters with a jolt, turned to Cyrus, and burst into applause. He laughed awkwardly and bowed.

"Amazing!" Donny crowed, standing with his ovation. "Superb! *Bravo!*"

"All right, all right," Cyrus waved his hands, chuckling.

"So—how exactly did you *do* that?" Aliyah asked.

"It's pretty simple," Cyrus replied. "Gravity is an attractive force."

"I'll say," Donny purred.

"Now stop that," Cyrus glared out of the corner of his eye. "Simply put, I made the ceiling as attractive to us right now as the whole planet is. The forces cancelled out and we became weightless." He nodded toward the foyer. "I only expanded the field within this room, though."

"How big *could* you make it?" asked Olive.

"Uh..." Cyrus looked at the ceiling and murmured inaudibly to himself. "Probably...the whole house is as far as I could stretch it without straining the gauntlets. This takes a lot of power."

"How small could you make it?"

"Um...well, as small as I need to, I guess," he picked up a pen and with a shorter hum let it fall to the ceiling. "I showed you with the bolt last night. Why do you ask?"

"Well, I was just wondering if you could make yourself fly," she explained. Donny and Aliyah turned to her and grinned. Cyrus raised his eyebrows. All at once, they made a mad dash for the door, with Donny carrying Maria. Cyrus stepped out into the street, waving his hand for them to stay back. He held out his hands; they heard the deep hum. The dust on the road rose in a perfect circle to orbit around him, forming faint rings like Saturn's around his palms. Cyrus squatted, tensing his knees, then kicked off. He went flying into the air back towards his house.

His friends ran out into the street to see him cautiously standing up again on the side of his house, a couple of meters above the door. After a few moments, with his body parallel to the ground, he began walking normally around the windows. He laughed again and jumped to the house across the street, leaping and flipping weightlessly onto the roof, then over to the next house. His friends jogged to keep

in sight of him as he jumped from house to house, doing tricks in the air. But as he kicked off a porch his gauntlets suddenly popped, and he fell a few meters before skidding across an abandoned lawn. His friends ran over to meet him, and Donny helped him to his feet and brushed clods of grass off him.

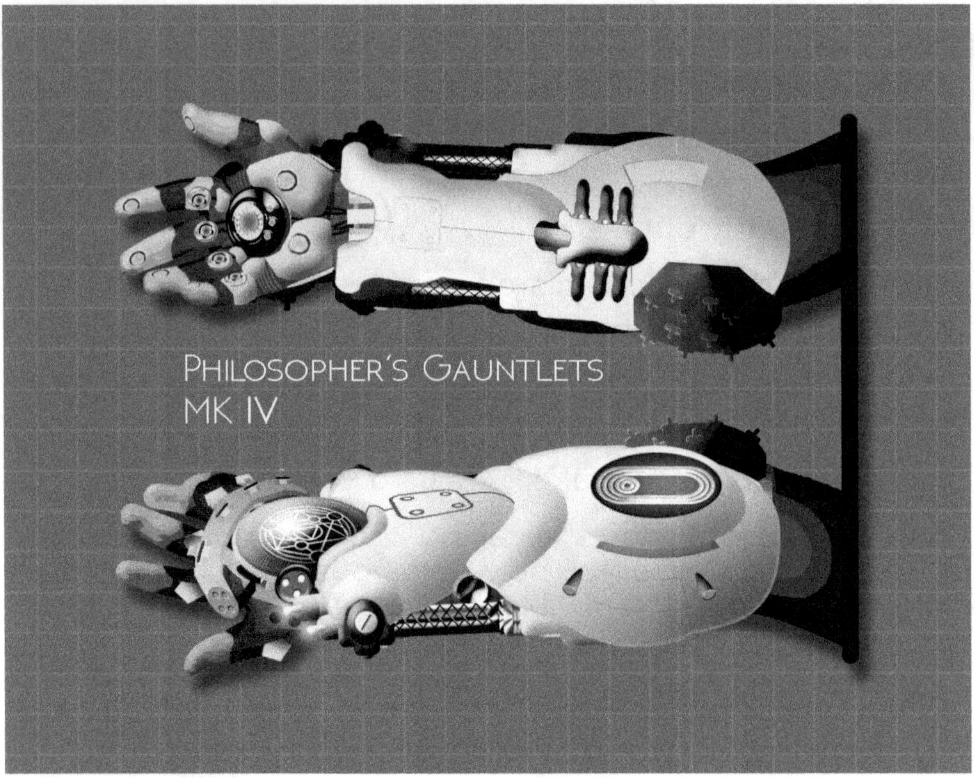

"Well," Cyrus groaned, carefully working his shoulders, "clearly I still have a few things to work on. But I think that substantiates the hypothesis." He grinned at them, "I can *totally* fly."

"Aliyah said you need somethin'?" said Donny, entering Cyrus' workroom a few hours later. Maria waved from a chair off to the side.

"Yeah, thanks for coming!" Cyrus finished ratcheting a small bolt in his gauntlets and set them aside, gesturing for Donny to sit. "Remind me which fighting style you know?"

"...Karate?" said Donny, sitting.

"Yeah, nice!" Cyrus nodded enthusiastically. "And Maria knows Taekwondo. What I want to do is design a martial arts-based input for the gauntlets. I think it'll make my combat ability more efficient."

"Sure, that makes sense," Donny agreed. "Put some physics behind that chemistry. Smart."

"Exactly!" Cyrus smiled. "I have to build some stuff first— I've upgraded the gauntlets again. I need gyroscopic sensors, and I'm completely rebuilding the graphic interface. It's going to have a complete periodic table of the elements and a reaction array. I'm excited about it!" Donny and Maria exchanged a knowing look. "Anyway, so I need to get a bunch of parts from the Pipeworks. In the meantime, maybe you and Maria can work out some ideas?...Thanks!" He patted the table and left the room.

"It's a shame he asked for *your* help," Donny goaded Maria, "he'd fight better if he left out the glorified yoga."

"I can't hear you over my current score of three to nothing," Maria signed back. "I seem to remember you having trouble defending against my flying kicks."

"I was going easy on you! My knees hurt."

"Your knees, or your *ego*?"

When Cyrus arrived under the basement later that evening, he found Adhara coming down to meet him. She returned his wave as he approached and helped him guide the freight platform, laden with spoils of scrap, to park at the foot of the stairs.

"Did you find everything you were looking for?" she asked in a placid voice like a cashier.

"And then some," Cyrus grunted, rearranging a pile. "Can you help me carry this upstairs? I found some really nice stuff. Check this out!" He held up a helmet with three lenses protruding from the face, like three eyes. "It has a bispectral imaging system in it! The navy makes these helmets. With this, I could see in infrared!"

"Cyrus, you shouldn't take that." Her voice and face were suddenly hard.

His face fell. "Why not?"

"I know it's hard for you to trust me when I tell you so little," she answered, "but please. For me, leave it behind." She smiled.

Cyrus tutted and set the helmet aside. "Well, the rest of this is for my gauntlets, and I need it. Will you help me?" He stumbled under the stack he was carrying, almost falling before Adhara reached forward and took half of the weight from him.

"*Wait* a minute!" Cyrus exclaimed, and dashed upstairs. He returned minutes later wearing his gauntlets and tapped each piece of scrap, bending their local gravity, so he could push the weightless heap upstairs. Adhara followed, effortlessly carrying some of the heaviest items. The wooden stairs sagged beneath her weight.

When they finished moving everything upstairs, Cyrus got to work right away installing his new hardware. Every now and then he would take a break for a few minutes and watch Donny and Maria from his window as they practiced maneuvers for him to try outside on the front lawn. When the sun set, they came inside to check on Cyrus' progress.

"We think we've got a good system worked out," said Donny as Maria nodded. "We'll start you off with basic principles so you can adapt it however you need. How's it going up here?"

"Check it out," Cyrus grinned, beckoning them over. He had built up the armor around the gauntlets even more than before. Each arm had two touchscreens, one mounted to the forearm and the other to the back of the hand. The forearm screens displayed a periodic table of the elements, but not the one Donny and Maria were used to—it had a bit of a spiral to it in the center and was overall shaped like a pill. As Cyrus put the gauntlets on, they could see a collection of polygons displayed on the back of his hands, along with a collection of unfamiliar symbols.

"I set up some reaction shortcuts, and I based the graphics off of traditional alchemy," Cyrus explained. He tapped a triangle pointing up and dragged a smaller triangle pointing down to intersect with the larger one. Then he selected a symbol like the omega character with a line beneath it and wrapped the whole array in a circle. A blue flame burst from his palm. "That's the shortcut for, y'know, splitting water and igniting the oxyhydrogen. The triangles refer to fire and water, respectively, and this symbol means 'decomposition.'" He tapped at the screen, scrolling through different shapes and symbols while Maria and Donny watched blankly.

"It's really cool that you were able to use alchemy!" Maria signed. "It gives your gauntlets kind of a mystic vibe."

"They're gonna have even *more* of a mystical vibe," Cyrus grinned, "after you guys teach me some sick kung fu moves."

"Neither of us knows Kung Fu. Anyway, how is this going to work, exactly?" asked Donny. "I mean, we can teach you the basics of our disciplines, but how is it supposed to translate into your gauntlets?"

"Good question!" Cyrus finished adjusting his gauntlets and tightened them around his arms. "As I was working on them today, I discovered that I can calibrate the graviton waveform to affect matter on an atomic scale, affecting atomic oscillation."

Maria and Donny stared at him flatly.

"Why does he do that, do you think?" Donny asked Maria.

"He *knows* we can't understand him," she replied. "Maybe he's trying to be impressive."

"I can change states of matter," Cyrus explained finally. "You know, melting, boiling, freezing, that sort of thing."

"Why didn't you say that from the beginning?" Maria signed.

"Welcome to my inner dialogue," said Cyrus. "I read text-books and research papers more than I talk to other human beings."

"So then, you want to associate...certain gestures and movements with states of matter?" Donny asked.

"Yes, and there's a few other reactions I'd like to dedicate," Cyrus nodded. "Some things I don't want to take the time to type in, you know? I want them to be easily accessible and intuitive."

"I gotcha," Donny nodded. "Although...I'd think karate moves are a little too *flamboyant* for simple stuff. And that's me talking."

"Oh! Well actually, I programmed in some sign language words for the basic reactions, or when I only need a small-scale reaction." He made the sign for "fire" and a flame burst from his palm, exactly as it had when he'd input the symbols before. "The karate and taekwondo moves are just for combat shortcuts. I'd have a move that would also make fire in the same way, but instead of this tiny flame, it would be like a huge blast!"

"That's so *cool*!" Maria beamed, excitedly staring at his hands. "Can you do that with my gauntlets?"

Cyrus laughed. "Sure, as soon as I finish this upgrade with mine. Ready to start practicing?"

Donny nodded. "Let's get started."

They regrouped in the living room and cleared out all the furniture to make room. Maria sat on the back of one of the couches, just outside the room, and Donny instructed Cyrus on the proper stance.

"Okay," Donny began, facing Cyrus, "I'm guessing you want to focus on moves that use the arms rather than the legs. And I won't bother teaching you the names of the moves, because, well." He shrugged. "They're in Japanese, and they don't really matter to you. So just do what I do." He whipped his forearms around in a circle in front of him.

"Oh, go on," said Cyrus, copying him. "What's that move called?"

"Mac Shuto Mawashi Uke."

"Okay yeah, I'm not going to remember that," Cyrus muttered, setting his gauntlets to record the gesture. "Let's see, I'm gonna say...that feels like an explosion."

"You *better* keep those turned off," Donny warned.

As they worked into the night, Cyrus fortunately avoided burning, freezing, or blowing up Donny. He was careful to merely record the movement as he learned to jab, chop, and punch, and he assigned each gesture to a command for the gauntlets. He also assigned a magnitude based on the inertia the gauntlets sensed—so Maria and Donny also taught him the proper forms and how to clench at the last second and whip his body around, so that he would deliver maximum force with each blow.

"You have to Kihap," Maria suggested.

"Kai...happ?" said Cyrus, trying to interpret her fingerspelling phonetically.

"She's saying 'Kihap,'" Donny translated. "It means a 'spirited yell.' Like...*HIYAH!*" he cried as he brought his hand down, chopping the air ferociously.

"It helps you to focus your energy," Maria explained.

"But the Lorentz field already does that."

They glared at him.

By midnight Olive and Aliyah had joined Maria to watch, and he had almost finished programming an elegant and intuitive gesture-based combat system. However, they continued to practice at Maria and Donny's insistence, because they agreed he would always benefit from reinforcing his muscle memory. One by one, their audience went to bed as they continued to practice, until Donny finally allowed respite to aching Cyrus.

The next morning, to Cyrus' surprise, Donny let him sleep in. Sore in every muscle, he dragged himself from bed and downstairs to find his friends in the living room.

"Good morning, sleepyhead," Donny crooned, "or should I say, *evening*."

"I wouldn't have asked you to train me if I knew you were going to push me that hard," Cyrus groaned.

"You can thank me later. Ready to see how much you remember?"

"Yes, actually." Cyrus straightened. "But this time, we're going to do it my way. Where's that *robot*?"

"You want to...*spar* with me?" Adhara asked after they found her cleaning the kitchen and Cyrus explained his plan. "That seems unwise."

"I don't actually want you to fight *back*," Cyrus explained. "It's just so I can practice and demonstrate the gestures."

"You want me to let you beat me up."

"Basically, yeah!" Cyrus grinned.

"All right," she shrugged. "Lead the way."

They convened in the tunnel under the basement. Adhara undressed to prepare for their fight as Cyrus moved the freight platform out of harm's way, and Donny drew a circle on the ground to serve as a ring.

"Hmm..." Cyrus tapped a finger on his lips, regarding the circle.

"Are you mentally criticizing my circle?" Donny demanded.

"No, no," said Cyrus. "I would never! It's a beautiful circle! I just feel like, for something like this we need more of an... arena." He looked at his friends. "Could you wait on the stairs, please?"

When they were out of range, Cyrus put his palms to the ground. The concrete beneath his fingers shifted, sinking down to form a meter-deep pit. His friends gathered at the edge.

"Impressive," Adhara remarked, looking at the pit wall behind her. "What did you do?"

"I increased the density of the concrete, so it contracted," Cyrus smirked. He crouched into his fighting stance. "I've learned a few new tricks."

"What do you want me to do?" she asked, turning back to him. "Just stand still?"

"Well no, you can...*react*." He loosened his stance. "Don't hurt me, but you can try to dodge, and block, and stuff."

"Very well." Adhara's eyes glowed and her jets fired. She adopted her own fighting stance and waited.

"Ready?" Donny asked, acting as referee. Cyrus nodded. Adhara nodded back. "Then...FIGHT!"

Adhara sprang high into the air and in an instant appeared behind him. Cyrus whipped around and released a blast of fire, thicker and brighter than oxyhydrogen flame. She twisted her body in midair to dodge it and landed to the side. Cyrus waved his arms and the concrete beneath him shattered—he grabbed chunks and melted them into glowing orange blobs before hurling them back at her. The training had paid off. Limited though it was, Donny had successfully taught Cyrus to move more deliberately, and he now took physics into account with every graceful movement.

Adhara knocked away the onslaught of molten concrete, but a few blobs stuck to her body and solidified. They reduced her range of movement until she twisted, and the brittle stuff crumbled away. Cyrus switched tactics, assuming solid poses and releasing deafening shockwaves from his fingertips. When they passed over Adhara harmlessly, he grabbed more shards of concrete and propelled them like shrapnel. She dodged aptly again, but the few shards that made contact merely ricocheted off her, embedding themselves in the tunnel wall.

While she was distracted with the shrapnel, Cyrus brought his hands together and engulfed her in a mass of ice. Once again, she momentarily seemed immobilized. Then she flexed her arms, shattering the ice and melting it in her own wave of fire. Cyrus redirected the fire as it passed over him, clenched his fists at his sides, and discharged a bolt of lightning to Adhara. Her body went rigid and the arc lashed out to light fixtures and metal objects, spitting cascades of sparks and making Cyrus' friends jump back. As he disconnected, he flung a hissing ball of swirling fluid at her with his other hand.

On contact, the ball exploded and knocked her to the ground. Without missing a beat, Cyrus reached forward and melted the cement into lava beneath her. Within seconds, she was ankle-deep, but she merely looked down curiously. When her body was half sunken, he froze the concrete again, finally immobilizing her, and approached her slowly. She looked up at him calmly as he raised his hand and produced a flickering sphere of energy. Her expression remained unchanged as the sphere grew, pulsating angrily, trying to escape Cyrus' force field. He reared back, preparing to strike—and shot the energy down the tunnel. It disappeared into the darkness and after a short delay, they saw a distant explosion. The shockwave blew back the tunnel past them, rippling Cyrus' hair.

"Well?" Cyrus turned, grinning, his hands raised in bravado. "Impressive, right?" They approached carefully, led by Donny.

"Uh...is Adhara *okay*?" Donny asked, concerned. They looked back at her.

"No need to be concerned. I am fine," she assured them, though still encased in cement. Her body glowed and they heard crackling, then she burst forth from the ground. When she joined the group, they could see that she didn't have as much as a scratch.

Olive sighed, relieved. "Oh man, I thought Cyrus almost *wrecked* you!"

"Yeah, that was pretty *scary*, Cy!" Aliyah added. "Remind me not to get on your bad side."

"Hey now, c'mon," Cyrus finally realized how shaken his friends looked. "It's a lot of power, I know. But I'm aware of the responsibility that comes with it. I promise, I'm only going to use these for the good of the city."

"Promise you won't go mad with power?" Donny asked.

"I promise I won't go mad with power."

They seemed reassured, if only slightly. In time, they would see what he meant— He finally had the *means* to do what really needed to be done! But he was getting ahead of himself. For the time being, there were more pressing matters.

"Good things are coming!" Cyrus declared, "I'm going to do *whatever it takes* to fix this city. But right now, I'm gonna do whatever it takes to get a *sandwich*."

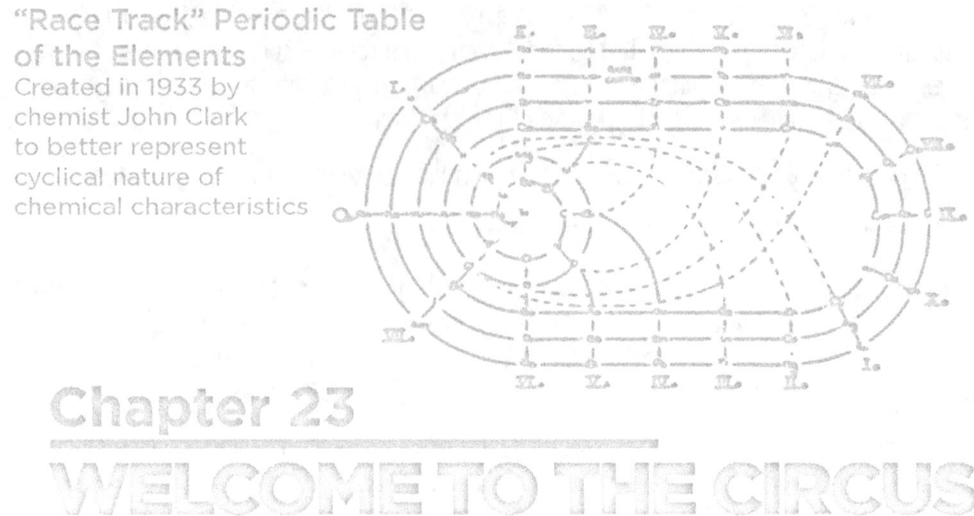

Chapter 23
WELCOME TO THE CIRCUS

"Hey man," said Olive quietly, slipping into the kitchen and sitting next to him. She wrinkled her nose at his sandwich. "So, um...I thought it was really cool, what you said earlier about doing whatever it takes to fix things? Takes a lot of guts to have that kind of dedication."

"Fanks," said Cyrus through a mouthful. He swallowed hard. "I figure, no one else really has the means, you know? Feels like I have an obligation." He took another bite, chewed thoughtfully, and swallowed again. "I guess that's what Adhara's been trying to tell me all along, huh?"

"Right, yeah," Olive nodded. "Hey Cyrus," she said suddenly. "You wanna come visit my crib? I wanna show you something."

"Uh..." he swallowed again. "Sure? You mean right now, or—"

"Yeah, or, when you finish...that." She glanced down at his sandwich's remains. "Meet me in the basement. And uh, you should probably wear your disguise...it's in the city. Don't want anyone to recognize ya." With that she slipped out of the kitchen again.

"So, you're being super weird," said Cyrus, fully suited up, as they boarded the freight platform half an hour later. "What's that all about?"

"What...do you mean?" said Olive absently as she chewed on her lip. She selected their destination on the control panel, then muttered under her breath. "Look man, I can't level with you just yet. But when we get there, I'll explain everything, I promise."

Apprehensive but intrigued, Cyrus shrugged. They spent the rest of the ride through the Pipeworks in silence. They entered a system of defunct subway tunnels and stopped in an abandoned station.

"Here's the deal," Olive told him as they disembarked. "I'm gonna show you something that might seem kinda whack. But just give it a chance and let it sink in, okay? I know it's edgy, but don't make a snap judgment."

"Are we still going to your house?" Cyrus asked, growing concerned as they pushed through rusty turnstiles. "Look, Aliyah and Maria are—heh." He chuckled to himself. "Aliyah and Maria. That kind of rhymes. Anyway—they're working on cross-species genetic modification. I'm sure whatever you're working on isn't that bad."

"Just promise me you'll be cool, man. I've overlooked some wild stuff you've done."

Cyrus abruptly clamped his mouth shut. "I'll be cool," he assured her. "No worries."

She nodded, tying a handkerchief over her mouth and nose, and led him out of the station up to the surface. They dashed through back alleyways, skulking past dumpsters and catching glimpses of police between the buildings, who were chasing citizens out past curfew. Cyrus spotted a young woman fall to the ground, convulsing after being hit with a taser, and lingered to watch until Olive dragged him away.

"Not much good you can do for her right now," Olive muttered. "You'll be helping everyone if you set Acryogen straight."

"I had no idea it was this bad," Cyrus admitted.

"Yeah, well, you live outside the city." She tapped a chain-link fence to ask Cyrus to cut through it. "These days, it's like a war zone down here."

Olive led them deeper into shadowy corners of the city, past warehouses and garages, stopping finally in front of a metal door at the end of a narrow alley. She knocked on the door and an eye slot opened.

"Olive?" said a man behind the door. "Good to see you. Been a while."

"You too, Reilley. Let us in, huh?"

"Who's this with you...?" The eyes behind the door widened. Cyrus nervously tightened his mask around his chin and pulled his hood forward. They heard a series of metallic clicks and the door swung inward. Olive pushed him inside and the door closed behind them.

"It's *you*!" said Reilley. A tall, stocky, and tired looking man with sandy hair. Cyrus inferred from his overalls and calloused hands that he was a laborer—a member of the half of the city who didn't work in a lab. "You're...the Alchemist!" Cyrus snapped out of his thoughts.

"Uh...yes, I am." he answered. "Who are you? Olive's roommate...?"

"Cy—I mean, dude—" Olive cut in before Reilley could answer. "Just hold on a second and I'll explain, okay?" She turned to Reilley. "I'm gonna take him to the great room, okay?"

"Sure," Reilley nodded. "There's a meeting soon. You should hurry." He stared at Cyrus as Olive led him away.

They passed through a few halls—they seemed to be in an old factory, but all the smaller rooms were furnished with makeshift beds or mattresses, old furniture, the occasional salvaged poster, and crude fixtures. They were occupied by families or small groups of people, like a shantytown apartment building. Cyrus stared stubbornly at the back of Olive's head but couldn't help but feel the stares as they walked past. Eventually she led him into an expansive room, the main floor of the factory, still equipped with decrepit machinery and steel girders. But in between the girders, a miniature city grid of tents made from mismatched salvage: discarded bedsheets and canvas, patched and haphazardly sewn together. Not a city of tents—this was a refugee camp. Setting sunlight streamed in from vast windows patched with pasted newspaper.

As Olive led him down an aisle, he came up next to her and whispered, "Olive? *Where* are we?"

She stopped in the middle of the room and sighed, then turned to him and smiled sadly. "Welcome to the rebellion, Cyrus."

Before he could respond, someone from the crowd yelled, "It's the Alchemist!" and the excitement rippled through the room. In minutes he was surrounded by adoring fans, praising him and crying, asking him questions he couldn't make out, and applauding. Olive had disappeared and he was surrounded; it seemed everyone in the entire room had gathered around him in a thick barrier. As he turned, he saw the crowd parting to allow a tall man to pass through. The man stopped in front of Cyrus and held up a hand, waiting until the crowd was settled and watching quietly before he turned to Cyrus.

He greeted Cyrus with a polite, "Good evening," inclining his head. His voice was gravelly but sonorous, and though his chiseled features seemed rough, his bushy beard obscured half his face, and his breadth was intimidating, Cyrus noticed smile wrinkles around his eyes.

"Good evening," Cyrus replied, returning the bow. "Thank you for having me."

"Thank you for visiting us. My name is Keith." He extended his hand to Cyrus, who took it. Keith gently rotated his hand so that Cyrus' was on top. "So," he nodded at the gauntlet, "it's true what they're saying? You're the Alchemist."

Cyrus hesitated, studying the crowd's expressions. They seemed as on-edge as he was. "It's true," he admitted finally. Excited whispers echoed out from all directions.

Keith released his hand. "I have to say, it's a pleasure to meet you, sir. We've all been following your...activities with great interest." One corner of his mouth twitched under his beard. "What brings you here?"

"I'm...my friend, Olive...?" Cyrus looked around, trying again to find Olive in the crowd.

"Olive, you said. Tall blonde girl, about your age?" Keith asked gently. Cyrus nodded. Keith cupped his hands over his mouth and barked, "Excuse me, everyone! We're trying to find Olive Menlo!"

After a few minutes of murmuring, the crowd parted, and Olive burst through. "Phew!" she gasped, "Sorry, buddy! Lost you in the crowd there for a minute. Howdy, Keith!"

"You two are friends?" Keith asked. The crowd gradually began to disperse but Cyrus still felt the long looks as people passed.

"He wants his identity to remain a secret; I'm sure you understand," said Olive. "But I was hoping you could explain to him what we're fighting for here, what our goals are. I think you guys have a lot in common."

"I'd be delighted," Keith smiled. He waved an open hand. "We have a meeting soon, but I think we have time for a quick tour. If you'd like to follow me?"

"I'll catch up with you later, Cyrus," whispered Olive, and she disappeared back into the crowd. Cyrus felt his stomach tighten.

"I have to admit," said Cyrus uneasily, "this isn't what I expected the rebellion to be like."

"It's sad," said Keith simply. "It's all right," he added quickly before Cyrus could backpedal, "there's no need to mince words. Acryogen makes us out to be this...radical guerrilla military force, lurking in the shadows and waiting to overthrow the city. But the truth is..." he gestured to a weary man squatting in the dust, making tea with a dingy pot on a hot plate that looked like an electrical fire waiting to happen. "We're just a community of the people who couldn't keep up. Trying to keep our heads above water."

"There are a few different kinds of people here," Keith explained as he led Cyrus through the rows of makeshift shelters. "Most people just don't have anywhere else to go—they're refugees. Displaced by a burst water main, or a fire, or what have you. Couldn't afford somewhere else, so..." he gestured to a group of college students, huddled with their textbooks around a battery-powered lantern. "Then we have what I call the 'offenders'— people who have committed a crime, like repair something they weren't supposed to, or invent something illegal. Take Steve here, for example." He gestured to a thin man working on a pipe manifold.

"Hullo there, Keith," Steve nodded, looking up. He turned to Cyrus and dropped his wrench. "Y—you're *the Alchemist*!" Steve chortled and grabbed Cyrus' hand, pumping it enthusiastically. "Man! It's a pleasure to meet you, I've gotta say. The impact you've had on this city, and the, uh..." he eyed Cyrus' gauntlets curiously, "things you've built? It makes an old mechanic proud. If I were, oh, ten or so years younger, I'd be tempted to join you!"

"Don't work too hard now, Steve," said Keith as they turned away. Grinning, Steve returned to his work. They passed through some more halls and Cyrus received more admiration from passersby. Then Keith led them down a staircase heading belowground. It was darker and cooler, their path lit by only a few dim bulbs.

"We have to keep some down here, for their safety. I'm sure you've heard of the work camps the Mongols have set up around the continent?"

"Sure," said Cyrus. "They're horrible, like work camps historically are." Keith led them through a dim hallway into a wider room, where a few clusters of people read books or listened to a radio in candlelight.

"I want you to meet Aubrey," he gestured to a woman curled up in a nearby chair. She extended a hand to him but didn't stand.

"Mr. Alchemist," she croaked. "It's a pleasure to meet you again. I don't know if you remember me, but you saved me that night from one of those skeleton monsters."

"I do remember you!" Cyrus realized. "It's…good to see you again. Though I wish it were under better circumstances."

"Forgive me for not getting up," she coughed. "My legs are still too weak."

"Aubrey recently escaped from a work camp," Keith explained.

"*Seriously*?" Cyrus breathed. "Why were you arrested? Did you go into the wasteland? How did you escape and get back inside the city?"

"Get back?" Aubrey squinted at him. "I never left the city. I was in the mines under the bay."

"I…don't understand," said Cyrus.

"What happens when you're convicted of a felony in Hudson City?" asked Keith.

"You…go to prison?"

"That's what they tell us," Keith nodded. "They call it prison so that it's easier for the public to swallow."

"It's not a prison," Aubrey breathed, leaning back and closing her eyes. "It's a work camp. Slavery."

"What?" Cyrus whispered.

"Acryogen claims that most of its labor is automated," Keith explained quietly. "But everyone in this room has escaped from one of their secret work camps. They're fugitives. They twist them up in the system so that they get free labor for the rest of their lives. Which usually isn't long," he nodded at Aubrey. "She escaped just a week ago and made her way here. She'd only been in for a few months." He shook his head, tutting, then patted Aubrey's shoulder. "Get some rest now, Aubrey. We'll leave you in peace." She nodded faintly.

"I guess I shouldn't be so surprised," Cyrus muttered as they turned away. "Recently, I found one of Acryogen's abandoned labs—they were experimenting with bioweapons. Combining animals with…technology for combat."

"It's repulsive to even think about," Keith shook his head. "But I'll admit. It doesn't surprise me, either. When Acryogen has a goal, they'll use any means to achieve it."

"What on earth did she even do to be charged with a felony?"

Keith looked down, uncomfortable. "She was defending you. She organized a petition to clear you of all charges after Acryogen named you public enemy number one. She argued you were a hero —and they accused her of colluding with a known terrorist."

Cyrus' heart sank. "I never meant, I'm...I'm so sorry—"

"You don't need to apologize," he insisted. "And here's why. Olive wants me to explain what we're fighting for," Keith added as he led the way back upstairs. "It's simple, really. Everyone in this building has been hurt in some way by Acryogen Industries." He rubbed his arm where long scars crisscrossed his dark skin. "Every single person. We want to change that. We want this city to be a place where innocent people," he gestured around him, "don't have to live in fear of a super-powerful corporation. We want to take responsibility and control and put it back in the hands of the people—and we're...*determined* to achieve that goal."

"That seems reasonable," Cyrus murmured.

He shrugged. "Some would call us radicals for it. But the way I see it, we're just fighting for equality and fairness. We know Acryogen protected us during the war, and we're not unappreciative of that, but I know we can do better than this. We shouldn't have to settle for 'good enough.' But to tell you the truth—" he chuckled. "We had *almost* given up! Last year, morale was low. We weren't making any progress. Then, out of nowhere," he turned to Cyrus, smirking proudly. "The Alchemist appears. There's a fire in Hudson City and it's extinguished *before* it spreads to other buildings, destroying people's livelihood and homes? Man, that gave people around here hope!" he grinned. "That and everything you did after it inspired us to keep fighting. It's why you see stuff like that." Keith pointed to a mural at the end of the hall.

Cyrus followed his finger to the wall slowly, like he was walking underwater. In black, white, and red, the mural depicted the visage of the Alchemist in dichromatic contrast, in his traditional costume but with beams of energy springing from his palms. In stark white letters above his head, the artist had painted, "REBIRTH."

"And of course, when...*that* guy showed up, we knew big changes were on the horizon." Keith was standing beside him, gesturing to the wall next to the mural of the Alchemist. Cyrus hadn't noticed, but there was another mural beside his. A dark figure, hulking and completely black except for three white circles instead of eyes. Above his head, in stark white letters: "DEATH."

"Mystery Man," Cyrus whispered.

"Quite the mystery indeed," Keith continued, unaware of the cold sweat beading on Cyrus' forehead. "Even more so than you. The media *never* covers him, like they do with you, but we have people who bring us reports. They only see him from afar, but they all give the same physical description. Actually, for a while we thought he was a pilot wearing some kind of secret Acryogen super-soldier power armor," he chuckled, "but he only ever attacks Acryogen facilities! No communication, no demands, no reasoning. Can't puzzle it out...no one knows where he came from or who he is." He scratched his chin. "Some of the more...*superstitious* folk around here think that he's here to destroy everything Acryogen related, and you're here to rebuild the city. Local mythos. That's why those words are painted on there, but...don't take them too seriously." He winked.

"Thank you for showing me all of this," said Cyrus suddenly. "But I have to go. There's somewhere I need to be."

"Ah—I understand," said Keith quickly, trying to hide his disappointment. "But before you go, please, let me ask you one thing."

"...What is it?" Cyrus asked cautiously.

"What are you fighting for?" he looked at Cyrus intently. "Really? I just...don't want folks to have false hope, you know?"

"Ah," said Cyrus. His mouth was full of cotton and he felt an odd pulling sensation, as if his very soul were tugging on him to turn away and run. "Well...I'm fighting for the same thing you are, I guess," he answered finally. Keith waited expectantly. "I'm trying to fix all the things wrong with the city. One problem at a time. I want to help people."

"I'm glad to hear it," Keith sighed. "If that's true, we're right to place our trust in you. And if you really believe that, then I have an offer for you."

"What's that?" Cyrus croaked.

"These people need a *leader*," Keith pleaded quietly. "They need someone to unify and inspire them. Someone to follow in this fight. Someone like you." He looked him dead in the eye, making Cyrus feel intense discomfort. "You don't have to say anything right now, but," Keith nodded slowly. "Please. Think about it."

"Huh? What about you?"

"Me?" Keith laughed. "You thought *I* was in charge? No, I'm more of a...mediator. I'm no leader."

"I'll think about it," Cyrus assured him. He tapped his fingers on his legs nervously.

"Good man." Keith smiled. "Do you need directions...?"

"No, I can manage, thank you for the tour, bye," Cyrus shouted behind as he hurried down the hallway. He pushed past groups of people smiling and exclaiming at him, and when he had passed Reilley again and burst out the door, he ran. He ran between buildings, vaulting dumpsters, and then he started firing shockwaves from his gauntlets to blast obstacles out of his way. When riot police noticed the commotion and tried to cut him off, he used his gauntlets to leap up to a fire escape, dash across a platform, and when he landed on the pavement again a block away, he kept running. Anything to put as much distance behind him as fast as possible.

REBIRTH

Chapter 24
IN THE BALANCE

When Cyrus got home after his visit with the rebellion, he crept through the darkness straight to his bedroom. He collapsed on his bed. But despite desperate, tireless efforts to find relief, he couldn't rest until after the sun pushed through his curtains. In the absence of sleep, Cyrus eventually found comfort in the familiarity of working.

Cyrus began to avoid sleep as much as he avoided his thoughts and his friends, especially Olive. He was giving himself time to absorb, he told himself, just time to get used to the idea of everything. Who could carry the weight of the future? He couldn't bear the overwhelming tide of his thoughts, all the players in this game: his friends, the rebellion, the police, the citizens, Acryogen, the riots, the future... his destiny. Adhara. Mason Smithy. Mystery Man. Anubis. Who was playing and who was being played? And whose side was *he* on? Two sides of his brain were constantly at war: one which regarded the entire situation as too ridiculous to dwell on or even be involved with in the first place, and the other which felt obligated to be involved, and filled him with guilt for even considering walking away.

There was only one thing Cyrus could coherently focus on. Every night he snuck past his friends, out of his house through the Pipeworks, and fixed as many things as he could find in the city, working himself to exhaustion before retreating home, collapsing around sunrise, and sleeping fitfully until sunset to do it again. Repairs made sense to him—they were something he could still control. They helped him to bring the world into focus, especially taking things one step at a time, finding something to fix, fixing it, then onto the next. The job was always the same: find what the thing is supposed to do, and make it work. He re-wired, realigned, and welded, wiring and plumbing that ran through the Pipeworks, small jobs at first. But before long he was repairing even roofs and foundations, preventing entire buildings from collapsing.

The gauntlets, of course, made the work easy. He waved his hand and erected a wall of rock. A snap of his fingers, and thick steel girders split in half. At his touch, massive structures became weightless; this wasn't even to mention the convenience of leaping weightlessly from one building to another. It was incredible power, he acknowledged to himself. But he was using it to help people. He was doing his best, as anyone should. Thinking this made him feel better.

Sometimes when Cyrus came home into the basement, the lights were still on in the house, and he could hear his friends' voices upstairs. He'd been avoiding them for too long, now—facing them seemed unbearably awkward. So, he backtracked to the street and slipped out from a man-hole cover, hopping gracefully up the side of his house and onto the roof. There he waited, night after night, watching the stars and cerulean clouds until he heard nothing but crickets. One night like this, he laid on the roof with his arms folded behind his head, wondering if Adhara would leave when the threat of Anubis was gone. If she did, what would *he* do next? What do you do after your destiny is ful-filled?

As though the thought summoned her, Cyrus heard Adhara's jets whine softly. To his left, she floated above the roofline and touched down softly before padding over and lying down next to him.

"Everyone misses you," she said gently, folding her arms behind her head as he had.

"Do they?" he asked dryly. "Then why aren't they up here instead of you?"

"I suspect it is because they are incapable of flight." Adhara frowned. "I'm sorry. I didn't mean to offend you. I thought the affection of your friends would be the most compelling argument for you to stop avoiding them."

"I'm not offended," he smirked. "Did someone send you to check up on me?"

"I came of my own accord. However, they *are* all concerned about you. Olive seems particularly distressed."

"Yeah..." he leaned back, searching for Andromeda in the moonless sky. "I just needed to be alone for a while. I have a lot on my mind."

"I know," she nodded. "That is perfectly justifiable. You're going through a lot, lately."

He turned and smiled at her. "Thanks for understanding."

"Take as much time as you need to care for yourself," said Adhara. She stood and approached the edge of the roof. "But, Cyrus," she turned and smiled at him gently. "Remember. You'll only be alone as long as you want to be."

He returned her smile and nodded, and she disappeared over the edge.

"What did he say?" Maria signed as Adhara came back inside. Aliyah, Donny, and Olive waited expectantly around her.

"He has a lot on his mind, and he needs some time to himself," she answered. "It would be unwise to press him further. He will rejoin our company when he is ready."

"Yeah. We should probably just let him have his space," Aliyah sighed.They returned to the living room, flopping defeated onto the couches.

"I just wish we knew *what* was bothering him, you know?" said Donny quietly. "I mean, it's not just *me*, right? He sparred with Adhara...and then suddenly, he starts avoiding us. Nothing happened to freak him out, did it?" he asked Adhara.

"I do not know what triggered this antisocial episode," she answered.

"Maybe he scared *himself*," Maria signed. "He got pretty intense in that fight. It's not like him to be violent—maybe he's afraid of his own power?"

"That makes sense," Donny nodded. "I remember when I started learning karate and I accidentally cracked my sparring partner's ribs. I quit for a *week* because I was so scared. Did you have an experience like that?"

Maria nodded.

"I can see that. The fights with Grimlords, him being in the news, and all this destiny talk...the pressure must be getting to him."

"It's not that," Olive finally spoke up. "He's—" something caught her eye and she turned suddenly, "Cyrus!"

They all whirled to see Cyrus, smiling apologetically, standing in the doorway.

"Hey, man!" Donny grinned as they all came forward, wanting to hug Cyrus but unsure if he would allow it. "How are you feeling? We've missed you."

"I know, and I'm sorry," Cyrus said quickly. "I just needed some time to think about stuff. But right now, we have a big problem." He turned to Adhara. "Animal King is back."

Maria paled, backing slowly against the wall. Donny held out his arm to support her—she seemed to not be able to put weight on her leg.

"Did you see it?" Adhara asked, ignoring the others' shock.

"I saw it from the roof. Or...I saw the thing it made." He grimaced. "There's a huge cloud of smoke coming from the tallest mountain. I thought it had become active again, so I looked through the telescope we mounted on the roof, for stargazing," he explained, nodding at Maria, who had helped him with the project. "It's built...a bigger version of itself. It has big horns, and it's gotta be almost...eight stories tall. It was surrounded by a horde of Grimlords and those rat creatures—there's *hundreds* of them, coming out of the huge fire they built inside the crater."

Maria clenched her jaw. "What's it doing?" She signed.

"I watched it climb out of the crater. It's heading towards the city—it's slow, but it'll be through the forest in hours."

"Don't worry," he reassured them. "I have a plan. I know I haven't been around lately. But will you help me?"

"Of course," said Donny, with Aliyah and Olive nodding in support. "You don't have to ask, brother. We always have your back."

"Good, because I don't know if I can pull this off without you," Cyrus admitted. "We'll work in teams of two. Donny, you'll be with Maria. Aliyah, you're with Olive. You guys are going to have a supporting role while Adhara and I face An-imal King head-on with our *secret weapon*." He turned to Adhara intently. "*This time*, we're killing that thing for good."

Chapter 25
LONG LIVE THE KING

"What's this secret weapon?" Adhara asked Cyrus after they dropped off his friends at designated points in the city. Cyrus had directed the freight platform to take them deep into the Pipeworks under the southern mountains.

"Remember the first time you took me into the Pipeworks, and we saw a massive excavation drone? You called it a Grunger."

"Of course, I remember," she replied. "My memory is faultless."

"As I've been exploring the Pipeworks looking for salvage for my gauntlets, I stumbled upon another one, in the deeper parts." He looked down, remembering. "Not a Grunger, and not as big, but...still huge. It has six legs and great big jaws like a beetle."

"You found a Pipe Grinder," she realized.

"Is that what they're called?" he nodded. "It was terrifying, just being near it, even though it was dead. And *way* too big to salvage for parts. But now..." he looked up, smiling ruefully. "I have a stupid idea."

"There it is," Maria whispered to Donny. From the rooftop of one of the buildings at the edge of the city where Cyrus had told them to wait, they had just spotted Animal King's colossus emerging from the trees. It was bigger than he had described, head and shoulders above a nearby transmission tower. But just as he had said, it seemed to be a larger version of Animal King itself, with its long limbs and horns and obscene leer. With a purposeful grimace and a terrible scream, it pulled the spitting high-tension wires down as it passed. Burning cinders from the mountain covered its body, draping it in smoke, giving it the appearance of a coaly demon just emerged from brimstone. Its eyes glowed with burning embers. The horde of Grimlords scuttled around its feet.

Donny and Maria hefted the huge magnetron Gatling guns Cyrus had made for them and balanced their barrels on the ledge. On the roof of the building across the way, they saw Olive and Aliyah do the same. They each flipped a switch and the magnetrons began to hum.

As the giant approached, they felt the earth shudder. With each footfall as it drew closer, the ground heaved and lurched—but asynchronously. Maria pressed her hand to the ground and shared a quizzical look with Donny. An earthquake? Or....

A nearby manhole cover burst out like a cork popping out of a bottle. From underground Cyrus careened high into the air before falling in a graceful arc and landing before them.

"I hope you're ready," he huffed.

"Ready for *what*?" shouted Donny over the rumble. "Where's Adhara—"

He was cut off by the very earth giving way in a spider-web of deep fissures, just in front of Animal King's giant. It stopped, seeming curious, and Cyrus sprang into the air again like a man on the moon. He came down close to the

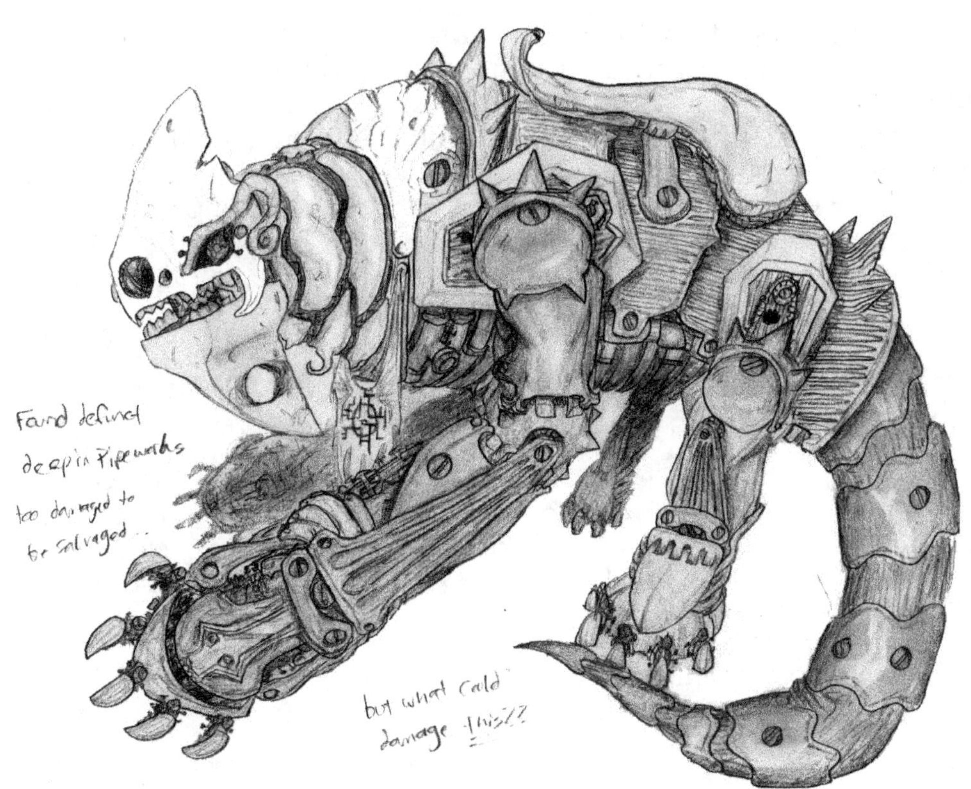

monster—too close, Donny and Maria thought. But at the end of his arc, he landed on the transmission tower. The metal began to glow—Cyrus was heating it. As the creature lunged towards him Cyrus leapt away, letting it collide with the tower. The softened transmission tower ensnared it like brambles. As the thing struggled to escape, the ground finally gave way, and the terrible Pipegrinder burst forth in a deafening tremor. It cleaved the earth and clenched its dreadful pincers around the golem's neck.

What a machine! Donny and Maria lowered their guns as they watched the titanic predator in awe. Animal King's ward scrabbled and clawed to escape, but the Pipegrinder didn't budge as it bore down harder, securing its grip. Almost too gigantic to see all of it at once, its legs were like the arm of a bulldozer, with hydraulic actuators as thick as trees, and ended in claws that pulverized soil and rock alike. It dwarfed the demon—its orange shell, in three stout segments like an ant with armoring like a beetle's, made of thick geometric metal plating painted industrial orange. It had to be three times longer than it stood tall. Steam burst from every seam and each joint moaned so earnestly that Maria could feel it resonate in her chest. The shell's surface was crisscrossed with ladders, stairs, hatches, lights, and stenciled markings—it was as if someone had taken apart a fleet of mining and construction vehicles to build an insect capable of razing a city in an afternoon. They were so stricken that they hardly noticed Cyrus alighting behind them.

"Phew!" he sighed, making Donny jump. "Wouldn't wanna be anywhere near all that right now."

"What on earth is that thing?" Donny implored.

"Adhara calls it a Pipegrinder," Cyrus explained. Maria turned, saw him, and jumped too. "It's one of the machines they used to build the Pipeworks. It was just lying down there, dead and buried beneath the city for decades. Until today."

"How are you making it do that?" Donny asked, turning back to the fight.

"I'm not," Cyrus pointed into the air. "These machines are remotely operated drones; I hacked into it and Adhara is controlling it." Sure enough, hovering in the air over the Pipegrinder, Adhara watched intently. "By the way, I figured something out: that thing? Not one of Animal King's monsters. That *is* Animal King. It made itself bigger. Fun fact."

Suddenly a Grimlord reached over the edge of the roof. It screamed, making Donny and Maria recoil. Cyrus lifted a hand and liquefied it.

"Here come the little ones!" Cyrus flipped off the edge of the roof as Maria and Donny readied their guns. They nodded across to Olive and Aliyah and began to turn their cranks—in each of the eight barrels a capacitor whined as it made temporary contact with the magnetron, then discharged after making a full revolution. Once the speed built up, each electromagnetic Gatling gun produced one hundred and twenty focused pulses per minute. The four of them cut through the horde of approaching Grimlords before they could enter the city.

As the fight wore on, Animal King finally gained some leverage against the Pipegrinder and pried the jaws apart before shoving it away. It screeched, an unearthly sound from an unearthly ghoul. The machine returned with its own cry: much louder, and like a tornado siren. It echoed through the mountains. They clashed again; the Grimlord giant struggled against the Pipegrinder and Cyrus as he shot lightning through its chest. Before long it was forced to kneel and the Pipegrinder had the creature in its jaws again, then clamped them around its skull.

Animal King's body contorted, shifting bone and munge to ensnare the Pipegrinder. It heaved the behemoth upwards, bringing it down in a titanic suplex. The Pipegrinder recovered quickly, though, righting itself and approaching again. Animal King swung a fierce right hook—but on impact the bone shattered, and the Pipegrinder was unfazed. It bore down and clamped the skull again, this time driving all six of its legs through Animal King's body and into the ground.

Meanwhile, the foot soldiers had grown overwhelming. Cyrus' friends cranked their guns as fast as they could, but the capacitors could only charge so fast. The Grimlords scrambled up the sides of the buildings. The Pipegrinder clenched the struggling Animal King. Donny and Maria's guns were snatched from their grasps; they looked over to see Olive and Aliyah overwhelmed too. Animal King's skull began to crack. It howled and wailed. The Grimlords tore at Donny and Maria's clothes, their skin; they could feel them biting. Animal King's skull cracked. Then crumbled. The munge liquefied and they cried out as it burned their skin. In the distance, Animal King melted from the Pipegrinder's grip onto the hillside, lifeless at last.

Out of the corner of his eye, Cyrus saw his friends drowning in the munge. His heart jumped and so did he. As he rushed to their aid, he spotted Mystery Man watching calmly from the roof of a nearby building. Just watching.

His friends ended up in the hospital. Multiple contusions, lacerations, aggressive bacterial infection, and chemical burns all over their bodies—not unusual wounds in Hudson City, fortunately. Not suspicious enough for them to be refused treatment, or worse, criminalized.

He should be with them. Instead, they and Adhara had urged him to repair the earthquake damage. Help the people, they'd said. We'll be all right.

So, he was out yet another night, as he had been for countless nights previously, angrily repairing damage he had just recently fixed. Entire buildings torn apart, wiring and pipes ripped from their housing. And why? It all came back to Acryogen.

Acryogen created the Grimlords. Acryogen neglected to destroy the Grimlords and left them where they could be reactivated and threaten the city. Acryogen had the Airshift towers running low. They neglected the water pressure. They neglected the whole city, leaving fires to burn and the rest to decay. Acryogen made the messes. And Cyrus always had to clean them up.

Or rather, it all came back to Mason Smithy. Cyrus thought about Mystery Man. At first the idea of Mason Smithy gallivanting around in a high-tech suit of body armor was just a whimsical notion, but the idea had marinated in his mind and taken hold, attracting pieces of the puzzle like iron filings to a magnet. Now, he could see no other candidate. Who else would wander around the city, destroying things as he pleased? Who else could wield weaponized technology without ever drawing attention from the police and drones? Who else had reason to spy on Cyrus and the indifference to witness senseless destruction without intervening? And, Cyrus realized, Mason Smithy had been mysteriously absent from the public eye for months. He hadn't even been seen since Christmas, when he declared the Alchemist public enemy number one.

And while he was considering candidacy—Anubis was still out there, his narrative perfectly fitting both Mystery Man and Mason Smithy. Who else could it be?

Cyrus was looking for an inventor with a god complex. And he knew where to find one.

Enough was enough. It was time for answers, one way or another. If Mason didn't turn out to be Anubis, at least he would be ruled out. And if he did...Adhara had already told him what would have to be done.

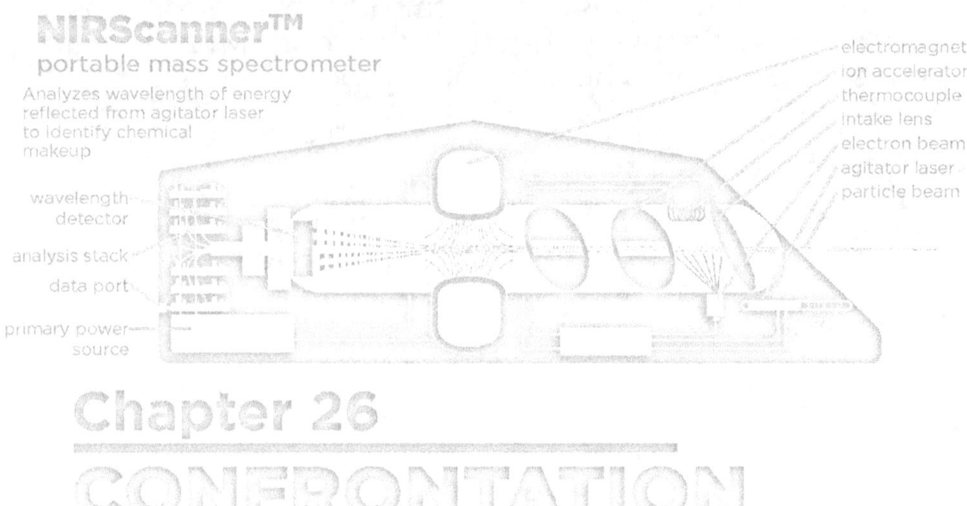

Chapter 26
CONFRONTATION

Cyrus arrived outside Acryogen Industries' corporate headquarters in the early hours after midnight. He had been here a few times before; Acryogen University's corporate offices were in this building, on the lower floors of the triple skyscraper. Mason would be on the upper floors.

He knew from previous visits that the security measures in the headquarters were more thorough than anywhere else in Hudson City, but mostly clustered around the ground-floor entrances. He could see the winking red lights of automated gun turrets perched like gargoyles in the shadows. They would delight in mowing him down before he made it past the lobby. Fortunately, from a former classmate whose mother was in the navy, he knew that there was a secret underwater docking bay, and where to find it.

The headquarters stood in the center of the crescent-shaped city, only a dozen or so yards from the deeper part of the bay which formed a harbor rather than a beach. Cyrus slipped through the shadows to the end of a dock. He paused beneath a dock lamp. By its flashing green light, he checked the seals around his mask and gauntlets. Then he took a deep breath and stepped off the dock, plunging into the water.

He didn't actually need the breath. As one last upgrade before confronting the Industry itself, Cyrus had connected his backpack to the filter cartridges on his gas mask. As soon as he submerged, a miniaturized Lorentz field and electrolysis array began splitting the water molecules, providing him with as much clean oxygen as he needed and refilling his backpack's proton supply from the hydrogen. Cyrus chuckled to himself at his cleverness.

The weight of his equipment dragged him down, and in seconds he touched the bottom of the bay in a cloud of silt. Even after it settled, he couldn't see around him, not even back up to the surface. Although, even in daylight, it was unlikely that the murky water would have allowed much visibility. He had brought a flashlight, of course—but Cyrus had read recently that a certain microwave frequency emitted through saltwater would produce plasma, and he couldn't resist trying it. He entered the frequency and raised his hand tentatively. After a few fizzles and some trial and error, a sputtering flame burst from his palm like a flare.

Hand held high, Cyrus sallied forth. The glowing plasma illuminated only a meter around him, but he knew where he was bound and marched unwaveringly. The sound of his breath filled his ears; all other sounds faded away. After several long minutes his feet found the edge of a drop-off. He pushed off, falling deeper and deeper before his feet found the bottom again. The ground was more rock and sand now and sloped downward. He continued onward and had just started to worry about the depth when a crack suddenly split a lens in his mask. He recoiled backwards as if struck; water forced through the crack and sprayed him in the eye. He panicked and began to claw at the mask as if he could stop the flow by holding his hand, clumsy inside the gauntlet, over the breach. The other lens cracked, and he finally flung his hands outward, pushing the water away behind a force field. He ripped off his mask and fell to his knees in the damp sand to catch his breath.

When he had calmed, he looked around. It was dark again so he couldn't see the water, but he heard it rushing all around him at the edge of his force field, which seemed *so* thin. He slowly stood, shivering. But in the dark he could see something. A distant yellow glow. Hands outstretched to maintain his bubble, he tiptoed forward carefully. As he approached the light and it grew brighter, he realized he had finally found the secret bay.

But as he grew closer still, he realized it was not a docking bay. It was a giant robot, half buried in the silt.

He couldn't help but giggle excitedly.

After sneaking in through a moon pool, relieved to find it deserted, Cyrus sat on a low pipe and took off his equipment so he could wring out his clothes. In this moment, the stress of the past months melted away and all he could see was the humor. He couldn't help but laugh to the empty room. Was the undead army not *enough*? Were the police with street-legal tanks, the weaponized robots and the wall of volcanoes and an artificial hurricane surrounding the city insufficient? They needed a giant robot to guard their secret underwater entrance as *well*? "Talk about overkill!" Cyrus quipped to the empty room. It answered with a pneumatic hiss. Only in Hudson City, Cyrus thought to himself, could things like this become the norm. He wondered, if someone from outside the city visited and saw how they lived...would they be able to stand it?

After Cyrus got dressed again, he hacked into a nearby computer terminal to do some snooping. The sixty-story behemoth he was standing in was indeed a weapon, a last resort in case of military invasion. As he perused the specs, Cyrus exhaled slowly. This thing could rip the Pipegrinder in half without a second thought. Then he snorted when he found the official designation. "*Bigger Brother*."

Cyrus shook his head as he connected the terminal to his gauntlets through a cable, downloading some key pieces of data for later. He was tired of hating Acryogen Industries and Mason Smithy. All he had left was pity. All these resources, all this money and time and so many bright scientists working with him, not to mention his own intelligence, and all Mason could spend it on was bigger guns.

The data finished downloading, and with it he located an elevator and rode it to the penthouse.

Cyrus only had a few minutes to prepare himself before the doors opened again. He stepped out onto a rectangle of light—it grew thinner as the elevator closed again, leaving him in darkness. He was standing in an office room, perhaps some kind of lobby. He could make out the shapes of desks and chairs and twin sofas arranged around a coffee table. It was raining outside, thundering. A flash of lightning revealed a silhouette seated in the center of the room. The figure stood; three lights came on over its face—Mystery Man loomed over him.

"Well, well," said Cyrus quietly. "Why am I not surprised? I always had a feeling that it was you...Mason."

Cyrus waited for a response but was rewarded with only a lingering stare.

"It seems like you've been expecting me," Cyrus continued. "You did a good job trying to criminalize me and make me a scapegoat, use me to shift the blame away from you. But guess what? It didn't work."

No response.

"It backfired, actually! You weren't as stealthy as you thought. The rebellion *knows* about you—they think we're both heroes! Champions of *their* cause!" He was shouting now. "What I can't understand, *Mason*, is *why*? Why would you do this to your own company, your own city? Are you so arrogant that you think you can do whatever you want? Do you get some kind of sick thrill out of manipulating people who trust you? I used to *idolize you!*"

He stepped aggressively toward the unrelenting statue.

"But you don't even know who I am beneath the mask. And it doesn't matter, really—who I was. What matters is that I *became* the Alchemist, and I'll tell you why. I did all of this to *help* people. Because you won't. And maybe you can't. Maybe you're just a cold, selfish old man who does nothing but hurt people."

He stepped forward further, growing more daring. Soon they were face to face.

"You may think that you're *untouchable*, but I know something you don't. I know how this all plays out." Cyrus raised his fists and they burst into flame. "You've devastated the safety of this city and the people who live in it. It's time for you to answer for what you've done."

Cyrus lashed out. His opponent reacted quickly, but not quickly enough. The gauntlets sparked and melted the armored plates, fusing them together. In one fluid movement Cyrus grabbed his shoulders, spun them around, and gripped his chin. He pulled upwards as he kicked off in the center of his back, intending to pull off the mask, but ripping off the entire head as he kicked the body through the opposite wall.

Cyrus dropped the head and recoiled in revulsion. But as he stared, horrified. he realized the broken neck exposed only wiring.The suit was empty? A decoy? He picked up the head again, turning it over—it was a robot. Not a man in a suit. A *robot*?

Cyrus ventured through the hole in the wall to find the body. The adjacent room where it lay was a darkened board room, with an entire wall of windows letting in the colorful light of the city below. Rain pattered on the glass. Cyrus knelt beside the body and rolled it over. Still a robot. Unnervingly familiar.

"Well, you destroyed it," came a voice like honeyed chocolate from the shadows at the end of the room. "Can't say I'm surprised. Though I am impressed by how *easy* it was for you—and I must say, decapitation shows almost uncharacteristic..." he lingered, as if tasting the word, "*ferocity.*"

Cyrus stood. His blood turned to ice.

"Hello, Cyrus." Mason Smithy stood, stepping forward out of the shadows, wearing his trademark smirk.

"You...know who I am?"

"I've *always* known," he chortled in his rich baritone, as though they were sharing a friendly chat. "Oh, you're pretty diligent about your disguise. But your friends?" he sauntered forward, picking up a small stack of files on the table and shuffling through them. "Adonis 'Donny' Theodore Paine?" he read from one. "Aliyah Alexis Vogelstein...Olive Helena Menlo...Maria Rowena Iadanza?" He shook the files as if fanning himself as Cyrus clenched his fists. "Acryogen Industries has files on *all* of them. Some are students. Some are employees. And *all* of them have been caught on surveillance footage committing crimes—some small, and some large...and all can be traced back to *you*. I'll admit," he tutted, "there is *one* girl in your entourage that we never identified, but that's no issue. We knew who the ringleader was from the start."

"Then...why did you never come after me?" Cyrus asked incredulously. "You knew *exactly* where I lived! The headhunting, the house-to-house searches, declaring me as public enemy number one...what was the point?!"

"Well, it made a great excuse to go after the rebellion!" Mason guffawed. "We couldn't get away with searching people's homes and businesses just to see if they're not 'loyal,'" he used air quotes, "to the company. Can you *imagine*? But...if we're looking for a specific person?" His eyes lit up. "Well, people are more accepting of that! We found *hundreds* of radicals thanks to you! Sure, there was some retaliation from the community, but not *nearly* as much as there would have been otherwise."

"How...could you do this?" Cyrus spat, crossing to the window. "Don't you realize what you've done? The city is falling *apart*, tearing itself to pieces! It's on the brink of civil war because of your ego!"

"My ego? Now Cyrus, really." Mason looked genuinely confused. "You've got it all wrong; can't you see that? I've been doing what's best for the city, as I always have. It isn't like this because of me. You did this."

"Come on," Cyrus scoffed. "You can't honestly still be trying that tactic. It won't work on me."

"Now, just listen, Cyrus," said Mason calmly. "I've been running this city since before you were born. People don't like Roadsters patrolling the streets or police searching homes, but they can endure it. They've had to before—maybe you're too young to remember, but the war was a challenging time for everyone."

Cyrus folded his arms.

"What threatens the stability of the city now," Mason continued, "is a series of jarring events that cause damage and unrest. Blackouts without notice or explanation. Pipes bursting across the city. The Airshift towers, which many look to as a symbol of safety, malfunctioning, and causing the weather to be unpredictable for days. An army of Grimlords running rampant through the city."

"Those..." Cyrus shook a finger at Mason, "were not my fault. The Grimlords—"

"Were designed and manufactured by Acryogen Industries, yes!" Mason crowed. "A controversial decision, of course, but what would you have preferred? That I send healthy citizens away from their families, off to war?"

"I realize that!" Cyrus snapped. "But you should have destroyed them, not kept them under the city where they could have gotten loose!"

"As I recall, *you* hacked into our system and activated them," Mason countered. "Every employee who worked in those areas knew the reactivation protocol and how to avoid it. We can debate the ethical ramifications of the entire project at another time, as I already have with each of the shareholders and the city board, but the fact of the matter is that they would have *never* turned on the people of Hudson City by our hand."

"W-well..." Cyrus faltered, "Fine. But—you had the Airshift towers running way too low. Facilities all over the city are being neglected!"

"Oh, I do apologize, sir," Mason chortled. "I didn't realize we had hired you to be an optimization assessor!" He shook his head, his eyes filled with disappointment. "Look, the truth is Cyrus...we're stretched thin. Not enough people, not enough money, too much work. For the sake of priorities, we've had to turn our attention away from some things. Regardless of how *you* believe things should be run, you can't go around flipping an Airshift tower from zero to sixty all of a sudden! That takes *weeks* to adjust! You know those things have fusion reactors in them, don't you?"

"Fine," Cyrus snapped. "If you think I'm a horrible criminal, why haven't you arrested me already?"

"We wanted to see what you'd do," Mason answered. "With those."

"My...gauntlets?"

"Very interesting invention," he nodded. "Amateur invention is illegal in the city, of course. Shame to discourage creativity, but..." he shook his head. "We've had too many fires. But *your* invention could revolutionize chemical engineering; make it so we're not so thin on resources. That's significant enough to turn a blind eye...to a *point*."

"What's so important that you have to divert resources away from the people, anyway?" Cyrus interjected.

"If you must know, we're working on a project. Something big. It's unfortunate that the city has to suffer for it, but if we can bear it for a little while longer...." He nodded at Mystery Man's body on the floor behind Cyrus. "It could change the world. Make life easier for *everyone*."

"What do you..." Cyrus turned to look at the body. "What is that?"

"It's an android; it's got some pretty neat gadgets crammed in it. You tearing it apart is inconvenient, but the body isn't even the best part. And we can repair it, anyway." His eyes twinkled. "This prototype has dozens of other 'brothers,' so to speak. They're all controlled by a super-powered artificial intelligence, broadcast from servers here in this building through a big antenna on the roof."

Cyrus opened his mouth, but no sound came out. His heart was pumping ice.

"I've had that one keep an eye on you; occasionally commit some vandalism of its own to see what you'd do; feel out your intentions. As a test run. They're still a..." he winced. "Work in progress. But when they're done..." his eyes sparkled again, and he grinned. "They'll be like *superheroes*! Indestructible and omnipotent. Flying around and fixing problems, all over the world maybe; saving people. My greatest creation."

"What do you call them?" Cyrus asked quietly.

"Well, the androids themselves each have a long, boring technical designation," Mason answered, furrowing his brow. "The lab boys nicknamed the AI after a star. It was, uh…"

"Adhara," Cyrus whispered.

As he said this, two blinding spotlights shone through the windows. The floor shook with the thrumming of impulsion engines. Two drones, hovering outside the windows, aimed their guns at Cyrus.

"ALL UNREGISTERED WEAPONS AND ENERGY TECHNOLOGY MUST BE DESTROYED."

"I'm sorry, Cyrus!" Mason shouted over the din. "For the record, I always liked you—I see a lot of myself in you! But you've become too much of a threat to my city, and I can't ignore it anymore!"

They heard two thunderous explosions, less than a second apart. The drones fell away from the window as Adhara burst through the glass with a spray of rain in front of Mason. She backhanded him, delivering him a sedative that knocked him unconscious.

"Adhara—" Cyrus spluttered, "I—"

"He was stalling you," she said flatly as she walked over to him. "We need to go, now." She grabbed Cyrus under his arms and jumped back out the window into the rain, falling seven agonizing seconds down the side of the tower before finally firing her jets a few stories above the street. They flew a few blocks to an old subway entrance and slipped back into the Pipeworks.

"I would have been fine!" Cyrus snapped when she finally let him go on the freight platform. "You didn't have to save me."

"Then you don't realize what you just risked," she replied, her voice hard. "I told you Mason Smithy is not Anubis."

"Yeah, well…" Cyrus stammered, "I realize that *now*. But at least we ruled him out!" As many men do, Cyrus buried his wounded pride beneath aggressive reassertion. "Look, I don't know what your *deal* is or what kind of plan you're working on, but *I* say we need to be looking for Anubis! The city is getting more unstable every day—he could appear any day now and take advantage; make things worse than they already are, and I want to be prepared! Unless...you've been lying to me? And there is no Anubis." He scoffed, thinking he'd caught her.

"Anubis is real," Adhara said coldly. "And I know who he is. I always have."

"Then..." Cyrus blinked quickly, confusion building to rage. "Then tell me who he is, instead of leading me on a ridiculous scavenger hunt around the city! Tell me who he is, and I'll go take care of him right *now*!"

Adhara only stared back at him. They passed through a darker section of the tunnel and he could only see her by the glow of her eyes.

"...Tell me who Anubis is, Adhara," he repeated, more quietly.

She still didn't answer. The longer they waited in silence, the harder his heart pounded. A dreadful realization was creeping upon him. The echoing tunnel walls seemed miles wider, vast and empty and ready to swallow him whole.

"Is it—" he whispered. He panted; he couldn't seem to get enough breath out to form words. He could hardly seem to breathe. He was being pulled away, like he was outside his body, watching a stranger from afar.

"It's me."

She nodded. "You have said so."

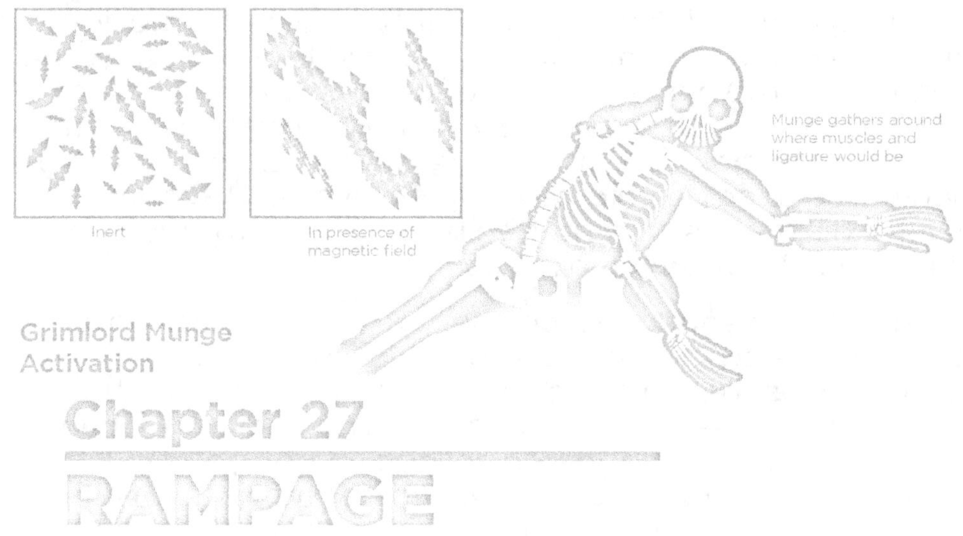

Chapter 27
RAMPAGE

Cyrus didn't remember waking up the next morning. Suddenly he had been lying in bed, staring at his ceiling for hours. The sun had risen long ago but he couldn't have guessed what time it was.

He inhaled, a deep sigh, as though he hadn't taken a breath since the night before. Breathing, blinking, moving—things Cyrus had been avoiding so that he would avoid setting time in motion again. He couldn't bear the past, he dreaded the future, and so he lingered in the present where he could simply exist, without blame or responsibility. His thoughts went to relativity. Time, Cyrus figured, was nothing more than movement, vibration of atoms, and position in space. To stand outside time was to completely stand still. In this single moment, there was nothing more for Cyrus than to stare at the ceiling and think about relativity, trying to remain completely still.

But eventually the breath ended. Cyrus had stopped but time moved on without him. Though he was still, the world moved regardless, and time became the motion of everything else. And try as he might to be unmoved, he was never truly still. He took another breath, a sharp one to steel himself, and rolled out of bed.

Cyrus wandered through his empty house. The previous night, he had texted his friends and told them not to come home from the hospital. He had told them what he had done and why it wasn't safe. Even now, he glanced out the window—he didn't see anyone yet, but he expected Acryogen police to arrive in force at any time now. He couldn't involve his friends with that, so he told them to stay away. He did not tell them who he was.

Who he was—and who *was* he, Cyrus wondered morosely as he lumbered into the bathroom. He looked in the mirror. Who was that, in there? A notorious, mass-murdering supervillain? No—he was the same as he had always been, surely! Just a mild-mannered college student, albeit with a theatrical streak and a proclivity for pyrotechnics. Mere quirks—one of dozens like him in the city. No one special. Certainly not worth singling out above everyone else—not as a threat to the city. Not even as the "chosen one" to save it. Just another citizen.

No, Cyrus decided, Adhara must have made a mistake. Perhaps, he reasoned, by the very *act* of going back in time, she had changed events on the timeline! Yes, that was it! Hadn't she once said that "Time travel has an inexact effect on sequential events?" The things she had described to him from her own timeline didn't match what was happening in his Hudson City. She was wrong, she *had* to be. Perhaps the Cyrus Agrah from her time became a monster, but he wasn't. He wouldn't. He nodded to himself in the mirror, strengthening his resolve before marching downstairs.

This was all just a big misunderstanding, he decided as he poured himself a bowl of cereal. And it wasn't too late to make things right. But as he opened his silverware drawer, he noticed that the spoon he sought was quivering. The milk in his bowl quivered too, and eventually he felt the tremors vibrating up through his feet. He rushed to the window. Coming over the hilltop was an army of Grimlords and police officers, side by side, around a fleet of Roadsters and drones. Mason must have finally found a way to regain control of them. Cyrus rolled his eyes and grumbled, setting his cereal down on the table hard before rushing upstairs to find his gauntlets.

By the time Cyrus had put his suit on and stepped outside, his house was surrounded. Standing at the forefront, directly facing him from across the wide perimeter, was a curious hybrid. It was an Acryogen-made android; there was no mistaking the telltale manufacturing style—another Adhara prototype. Cyrus figured it to be a model one or two generations newer than Mystery Man. But its body had been fused with a Grimlord. The human skull, tiny on the massive shoulders, would have been almost comical if not for its glowing red eyes and pulsating black body.

"Efficient!" Cyrus called. "Combining a combat android with a Grimlord. Best of both worlds, right?" he stepped forward boldly. "You probably figured they would cancel out each other's weaknesses, right Mason?" He looked around as if expecting to find Mason in the crowd, resting his hands condescendingly on sassy hips. "I thought you would have learned by now. I don't *need* weaknesses."

Cyrus slammed his palms into the ground, and from them burst a shockwave that buckled the ground in its wake. A wave of fire followed, melting the asphalt into a field of steaming lava between Cyrus and the mob. When the lava formed a burning moat protecting Cyrus and his house,

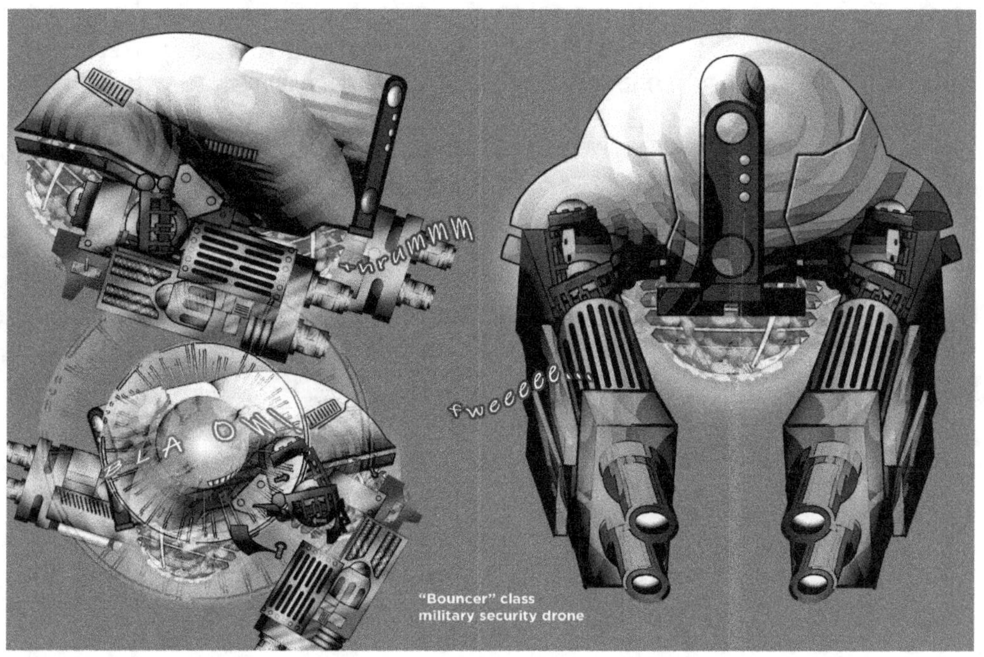

he stood again, daring his opponents to approach. From the back of the crowd, a group of drones rose, aiming their lasers and guns at him.

He swept his gaze over the crowd. The Grimlords' twisted expressions remained neutral, and most of the police officers wore riot helmets over their faces, but the ones who didn't looked terrified. He could see them looking back and forth between the lava and Cyrus' gauntlets, murmuring amongst themselves, holding their ground but finding it increasingly difficult. There was one thing he knew that kept them from fleeing—the pain and hatred he could see in their eyes. Though he was only defending himself, they looked at him like he was a monster.

"Put down the weapons," said a police officer with a bull-horn. "And you won't be harmed."

Cyrus scoffed.

Aiming his palm at each of them, he released a burst of energy that sent the drones spiraling. The crowd scattered to avoid them as they fell to the ground and each crashed into a fiery heap. Cyrus raised his arms, inviting their next gambit.

The Grimlord hybrid stepped forward, walking slowly across the river of fire. Its feet hissed with each step and sank to the ankle; its black body distorted through the rippling waves of heat. But those beady red eyes still shone, never wavering from Cyrus. When it stepped back into solid ground its feet reformed from the damage. It leered down at Cyrus, watching him and waiting silently as the crowd did.

"I have to say, I preferred Animal King's golems, Mason." Though it loomed a full meter over him, Cyrus looked the hybrid up and down and scoffed. "This...Grim Hybrid...lacks a certain elegance. It's clumsy. Feels like you sacrificed craftsmanship in desperation."

The Grim Hybrid's eyes flashed and it lunged forwards—Cyrus felt a jab of rage and he pushed it back with a brief force field. Its feet skidded, digging into the ground and leaping forwards again as soon as Cyrus released it. He calibrated his gauntlets for maximum gravity distortion, then spun around and caught the Grim Hybrid with a backhand that sent it tumbling back into the lava. The shockwave, like a clap of thunder, echoed off the empty houses.

As his opponent leapt back into battle, Cyrus beat it away over and over, growing more furious with each thundering blow. *Just* as he had decided to turn things around, Mason had to send an army after him. Clap. Mason had made his *own* demons. He just couldn't live with the consequences. Clap. With the unrest of the people. Of course, people would be angry and fight back! Clap! Cyrus hadn't founded the rebellion; Mason's failings were only catching up to him! *Clap*! And he had the *nerve* to try and blame Cyrus! Ca-CLAP!

Cyrus' devastating one-two punch sent the Grim Hybrid flying into the crowd—its body crushed two police officers beneath it and absorbed them, growing larger. The other officers backed away in horror. It was time to stop toying with this thing and take it out. As it rose up again, munge writhing furiously around its twisted metal workings, Cyrus tried an EMP—the Grim Hybrid deformed momentarily but kept coming. A stronger magnetic field, and probably shielding, Cyrus realized. But what if that magnetic field was too strong for its own good?

Cyrus beat the Golem back again and while it scrambled to its feet, Cyrus reached out and plucked a smaller Grimlord from the crowd with gravity, frying it with a quick EMP then flinging the pile of munge and bones towards the Grim Golem. It was absorbed immediately, and the Golem grew taller. It howled and lunged for him again.

Again and again Cyrus beat the Golem back and threw another deactivated Grimlord at it, and with each body added the monster grew taller and more bulbous. And, Cyrus noted smugly, clumsier. After Cyrus missed a Grimlord and accidentally flung a police officer, the Grim Golem had lost its original agility, reduced to a gurgling, lumbering mass. And it was massively engorged—Cyrus leapt into the air to avoid the flailing arms, now thick as trees. From his midair vantage point, Cyrus produced a gravity well under the Golem. Most of the officers escaped the pull, but the Grimlords fell into the amorphous blob. Cyrus shot a final EMP into the munge, destroying all the smaller units, and touched down beside it.

Cyrus released the gravity well, but the Grim Golem remained immobile. The weight of the additional munge was too much for it. Cyrus stepped around it, facing the crowd. As they watched he raised his hand and snapped his fingers—the quivering munge behind him erupted into burning plasma.

"You're no match for me!" Cyrus shouted as the officers stared, transfixed by the fire. "If you try to fight me now, the cost will be higher than it's worth. Leave," he ordered. "Regroup. Come back with something stronger." Cyrus retreated to his front steps and sat, calmly watching while the officers retreated to their Roadsters and vans and left with their army of Grimlords.

Long after the army had gone, as the sun was setting, Cyrus' bravado faded. Who was he kidding, he thought as he stared at the debris from the battle. Maybe he wasn't the Anubis that Adhara had known. But how could he deny he was a menace to the city? He was out of control. He'd always had good intentions, but Mason had been right—his actions had hurt people. And he'd never truly considered the consequences seriously.

Cyrus trudged back inside and gasped in despair at the state of his house. The shockwaves and tremors he'd made in the battle had rebounded on the structure; the walls and floors had deep cracks, some of the lights had fallen from the ceiling, and a layer of dust coated every surface. The picture of his parents that hung in the foyer had fallen, and it lay on the floor surrounded by its broken glass. Cyrus carefully picked his way through the rubble into the kitchen. He sat at the table, sighing deeply and staring at his forgotten bowl of cereal, now soggy and filled with sawdust.

Was redemption even possible, at this point? Was he too far gone? Cyrus wanted desperately to make things right. To do something good for the city, as he'd always meant to. But since Adhara abandoned him, and the reputation he had, he wasn't sure what he…

Maria. Cyrus clapped a hand to his forehead. Of course, Maria. His best friend for so long, his only family, who was kinder than anyone he knew, so selfless, and idolized Norman Borlaug, of all people! She'd been the answer the whole time, right under his nose—he had been so concerned with Adhara's talk of destiny and saving the city. He had almost ignored the project Maria had been working on with Aliyah, even when she had asked for his help. Cyrus felt tears well up in his eyes from a wave of remorse and self-loathing. He didn't know if she would even accept his help; he'd let her down so many times. But now, she might be his last chance to do the right thing.

He looked at his hands and nodded to himself slowly. No more Alchemist. No more Anubis.

Cyrus unfastened his gauntlets, throwing them and his mask on the table before dashing out the door.

Cyrus made his way carefully to the address Maria had texted him, inviting him to visit if ever he processed what he was going through. Cyrus marveled at her undeserved patience as he ducked through alleys and lingered in doorways, avoiding police patrols enforcing the curfew. The city really had become a rough place. Garbage and remnants of riots littered the street, some still burning, and his or Mystery Man's graffitied likeness adorned secluded corners. Cyrus could hear distant sirens, shouting, then gunfire. He pulled his hood forward and hurried along.

Fortunately, the closer he got to Maria's new apartment, the fewer police he saw. He remained in the shadows, however, hoping to avoid the attention of any overhead drones. He arrived at the last turn before her building and stopped for a moment to catch his breath and rehearse what he was going to say— "Sorry" didn't quite capture the magnitude of his penitence. He would need to be armed with stronger proclamations to make up for his lack of appreciation. He took a deep breath, muttering to himself nervously, but with hope beating in his chest. Hope of a second chance.

Cyrus turned the corner to flickering firelight. At first, he expected more burning garbage, but his eyes widened as he found Maria's entire apartment building ablaze. The fire crackled quietly, like that in a cozy fireplace, as Cyrus ran up and down the street, calling, screaming for help. But no one came. He looked down at his empty hands and sank to his knees, crying and beating his bare fists on the ground, as the building collapsed.

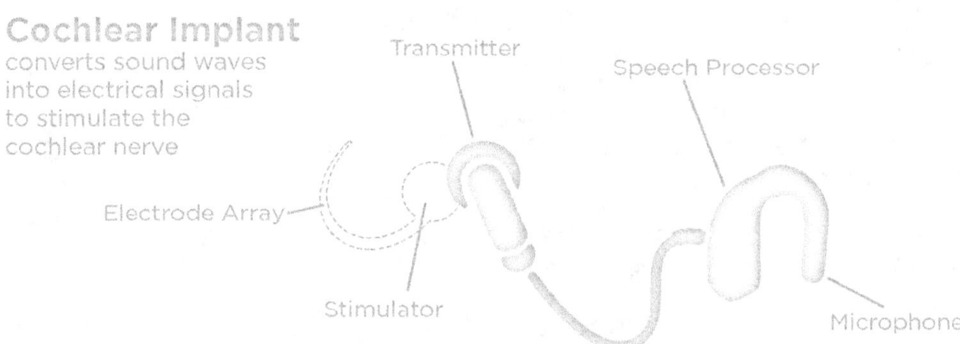

Chapter 28
DEVASTATION

"Cyrus?"

He whirled. Olive came down the stairs. He turned back to the floor.

"Cyrus," she repeated. She was sitting next to him on the freight platform. "I came as soon as I heard. I'm so sorry."

"Are you?" he asked quietly, then fell silent again.

"What...happened to your house?"

"I destroyed it," he looked to the top of the stairs where sunlight was streaming in. "If they came back...I wanted them to think I was gone."

"You mean...Acryogen?"

He nodded.

"Cyrus, I don't know what to say." She was crying. "This is all my fault. I know you must blame me. If I hadn't taken you to see the rebels, you wouldn't have gone after Mason, and Maria and Aliyah would...would never have..." her words became lost in her sobs.

"No," said Cyrus, quietly but firmly. "I don't blame you."

"You..." she took a shuddering breath and cleared her throat. "You don't?"

"No," he repeated. "The fire killed everyone in the building. Twenty-three people. If it hadn't been Maria, it would have been someone else."

"What's that?" she nodded to the smartphone he was turning over in his hands.

"It was hers," he whispered. "She forgot it...in her bicycle basket. So, it survived." He turned the phone on and began scrolling through her photos, then handed the phone to Olive. She browsed the photos then looked up at Cyrus.

"I remember this," she said quietly. "This...was when we built the fusion reactor. And we had that picnic." She scrolled to the next picture. "And this, it's when we had Christmas in your room." She blinked a tear away.

"Maria always wanted a family," Cyrus sighed. "And all she had for a long time was me. Sorry excuse." He shook his head bitterly.

"But *look* at these!" she exclaimed, scrolling through the photos. "At least...it seems like she did have a family. For a little while... Cyrus, I know we haven't known each other long. But she loved you."

"I suppose it's only fitting. Her last day is the day I finally appreciate that."

Olive looked down, turning the phone off and handing it back to him. "Do they...know what started it?"

"Ruptured gas line. From lack of maintenance."

Olive nodded slowly. "Just another accident."

Cyrus exhaled shortly through his nose. "If you can call it that."

"What do you mean?"

"I *waited*, Olive." He stared at the ground. "I waited and *watched* as the building burned. As it collapsed. Do you want to guess how long it took for the fire drones to arrive?"

She shook her head.

"Forty minutes. I counted." He shook his head grimly. "By the time they got there, the fire was almost out."

"I..." Olive looked down at his hands. He was wearing his gauntlets again. "Were...your gauntlets not working?"

"They were working perfectly. I could have saved her." He sighed bitterly, gritting his teeth. "I left them...I left them at home when I went to visit her."

"But...why?"

"I thought that I needed to leave this life behind." He looked up, finally meeting her eyes. "Now I see that I've only just started."

A shadow passed over the staircase. Adhara looked down from the hatch.

"Come back here tomorrow, at sunset," Cyrus muttered to Olive. She nodded, wiping her eyes, and passed Adhara on the stairs.

"Why are you here?" he called to Adhara when Olive had gone.

"I know you must be angry with me," she said quietly. "I can't imagine what you're going through."

"No. You can't."

"Cyrus..." she tried to rest her hand on his shoulder, but he brushed her off. She let out a gentle sigh and sat near to him, maintaining a respectful distance.

"...I know," she began, "that there is nothing I can say that will ease the pain right now." She folded her hands and kept her gaze low. "And I realize that I am in no position to empathize, having never experienced the kind of loss you're suffering." She glanced over at him, but he didn't respond.

"Though I can't offer empathy, what I can offer is sympathy," she continued, "as much as you need for as long as you need it. And perhaps," she glanced over again, "If you'll allow me...I can offer some perspective that may give you some comfort."

He didn't reply—but he didn't stop her, so she continued.

"When you love someone, you accept the price that comes with it…which is, that you will experience pain, equal in magnitude to the love you had for them, when they're gone. At first all you can feel is the pain. And it's agony. But in time…the pain fades, and you can remember the love again. Though they're gone, and you mourned for them, one day the love will make those memories happy again." She smiled softly at Cyrus, who had turned away.

"But for now, I know all you can feel is the pain," she said soothingly. "And that pain, from love, is what Maria deserves. She deserves to be mourned. So for now, I'll just sit here with you. And we'll be sad together for as long as you want."

Cyrus finally unclenched his jaw. He let out a deep, shuddering sigh and his eyes welled with tears. They rolled down his cheeks, slowly at first. He sobbed into Adhara's shoulder, gripping her hand tightly. His quiet sobs echoed off the tunnel walls, mingling with the distant sound of cicadas and wind through the trees from the hole above. Eventually his breathing evened; the tears stopped. Cyrus pulled away, wiping his eyes and rubbing his face.

"I feel…almost serene," he murmured. "At peace. I feel like I haven't had this kind of calm in…years."

"Crying releases stress hormones, which provides a feeling of tranquility."

"I suppose it does," he murmured. "It's strange…I feel so free. I finally know exactly what I have to do."

His gauntlets buzzed; Cyrus flung his hand towards Adhara, throwing her off the freight platform and embedding her into the wall of the cavern.

"Cyrus!" she exclaimed. "What are you doing?"

"Too many people have died because of Acryogen's negligence, just like Maria did," said Cyrus as he approached her. "I'm going to avenge her. And I'm going to make sure their suffering ends by taking out Acryogen once and for all— starting with you." He nodded darkly. "I know they made you. They sent you back in time to stop me from taking them down, by tricking me into thinking I'm 'the chosen one.'"

"Cyrus, please stop this. Let me explain."

He raised his hand. In the palm he produced a ball of blinding, concentrated energy, like a fallen star. Its light threw his face into sharp relief. "I'm done being manipulated by Acryogen."

As he reached for her face, Adhara surged forward, deflecting his arm and making him fling the fallen star into the far wall. The explosion collapsed half the tunnel as she gripped his gauntlet, eyes glowing in her hard, merciless face. She ripped the gauntlet from his arm and bent it in half, cast the mangled heap aside then shoved him away. She blasted up through the ceiling, leaving him on the ground, looking up through the hole and squinting in the new patch of sunlight.

"Hey...Cyrus?" At sunset the next day, as promised, Olive returned, and carefully came down the stairs as she regarded the piles of rubble. "What happened here? Where's Adhara?"

"She attacked me," said Cyrus, not looking up. "But only because I attacked her first."

"What? *Dude*, why on earth?"

"I discovered that Adhara was...made by Acryogen Industries. By Mason," he muttered. "He'd been manipulating me this whole time."

"Acryogen...of course." Olive's face hardened and she shook her head. "It...all comes together. I'm so sorry." When he didn't respond, she added, "You've been busy." She nodded at his hands—the gauntlets were twice as thick as they had been before, armored and reinforced. He was modifying the helmet Adhara had forbidden him from using, with the bispectral imaging system, upgrading it with various filters and sensors.

"I've been using parts I salvaged from the Pipegrinder. I think I'll be a match for anything Acryogen can throw at me."

"So, you have a plan," she nodded approvingly as he slipped the helmet over his head. "How can I help?"

"Take me to the rebellion headquarters," he answered, activating the helmet. The triple lights over his eyes glowed, and he saw Olive in shades of infrared. He switched the input back to visible light and her familiar face returned. "I'll need their help. It's time to put an end to Acryogen's reign of terror." The helmet distorted his voice—the built-in amplifier must have been damaged, making his voice sound unnaturally deep and garbled.

"They'll like that news," she nodded, then squinted at him. "Anu...bis?"

"What?" He turned to her sharply. "What did you call me?"

"I...I'm sorry," she pointed at his head, taken aback. "I was just reading the side of your helmet. Authorized Naval Use, Bispectral Imaging System. ANU-BIS."

"Oh. I..." Cyrus' thoughts drifted. Then he snapped back to the present, nodded and said, "Let's go."

As Olive led him back to the rebellion's hideout, Cyrus saw the pieces fitting together and wondered: could he ever have escaped his destiny? Was Adhara's mission futile from the start? He had never been forced into anything, and yet... left to his free will, he had followed a hauntingly similar path. Was he simply a case of self-fulfilling prophecy? Or was there, after all, something immutable about the flow of time? If that were true...it meant he had made this choice before. And he would make it again, if given the chance to do it over. For something so significant to be constant, Cyrus believed...there had to be a very good reason.

They made their way to the hideout in a daze which Cyrus didn't wake from until they were at the door. They were again allowed entry, and before long, Keith came to meet them.

"Hello again," he greeted them breathlessly. "You...look different. Like him." Keith pointed to the mural of Mystery Man.

"You shouldn't have put your faith in him," said Cyrus coldly. "He was nothing but an android made by Acryogen."

"Really?" Keith stepped back, intimidated by Cyrus' voice. "Well, that's...certainly a surprise. And of course, disappointing. But are you...?"

"Yes," Cyrus interjected. "I've come to lead your people to liberation."

"That's excellent news. What do you need?"

"I need to address everyone."

Keith led Cyrus toward the big stage in the main room, all the while spreading the word to gather. By the time Keith and Cyrus took the stage, everyone in the rebellion had crowded into the vast warehouse floor—Cyrus estimated close to four or five hundred.

"I'll introduce you," Keith whispered, covering a microphone with his hand, "then you can take the stage. Should I just call you 'the Alchemist?' or—"

"No," Cyrus interjected. He leaned forward and whispered in Keith's ear. He nodded and uncovered the microphone.

"Brothers and sisters!" Keith cried. "For too long we have wasted away, struggling to even survive against Acryogen's tyranny." The crowd booed and hissed, and some shook their fists. "Too long have we not been able to resist their injustice! But now, everything will change, my friends! It is with joy and hope that I introduce a man who needs no testament to his capabilities, who is here to lead us *out* of the darkness and into *liberation*. Please join me in welcoming our powerful and fearless new leader: *ANUBIS!*"

Keith handed the microphone to Cyrus. As Cyrus stepped to the front of the stage, the crowd chanted:

"ANUBIS! ANUBIS! ANUBIS! ANUBIS!"

Chapter 29
STOCKPILE

"You have waited patiently for a revolution," Cyrus began, and he could see the crowd recoil. His voice, distorted already from the mask, sounded demonic through the microphone. He waited for them to calm before resuming. "In three days...I will destroy Acryogen Industries."

The crowd's apprehension faded as they burst into stoic applause. Some nodded their approval, while others thrust their fists into the air.

"I have a confession to make to you," he continued, "I want our relationship to be founded in trust, because I know Acryogen has broken yours so many times. I am...*was* an employee of Acryogen."

They murmured uncertainly, and Cyrus could see disapproval flash across some faces. But they permitted him to continue.

"More specifically, I was a graduate student, working in a research and development lab—and I used to think that I was so lucky for that. You see, I used to admire Acryogen. In fact, you might have said, at one time, Mason Smithy was like an idol to me—as a scientist I aspired to be like him. There's a lot to admire, I admit," Cyrus confessed, holding his hand out conversationally. "Acryogen has achieved remarkable things—artificial intelligence, weaponry…their impulsion technology alone has revolutionized transportation in this city!" His audience grumbled their reluctant agreement. "They've molded the very earth and sky like clay. These are great feats; there's no denying it. But…does the good outweigh the bad?"

Now he had their attention. They knew the answer already—but their excitement was palpable for how he would arrive at it.

"Do their drones make up for the fires that plague our city?" he asked. "Do flying cars and advanced robotics give them the right to make decisions for our city without us?"

"*No!*" they shouted.

"Do clever ideas and efficient manufacturing excuse them for prioritizing their private projects over the people in need, like *you*?"

"*NO!*"

"The greatest intelligence in the *world* does *not* compensate for *lack of moral fiber!*" Riled, the crowd cheered affirmation.

"You may be wondering," Cyrus continued as the enraptured silence returned. "Why I've chosen to join you now? And why *Anubis*?" he paced across the stage. "I'm ashamed to confess…the reason for my timing is… selfish." His voice lowered. Still audible, but grim. "Recently, I lost someone close to me. Some of you may have heard of the most recent fire the other night, which destroyed an entire apartment building and with it, twenty-three people. Including someone I loved." Cyrus scanned their faces. Some held his gaze, but most looked to the floor.

"I can tell by your faces…that you have all been touched by the callousness of Acryogen. This fire, like so many others, was preventable. But accidents happen; fires happen in any city. But Acryogen's *response*, their chance to make it *right*—" his voice was rising, and with it, the agitation of the crowd, "was *too late* to make a difference!" Cyrus shook his head, angrily pacing.

"I believe that if you have *power*, if you have the ability to help people and do good, then with that power comes an obligation. A responsibility. Acryogen has neglected that responsibility. They have neglected *us*." A scattering of applause punctuated the accusation. "Since they've neglected the responsibility of their power," he raised his hands, presenting his gauntlets, "I must accept responsibility of my own. They have used their power and resources to oppress you and keep you down, but now they face an opponent with power to rival *theirs*!" For effect, he made snapping arcs of electricity leap from his fingertips to light fixtures high above, entrancing his audience.

"I chose the name Anubis for the ancient Egyptian god of judgment, judgment which Acryogen has escaped for too long. But it's time for change. The time has come," Cyrus declared, "for the powerful to be held accountable. It's time that their abuse of our patience and subservience be rectified! It's *time*!" Cyrus thrust his fist in the air as he had seen them do. "For them to face *judgment* for their sins."

The crowd roared, standing and shaking their fists. Cyrus dropped the microphone and walked away. He found Keith with the other rebellion leaders and began to give instructions for his plan.

"Mister, ah, uh...Anubis? Sir?" Cyrus turned away from the workspace they had set up for him in the basement. A young man was waiting awkwardly on the stairs. They stared at each other expectantly.

"Yes?" Cyrus asked finally.

"There's a, uh..." he gestured limply. "Visitor. For you. We told him you were busy but he's insisting."

"What does he look like?"

"It's me, Cyrus," came Donny's irritated voice. "Tell your goons to let me through."

"It's fine, let him in." Cyrus waved his hand and turned back to his work.

"I see you've finally gone and lost your mind," Donny began sternly. Cyrus glanced back at him and saw that he was still healing from the chemical burns. "I saw what you did to your parents' house, and your fight with the police was on the news. And now you've joined the rebellion!" But his nerve faltered as he approached the center of the room, from which emitted the only light.

Cyrus had drawn a series of complex polygons on the ground with charcoal, a few meters in diameter, like the graphics on his gauntlets but more elaborate. They formed a boundary around a swirling pool of chartreuse fluid, casting the room into eerie shades, spiraling inwards towards a central nexus. Donny could just make out spiraling rectangular shapes in the centers, glowing brilliantly white. Cyrus stepped carefully around the ring, adjusting the brew with energy from his gauntlets.

"What...is that?"

"It's a transmutation array," Cyrus answered. "The gauntlets read the symbols as instructions."

"And what...are you making?"

"I'm bombarding an isotope of bismuth with neutrons to make polonium-210. It's nuclear fuel."

"Why do you need nuclear fuel, Cyrus?" The edge to his voice returned, but it was colder now, more uneasy.

Cyrus finally turned to him, unreadable under his mask. "I have a plan," he answered simply.

"And that," Donny nodded to a corner of the room, which contained crates labelled "explosive," pressure tanks, and enormous bullets over half a meter wide, partially hidden beneath a tarp. "Is all of that for your 'plan' too?"

"Yes," Cyrus answered, unapologetic, turning back to his isotopes. "Depleted uranium bullets and astatine-213 powder to coat them with, and an explosive propellant. The propellant was tricky to make—it's a nitration of hexamine in the presence of acetic anhydride, paraformaldehyde and ammonium nitrate." He nodded at the modest stockpile. "I realize you can't appreciate the complexity of the chemicals, but it helps me to review these things verbally. Each bullet should be able to level a building."

"Level a *building*...?" Donny stared, dumbfounded. Cyrus, unfazed, crossed to the far side of his glowing pool, waving his hands at it soothingly. "What could you *possibly* need that kind of firepower for?"

Cyrus looked up slowly. "I face an insurmountable enemy. I won't have a second chance—I need to be prepared." He looked down again. "Besides, I've only just gotten started."

"Clearly. On top of that, you need an army, too?" Donny flicked his head towards the stairs. "I see that you've replicated your gauntlets for all your radical buddies."

"I just taught them how to build a basic version. Like Maria's, they can make fire and EMPs, but these...can also freeze," Cyrus explained quietly. "They will need to be able to defend themselves in the coming fight."

"Cyrus, this is a fight you *don't* need to have," Donny pleaded. "I *know* you're hurting after Maria's death."

Cyrus turned to him sharply but didn't respond.

"And I *know* it's easier to channel all your anger into blaming Acryogen and taking revenge on them. I don't like Acryogen either! You *know* that! I never told you, but even since Christmas, I've attended peaceful protests! I defended you! But starting a war won't make things better. 'Violence for violence is the rule of beasts!'"

"Ah, Donny," Cyrus said calmly." You always did have a dramatic streak."

Donny sighed bitterly. "You're one to talk."

"Would you like to see what else I'm working on?" Cyrus led Donny to a nearby table and picked up two handles which were attached to spindly framing, like the wireframe of a sword. He attached one to the corresponding gauntlet and raised it high. The gauntlet hummed, and shining crystals grew from the frames until they formed a short yet broad translucent saber. Donny covered his ears at a shrill whistle which grew higher in pitch as the blade glowed red, then orange, then pale yellow. Donny stepped back as Cyrus lowered the blade, and arcs of electricity snapped from its edges to the ground and through the table. The air smelled of metal and seared meat.

"I call this a conductor blade," Cyrus explained. "It's made of palladium micro-alloy glass, but—" a particularly harsh bolt of electricity snapped through the blade, cracking it. Cyrus powered down his gauntlet and the rest of the glass crumbled onto the floor. "The molecular structure isn't stable yet; I haven't finished calibrating it. But when it's done, it will be able to conduct as much electricity as a lightning bolt and reach...somewhere around 2,800 degrees Celsius. If my math is right, it will even phase through some metals."

Cyrus set the conductor blade handle back on the table and raised the other handle. Having connected this handle to the other gauntlet, it began to hum immediately, and a metallic liquid dribbled across the framing. It warped to form a smooth, slim blade, and with a burst of mist it solidified. A constant stream of heated vapor escaped from the gauntlet. The blade emitted quiet crackles, like ice cubes rubbing against each other.

"I call this one a shear blade," Cyrus continued, turning the sword over so it caught the light. "It's made of mercury, if you can believe that. It's cooled to just above absolute zero; the gauntlets have to constantly divert heat from it. I still haven't gotten it as cold as I want, and when it shatters—" he broke the sword against the table leg. The broken pieces, like sheets of frost, quickly melted back into shiny pools of mercury. But as Donny watched, the broken end of the sword began to reform. "It reforms slowly. Too slowly for combat." He placed the sword back on the table and the whole blade melted. "I'm also intending to make some armor—aggregated diamond nanorod is promising, but I'll save that until later."

"Classic Cyrus," said Donny. "You always do this. When you can't cope with what's going on around you, you just throw yourself into your work and shut out the rest of the world."

"That's worked out pretty well for me so far," Cyrus shrugged. "Besides, I'm not shutting out the world. I'm trying to save it."

"Save it?" Donny laughed. "*Save* it? You call—you think all of this will *save* the city?"

"I don't expect you to understand." Cyrus crossed back over to his green pool, guiding tendrils of escaping fluids back into the vortex. "I don't expect thanks or appreciation. But when I'm done, this city will be a better place. The negatives of Acryogen's existence outweigh the positives—without them, we can start over. We can rebuild and do better."

"And what will that *cost*?" Donny snapped. "Destroying half the city? *Thousands* of lives? And by the end of it, your *soul*? Don't you see, Cyrus? You've become exactly what Adhara warned you about."

"Adhara *lied*."

"Maybe so," Donny admitted, his voice breaking, "But you're not in your right mind, Cyrus. Please, see that. You're *grieving*, and I know that because *I'm grieving too*. I lost my *sister* that night, Cyrus! You're so obsessed that you missed Maria and Aliyah's funeral!"

Cyrus said nothing for a few moments. "I know," he said quietly. "I'm sorry. But I couldn't...face her. Not until I made it right."

"You think this will make it *right*?" Donny repeated in a low voice. "Maria would be *disgusted* by what you're planning."

"Maybe you didn't know her as well as I did," Cyrus turned away. "And if you're not willing to go to the lengths that I am to avenge their deaths, maybe you didn't love them as much as I did."

"*How dare you say—*" Donny spat, starting forward, but he stepped back when Cyrus clenched his fists, making his gauntlets whine menacingly.

“You should leave town tonight,” Cyrus suggested, relaxing. “Tomorrow, it won't be safe anymore for people who aren't ready to embrace change.”

Chapter 30
ANUBIS

The next morning, from atop the tallest mountain Cyrus could see the city below. It was still in shadow as the sun rose from the far side of the expansive wasteland outside the city. He had been up for hours already, disintegrating blocks of cast aluminum and iron into powder to fill the bottom of the mountains' craters with thermite, but it wasn't until the sunrise that he felt the gravity of the day. This day. Somehow, it didn't feel like he had expected it to. He had been building up to this point, this apex of his destiny, for so long, and now...it was almost anticlimactic. After adjusting his diamond nanorod armor under his clothes, Cyrus removed his helmet and sat on the edge of the crater, watching the clear morning dawn.

The city looked so peaceful from up here, Cyrus thought to himself. Was it right of him, he wondered, to disrupt that peace, and throw the city into chaos? He wondered if he were doing the right thing—how history would remember him. *Had* he become the Anubis that Adhara had warned him about so long ago?

And yet, Adhara had taught him an important lesson. "There are always growing pains that come with change." Human beings don't like change, as is their nature—but the alternative is stagnation and eventually death. To survive and move forward fell on the shoulders of those brave enough to face the unknown—and brave enough to face the hatred of his or her fellow man.

Growing pains. It was okay to be afraid, Cyrus told himself. As long as he was doing what he knew, in the end, was for the best. And to that end, sacrifice was inevitable.

He put his helmet back on.

With a snap of his fingers, Cyrus ignited the thermite. The fizzling flames followed trails to the other mountains, and in less than an hour the mountain range was engulfed in fire. A few more minutes and the thermite started to melt through the rock, and streams of lava pushed out of the craters and began to run down the mountainside towards the city.

In a single bound, Cyrus leapt from the mountaintops over to the master AirShift tower, landing at its base.Glancing up occasionally to watch the lava's progress, he hacked into the AirShift system and sent it into overdrive. The towers wailed. High above, the dark clouds swelled, fed by the noxious fumes billowing from the reawakened volcanoes. The storm spread towards the bay, slowly closing its eye over the city. As its shadow passed over him, Cyrus leapt into the air again, high enough to hear a murmur of thunder before landing just outside an entrance to the Pipeworks.

The freight platform waited for him just inside the tunnels, laden with his astatine-coated uranium bullets and other weaponry. The platform took him towards the center of the city. He finished mounting his shear blade and conductor blade, to his left wrist and right wrist respectively, as he sped through the tunnels, passing some that were already filling with lava.

He finished mounting the retractable blades as the freight platform stopped, just beneath the city square. Cyrus unloaded the bullets and propellant, and in a small, latched metal container, the polonium-210, which he clipped to his belt. He left an explosive, like an over-sized pipe bomb, on the freight platform. When he had finished unloading his stockpile, he covered the bomb with a tarp and sent the platform through the tunnels towards Acryogen headquarters. After watching it disappear, he reversed the gravity around him, levitating himself and his weapons up to the surface.

The city square was deserted, but Cyrus could hear the fallout siren echo through the empty streets. That was good—most people will have evacuated or be taking shelter. Fewer innocent lives lost this way. And by now, the members of the rebellion equipped with gauntlets would be in position.

Cyrus felt the explosion before he saw it, and he turned to Acryogen headquarters, the triple towers looming in the distance. A pillar of fire burst from the top of the middle tower. Cyrus smiled as the clouds closed in, watching his plan come together. Then he frowned as a blast of energy shot past him, missing his head by centimeters. He turned calmly to see a Bouncer drone looming behind him.

"ALL UNREGISTERED WEAPONS AND ENERGY TECHNOLOGY MUST BE DESTROYED."

"I am getting *really* tired of hearing that," Cyrus muttered as he raised his hand.

A red bubble of fire formed in his palm, swelling to the size of a softball before bursting. The splatter hit the drone and began to hiss, burning through its shell in seconds before the drone darkened and fell to the ground. Silence returned for a few moments until three more drones followed, emerging from over and around buildings. Dodging their bullets, Cyrus spat a bubble of fire at each of them, dropping one after another as the Bouncer drones kept coming. Eventually Cyrus grew impatient and he thrust his hand to the sky.

The conductor blade erupted out of his wrist, perfect and glassy, and from it shot a bolt of electricity into the clouds. There was a deep rumble, and the electricity returned in a massive lightning strike, which rebounded from Cyrus' hand through the remaining drones. They fell to the ground smoking and at last, Acryogen seemed to have run out of Bouncer drones. But with a squeal of tires, a Roadster appeared on the other side of the square. The back doors opened; guns protruded. Its engine roared. "Level two," Cyrus smirked, and leapt into the air.

After a terrific midair cartwheel, Cyrus came down on the Roadster, reversing his gravitational field at the last second and crushing it beneath him. Cyrus heard a sharp patter of gunfire behind him—another Roadster had arrived behind him and wisely opted to open fire without hesitation. He sidestepped then flipped behind the Roadster he had just crushed. He grabbed the bumper, and from his fingertips a wave of fire swept over the surface of the metal, leaving it warped and crackling. With a boost from his gauntlets, he kicked the Roadster skidding across the lot. On contact the burning car fused to the other, giving Cyrus an opening to rush forward and use his shear blade to cut the guns off.

Two more Roadsters pulled into the lot, larger than the sedans. One opened its back doors and fired a rocket at him, but the rocket stopped in Cyrus' outstretched hand and grew cold as he transmuted it into lead. He flipped the leaden rocket in midair, and with a snap of his fingers sent it back, hurtling so fast that it plowed through both Roadsters and disappeared into a building on the other side. Then the ground shook, so violently that Cyrus jumped and almost fell on his knees. He turned and back-flipped just in time to avoid a gigantic robot's arm driving into the pavement.

Now things were getting interesting, Cyrus thought, as the robot retracted its arm. He recognized the model—fifteen meters tall, covered in swiveling turrets, humanoid but reminiscent of a horseshoe crab. Acari drones were distinctive. They were used frequently during the war, but never since. As two more landed from the sky, flanking him, Cyrus smirked. If they were sending guns this big and old after him, they were growing desperate. All according to plan.

In perfect coordination the Acari took aim at him, but Cyrus pushed them back with twin shockwaves from each palm. He jumped onto the nearest, driving the shear blade through its brain and breaking the mercury off inside, and released a wave of oxidization for good measure. As another swiped, he flipped backwards and embedded the conductor blade into its chest. It still reached for him and its brother approached as well, so Cyrus twisted the blade, and with his other hand released a burst of electricity, sucking the energy from one drone and shooting it into the other.

The shock immobilized them, but he knew they would recover soon, so Cyrus used the brief opening to return to his stockpile. The drones began to move and regained their focus on him. He lifted a uranium bullet, letting it float in front of him with a globule of propellant behind it, as the Acari drones opened compartments of missiles on their bodies and took aim towards Cyrus. But Cyrus fired first.

In a matter of seconds, the following events occurred. When Cyrus ignited the propellant, he used his gauntlets to contain the pressure in a narrow chute, like the barrel of the gun. The pressure accelerated the six-kilogram uranium bullet so that it was traveling at almost eight hundred meters per second when it touched the first Acari. The uranium sharpened with each layer of armor it penetrated, depositing burning astatine on the inner surfaces before

passing through and lancing the second. Cyrus couldn't even see it happen. He flexed his hand, igniting the propellant, and in the next moment he stumbled backwards from the sonic shockwave. The bullet was gone, and the two towering drones laid in a crumpled, burning heap.

Cyrus stepped back, looking around for his next opponent, but none came. Then, from the rooftops, a spray of bullets pocked the ground around him. As a second spray of bullets from another high angle bore down on him, Cyrus took shelter behind the crippled Acari corpses. But as he weighed his options, he noticed the river of lava creeping through a nearby alley. He looked to the other side of the square—through a hailstorm of bullets, he could see lava flowing from the other side as well. That explained why he hadn't seen more Roadsters.

Trusting in his armor, Cyrus winced and leapt into the air, trying to gain as much altitude as quickly as possible. He felt a few bullets graze him and a few hit him directly as he ascended through clouds of smoke and embers, and although they stung badly, he didn't feel any lasting pain. When he reached the apex of his arc he spun in midair, coaxing another bolt of lightning from the black clouds to arc indiscriminately through the buildings below until the gunfire stopped.

Cyrus landed on one of the taller buildings. Lava flooded the streets, filling the alleys with smoke as the gelatinous flow swallowed random debris and wreckage from his battle. The dark sky, reflecting the red glow, rumbled more and more loudly, then all at once opened up into a deluge. Thick clouds of steam filled the city with a dim haze. Deafening cracks of thunder burst from nearby lightning strikes. The ground rumbled. A deep hum resonated up through the city and through Cyrus' chest. He jumped into the air again—in the distance he could see the water churning. The yellow glow beneath the waves grew brighter.

Bigger Brother emerged steadily from the water, rumbling like the thunder. In the distance the colossus appeared to move slowly, but Cyrus knew it had to be rising at least a few meters every second. When it was upright it paused, with rivers cascading over its body, misting into waterfalls as they reached the open air. The body was humanoid without a head, but its broad shoulders and hulking form made it look like a moving mountain. Its surface was an oxidized umber, like the underside of an old boat, except for a huge dome in the center of its chest. The dome, crisscrossed with support struts, revealed five decks inside, and glowed with yellow light from the interior. Rectangular panels popped open on the shoulders. From within the left shoulder a missile, visible by its smoke trail, flew high into the sky before arcing towards Cyrus.

Cyrus waited calmly as it approached, then braced his knees and produced a gravity well down on the street. The missile swung dramatically, careening into the gravity well and disappearing into the lava. After a few seconds it exploded, throwing a splatter of lava onto the surrounding buildings. More missiles followed, bursting sequentially from Bigger Brother's shoulders. When they were in range Cyrus hit them with an EMP, frying their navigation. The missiles spiraled randomly around him in a series of explosions, blowing out some buildings and even causing others to tip over into the lava. Cyrus scoffed. Clearly, Acryogen's fixation with killing him came at any price.

Then, faintly, Cyrus heard a familiar sound. The scream of jet engines. Out of the corner of his eye, he saw a bright streak—Adhara was on the street, knee deep in lava, trying to save a building from collapse. She was firing her jets to push the structure back into balance, and as soon as it was, she flew off to the next job. As he watched, she caught rubble, lifted collapsing beams, and even...rescued people. His heart dropped. Some of the burning buildings still had people inside them. If it hadn't been for Adhara, they would have died like Maria had.

Cyrus grit his teeth and sat on the edge of the roof. Maria had died thinking that Cyrus was a hero—maybe not always successfully, but she thought he was trying his best to help people with Adhara. She *believed* in him. And now he realized Donny was right—she'd be horrified by what he was doing! Would she? She knew Acryogen caused the problems in the city, didn't she? Wouldn't she see that his plan, although extreme...was necessary?

But Adhara was throwing this in his face. Insulting him by taking the moral high ground, as if she had any right to, after he had welcomed her into his home and his life while she lied to him. She was an extension of Acryogen. What they had done to him, the pain they had caused him personally—he couldn't leave it alone.

Cyrus swept down to the street and gathered his giant bullets from the scrap pile where he had stashed them above the lava. As he rose to the rooftops again, he arranged the bullets in a floating circle behind him, and one by one, he fired them at Bigger Brother. With each shockwave a new hole appeared. Cyrus made a lucky shot and hit a critical point in the shoulder; the arm fell off into the bay and set the colossus off balance. The next bullet pierced the dome and the interior burst into flame. Cyrus fired the last shot at a knee. Bigger Brother lurched forward, electrical lights flickering off but firelight glowing brighter, and fell with an incredible shudder that shook the entire city, crushing all the buildings beneath it like sandcastles and barely missing the Acryogen towers.

Around the city, Cyrus heard faint applause echo through the streets. He looked around and saw members of the rebellion—the ones armed with gauntlets shot bursts of fire into the air. A small group nearby hooted and cheered, standing on a defeated Bouncer.

"Go get 'em, Anubis! Finish it!"

It was finally almost over, Cyrus thought. Only one more thing to do. He bounded across the rooftops towards Acryogen headquarters.

Matter	Antimatter
particles	antiparticles
protons +	-antiprotons
neutrons x	x antineutrons
electrons -	+ positrons

Chapter 31

JUDGEMENT

With his final leap, Cyrus dropped gracefully through the broken penthouse window, burning through the plastic they had taped over the hole. The room was quiet. He looked around slowly, remembering the night he had confronted Mason. The broken glass had been cleared and the wall he'd kicked Mystery Man's body through had already been patched, but aside from some tools left by a contractor, the empty board room had been almost returned to normal. Somehow it seemed wrong, that a location so significant for him should look so mundane.

He crossed into the next room, the central room with the elevator. This room wasn't as dull because there was a giant hole burned through the middle of the floor. He stood on the edge, peering into the abyss—the hole shot straight down through the floors of the skyscraper into the Pipeworks, where he had positioned the freight platform.

"Hello again...Cyrus."

Cyrus looked up. On the other side of the hole, Mason Smithy was pointing a device at him—something like a gun, presumably.

"What do you have there, Mason?"

"It's a sort of harmonic pulse laser gun," he answered, trying to sound casual. "Something new we've been working on. I'm sure you'd appreciate the science behind it, but I'm afraid I'm in no mood for a lecture just now." He flicked a switch on the side of the gun and a capacitor whined. He leveled the barrel at Cyrus, and though his jaw was set, Cyrus could see his hair was frazzled and his clothes were disheveled. He was determined but desperate. "I'm going to have to ask you to take off the gauntlets," Mason added slowly.

Cyrus flicked his hand as Mason fired, and the pulse rebounded. With his other hand Cyrus reached forward and hit it with an energy pulse of his own, making the prototype gun burst into fizzling sparks. Mason threw it instinctively. Cyrus was finally in control—Mason Smithy was before him, defenseless, holding up his hands in surrender and outmatched by Cyrus' superior technology. Why did that feel so hollow?

"Please," Mason whispered hoarsely, "*please* stop. You *win*. We're outmatched—nothing I have stands a chance against you. I know you're angry with us, but please don't take it out on the city. Please, no more of this..." he kneeled. "If the price of your wrath is my life, then I'll give it. Just don't hurt anyone else. We are at your mercy."

Mason Smithy...offering his life for the safety of the city? Cyrus cocked his head at him. This meek man before him... didn't at all fit into Cyrus' impression of Mason. Was this an act? A trick, a manipulation? Or perhaps, Cyrus had the wrong idea about him all along.

"As gratifying as I find you begging for mercy, I don't intend to kill you, Mason."

"Then..." Mason's eyes wandered to the hole. "What are your intentions?"

Good question, Cyrus thought. Did his plan still make sense?

"I'm going to use this," Cyrus answered, removing the polonium-210 from his belt and releasing its containment. The green sphere of polonium glowed so brightly it was almost white and cast the room into harsh relief. "It's polonium-210; a highly radioactive isotope. I'm going to drive it into a fission reaction and drop it down this hole," he continued, reciting as much for his own benefit as for Mason's. "The thermonuclear reaction will level this building and produce a massive electromagnetic pulse."

"But that's..." Mason wiped his brow under his glasses. "Cyrus, please don't do that. You'll destroy the whole city."

"Not the whole city," Cyrus corrected. "Just Acryogen. Three days ago, I told the rebellion to spread a message. When all of this started," he gestured to the chaos out the window, "everyone who isn't a part of Acryogen went off-grid. They cut wires, unplugged, pulled out. When the EMP hits, it'll pass over everyone loyal to me." Loyal to me? Did he *really* just say that? He sounded like a tyrant! And his plan sounded like it came from a mad scientist or a supervillain, or maybe a combination of both. It sounded like something he would have expected Mason to say.

"The EMP would cause a chain reaction..." Mason realized, "a power surge from this building outward. It would fry every Acryogen facility in the city. We'd never recover," he accepted finally. "Well done, Cyrus. It's a ruthless, efficient, and clever strategy against us. I can see...that your mind is made up."

"Well, it *was*." Cyrus sighed and sat on the edge of the hole, still cradling the polonium.

"...and now?" Mason asked warily.

"Well..." Cyrus sighed again. "Do you believe in free will, Mason?"

"Free...will?"

"Or, fate. Are we masters of our own destiny? Or are we all hurtling towards a pre-determined outcome?"

"Well, I," Mason cleared his throat, regaining some composure. "I believe we have full control over our choices, and therefore responsibility for them."

Cyrus nodded sagely, taking off his helmet and setting it gently beside him. "I used to believe that too—without question. If you had told me two years ago that I would become..." He looked down at his hands. "This? I wouldn't have believed you. I was...trying to *fight* this, *actively* avoiding it. And it still happened." He shook his head in wonder. "It makes me wonder if all those old movies were right. If the timeline is fixed. To tell you the truth, I'm not sure anymore who's the bad guy in this story."

"I'm not...following you," said Mason uncertainly.

"Well, it doesn't matter now, anyway. It's too late." Cyrus got to his feet, still at the edge of the hole. "All this damage, the loss of life, the pain I've caused...I can't take back what I've done. Might as well stop trying to hide from it." He dropped his helmet into the hole and watched as it disappeared into the darkness. "It's just like you said. Our choices come with responsibility."

There was a terrific crash as Adhara burst into the room. She flew past Cyrus, snatching the polonium from his hand before skidding to a stop on the other side of the room. He watched incredulously as she placed the polonium ball in her mouth and swallowed it. Blue flame burst from the depths of her body, escaping from the seams and joints of her shell for several seconds before quieting again, but her eyes still glowed with power.

"Speaking of destiny," Cyrus muttered, clenching his fists, "it's time I embraced mine."

As Mason scrambled out of the room, Cyrus lunged for Adhara with a fist full of fire. The conflagration burst around her, throwing the room into an inferno, but she remained unfazed, immutable. Her eyes glowed through the smoke.

Cyrus hit her with a series of quick jabs Maria and Donny had taught him. She blocked each move easily, and Cyrus noticed that when she blocked, she gave just enough that he wouldn't be hurt by the recoil. She *still* didn't consider him as a genuine threat—she was humoring him! Like a babysitter with a tantruming child! Cyrus grit his teeth and twisted his fist, throwing a splatter of phosphorus over her. It burned in the air—harmlessly.

"You have still not learned that I am fireproof," she commented.

"It's *REFLEXIVE*!" he shouted, encasing her in ice. He continued to spray ice around her even after she was encased in a massive block. When the ice was meters thick, he blew a hole in the wall and pushed her out. He waited at the edge, watching the block fall towards the street—but he could see the block glow red before she burst out and began to ascend again. He drew the conductor blade and the sky rumbled in response as he aimed at Adhara. The lightning came down hard, but just as she had told Cyrus long ago, she was impervious, and the electricity flowed around her body and straight toward the ground.

As she continued to ascend Cyrus typed some equations into his gauntlets, and when she appeared outside the room again, he threw burning magnesium flakes at her face. She recoiled from the flash, and in the opening, he attempted a direct approach by placing his palm on her body. When the NIRScanner returned the results, his heart jumped into his throat. The surface of her body was chemically inert. There was nothing he could do to her.

He cartwheeled backwards and plunged his hand through drywall into the structure of the building, melting steel beams which fell into a twisted haystack around her. But she was *still* unfazed, and with the torches in her hands began cutting the beams away from her. While she was distracted, Cyrus took cover in the next room and prepared his last resort.

Adhara burst into the room seconds later, and Cyrus, just in time, flicked a cluster of antimatter towards her. Just before it touched her body, she became a blur and disappeared; the antimatter hit the wall and with a burst of light, annihilated a colossal crater from it. Cyrus stepped forward cautiously, looking around with his gauntlets primed.

In a blur, she was behind him—he whirled and shot an explosion, but the recoil pushed him backwards. He was in the air, outside the towers, falling. He saw Adhara jump out the window after him—she was flying down to meet him, her hand reaching towards him. Impulsively he thrust his hand forward, engulfing her in an eruption of fire. But she drew closer, her hand reached through the fire—and grabbed his.

She pulled him towards her and grabbed Cyrus under his arms, firing her jets a few stories above the street and flying with him back up to the top of the building—no, to the roof, where she set him down gently and landed before him.

Cyrus fell to his knees. Adhara looked down at him calmly and the glow faded from her eyes.

"You shouldn't have saved me," he whispered.

Adhara angled her head.

"We both know how this has to end," he continued, tears streaming down his face. "How it *always* had to end. But I appreciate…you giving me a chance. Letting me hope, if just for a little while."

Cyrus looked up. The clouds were clearing; the blue was returning to the sky.

"It's okay. I accept my fate."

Adhara reached towards him.

He closed his eyes.

Fractal Multiverse Model

"Time" is represented by a branching pathway of potential outcomes, made up of indidivual moments each lasting 1 Planck Time, or, 10^{-44} seconds.

Each moment's potential outcome is represented by a branch, including variations from atomic vibration to human decision-making.

As elapsed universal time increases, potential outcomes increases exponentially.

Time expands outwards from a point of origin that represents the beginning of time, branching out to represent every potential sequence of events.

Branches form an overall spherical shape, arranged around poles of probability, most likely events branching opposite from least likely events.

Due to the branching shape, one can only move backwards in time along a set path but forward into infinite potential futures.

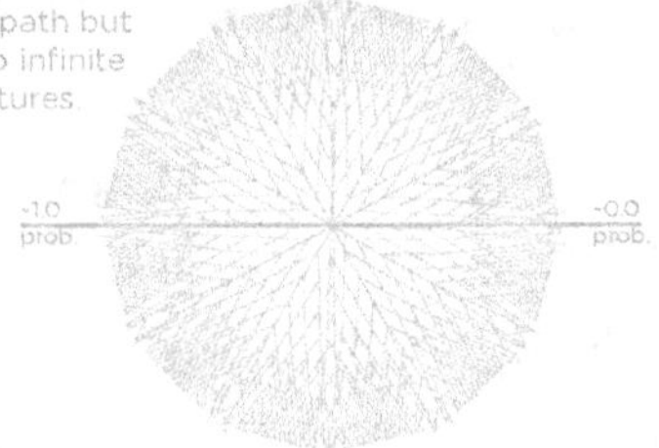

Chapter 32
THE TURNING POINT

"You're wrong."

His eyes blinked open again. Adhara was sitting across from him, a comforting hand on his shoulder.

"Wh…what?" he whispered.

"You believe…that what happens is immutable," she answered. "That the future cannot be changed. But it never had to be this way."

"But…" Cyrus wiped his eyes, "you're *from* the future. You already know what's going to happen, and you told me. And look," he chuckled sadly, gesturing at the destruction around them. "It came *true*."

"I'm from *a* future, Cyrus." She shook her head. "You're not the first Cyrus I've met. And you're far from the last."

"You mean you're…" Cyrus furrowed his brow over widening eyes. "You're from a parallel universe? An… alternate timeline?"

"That's correct," she nodded. "There's never been another Cyrus just like you, and there's never been a Cyrus who made the same choices as you. You were never bound by what you did in another life, in another universe. You are, and always have been, the one and only master of your own destiny."

"That's...incredible," he breathed, then sighed. "I wish I'd known that all along. I got so wrapped up in everything... but I guess hindsight is twenty-twenty, huh?" he chuckled humorlessly again. "There's no excuse, though. Even if I didn't know it...I was always responsible for my choices."

"There's still time. You have a choice to make, right now."

"But...I let you and Maria and everyone down so much." He gazed out over the skyline. "How can you forgive me? Isn't it too late for me?"

"Oh, Cyrus," she smiled, "It's never too late to do the right thing."

Cyrus met her eyes resolutely. "Then there's something I need to do, right now."

With Adhara closely following, Cyrus returned to the penthouse and discovered Mason Smithy hiding in a supply closet.

"Cyrus!" he exclaimed, then shouted incomprehensibly when he saw Adhara.

"Mason, I know I'm the last person you want to see right now but listen to me." Cyrus reached out his hand unthreateningly. "I don't expect you to forgive me. But I have a chance to make this right, and I need your help. I need you to come with me, okay?"

Though probably out of fear, Mason took his hand and allowed Cyrus to pull him upright. He followed wordlessly as Cyrus led him and Adhara down the elevator, miraculously still working, and onto the street. Cyrus approached the edge of the lava flow, and with a gentle wave of his hand, the lava grew cold and dark. He stepped up onto the flow and beckoned them to follow as he walked calmly through the streets, freezing the lava back into rock as they went.

As they walked through the city, smoothly repaving the roads, Cyrus saw the members of the rebellion peeking over the edges of the buildings to watch him.

"What's he doing?" he heard them ask. "He's undoing it. Is this part of the plan?"

"Look!" said another. "He's with Smithy!"

"They must have gotten to him; made a deal! He's brainwashed!"

"What does it mean?"

But Cyrus ignored their cries of confusion, and silently continued to freeze the lava. They turned a corner and saw a building sinking into the flow—Adhara waded into the lava and grabbed the edge of the wall, slowly lifting it until it was high enough that Cyrus could resolidify its foundation. She smiled at him as he led them further.

Cyrus tirelessly marched through the city, repairing everything he could find. Adhara helped whenever he needed her, and before long Mason had relaxed and offered advice for how certain things fit together. And at one point, when Cyrus led them through an alley onto a larger street, they ran into some members of the rebellion. They were using the gauntlets Cyrus had designed to fix things, as well. They smiled sheepishly, glanced at Mason, and turned to find something else to repair.

When Cyrus was satisfied with his work and all the fires had been extinguished, he led Mason and Adhara to the city square, where a small crowd had already gathered. As they approached the crowd parted. Cyrus climbed onto the roof of one of the Roadsters he had destroyed.

"I was *WRONG!*" he shouted, straining to be heard without a microphone. His words echoed nevertheless, and the crowd recoiled in surprise. Mason stepped forward and whispered something into Cyrus' ear. Cyrus nodded and raised one hand to his mouth, lifting the other over his head, and used the gauntlets to amplify his voice.

"I was wrong," Cyrus repeated into the gauntlets. "Please, listen to me. Listen to what I have to say, and then you can believe whatever you like. But this man," he gestured to Mason, who looked uncomfortable. "This man is not a menace. I am."

The audience murmured indignantly but grew more attentive.

"I was wrong," Cyrus croaked a third time, his voice breaking. "I thought I was fighting on the right side. I thought we all were. I told you that I believe that if you have power, if you are able help people and do good things, then with that power comes responsibility." He stepped forward, squaring his shoulders. "But I used my power to cause destruction and suffering!" he shouted. "Until now, I've let you believe that Acryogen is to blame for the state of the city, but that's not true. I must confess the truth: *I* caused the overgrowth," he heard gasps, "and the water pipes bursting. I tampered with the AirShift towers. I released an army of monsters into the city. Acryogen has been taking the blame while they try to clean up after my mistakes."

The crowd murmured and some faces grew dark. He could feel Mason looking at him.

"This city has problems. And we can fix them *without* hurting people. I led you to believe that war is the answer. But we need to work together...towards *peace* and *balance*." He took a shuddering breath. "I've done terrible things. I don't make any excuse for them, and I will answer for what I've done. I won't run from the consequences...all I can do is beg for your forgiveness, and vow to do everything I can to make it right."

Cyrus looked down, clenching his jaw and shaking with nerves. He felt a comforting hand on his shoulder—he turned and expected Adhara, but it was Mason standing next to him, smiling and nodding reassuringly.

"Ladies and gentlemen," he began regally, having regained his old panache, "I believe I owe you a substantial apology as well."

Cyrus looked to him in surprise.

"It took me too long to understand the justification of your battle," he continued gravely. "We, that is, Acryogen...have made mistakes. Too many. And more often than not, innocent people are hurt by them. I see now that you, the rebellion...and even Cyrus," he looked over to Cyrus, his eyes full of sorrow, "are demons of our own creation. How else were innocent people supposed to respond to an indifferent government than with protest?"

As Mason paused, Cyrus marveled again at how much he had falsely assumed.

"I would like to follow Cyrus' example," he added, "and take responsibility for my personal actions, as well as those in the name of Acryogen Industries. Today, I make a change. No more prioritizing science projects over people; no more taking advantage of your patience. From now on, I vow to you that we are going to focus on the community, and I will begin that process," he thrust a finger into the air pointedly, "by stepping down as CEO of Acryogen Industries, effective *immediately*, to be replaced by a democratically elected board of citizen directors. I vow to you that from this day forward...we *will* do better!"

There was agonizing silence, then near the front of the stage, clapping. Keith. Others around him followed, and slowly at first, the trend picked up. The applause grew to a roar; Cyrus could see people crying and hugging. Mason returned to his side, patting his shoulder. He looked over to see Mason smiling at him, and over his shoulder, in the corner—Adhara was smiling too.

"I expected to find you here."

Cyrus turned to see Adhara over the grassy hill and smiled. She sat beside him in the shade of the tree near Maria's grave.

"You're leaving, aren't you?"

"Yes," she nodded. "I'm satisfied with the outcome of this timeline. It's time for me to move on."

Cyrus nodded, gazing towards the horizon. For a few moments, they sat together quietly, listening to the birds.

"These past few weeks...you've been keeping an eye on me, haven't you? Making sure that I stay good?"

"Something like that," she chuckled.

"So, I'm doing well, right? You wouldn't be leaving otherwise."

"I have to admit, I'm impressed," she smiled. "I've never met a Cyrus who was so proactively altruistic. You're really doing a lot to make things right and help your community."

"Actually, I..." Cyrus' face grew serious. "I had some questions about the *other* Cyrus...es. Now that you're leaving, can you tell me...what happened to them?"

"In the end, they all chose destruction. They embraced Anubis."

"So, you...had to..."

"Yes," she answered calmly. "To save the city, I had to destroy Anubis."

"Every single one?" Cyrus winced. "How many times have you done this?"

"So far?" She picked a wildflower and twirled it between her fingertips. "Not many. Four hundred and thirty-eight."

"And they all..."

"They all would have destroyed the city if I had let them. But *this* city," she patted his shoulder as she stood, "is in good hands. You don't need me anymore."

"Wait," he cried, jumping to his feet. "I have so many more questions! Are you just...going to a new timeline after this? To start it *all* over again?"

"Yes."

"Isn't that...I don't know, kind of depressing? To do all of this and then have to start over from the beginning, and convince me not to turn evil over and over again?"

"I'm a machine, Cyrus."

"I know, but still." He sighed. "Will you ever get to...stop? Do something else?"

"No. I will continue to pursue my directive indefinitely, traveling to new timelines. It's not what Acryogen intended when they programmed me, but...that's how it worked out. My directive applies to all potential scenarios. There are billions and billions of potential futures for me to visit, each with a unique Cyrus who's had a unique experience. But, my time here with you," she smiled fondly, "has changed my parameters for the probability of potential outcomes. In a way...it's given me hope."

Cyrus smiled meekly. She turned towards the city, surveying the skyline.

"What will *you* do, now?"

"I've been thinking about that," Cyrus answered. "Before they died, Maria and Aliyah were working on a genome mapping project. I'm not great at biology, but I'd like to pick up where they left off. I think they were onto something that could really change the world for the better."

He followed her gaze, towards the Acryogen headquarters. The penthouse windows had been repaired long ago, and he knew within them the representative council would be having their first meeting to decide which direction they would lead Hudson City.

"After that...I might leave the city; there's a lot of bad memories for me here. I don't know if Donny will ever talk to me again, and things are weird with Olive...I don't think Mason likes it when I visit him in jail...I might go see what the rest of the world has to offer. Start fresh."

Adhara nodded understandingly.

"But for now," he nodded at Maria's headstone, "I think I'll just sit here a while. It's been a long time since I was able to just...live the present."

"You *should* enjoy it; you're on a good path. No more living for the future."

"Thank you for helping me find my way." He held out his hand. "Goodbye, Adhara. I'll miss you. Honestly."

"Goodbye, Cyrus." She shook his hand and smiled. "It was nice to meet you."